He *was* jealous.

The thought reverberated through her, but for the first time in two years, what Lucas wanted wasn't a priority. *Her* rules had just changed. From now on it was commitment or nothing.

Her chin firmed. "No. I have an escort. He can take me back to the party."

For a long, tension-filled moment Carla thought Lucas would argue, but then the demanding, possessive gleam was replaced by a familiar control. He nodded curtly, then sent her escort a long, cold look that conveyed a hands-off message that left Carla feeling doubly confused. Lucas didn't want her, but neither did he want anyone else near her.

And if Lucas no longer wanted her, if they really were finished, why had he bothered to search her out?

Dear Reader,

The second story in THE PEARL HOUSE series centers on Lucas Atraeus and Carla Ambrosi—both gorgeous and high profile, but actually pretty nice beneath all the media hype. They've chosen to keep their passion secret because of the tension and hurt surrounding Constantine Atraeus and Sienna Ambrosi's broken engagement two years previously.

With a wedding for Sienna and Constantine suddenly in the mix, all the obstacles to true love and happiness for Carla and Lucas finally seem to be dissolved. But Lucas has other ideas.

Wary of a past mistake and the fatal attraction to Carla that has seen him breaking every one of the emotional rules he had sworn to live by—and the streak of niceness that makes it hard for him to say no to women and fluffy pets—Lucas needs a foolproof strategy. But no matter what lengths he goes to to finish things with his ex, Lucas can't seem to stay away from an unexpectedly vulnerable Carla. Let's face it, he's dazzled. To the extent that he has to ask himself the question…

What if, this time, the fatal attraction is the real thing?

Fiona Brand

Fiona Brand lives in the sunny Bay of Islands, New Zealand. Now that both her sons are grown, she continues to love writing books and gardening. After a life-changing time in which she met Christ, she has undertaken study for a bachelor of theology and has become a member of The Order of St Luke, Christ's healing ministry.

For the Lord. Thank you.

The kingdom of heaven
a merchant in search of fine pearls.
—*Matthew* 13:45

One

The vibration of Lucas Atraeus's cell phone disrupted the measured bunch and slide of muscle as he smoothly bench-pressed his own weight.

Gray sweatpants clinging low on narrow hips, broad shoulders bronzed by the early morning light that flooded his private gym, he flowed up from the weight bench and checked the screen of his cell. Few people had his private number; of those only two dared interrupt his early morning workout.

"Si." His voice was curt as he picked up the call.

The conversation with his older brother, Constantine, the CEO of The Atraeus Group, a family-owned multibillion-dollar network of companies, was brief. When he terminated the call, Lucas was grimly aware that within the space of a few seconds a great many things had changed.

Constantine intended to marry in less than a fortnight's

time and, in so doing, he had irretrievably complicated Lucas's life.

The bride, Sienna Ambrosi, was the head of a Sydney-based company, Ambrosi Pearls. She also happened to be the sister of the woman with whom Lucas was currently involved. Although *involved* was an inadequate word to describe the passionate, addictive attraction that had held him in reluctant thrall for the past two years.

The phone vibrated again. Lucas didn't need to see the number to know who the second caller was; his gut reaction was enough. Carla Ambrosi. Long, luscious dark hair, honey-tanned skin, light blue eyes and the kind of taut, curvy body that regularly disrupted traffic and stopped him in his tracks.

Desire kicked, raw and powerful, almost overturning the rigid discipline he had instilled in himself after his girl-friend had plunged to her death in a car accident almost five years ago. Ever since Sophie's death he had pledged not to be ruled by passion or fall into such a destructive relationship ever again.

Lately, a whole two years lately, he had been breaking that rule on a regular basis.

But not anymore.

With an effort of will he resisted the almost overwhelming urge to pick up the call. Seconds later, to his intense relief, the phone fell silent.

Shoving damp, jet-black hair back from his face, he strolled across the pale marble floor to the shower with the loose-limbed power of a natural athlete. In centuries past, his build and physical prowess would have made him a formidable warrior. These days, however, Medinian battle was fought across boardroom tables with extensive share portfolios and gold mined from the arid backbone of the main island.

In the corporate arena, Lucas was undefeated. Relationships, however, had proved somewhat less straightforward.

All benefit from the workout burned away by tension and the fierce, unwanted jolt of desire, he stripped off his clothes, flicked the shower controls and stepped beneath a stream of icy water.

If he did nothing and continued an affair that had become increasingly irresistible and risky, he would find himself engaged to a woman who was the exact opposite of the kind of wife he needed.

A second fatal attraction. A second Sophie.

His only honorable course now was to step away from the emotion and the desire and use the ruthless streak he had hammered into himself when dealing with business acquisitions. He had to form a strategy to end a relationship that had always been destined for disaster, for both of their sakes.

He had tried to finish with Carla once before and failed. This time he would make sure of it.

It was over.

Lucas was finally going to propose.

The glow of a full moon flooded the Mediterranean island of Medinos as Carla Ambrosi brought her rented sports car to a halt outside the forbidding gates of Castello Atraeus.

Giddy delight coupled with nervous tension zinged through her as the paparazzi, on Medinos for her sister's wedding to Constantine Atraeus tomorrow, converged on the tiny sky-blue car. So much for arriving deliberately late and under cover of darkness.

A security guard tapped on her window. She wound the glass down a bare two inches and handed him the cream-colored, embossed invitation to the prewedding dinner.

With a curt nod, he slid the card back through the narrow gap and waved her on.

A flash temporarily blinded her as she inched the tiny rental through the crush, making her wish she had ignored the impulse that had seized her and chosen a sensible, solid four-door sedan instead of opting for a low-slung fun and flimsy sports car. But she had wanted to look breezy and casual, as if she didn't have a care in the world—

A sharp rap on her passenger-side window jerked her head around.

"Ms. Ambrosi, are you aware that Lucas Atraeus arrived in Medinos this morning?"

A heady jolt of anticipation momentarily turned her bones to liquid. She had seen Lucas's arrival on the breakfast news. Minutes later, she had glimpsed what she was sure must be his car as she had strolled along the waterfront to buy coffee and rolls for breakfast.

Flanked by security, the limousine had been hard to miss but, frustratingly, the darkly tinted windows had hidden the occupants from sight. Breakfast forgotten, she had both called and texted Lucas. They had arranged to meet but, frustratingly, a late interview request from a popular American TV talk-show host had taken that time slot. With Ambrosi's new collection due for release in under a week, the opportunity to use the publicity surrounding Sienna's wedding to showcase their range and mainstream Ambrosi's brand had been pure gold. Carla had hated canceling but she had known that Lucas, with his clinical approach to business, would understand. Besides, she was seeing him tonight.

Another camera flash made the tension headache she had been fighting since midafternoon spike out of control. The headache was a sharp reminder that she needed to slow down, chill out, de-stress. Difficult to do with the type A personality her doctor had diagnosed just over two years ago, along with a stomach ulcer.

The doctor, who also happened to be a girlfriend, had

advised her to lose her controlling, perfectionist streak, to stop micromanaging every detail of her life including her slavish need to color coordinate her wardrobe and plan her outfits a week in advance. Her approach to relationships was a case in point. Her current system of spreadsheet appraisal was hopelessly punitive. How could she find Mr. Right if no one ever qualified for a second date? Stress was a killer. She needed to loosen up, have some fun, maybe even consider actually sleeping with someone, before she ended up with even worse medical complications.

Carla had taken Jennifer at her word. A week later she had met Lucas Atraeus.

"Ms. Ambrosi, now that your sister is marrying Constantine, is there any chance of resurrecting your relationship with Lucas?"

Jaw tight, Carla continued to inch forward, her heart pounding at the reporter's intrusive question, which had been fired at her like a hot bullet.

And which had been eating at her ever since Sienna had broken the news two weeks ago that she had agreed to marry Constantine.

Tonight, though, she was determined not to resent the questions or the attention. After two years of avoiding being publicly linked with Lucas after the one night the press claimed they had spent together, she was now finally free to come clean about the relationship.

The financial feud that had torn the Atraeus and Ambrosi families apart, and the grief of her sister's first broken engagement to Constantine, were now in the past. Sienna and Constantine had their happy ending. Now, tonight, she and Lucas could finally have theirs.

A throaty rumble presaged the glare of headlights as a gleaming, muscular black car glided in behind her.

Lucas.

Her heart slammed against the wall of her chest. He was staying at the *castello,* which meant he had probably been at a meeting in town and was just returning. Or he could have driven to the small town house she and Sienna and their mother were renting in order to collect her. The possibility of the second option filled her with relieved pleasure.

A split second later the way ahead was clear as the media deserted her in favor of clustering around Lucas's Maserati. Automatically, Carla's foot depressed the accelerator, sending her small sports car rocketing up the steep, winding slope. Scant minutes later, she rounded a sweeping bend and the spare lines of the *castello* she had only ever seen in magazine articles jumped into full view.

The headlights of the Maserati pinned her as she parked on the smooth sweep of gravel fronting the colonnaded entrance. Feeling suddenly, absurdly vulnerable, she retrieved the flame-red silk clutch that matched her dress and got out of the car.

The Maserati's lights winked out, plunging her into comparative darkness as she closed her door and locked the car.

She started toward the Maserati, still battling the after-effects of the bright halogen lights. The sensitivity of her eyes was uncomfortably close to a symptom she had experienced two months ago when she had contracted a virus while holidaying with Lucas in Thailand.

Instead of the romantic interlude she had so carefully planned and which would have generated the proposal she wanted, Lucas had been forced into the role of nursemaid. On her return home, when she had continued to feel off-color, further tests had revealed that the stomach ulcer she thought she had beaten had flared up again.

The driver's side door of the car swung open. Her pulse rate rocketed off the charts. Finally, after a day of anxious waiting, they would meet.

Meet.

Her mouth went dry at a euphemism that couldn't begin to describe the explosive encounters that, over the past year, had become increasingly intense.

The reporter at the gate had put his finger on an increasingly tender and painful pulse. Resurrect her relationship with Lucas?

Technically, she was not certain they had ever had anything as balanced as a relationship. Her attempt to create a relaxed, fun atmosphere with no stressful strings had not succeeded. Lucas had seemed content with brief, crazily passionate interludes, but she was not. As hard as she had tried to suppress her type A tendencies and play the glamorous, carefree lover, she had failed. Passion was wonderful, but she *liked* to be in control, to personally dot every *i* and cross every *t*. For Carla, leaving things "open" had created even more stress.

Heart pounding, she started toward the car. The gown she had bought with Lucas in mind was unashamedly spectacular and clung where it touched. Split down one side, it revealed the long, tanned length of her legs. The draped neckline added a sensual Grecian touch to the swell of her breasts and also hid the fact that she had lost weight over the past few weeks.

Her chest squeezed tight as Lucas climbed out of the car with a fluid muscularity she would always recognize.

She drank in midnight eyes veiled by inky lashes, taut cheekbones, the faintly battered nose, courtesy of two seasons playing professional rugby; his strong jaw and firm, well-cut mouth. Despite the sleek designer suit and the ebony seal ring that gleamed on one finger, Lucas looked somewhat less than civilized. A graphic image of him naked and in her bed, his shoulders muscled and broad, his skin dark against crisp white sheets, made her stomach clench.

His gaze captured hers and the idea that they could keep the chemistry that exploded between them a secret until after the wedding died a fiery death. She wanted him. She had waited two years, hamstrung by Sienna's grief at losing Constantine. She loved her sister and was fiercely loyal. Dating the younger and spectacularly better looking Atraeus brother when Sienna had been publicly dumped by Constantine would have been an unconscionable betrayal.

Tonight, she and Lucas could publicly acknowledge their desire to be together. Not in a heavy-handed, possessive way that would hint at the secretive liaison that had disrupted both of their lives for the past two years, but with a low-key assurance that would hint at the future.

As Ambrosi's public relations "face," she understood exactly how this would be handled. There would be no return to the turgid headlines that had followed their first passionate night together. There would be no announcements, no fanfare...at least, not until after tomorrow's wedding.

Despite the fact that her strappy high heels, a perfect color match for the dress, made her more than a little unstable on the gravel, she jogged the last few yards and flung herself into Lucas's arms.

The clean scent that was definitively Lucas, mingled with the masculine, faintly exotic undernote of sandalwood, filled her nostrils, making her head spin. Or maybe it was the delight of simply touching him again after a separation that had run into two long months.

The cool sea breeze whipped long silky coils of hair across her face as she lifted up on her toes. Her arms looped around his neck, her body slid against his, instantly responding to his heat, the utter familiarity of broad shoulders and sleek, hard-packed muscle. His sudden intake of breath, the unmistakable feel of him hardening against the soft contours of her belly filled her with mindless relief.

Ridiculous tears blurred her vision. This was so *not* playing it cool, but it had been two months since she had touched, kissed, made love to her man. Endless days while she had waited for the annoying, debilitating ulcer—clear evidence that she had not coped with her unresolved emotional situation—to heal. Long weeks while she had battled the niggling anxiety that had its roots in the disastrous bout of illness in Thailand, as if she was waiting for the next shoe to drop.

She realized that one of the reasons she had not told Lucas about the complications following the virus was that she had been afraid of the outcome. Over the years he had dated a string of gorgeous, glamorous women so she usually took great care that he only ever saw her at her very best. There had been nothing pretty or romantic about the fever that had gripped her in Thailand. There had been even less glamour surrounding her hospital stay in Sydney.

Lucas's arms closed around her, his jaw brushed her cheek sending a sensual shiver the length of her spine. Automatically, she leaned into him and lifted her mouth to his, but instead of kissing her, he straightened and unlooped her arms from his neck. Cold air filled the space between them.

When she moved to close the frustrating distance he gripped her upper arms.

"Carla." His voice was clipped, the Medinian accent smoothed out by the more cosmopolitan overtones of the States, but still dark and sexy enough to send another shiver down her spine. "I tried to ring you. Why didn't you pick up the call?"

The mundane question, the edged tone pulled her back to earth with a thump. "I switched my phone off while I was being interviewed then I put it on charge."

But it had only been that way for about an hour. When she had left the private villa she was sharing with her mother and Sienna, she had grabbed the phone and dropped it in her purse. His hands fell away from her arms, leaving a palpable chill in place of the warm imprint of his palms. Extracting the phone from her clutch, she checked the screen and saw that, in her hurry, she had forgotten to turn it on.

She activated the phone, and instantly the missed calls registered on the screen. "Sorry," she said coolly. "Looks like I forgot to turn it back on."

She frowned at his lack of response. With an effort of will, she controlled the unruly emotions that had had the temerity to explode out of their carefully contained box and dropped the phone back in her clutch. So, okay, this was subtext for "let's play it cool."

Fine. Cool she could do, but not doormat. "I'm sorry I missed meeting you earlier but you've been here most of the day. If you'd wanted we could have met for lunch."

A discreet thunk snapped Carla's head around. Automatically, she tracked the unexpected sound and movement as the passenger door of the Maserati swing open.

Not male. Which ruled out her first thought, that the second occupant of the Maserati, hidden from her view by darkly tinted windows, was one of the security personnel who sometimes accompanied Lucas.

Not male. Female.

Out of nowhere her heart started to hammer. A series of freeze frames flickered: silky dark hair caught in a perfect chignon; a smooth, elegant body encased in shimmering, pale pearlized silk.

She went hot then cold, then hot again. She had the abrupt sensation that she was caught in a dream. A *bad* dream.

She and Lucas had an agreement whereby they could date others in order to distract the press and preserve the privacy she had insisted upon. But not here, not now.

Jerkily, Carla completed the movement she realized Lucas wanted from her: she stepped back.

She focused on his face, for the first time fully absorbing the remoteness of his dark gaze. It was the same cool neutrality she had seen on the odd occasion when they had been together and he'd had to take a work call.

The throbbing in her head increased, intensified by a shivery sensitivity that swept her spine. Her fingers tightened on her clutch as she resisted the sudden, childish urge to hug away the chill.

She drew an impeded breath. Another woman? She had not seen that coming.

Her mind worked frantically. No. It couldn't be.

But, if she hadn't felt that moment of heated response she *could* almost think that Lucas—

Emotion flickered in his gaze, gone almost before she registered it. "I believe you've met Lilah."

Recognition followed as Lilah turned and the light from the portico illuminated delicate cheekbones and exotic eyes. "Of course." She acknowledged Ambrosi's spectacularly talented head designer with a stiff nod.

Of course she knew Lilah, and Lilah knew her.

And all about her situation with Lucas, if she correctly interpreted the sympathy in Lilah's eyes.

Confusion rocked her again. How dare Lucas confide their secret to anyone without her permission? And Lilah Cole wasn't just anyone. The Coles had worked for Ambrosi's for as long as Carla could remember. Carla's grandfather, Sebastien, had employed Lilah's mother in Broome. Lilah, herself, had worked for Ambrosi for the past five years, the last two as their head designer, creating some of their most exquisite jewelry.

Lilah's smile and polite greeting were more than a little wary as she closed the door of the Maserati and strolled around the front of the car to join them.

The sudden uncomfortable silence was broken as the front

door of the *castello* was pushed wide. Light flared across the smooth expanse of gravel, the soft strains of classical music filtered through the haze of shock that still held Carla immobile.

A narrow, well-dressed man Carla recognized as Tomas, Constantine's personal assistant, spoke briefly in Medinian and motioned them all inside.

With a curt nod, Lucas indicated that both Carla and Lilah precede him. Feeling like an automaton, Carla walked toward the broad steps, no longer caring that the gravel was ruining her shoes. Exquisite confections she had chosen with Lucas in mind—along with every other item of jewelry and clothing she was wearing tonight, including her lingerie.

With each step she could feel the distance between them, a mystifying cold impersonality, growing by the second. When his hand landed in the small of Lilah's back, steadying her as she hitched up her gown with a poised, unutterably graceful movement, Carla's heart squeezed on a pang of misery. In those few seconds she finally acknowledged the insidious fear that had coexisted with her need to be with Lucas for almost two years.

She knew how dangerous Lucas was in business. As Constantine's right hand, by necessity he had to be coldly ruthless.

The other shoe had finally dropped. She had just been smoothly, ruthlessly dumped.

Two

Tucking a glossy strand of dark hair behind her ear—hair that suddenly seemed too lush and unruly for a formal family occasion—Carla stepped into the disorienting center of what felt like a crowd.

In reality there were only a handful of people present in the elegant reception room: Tomas and members of the Atraeus family including Constantine, his younger brother, Zane, and Lucas's mother, Maria Therese. To one side, Sienna was chatting with their mother, Margaret Ambrosi.

Sienna, wearing a sleek ivory dress and already looking distinctly bridal, was the first to greet her. The quick hug, the moment of warmth, despite the fact that they had spent most of the morning going over the details of the wedding together, made Carla's throat lock.

Sienna gripped her hands, frowning. "Are you okay? You look a little pale."

"I'm fine, just a little rushed and I didn't expect the media ambush at the gates." Carla forced a bright smile. "You know me. I do thrive on publicity, but the reporters were like a pack of wolves."

Constantine, tall and imposing, greeted her with a brief hug, the gesture conveying her new status as a soon-to-be member of Medinos's most wealthy, powerful family. He frowned as he released her. "Security should have kept them at bay."

His expression was remote, his light gray gaze controlled, belying the primitive fact that he had used financial coercion and had even gone so far as kidnapping Sienna to get his former fiancée back.

"The security was good." Carla hugged her mother, fighting the ridiculous urge to cling like a child. If she did that she would cry, and she refused to cry in front of Lucas.

A waiter offered champagne. As she lifted the flute from the tray her gaze clashed with Lucas's. Her fingers tightened reflexively on the delicate stem. The message in his dark eyes was clear.

Don't talk. Don't make trouble.

She took a long swallow of the champagne. "Unfortunately, the line of questioning the press took was disconcerting. Although I'm sure that when Lucas arrived with Lilah any misconceptions were cleared up."

Sienna's expression clouded. "Don't tell me they're trying to resurrect that old story about you and Lucas?"

Carla controlled her wince reflex at the use of the word *resurrect.* "I guess it's predictable that now that you and Constantine have your happy ending, the media are looking to generate something out of nothing."

Sienna lifted a brow. "So, do they need a medic down at the gates?"

"Not this time." Lucas frowned as Carla took another

long swallow of champagne. "Don't forget I was the original target two years ago, not the media."

And suddenly the past was alive between them, vibrating with hurtful accusations and misunderstandings she thought they had dealt with long ago. The first night of unplanned and irresistible passion they'd shared, followed by the revelation of the financial deal her father had leveraged on the basis of Sienna's engagement to Constantine. Lucas's accusation that Carla was more interested in publicity and her career than she had been in him.

Carla forced herself to loosen her grip on the stem of her glass. "But then the media are so very fascinated by your private life, aren't they?"

A muscle pulsed along the side of his jaw. "Only when someone decides to feed them information."

The flat statement, correct as it was, stung. Two years ago, hurt by his comments, she had reacted by publicly stating that she had absolutely no interest in being pursued by Lucas. The story had sparked weeks of uncomfortable conjecture for them both.

Sienna left them to greet more arrivals. Her anger under control, Carla examined the elegant proportions of the reception room, the exquisite marble floors and rich, Italianate decor. "And does that thought keep you awake at night?"

Lucas's gaze flared at her deliberate reference to the restless passion for her that he had once claimed kept him awake at nights. "I'm well used to dealing with the media."

"A shame there isn't a story. It could have benefited Ambrosi's upcoming product launch." She forced a brilliant smile. "You know what they say, any publicity is good publicity. Although in this case, I'm sure the story wouldn't be worth the effort, especially when it would involve dragging *my* private life through the mud."

Lucas's expression shuttered, the fire abruptly gone. "Then I suggest you sleep easy. *I* don't kiss and tell."

The sense of disorientation she had felt the past few minutes evaporated in a rush of anger. "Or commit to relationships."

"You were the one who set the ground rules."

Suddenly Lucas seemed a lot closer. "You know I had no other option."

His expression was grim. "The truth is always an option."

Her chin jerked up. "I was protecting Sienna and my family. What was I supposed to do? Turn up with you at Mom and Dad's house for Sunday dinner and admit that I was—"

"Sleeping with me?"

The soft register of his voice made her heart pound. Every nerve in her body jangled at his closeness, the knowledge that he was just as aware of her as she was of him. "I was about to say dating an Atraeus."

Sienna returned from her hostess duties to step neatly between them. "Time out, children."

Lucas lifted a brow, his mouth quirking in the wry half smile that regularly made women go weak at the knees. "My apologies."

As Constantine joined them, Lucas drew Lilah into the circle. "I know I don't need to introduce Lilah."

There was a moment of polite acknowledgment and brief handshakes as Lilah was accepted unconditionally into the Atraeus fold. The process of meeting Maria Therese was more formal and underlined a salient and well-publicized fact. Atraeus men didn't take their women home to meet their families on a casual basis. To her best knowledge, until now, Lucas had never taken a girlfriend home to meet his mother.

Lucas's *girlfriend*.

Lilah was smiling, her expression contained but lit with an unmistakable glow.

A second salient fact made Carla stiffen. A few months ago, while stuck overnight together at a sales expo in Europe, she and Lilah had discussed the subject of relationships. At age twenty-nine, despite possessing the kind of sensual dark-haired, white-skinned beauty that riveted male attention, Lilah was determinedly single.

She had told Carla a little of her background, which included a single mother, a solo grandmother and ongoing financial hardship. Born illegitimate, Lilah had early on given herself a rule. No sex before marriage. There was no way she was going to be left holding a baby.

While Carla had stressed about finding Mr. Right, Lilah was calmly focused on marrying him, her approach methodical and systematic. She had moved on a step from Carla's idea of a spreadsheet and had developed a list of qualifying attributes as precise and unwavering as an employment contract. Also, unlike Carla, Lilah had *saved* herself for marriage. She was that twenty-first century paragon: a virgin.

The simple fact that she was on Medinos with Lucas, thousands of miles from her Sydney apartment and rigorous work schedule, spoke volumes.

Lilah did not date. Carla knew that she occasionally accompanied a gay neighbor to his professional dinners and had him escort her to charity functions she supported. But their relationship was purely friendship, which suited them both. That was all.

Carla took another gulp of champagne. Her stomach clenched because the situation was suddenly blindingly obvious.

Lilah was dating Lucas because she had chosen him. He was her intended husband.

Anger churned in Carla's stomach and stiffened her spine. She and Lucas had conducted their relationship based on a set of rules that was the complete opposite of everything that

Lilah was holding out for: no strings, strictly casual and, because of the family feud, in secrecy.

An enticing, convenient arrangement for a man who clearly had never had any intention of offering *her* marriage.

Waiters served more chilled champagne and trays of tiny, exquisite canapés. Carla forced herself to eat a tiny pastry case filled with a delicate seafood mousse. She continued to sip her way through the champagne, which loosened the tightness of her throat but couldn't wash away the deepening sense of hurt.

Lilah Cole was beautiful, elegant and likable, but nothing could change the fact that Lilah's easy acceptance into the Atraeus fold should have been *her* moment.

The party swelled as more family and friends arrived. Abandoning her champagne flute on a nearby sideboard, Carla joined the movement out onto a large stone balcony overlooking the sea.

Feeling awkward and isolated amidst the crowd, she threaded her way through the revelers to the parapet and stared out at the expansive view. The breeze gusted, laced with the scent of the sea, sending coils of hair across her cheeks and teasing at the flimsy silk of her dress, briefly exposing more leg than she had planned.

Lucas's gaze burned over her, filled with censure, not the desire that had sizzled between them for the past two years.

Cheeks burning, she snapped her dress back into place, her mood plummeting further as Lilah joined Lucas. Despite the breeze, Lilah's hair was neat and perfect, her dress subtly sensual with a classic pureness of line that suddenly made Carla feel cheap and brassy, all sex and dazzle against Lilah's demure elegance. Her cheeks grew hotter as she considered what she was wearing under the red silk. Again, nothing with any degree of subtlety. Every flimsy stitch was designed to entice.

She had taken a crazy risk in dressing so flamboyantly, practically begging for the continuation of their relationship. After the distance of the past two months she should have had more sense than to wear her heart on her sleeve. Jerking her gaze away, she tried to concentrate on the moon sliding up over the horizon, the churning floodlit water below the *castello.*

A cool gust of wind sent more hair whipping around her cheeks. Temporarily blinded, she snatched at her billowing hemline. Strong fingers gripped her elbow, steadying her. Heart-stoppingly familiar dark eyes clashed with hers. Not Lucas, Zane Atraeus.

"Steady. I've got you. Come over here, out of the wind before we lose you over the side."

Zane's voice was deep, mild and low-key, more American than Medinian, thanks to his Californian mother and upbringing. With his checkered, illegitimate past and lady-killer reputation, Zane was, of the three brothers, definitely the most approachable and she wondered a little desperately why she hadn't been able to fall for him instead of Lucas. "Thanks for the rescue."

He sent her an enigmatic look. "Damsels in distress are always my business."

The warmth in her cheeks flared a little brighter. The suspicion that Zane wasn't just talking about the wind, that he knew about her affair with Lucas, coalesced into certainty.

He positioned her in the lee of a stone wall festooned with ivy. "Can I get you a drink?"

A reckless impulse seized Carla as she glanced across at Lucas. "Why not?"

With his arm draped casually across the stone parapet behind Lilah, his stance was male and protective, openly claiming Lilah as his, although he wasn't touching her in any way.

Unbidden, a small kernel of hope flared to life at that

small, polite distance. Ten minutes ago, Carla had been certain they were an established couple; that to be here, at a family wedding, Lucas would have had to have slept with Lilah. Now she was abruptly certain they had not yet progressed to the bedroom. There was a definite air of restraint underpinning the glow on Lilah's face, and despite his possessive stance, Lucas was preserving a definite distance.

A waiter swung by. Zane handed her a flute of champagne. "Do you think they've slept together?"

Carla's hand jerked at the question. Champagne splashed over her fingers. She dragged her gaze from the clean line of Lucas's profile and glanced at Zane. His expression was oddly grim, his jaw set. "I don't know why you're asking me that question."

Zane, who hadn't bothered with champagne, gave her a steady look, and humiliation curled through her. He knew.

Carla wondered a little wildly how he had found out and if everyone on the balcony knew that she was Lucas's ditched ex.

Zane's expression was dismissive. "Don't worry, it was a lucky guess."

Relief flooded her as she swallowed a mouthful of champagne. A few seconds later her head began to spin and she resolved not to drink any more.

Zane's attention was no longer on her; it was riveted on Lilah and realization hit. She wasn't the only one struggling here. "You want Lilah."

The grim anger she had glimpsed winked out of existence. "If I was in the market for marriage, maybe."

"Which, I take it, you're not."

Zane's dark gaze zeroed in on hers, but Carla realized he still barely logged her presence. "No. Are you interested in art?"

Carla blinked at the sudden change of subject. "Yes."

"If you want out of this wind, I'll be happy to show you the rogue's gallery."

She had glimpsed the broad gallery that housed the Atraeus family portraits, some painted by acknowledged masters, but hadn't had time to view them. "I would love to take a closer look at the family portraits."

Anything to get her off the balcony. "Just do me one favor. Put your arm around my waist."

"And make it look good?"

Carla's chin jerked up a fraction. "If you don't mind."

The unflattering lack of reaction to her suggestion should have rubbed salt into the wound, but Carla was beyond caring. She was dying by inches but she was determined not to be any more tragic than she had to be.

Lucas's gaze burned over her as she handed her drink to a waiter then allowed Zane's arm to settle around her waist. As they strolled past Lucas, she was forcibly struck by the notion that he was jealous.

Confusion rocked her. She hadn't consciously set out to make Lucas jealous; her main concern from the moment she had realized that Lucas and Lilah were together had been self-preservation. Lucas being jealous made no sense unless he still wanted her, and how could that be when he had already chosen another woman?

Carla was relieved when Zane dropped his arm the second they were out of sight of the balcony. After a short walk through flagged corridors, they entered the gallery. Along one wall, arched windows provided spectacular views of the moonlit sea. The opposite wall was softly lit and lined with exquisite paintings.

The tingling sense of alarm, as if at some level she was aware of Lucas's displeasure, continued as they strolled past rank after rank of gorgeous rich oils. Most had been painted pre-1900s, before the once wealthy and noble Atraeus family had fallen on hard times. Lucas's grandfather, after discovering an obscenely rich gold mine, had since purchased most of the paintings back from private collections and museums.

The men were clearly of the Atraeus bloodline, with strong jaws and aquiline profiles. The women, almost without exception, looked like Botticelli angels: beautiful, demure, virginal.

Zane paused beside a vibrant painting of an Atraeus ancestor who looked more like a pirate than a noble lord. His lady was a serene, quiet dove with a steely glint in her eye. With her long, slanting eyes and delicate bones, the woman bore an uncanny resemblance to Lilah. "As you can see it's a mixture of sinners and saints. It seemed that the more dissolute and marauding the Atraeus male, the more powerful his desire for a saint."

Carla heard the measured tread of footsteps. Her heart sped up because she was almost sure it was Lucas. "And is that what Atraeus men are searching for today?"

Zane shrugged. "I can't speak for my brothers. I'm not your typical Atraeus male."

Her jaw tightened. "But the idea of a pure, untouched bride still has a certain appeal."

"Maybe." He sent her a flashing grin that made him look startlingly like the Atraeus pirate in the painting. "Although, I'm always willing to be convinced that a sinner is the way to go."

"Because that generally means no commitment, right?"

Zane's dark brows jerked together. "How did we get on to commitment?"

Carla registered the abrupt silence as if whoever had just entered the gallery had seen them and stopped.

Her heart slammed in her chest as she caught Lucas's reflection in one of the windows. On impulse, she stepped close to Zane and tilted her head back, the move flirtatious and openly provocative. She was playing with fire, because Zane had a reputation that scorched.

Lucas would be furious with her. If he *was* jealous, her behavior would probably kill any feelings he had left for her, but she was beyond caring. He had hurt her too badly for her to pull back now. "If that's an invitation, the answer is yes."

Zane's gaze registered unflattering surprise.

Minor detail, because Lucas was now walking toward them. Gritting her teeth, she wound her finger in Zane's tie, applying just enough pressure that his head lowered until his mouth was mere inches from hers.

His gaze was disarmingly neutral. "I know what you're up to."

"You could at least be tempted."

"I'm trying."

"Try harder."

"Damn, you're type A. No wonder he went for Lilah."

Carla's fingers tightened on his tie. "Is it that obvious?"

"Only to me. And that's because I'm a control freak myself."

"I am *not* a control freak."

He unwound her fingers from his tie. "Whatever you say."

Cut adrift by Zane's calm patience, Carla had no choice but to step back and in so doing almost caromed into Lucas.

She flinched at the fiery trail of his gaze over the shadow of her cleavage, her mouth, the impression of heat and desire. If Zane hadn't been there she was almost certain he would have pulled her close and kissed her.

Lucas's expression was shuttered. "What are you up to?"

Carla didn't try to keep the bitterness out of her voice. "*I'm* not up to anything. Zane was showing me the paintings."

"Careful," Zane intervened, his gaze on Lucas. "Or I

might think you have a personal interest in Carla, and that couldn't possibly be, since you're dating the lovely Lilah."

A sharp pang went through Carla at the tension vibrating between the brothers, shifting undercurrents she didn't understand.

Spine rigid, she kept her gaze firmly on Zane's jaw. She hadn't liked behaving like that, but at least she had proved that Lucas did still want her. Although the knowledge was a bitter pill, because his reaction repeated a pattern that was depressingly familiar. In establishing a stress-free liaison with him based on her rules, she had somehow negotiated herself out of the very things she needed most: love, companionship and commitment.

Lucas had wanted her for two years, but that was all. The relationship had struggled to progress out of the bedroom. Even when she had finally gotten him to Thailand for a whole four-day minibreak, the longest period of time they had ever spent together, the plan had crashed and burned because she had gotten sick.

She wondered in what way she was lacking that Lucas didn't want a full relationship with her? That instead of allowing them to grow closer, he had kept her at an emotional arm's length and gone to Lilah for the very things that Carla needed from him.

She glanced apologetically at Zane in an effort to defuse the tension. "It's okay, Lucas and I are old news. If there was anything more we would be together now."

"Whereas marriage *is* Lilah's focus," Zane said softly.

Lucas frowned. "Back off, Zane."

Confusion gripped Carla along with another renegade glimmer of hope at Lucas's reaction. She was tired of thinking about everything that had gone wrong, but despite that, her mind grabbed on to the notion that maybe all he was doing *was* dating Lilah on a casual basis. Just because Lilah wanted marriage didn't necessarily mean she would get what she wanted.

Grimly, she forced herself to study the Atraeus bride in the painting again. It was the perfect reality check.

Her pale, demure gown was the epitome of all things virginal and pure. Nothing like Carla's flaming red silk dress, with its enticing glimpse of cleavage and leg. The serene eighteenth-century bride was no doubt every man's secret dream. A perfect wife, without a flirty bone in her body. Or a stress condition.

Lucas's gaze sliced back to Carla. "I'll take you back to the party. Dinner will be served in about fifteen minutes."

He *was* jealous.

The thought reverberated through her, but for the first time in two years what Lucas wanted wasn't a priority. *Her* rules had just changed. From now on it was commitment or nothing.

Her chin firmed. "No. I have an escort. Zane will take me back to the party."

For a long, tension-filled moment Carla thought Lucas would argue, but then the demanding, possessive gleam was replaced by a familiar control. He nodded curtly then sent Zane a long, cold look that conveyed a hands-off message that left Carla feeling doubly confused. Lucas didn't want her, but neither did he want Zane anywhere near her.

And if Lucas no longer wanted her, if they really were finished, why had he bothered to search her out?

Three

Lucas Atraeus strode into his private quarters and snapped the door closed behind him. Opening a set of French doors, he stepped out onto his balcony. The wind buffeted the weathered stone parapet and whipped night-dark hair around the obdurate line of his jaw. He tried to focus on the steady roar of the waves pounding the cliff face beneath and the stream of damp, salty air, while he waited for the self-destructive desire to reclaim Carla to dissolve.

The vibration of his cell phone drew him back inside. Sliding the phone out of his pocket, he checked the screen. Lilah. No doubt wondering where he was.

Jaw clenched, he allowed the call to go through to his voice mail. He couldn't stomach talking to Lilah right at that moment with his emotions still raw and his thoughts on another woman. Besides, with a relationship based on a few phone calls and a couple of conversations, most of them purely work based, they literally had nothing to say to each other.

The call terminated. Lucas found himself staring at a newspaper he had tossed down on the coffee table, the one he had read on the night flight from New York to Medinos. The paper was open at the society pages and a grainy shot of Carla in her capacity as the "face" of Ambrosi Pearls, twined intimately close with a rival millionaire businessman.

Picking up the newspaper, he reread the caption that hinted at a hot affair.

He had been away for two months but by all accounts she had not missed him.

Tossing the newspaper down on the coffee table, he strode back out onto the balcony. Before he could stop himself, he had punched in her number on his phone.

Calling her now made no kind of sense.

He held the sleek phone pressed to his ear and forced himself to remember the one overriding reason he should never have touched Carla Ambrosi.

Grimly, he noted that the hit of old grief and sharp-enough-to-taste guilt still wasn't powerful enough to bury the impulse to involve himself even more deeply in yet another fatal attraction.

When he had met Carla, somehow he had stepped away from the rigid discipline he had instilled in himself after Sophie's death.

The car accident hadn't been his fault, but he was still haunted by the argument that had instigated Sophie's headlong dash in her sports car after he had found out that she had aborted his child.

Sophie had been beautiful, headstrong and adept at winding him around her little finger. He should have stopped her, taken the car keys. He should have controlled the situation. It had been his responsibility to protect her, and he had failed.

They should never have been together in the first place.

They had been all wrong for each other. He had been disciplined, work focused and family orientated. Sophie had skimmed along the surface of life, thriving on bright lights, parties and media attention. Even the manner in which Sophie had died had garnered publicity and had been perceived in certain quarters as glamorous.

The ring tone continued. His fingers tightened on the cell. Carla had her phone with her; she should have picked up by now.

Unless she was otherwise occupied. *With Zane.*

His stomach clenched at the image of Carla, mouthwateringly gorgeous in red, her fingers twined in Zane's tie, poised for a kiss he had interrupted.

He didn't trust Zane. His younger brother had a reputation with women that literally burned.

The call went through to voice mail. Carla's voice filled his ear.

Despite the annoyance that gripped him that Carla had decided to ignore his call, Lucas was riveted by the velvet-cool sound of the recorded message. The brisk, businesslike tone so at odds with Carla's ultrasexy, ultrafeminine appearance and which never failed to fascinate.

During the two months he had been in the States he had refrained from contacting Carla. He had needed to distance himself from a relationship that during an intense few days in Thailand had suddenly stepped over an invisible boundary and become too gut-wrenchingly intimate. Too like his relationship with Sophie.

Carla, who was surprisingly businesslike and controlled when it came to communication, had left only one text and a single phone message to which he had replied. A few weeks ago he had seen her briefly, from a distance, at her father's funeral, but they hadn't spoken.

That was reason number two not to become involved with Carla.

The ground rules for their relationship had been based on what she had wanted: a no-strings fun fling, carried out in secret because of the financial scandal that had erupted between their two families.

Secrecy was not Lucas's thing, but since he had never planned on permanency he hadn't seen any harm in going along with Carla's plan. He had been based in the States, Carla was in Sydney. A relationship wasn't possible even if he had wanted one.

The line hummed expectantly.

Irritated with himself for not having done it sooner, Lucas terminated the call.

Grimly, he stared at the endless expanse of sea, the faint curve of the horizon. Carla not picking up the call was the best-case scenario. If she had, he was by no means certain he could have maintained his ruthless facade.

The problem was that, as tough and successful as he was in business, when it came to women his track record was patchy.

As an Atraeus he was expected to be coolly dominant. Despite the years he had spent trying to mold himself into the strong silent type who routinely got his way, he had not achieved Constantine's effortless self-possession. Little kids and fluffy dogs still targeted him; women of all ages gravitated to him as if they had no clue about his reputation as The Atraeus Group's key hatchet man.

Despite the long list of companies he had streamlined or clinically dismantled, he couldn't forget that he had not been able to establish any degree of control over his relationship with Sophie.

Jaw taut, Lucas padded inside. He barely noticed the

warm glow of lamplight, the richness of exquisite antiques and jewel-bright carpets.

His gaze zeroed in on the newspaper article again. A hot pulse of jealously burned through him as he studied the Greek millionaire who had his arm around Carla's waist.

Alex Panopoulos, an archrival across the boardroom table and a well-known playboy.

Given the limited basis of Lucas's relationship with Carla, they had agreed it had to be open; they were both free to date others. Like Lucas, Carla regularly dated as part of her career, although so far Lucas had not been able to bring himself to include another woman in his life on more than a strictly platonic basis.

Panopoulos was a guest at the wedding tomorrow.

Walking through to the kitchen, he tossed the paper into the trash. His jaw tightened at the thought that he would have fend off the Greek, as well.

He guessed he should be glad that it was Zane Carla seemed to be attracted to and not Panopoulos.

Zane had been controllable, so far. And if he stepped over the line, there was always the option that they could settle the issue in the old-fashioned way, down on the beach and without an audience.

Dinner passed in a polite, superficial haze. Carla made conversation, smiled on cue, and avoided looking at Lucas. Unfortunately, because he was seated almost directly opposite her, she was burningly aware of him through each course.

Dessert was served. Still caught between the raw misery that threatened to drag her under, and the need to maintain the appearance of normality, Carla ate. She had reached the dessert course when she registered how much wine she had drunk.

A small sharp shock went through her. She wasn't drunk, but alcohol and some of the foods she was eating did not mix happily with an ulcer. Strictly speaking, after the episode with the virus and the ulcer, she wasn't supposed to drink at all.

Setting her spoon down, she picked up her clutch and excused herself from the table. She asked one of the waitstaff to direct her to the nearest bathroom. Unfortunately, since her grasp of Medinian was far from perfect, she somehow managed to take a wrong turn.

After traversing a long corridor and opening a number of doors, one of which seemed to be the entrance to a private set of rooms, complete with a kitchenette, she opened a door and found herself on a terrace overlooking the sea. Shrugging, because the terrace would do as well as a bathroom since all she required was privacy to take the small cocktail of pills her doctor had prescribed, she walked to the stone parapet and studied the view.

The stiff sea breeze that had been blowing earlier had dropped away, leaving the night still, the air balmy and heavily scented with the pine and rosemary that grew wild on the hills. A huge full moon glowed a rich, buttery gold on the horizon.

Setting her handbag down on the stone pavers, she extracted the MediPACK of pills she had brought with her, tore open the plastic seal and swallowed them dry.

Dropping the plastic waste into her handbag, she straightened just as the door onto the terrace popped open. Her chest tightened when she recognized Lucas.

"I hope you weren't expecting Zane?"

"If I was, it wouldn't be any of your business."

"Zane won't give you what you want."

Carla swallowed to try and clear the dry bitterness in her

mouth. "A loving relationship? The kind of relationship I thought we could have had?"

He ignored the questions. "You should return to the dining room."

The flatness of Lucas's voice startled her. Lucas had always been exciting and difficult to pin down, but he had also been funny and unexpectedly tender. This was the first time she had ever seen this side of him. "Not yet. I have a…headache, I need some air." Which was no lie, because the headache was there, throbbing steadily at her temples.

She pretended to be absorbed by the spectacular view of the crystal-clear night and the vast expanse of sea gleaming like polished bronze beneath the moon. Just off the coast of Medinos, the island of Ambrus loomed, tonight seemingly almost close enough to touch. One of the more substantial islands in the Medinos group, Ambrus was intimately familiar to her because her family had once owned a chunk of it.

"How did you know these are my rooms?"

She spun, shocked at Lucas's closeness and what he'd just said. "I didn't. I was looking for a bathroom. I must have taken a wrong turn."

The coolness of his glance informed her that he didn't quite believe her. Any idea that Lucas would tell her that he had made a mistake and that he desperately wanted her back died a quick death.

A throb of grief hit her at the animosity that seemed to be growing by the second and she pulled herself up sharply. She had run the gamut of shock and anger. She was not going to wallow in self-pity.

It was clear Lucas wasn't going to leave until she did, so she picked up her bag and started toward the door.

Instead of moving aside, Lucas moved to block her path. "I'm sorry you found out this way. I did try to meet with you before dinner."

Her heart suddenly pounding off the register, she stared rigidly at his shoulder. "You could have told me when I called to cancel and given me some time. Even a text would have helped."

His dark brows jerked together. "I'm not in the habit of breaking off relationships over the phone or by text. I wanted to tell you face-to-face."

Her jaw tightened. It didn't help that his gaze was direct, that he was clearly intent on softening the blow. The last thing she wanted from Lucas was pity. "Did Lilah fly in with you?"

"She arrived this afternoon."

Relief made her feel faintly unsteady. So, Lilah hadn't been with Lucas in the limousine.

As insignificant as that detail was, it mattered, because when she had seen the limousine she had been crazily, sappily fantasizing about Lucas and the life they could now share. Although she should have known he hadn't arrived with Lilah, because there hadn't been any media reports that he had arrived at the airport with a female companion.

Lucas's gaze connected with hers. "Before you go back inside, I need to know if you intend to go to the press with a story about our affair."

Affair.

Her chin jerked up. For two years she had considered they had been involved in a relationship. "I'm here for Sienna's wedding. It's her day, and I don't intend to spoil it."

"Good. Because if you try to force my hand by going public with this, take it from me, I'm not playing."

Comprehension hit. She had been so absorbed with the publicity for Ambrosi's latest collection and the crazy rush to organize Sienna's wedding that she had barely had time to sleep, let alone think. When Sienna married Constantine, Carla would be inextricably bound to the Atraeus family.

The Atraeus family were traditionalists. If it were discovered that she and Lucas had been seeing each other secretly for two years, he would come under intense pressure from his family to marry her.

Now the comment about her looking for his rooms made sense.

What better way to force a commitment than to arrange for them both to be found together in his rooms at the *castello?* Anger and a burning sense of shame that he should think she would stoop that low sliced through her. "I hadn't considered that angle."

Why would she when she had assumed Lucas wanted her?

He ignored her statement. "If it's marriage you want, you won't get it by pressuring me."

Which meant he really had thought about the different ways she could force him to the altar. She took a deep breath against a sharp spasm of hurt. "At what point did I ever say I was after marriage?"

His gaze bored into hers, as fierce and obdurate as the dark stone from which the fortress was built. "Then we have an understanding?"

"Oh, I think so." She forced a bright smile. "I wouldn't marry you if you tied me up and dragged me down the aisle. Tell me," she said before she could gag her mouth and instruct her brain to never utter anything that would inform Lucas just how weak and vulnerable she really was. "Did you ever come close to loving me?"

He went still. "What we had wasn't exactly about love."

No. Silly her.

"There's something else we need to talk about."

"In that case, it'll have to wait. Now I really do have a headache." She fumbled in her clutch, searching for the painkillers she'd slipped in before she'd left the villa, just in case. In her haste the foil pack slipped out of her fingers and dropped to the terrace.

Lucas retrieved the pills before she could. "What are these?"

He held the foil pack out of her reach while he read the label. "Since when have you suffered from headaches?"

She snatched the pills from his grasp. "They're a left-over from the virus I caught in Thailand. I don't get them very often."

She ripped the foil open and swallowed two pills dry, grimacing at the extra wave of bitterness in her mouth when one of the pills lodged in her throat. She badly needed a glass of water.

Lucas frowned. "I didn't know you were still having problems."

She shoved the foil pack back in her clutch. "But then you never bothered to ask."

And the last thing she had wanted to do was let him know that she had been so stressed by the unresolved nature of their relationship that she had given herself an even worse stomach ulcer than she had started with two years ago.

After the growing distance between them in Thailand, she hadn't wanted to further undermine their relationship or give him an excuse to break up with her. Keeping silent had been a constant strain because she had wanted the comfort of his presence, had *needed* him near, but now she was glad she hadn't revealed how sick she really had been. It was one small corner of her life that he hadn't invaded, one small batch of memories that didn't contain him.

She felt like kicking herself for being so stupid over the past couple of months. If Lucas had wanted to be with her he would have arranged time together. Once, he had flown into Sydney with only a four-hour window before he'd had to fly out again. They had spent every available second of those four hours locked together in bed.

Cold settled in her stomach. In retrospect, their relationship had foundered in Thailand. Lucas hadn't liked crossing the line into caring; he had simply wanted a pretty, adoring lover and uncomplicated sex.

Lucas was still blocking her path. "You're pale and your eyes are dilated. I'll take you home."

"No." She stepped neatly around him and made a beeline for the open door. Her heart sped up when she realized he was close behind her. "I can drive myself. The last thing I want is to spend any more time with you."

"Too bad." His hand curled around her upper arm, sending a hot, tingling shock straight to the pit of her stomach as he propelled her into the hall. "You've had a couple of glasses of wine, and now a strong painkiller. The last thing you should do is get behind the wheel of that little sports car."

She shot him a coolly assessing look. "Or talk to the paparazzi at the gate."

"Right now it's the hairpin bends on the road back to the villa that worry me."

Something snapped inside her at the calm, matter-of-fact tone of his voice, as if he was conducting damage control in one of his business takeovers. "What do you think I'm going to do, Lucas? Drive off one of your cliffs into the sea?"

Unexpectedly his grip loosened. Twisting free, she grasped the handle of the door to the suite she had briefly checked out before, thinking it could be a bathroom. It was Lucas's suite, apparently. Forbidden territory.

Flinging the door wide, she stepped inside. She was about to prove that at least one of Lucas's fears was justified.

She was going to be her control-freak, ticked-off, stressed-out self for just a few minutes.

She was going to behave badly.

Four

The paralyzing fear that had gripped Lucas at the thought of Carla driving her sports car on Medinos's narrow roads turned to frustration as she stepped inside his suite.

Grimly, he wondered what had happened to the dominance and control with which he had started the evening.

Across boardroom tables, he was aware that his very presence often inspired actual fear. His own people jumped to do his bidding.

Unfortunately, when it came to Carla Ambrosi, concepts like power, control and discipline crashed and burned.

He closed the door behind him. "What do you think you're doing?"

Carla halted by an ebony cabinet that held a selection of bottles, a jug of ice water and a tray of glasses. "I need a drink."

Glass clinked on glass, liquid splashed. His frustration deepened. Carla seldom drank and when she did it had always been in moderation. Tonight he knew she'd had champagne, then wine with dinner. He had kept a watch on her intake, specifically so he could intervene if he thought she was in danger of drinking too much then making a scene. He had been looking for an opportunity to speak to her alone when she had walked out halfway through dessert. Until now he had been certain she wasn't drunk.

He reached her in two long strides and gripped her wrist. "How much have you had?"

Liquid splashed the front of her dress. He jerked his gaze away from the way the wet silk clung to the curve of her breasts.

Her gaze narrowed. A split second later cold liquid cascaded down his chest, soaking through to the skin.

Water, not alcohol.

Time seemed to slow, stop as he stared at her narrowed gaze, delicately molded cheekbones and firm jaw, the rapid pulse at her throat.

The thud of the glass hitting the thick kilim barely registered as she curled her fingers in the lapel of his jacket.

"What do you think you're doing?" His voice was husky, the question automatic as he stared at her face.

"Conducting an experiment."

Her arms slid around his neck; she lifted up onto her toes. Automatically, his head bent. The second his mouth touched hers he knew it was a mistake. Relief shuddered through him as her breasts flattened against his chest and the soft curve of her abdomen cradled his instant arousal.

His hands settled at her waist as he deepened the kiss. The soft, exotic perfume she wore rose up, beguiling him, and the fierce clamp of desire intensified. Two months. As intent as he had been on finishing with Carla, he didn't know how he had stayed away.

No one else did this to him; no one came close. To say he

made love with Carla didn't cover the fierceness of his need or the undisciplined emotion that grabbed at him every time he weakened and allowed himself the "fix" of a small window of time in her bed.

Following the tragedy with Sophie, he had kept his liaisons clear-cut and controlled, as disciplined as his heavy work schedule and workout routines. He had been too shell-shocked to do anything else. Carla was the antithesis of the sophisticated, emotionally secure women he usually chose. Women who didn't demand or do anything flamboyant or off-the-wall.

He dragged his mouth free, shrugged out of his jacket then sank back into the softness of her mouth. He felt her fingers dragging at the buttons of his shirt, the tactile pleasure of her palms sliding over his skin.

Long, drugging minutes passed as he simply kissed her, relearning her touch, her taste. When she moved restlessly against him, he smoothed his hands up over her back, knowing instinctively that if she was going to withdraw, this would be the moment.

Her gaze clashed with his and he logged her assent. It occurred to Lucas that if he had been a true gentleman, he would have eased away, slowed things down. Instead he gave into temptation, cupped her breasts through the flimsy silk of bodice and bra. She arched against him with a small cry. Heat jerked through him when he realized she had climaxed.

Every muscle taut, he swept her into his arms and carried her to the couch. Her arms wound around his neck as she pulled him down with her. At some point his shirt disappeared and Carla shimmied against him, lifting up the few centimeters he needed so he could peel away the flimsy scrap of silk and lace that served as underwear.

He felt her fingers tearing at the fastening of his trousers. In some distant part of his mind the fact that he didn't have a condom registered. A split second later her hands closed around him and he ceased to think.

Desire shivered and burned through Carla as Lucas's hands framed her hips. Still dazed by the unexpected power of her climax, she automatically tilted her hips, allowing him access. Shock reverberated through her when she registered that there was no condom.

She hadn't thought; he hadn't asked. In retrospect she hadn't wanted to ask. She had been drowning in sensation, caught and held by the sudden powerful conviction that if she walked away from Lucas now, everything they had shared, everything they had been to each other would be lost. She would never touch him, kiss him, make love with him again, and that thought was acutely painful.

It was wrong, crazily wrong, on a whole lot of levels. Lucas had broken up with her. He had chosen someone else.

His gaze locked with hers and the steady, focused heat, so utterly familiar—as if she really was the only woman in the world for him—steadied her.

Emotion squeezed her chest as the shattering intensity gripped her again, linking her more intensely with Lucas. She should pull back, disengage. Making love did not compute, and especially not without a condom, but the concept of stopping now was growing progressively more blurred and distant.

She didn't want distance. She loved making love with Lucas. She loved his scent, the satiny texture of skin, the masculine beauty of sleek, hard muscle. The tender way he touched her, kissed her, made love to her was indescribably singular and intimate. She had never made love with another man, and when they were together, for those moments, he was *hers*.

Sharp awareness flickered in his gaze. He muttered something in rapid, husky Medinian, an apology for his loss of control, and a wild sliver of hope made her tense. If Lucas had wanted her badly enough that he hadn't been able to stop long enough to take care of protection, then there had to be a future for them.

With a raw groan he tangled his fingers in her hair, a glint of rueful humor charming her as he bent and softly kissed her. Something small and hurt inside her relaxed. She wound her arms around his neck, holding him tight against her and the hot night shivered and dissolved around them.

For long minutes Carla lay locked beneath Lucas on the couch. She registered the warm internal tingle of lovemaking. It had been two months since they had last been together, and she took a moment to wallow in the sheer pleasure of his heat and scent, the uncomplicated sensuality of his weight pressing her down.

She rubbed her palms down his back and felt his instant response.

Lucas's head lifted up from its resting place on her shoulder. The abrupt wariness in his gaze reflected her own thoughts. They'd had unprotected sex once. Were they really going to repeat the mistake?

A sharp rap at the door completed the moment of separation.

"Wait," Lucas said softly.

She felt the cool flutter as he draped her dress over her thighs. Feeling dazed and guilty, Carla clambered to her feet, snatched up her panties and her bag and found her shoes.

"The bathroom is the second on the left."

Her head jerked up at the husky note in his voice, but Lucas's expression was back to closed, his gaze neutral.

He was already dressed. With his shirt buttoned, his jacket on, he looked smoothly powerful and unruffled, exactly as he had before they had made love. Somewhere in-

side her the sliver of hope that had flared to life when they
had been making love died a sudden death.

Nothing had changed. How many times had she seen him
distance himself from her in just that way when he had left
her apartment, as if he had already separated himself from
her emotionally?

As if what they had shared was already filed firmly in
the past and she had no place in his everyday life.

The moment was chilling, a reality check that was long
overdue. "Don't worry, I'll find it. I don't want anyone to
know I was here, either." Her own voice was husky but
steady. Despite the hurt she felt oddly distant and remote.

She stepped into the cool, tiled sanctuary of the bathroom and locked the door. After freshening up she set about
fixing her makeup. A sharp rap on the door made her jerk,
smearing her mascara.

"When you're ready, I'll take you home."

"Five minutes. And I'll take myself home."

She stared at her reflection, her too pale skin, the curious blankness in her eyes as if, like a turtle retreating into
its shell, the hurt inner part of her had already withdrawn.
With automatic movements, she cleaned away the smear and
reapplied the mascara.

When she stepped out of the bathroom the sitting room
was empty. For the first time she noticed the fine antiques
and jewel-bright rugs, the art that decorated the walls and
which was lit by glowing pools of light.

Lucas stepped in from the terrace, through an elegant set
of French doors.

She met his gaze squarely. "Who was at the door?"

"Lilah."

Oh, good. Her life had just officially gone to hell in a
handbasket. "Did she see me?"

"Unfortunately."

Lucas's choice of word finally succeeded in dissolving the curious blankness and suddenly she was fiercely angry. "What if I'm pregnant?"

A pulse worked in his jaw. "If you're pregnant, that changes things—we'll talk. Until you have confirmation, we forget this happened."

When Carla woke in the morning, the headache was still nagging, and she was definitely off-color. She stepped into the shower and washed her hair. When she'd soaped herself, she stood beneath the stream of hot water and waited to feel better.

She spread her palm over her flat abdomen, a sense of disorientation gripping her when she considered that she could be pregnant.

A baby.

The thought was as shocking as the fact that she had been weak enough to allow Lucas to make love to her.

If she was pregnant, she decided, there was no way she could terminate. She loved babies, the way they smelled, their downy softness and vulnerability, the gummy smiles— and she would adore her own.

Decision made. If—and it was a big *if*—she was pregnant she would have the child and manage as a single parent. Lucas wouldn't have to be involved. There was no way she would marry him without love, or exist in some kind of twilight state in his life that would allow him discreet access while he married someone else.

Turning off the water, she toweled herself dry, belted on a robe and padded down to breakfast. Her stomach felt vaguely nauseous and she wasn't hungry, but she forced herself to chew one of the sweet Medinian rolls she had enjoyed so much yesterday.

Half an hour later, she checked on Sienna, who was

smothered by attendants, then dressed for the wedding in an exquisite lilac-silk sheath. She sat for the hairdresser, who turned her hair into a glossy confection of curls piled on top of her head, then moved to another room where a cosmetician chatted cheerfully while she did her makeup.

Several hours later, with the wedding formalities finally completed and the dancing under way, she was finally free to leave her seat at the bridal table. Technically, as the maid of honor, her partner for the celebration was Lucas, who was the best man. Mercifully, he was seated to one side of the bride and groom, and she the other, so she had barely seen him all evening.

As she rose from the table and found the strap of her purse, which was looped over the back of her seat, lean brown fingers closed over hers, preventing her from lifting up the bag.

A short, sharp shock ran through her at the pressure. Lucas released his hold on her fingers almost immediately.

He indicated Constantine and Sienna drifting around the dance floor. "I know you probably don't want to dance, but tradition demands that we take the floor next."

She glanced away from the taut planes of his cheekbones and his chiseled jaw, the inky crescents of his lashes. In a morning suit, with its tight waistcoat, he looked even more devastatingly handsome than usual. "And is that what you do?" she said a little bitterly. "Follow tradition?"

Lucas waited patiently for her to acquiesce to the dance. "You know me better than that."

Yes, she did, unfortunately. As wealthy and privileged as Lucas was, he had done a number of unconventional things. One of them was to play professional rugby. Her gaze rested on the faintly battered line of his nose. An automatic tingle of awareness shot through her at the dangerous, sexy edge it added to features that would otherwise have been *GQ* perfect.

His gaze locked on hers and, as suddenly as if a switch had been thrown, the sizzling hum of attraction was intimately, crazily shared.

Her breath came in sharply. Not good.

Aware that they were now under intense scrutiny from guests at a nearby table, including Lilah, Carla placed her hand on Lucas's arm and allowed him to lead her to the dance floor.

Lucas's breath feathered her cheek as he pulled her close. "How likely is it that you are pregnant?"

She stiffened at the sudden hot flood of memory. On cue the music changed, slowing to a sultry waltz. Lucas pulled her into a closer hold. Heat shivered through her as her body automatically responded to his touch. "Not likely."

Since the virus she had caught in Thailand she hadn't had a regular cycle, mostly because, initially, she had lost so much weight. She had regained some of the weight but she hadn't yet had a period. Although she wasn't about to inform Lucas of that fact.

"How soon will you know?"

"I'm not sure. Two weeks, give or take."

"When you find out, one way or the other, I want to be informed, but that shouldn't be a problem. As of next week, I'm Ambrosi's new CEO."

She stumbled, missing a step. Lucas's arm tightened and she found herself briefly pressed against his muscular frame. Jerkily, she straightened, her cheeks burning at the intimate brush of his hips, a stark reminder of their lovemaking last night. "I thought Ben Vitalis was stepping in as CEO."

Lucas's specialty was managing hostile acquisitions. Since her family, embattled by long-term debt, had voluntarily offered The Atraeus Group a majority shareholding

of Ambrosi Pearls, the situation was cut-and-dried. Lucas
shouldn't have come within a mile of Ambrosi.

Unless he viewed *her* as a problem.

Her chin jerked up as another thought occurred to her.
"You told Constantine about us."

His brows jerked together. "No."

Relief flooded her. The thought that Lucas could have revealed their relationship now, when it was over, would have
finally succeeded in making her feel cheap and disposable.

She drew in a steadying breath. "When was the decision made?"

"A few weeks ago, when we knew Ambrosi was in trouble."

"It's not necessary for you to come to Sydney. In the un-
likely event that there is a baby, I will contact you."

His glance was impatient. "The decision is made."

She drew an impeded breath at the sudden graphic image
of herself round and heavy with his child. She didn't think a
pregnancy was possible, but clearly Lucas did.

The music wound to a sweeping, romantic halt. There was
a smattering of applause. Carla allowed Lucas to complete
the formalities by leading her off the dance floor.

The rest of the evening passed in a haze. Carla danced
with several men she didn't know, and twice with Alex Panopoulos, an Ambrosi client she'd had extensive dealings with
in Sydney. The wealthy owner of a successful chain of high-
end retail stores, Alex was a reptile when it came to women.
He was also in need of a public relations officer for a new
venture and spent the first dance fishing to see if she was
available. Halfway through the second dance, Lucas cut in.

His gaze clashed with hers as he spun her into a sweeping turn. "Damn. What are you doing with Panopoulos?"

"Nothing that's any of your business. Why? Do you think

I'm in danger of meeting a man who might actually propose?"

"Alex Panopoulos is a shrewd operator. When he marries, there will be a business connection."

She stared at the clean line of his jaw. "Are you suggesting that all he wants is an affair?"

His grip on her fingers tightened. "I have no idea what Panopoulos wants. All I know is that when it comes to women he doesn't have a very savory reputation."

"I'm surprised you think I need protection."

"Trust me, you don't want to get involved with Panopoulos."

Dragging free of his gaze, she stared at the muscular column of his throat. "Maybe he wanted something from me that has nothing to do with sex? Besides, you're wasting your breath trying to protect me. From now on, who I choose to be with is none of your business."

"It is if you're pregnant."

The flash of possessive heat in his gaze and the tightening of his hold finally succeeded in making her lose her temper. "I might have some say in that."

Five

Lucas leaned against the wall in a dim alcove, arms folded over his chest as he observed the final formality of the wedding, the throwing of the bouquet.

Zane joined him, shifting through the shadows with the fluid ease that was more a by-product of his time spent on the streets of L.A. than of the strict, conventional upbringing he'd received on Medinos. He nodded at Carla, who was part of a cluster of young women gathered on the dance floor. "Not your finest hour. But, if you hadn't rescued her, I was thinking of doing it myself."

"Touch Carla," Lucas said softly, "and you lose your hand."

Zane took a swallow of beer. "Thought so."

Lucas eyed his younger brother with irritation. Four years difference and he felt like Methuselah. "How long have you known?"

"About a year, give or take."

The bouquet arced through the air straight into Carla's hands. Lucas's jaw tightened as she briskly handed it to one of the pretty young flower girls and detached herself from the noisy group. She made a beeline for her table, picked up the lilac clutch that went with her dress, and made her way out of the *castello's* ballroom.

Lucas glanced at Zane. "Do me a favor and look after Lilah for me for the rest of the evening."

Zane's expression registered rare startlement. "Let me get this right, you won't let me near Carla, but with Lilah it's okay?"

Lucas frowned at his turn of phrase, but his attention was focused on the elegant line of Carla's back. "The party's almost over. An hour, max."

"That long."

Impatiently, he studied the now empty hallway. "She'll need a ride back to the villa."

"Not a problem. Aunts at six o'clock." With a jerk of his chin, indicating direction, Zane snagged his beer and made a swift exit.

Pushing away from the wall, Lucas started after Carla, and found himself the recipient of a shrewd glance from his mother and steely speculation from a gaggle of silver-haired great-aunts.

He groaned inwardly, annoyed that he had dropped his guard enough that not only Zane but his mother had become aware of his interest in Carla. The last thing he needed was his mother interfering in his love life.

Seconds later, he traversed the vaulted hallway and stepped outside onto the graveled driveway just as the sound of Constantine and Sienna's departing helicopter cut the air.

The sun was gone, the night thick with stars, but heat still flowed out of the sunbaked soil as he strode toward Carla.

The ambient temperature was still hot enough that he felt uncomfortable in his suit jacket.

A stiff sea breeze was blowing, tugging strands loose from the rich, dark coils piled on top of Carla's head, making her look sexily disheveled. The breeze also plastered her dress against her body, emphasizing just how much weight she had lost.

His frown deepened. A regular gym bunny, Carla had always been fit and toned, with firm but definite curves. The curves were still there but if he didn't miss his guess she had dropped at least a dress size. After the virus she had picked up in Thailand, weight loss was understandable, but she should have regained it by now.

She spun when she heard the crunch of gravel beneath his shoes. A small jolt went through him when he registered the blankness of her gaze.

Carla didn't do sad. She had always been confident, sassy and adept at using her feminine power to the max. For Carla, masculine conquest was as natural as breathing. He had assumed that when their relationship was at an end she would have a lineup of prospective boyfriends eager to fill the gap.

In that moment it hit him forcibly that as similar as Carla was to Sophie with her job and her lifestyle, there were some differences. Sophie had been immature and self-centered, while Carla was fiercely loyal to her sister and her family, to the point of putting her own needs aside so as not to hurt Sienna. Even though that loyalty had clashed with what he had wanted, he had respected it. It also occurred to him that in her own way, Carla had been fiercely loyal to him. She had dated other men, but only ever in a business context for Ambrosi Pearls.

Broodingly, he considered the fact that Carla had been a virgin the first time they had made love, that she had never slept with anyone but him. He realized he had conveniently pushed the knowledge aside because it hadn't fitted the picture of Carla he had wanted to see.

He had been the one who had held back and played it safe, not Carla, and now the sheer intimacy of their situation kept hitting him like a kick to the chest.

He should let her go, but the shattering fact that he could have made her pregnant had changed something vital in his hard drive.

They were linked, at least until he had ascertained whether or not she was carrying his child. Despite his need to end the relationship, he couldn't help but feel relieved about that fact. "The limousines are gone. If you want a lift, I'll drive you."

"That won't be necessary." Carla extracted a cell phone from her clutch. "I'll get a taxi."

"Unless you've prebooked, with all the guests on Medinos for the wedding, you'll have difficulty getting one tonight."

She frowned as she flipped the phone closed and slipped it back in her clutch. "Then I'll ask Constantine."

He jerked his head in the direction of the helicopter, which was rapidly turning into a small dot on the horizon. "Constantine is on honeymoon. I'll take you."

Her glare was pointed. "I don't understand what you're doing out here. Shouldn't you be looking after your new girlfriend?"

"Zane's taking care of Lilah." Before she could argue, he cupped her elbow and steered her in the direction of the *castello's* stable of garages.

She jerked free of his hold. "Why doesn't Zane take me home and you go and take care of Lilah?"

His jaw clamped. "Do you want the lift or not?"

She stared at a point somewhere just left of his shoulder. Enough time passed that his temper began to spiral out of control.

Carla shrugged. "I'll accept a lift because I need one, but please don't touch me again."

"I wasn't trying to 'touch' you."

Her gaze connected with his, shooting blue fire. "I know what you were doing. The same thing you tried to do on the dance floor. Save it for Lilah."

He suppressed the cavemanlike urge to simply pick her up and carry her to the car. "You don't look well. What's wrong with you?"

"Nothing that a good night's sleep won't fix." Her gaze narrowed. "Why don't you say what's really bothering you? That, with all the paparazzi still on the loose, you can't take the risk that I might give them a story? And I think we both know that I could give them quite a story, an exposé of the *real* Lucas—"

Lucas gave in to the caveman urge and picked her up. "Did I mention the paparazzi?"

She thumped his shoulder with her beaded purse. "Let me down!"

Obligingly, he set her down by the passenger door of the Maserati. He jerked the door open. "Get in. If you try to run I'll come after you."

"There has to be a law against this." But she climbed into the sleek leather bucket seat.

"On Medinos?" Despite his temper, Lucas's mouth twitched as he slid behind the wheel and turned the key in the ignition. For the first time in two months he felt oddly content. "Not for an Atraeus."

Carla's tension skyrocketed when, instead of responding to her request and parking out on the street, Lucas drove into the cobbled driveway of the villa. At that point, he insisted on taking the house key from her and unlocked the door. When she attempted to close the door on him, he simply stepped past her and walked into the small, elegant house, switching on lights.

A narky little tension headache throbbing at her temples, Carla made a beeline for the bathroom, filled the glass on the counter with water and took her pills. Refilling the glass, she sat down on the edge of the bath and sipped, waiting to feel better.

A sharp rap on the bathroom door made her temper soar. She had hoped Lucas would take the hint and leave, but apparently he was still in the house. Replacing the glass on the counter, she checked her appearance then unlocked the door and stepped out into the hall.

He was leaning against the wall, arms crossed over his chest. She tried not to notice that, though he was still wearing his jacket, his tie and waistcoat were gone and several buttons of his shirt were undone revealing a mouthwatering slice of bronzed skin. "I'm fine now. You can leave."

She stepped past him and headed for the front door. Her spine tightened as Lucas followed too close behind, and she remembered what had happened the last time they had been alone together.

Note to self, she thought grimly as he peeled off into the sitting room and picked up his tie and waistcoat, *do not allow yourself to be alone with Lucas again.*

Opening the front door, she stood to one side, allowing him plenty of space. "Thank you for the lift."

He paused at the open door, making her aware of his height, the width of his shoulders, the power and vitality that seemed to burn from him. "Maybe you should see a doctor."

"If I need medical help, I'll get it for myself." She glanced pointedly at her wristwatch, resisting the urge to squint because one of the annoying symptoms of the headache now seemed to be that her eyes were ultrasensitive to light.

Not good. Her doctor had warned her that stress could

cause a viral relapse. With her father's funeral, Sienna's wedding and the breakup with Lucas, she was most definitely under stress.

His hand landed on the wall beside her head. Suddenly he was close enough that his heat engulfed her, and his clean, faintly exotic scent filled her nostrils.

Grimly, she resisted the impulse to take the half step needed, wrap her arms around his neck and melt into a goodnight kiss that would very likely turn into something else. "Um, shouldn't you be getting back to Lilah?"

For the briefest of moments he hesitated. His gaze dropped to her mouth and despite the tiredness that pulled at her, she found herself holding her breath, awareness humming through every cell of her being.

He let out a breath. "We can't do this again."

"No." But it had been an effort to say that one little word, and humiliation burned through her that, despite everything, she was still weak enough to want him.

His hand closed into a fist beside her head, then he was gone, the door closing gently behind him.

Carla leaned her forehead against the cool cedar of the door, her face burning.

Darn, darn, darn. Why had she almost given in to him? Like a mindless, trained automaton responding to the merest suggestion that he might kiss her.

After the stern talking-to she had given herself following the episode on the dance floor, she had succeeded in making herself look needy, like a woman who would do anything to get him back into her bed.

The pressure at her temples sharpened. Feeling more unsteady by the second, as if she was coming down with the flu, Carla walked to her bedroom. The acute sensitivity of her eyes was making it difficult to stand being in a lit room. No doubt about it, the virus had taken hold.

Removing her jewelry, she changed into cool cotton drawstring pants and a tank. She pulled on a cotton sweatshirt and cozy slippers against the chill and walked through to the bathroom. After washing and moisturizing her face, she pulled the pins out of her hair, which was an instant relief.

A discreet vibration made her frown. Her cell phone had a musical ring tone, and so did Sienna's. Margaret Ambrosi didn't own a cell, which meant the phone must belong to Lucas.

She padded barefoot into the sitting room in time to see the phone vibrate itself off the coffee table and drop to the carpet. A small pinging sound followed.

Carla picked up the phone. Lucas had missed a call from Lilah; now he had a text message, also from Lilah.

Fingers shaking slightly, she attempted to read the text but was locked out. A message popped up requesting she unlock the phone.

Not a problem, unless Lucas had changed his PIN since the last time they had dated.

Not dated, she corrected, her mood taking another dive. *Slept together.*

The last time he had stayed over at her apartment, before the holiday in Thailand, Lucas had needed to buy a new phone. The PIN he had used had been her birth date. At the time she had been ridiculously happy at his sentimental streak. She had taken it as a definite, positive *sign* that their relationship was progressing in the right direction.

She held her breath as she keyed in the number. The mail menu opened up.

The message was simple and to the point. Lilah was waiting for Lucas to call and would stay up until she heard from him.

The sick feeling in her stomach, the prickling chill she'd felt when he had broken up with her the previous night, came back at her full force. If she'd needed reinforcement of her decision to stay clear of Lucas Atraeus, this was it.

He was involved with someone else. He had *chosen* someone else, and the new woman in his life was waiting for him.

Closing the message, she replaced the phone on the coffee table and walked back to the bathroom. She switched off lights as she went, leaving one lamp burning in the sitting room for her mother when she came home. The relief of semidarkness was immense.

In the space of the past few minutes, she realized, the throbbing in her head had intensified and her skin hurt to touch. She swallowed another headache tablet, washing it down with sips of water. The sound of the doorbell jerked her head up. The sharp movement sent a stab of hot pain through her skull.

Lucas, back for his phone.

Setting the glass down, she walked back out to the hall, which was lit by the glow from the porch light streaming through two frosted sidelight windows. The buzzer sounded again.

"Open up, Carla. All I want is my phone."

That particular request, she decided, was the equivalent of waving a red rag at a bull. "You can have the phone tomorrow."

"I still have the key to this door," he said quietly. "If you don't unlock it, I'll let myself in."

Over her dead body.

"Just a minute." Annoyed with herself for forgetting to reclaim the key, she reached for the chain and tried to engage it. In her haste it slipped from her fingers.

She heard Lucas say something short and sharp. Adrenaline pumped. He knew she was trying to chain the door against him. The metallic scrape of a key being inserted into the lock was preternaturally loud as she grabbed the chain again.

Before she could slot it into place the door swung open, pushing her back a half step. Normally, the half step back wouldn't have fazed her, but with the weird shakiness of the virus she was definitely not her normal, athletic self and had to clutch at the hall table to help with her balance. Something crashed to the floor; glass shattered. She registered that when she had grabbed at the table her shoulder must have brushed against a framed watercolor mounted on the wall.

Lucas frowned. "Don't move."

Ignoring him, she bent down and grasped the edge of the frame.

Lean fingers curled around her upper arms, hauling her upright. "Leave that. You'll cut yourself."

Too late. Curling her thumb in against her palm, she made a fist, hiding a tiny, stinging jab that as far as she was concerned was so small it didn't count as a cut. She blinked at the bright porch light. "I didn't give you permission to come in, and you don't have the right to give me orders."

"You *did* cut yourself." He muttered something in Medinian. She was pretty sure it was a curse word. "Give me the watercolor before you do any more damage."

Her grip on the watercolor firmed, even though his request made sense. If she got blood on the painting it would be ruined. "I don't need your help. Get your phone and go."

"You look terrible."

"Thanks!"

"You're as white as a sheet."

He released her so suddenly she swayed off balance. By the time she recovered he had laid claim to her sore thumb and was probing at the small cut. But she still had the painting. "Neat trick."

His gaze was oddly intent. "There doesn't seem to be any glass in it."

He wrapped a handkerchief around her thumb and closed her fingers around it to apply pressure. "How long have you been sick?"

Her jaw tightened. She was being childish, she knew, but she hated being sick. It literally brought out the worst in her. "I'm not sick. Like I said before, all I need is a good night's sleep, so if you don't mind—"

The brush of his fingers against her temple as he pushed hair away from her face distracted her.

"Does that hurt? Don't answer. I can see that it does."

He leaned close. Arrested by his nearness, she studied the taut line of his jaw, suddenly assaulted by a myriad of sensations—the heat from Lucas's body, the clean scent of his skin, the rasp of his indrawn breath. That was one of the weird things about the virus: it seemed to amplify everything, hearing, scent, emotions, as if protective layers had been peeled away, leaving her senses bare and open.

In a slick move, he took the watercolor while her attention was occupied by the intriguing shape of his cheekbones, which were meltdown material.

A small sound informed her that he had placed the painting on the hall table. Out of nowhere her stomach turned an uncomfortable somersault. "I think I'm going to be sick."

His hand closed around her upper arm, and the heat from his palm burned through the cotton sweatshirt. Then they were moving, glass crunching under the soles of her slippers as he guided her out of the entrance hall into the sitting room. Another turn and they were in the bathroom.

Long minutes later, she rinsed her mouth and washed her face. She had hoped that Lucas would have left, but he was leaning against the hallway wall looking patient and composed and drop-dead gorgeous. In contrast she felt bedraggled and washed-out and as limp as a noodle.

Disgust and a taut, burning humiliation filled her. It was a rerun of Thailand, everything she had never wanted to happen again.

He folded his arms across his chest. "I'm guessing this is a relapse of the virus."

Keeping one hand on the wall for steadiness, she made a beeline for her bedroom. "Apparently. This is the first recurrence I've had." Her head spun and for a split second she thought she might be sick again, although she was fairly certain there was nothing left in her stomach. Two more wavering steps then the blissful darkness of her bedroom enfolded her. "Don't turn on the light. And don't come in here. This is *my* room." And as such it was off-limits to men who didn't love her.

"You should have told me you were still ill."

Her temper flashed, but if it was measured on a color spectrum it would have been a washed-out pink, not the angry red it had been earlier in the evening. She didn't have the energy for anything more and she was fading fast. "I didn't *know* I was still ill."

"That's some temper you've got."

Her teeth would have gritted if she'd had the strength. "Inherited it from my mother." She dragged her coverlet back. "She'll be home soon." The thought filled her with extreme satisfaction. She hadn't been able to kick Lucas's butt out, but Margaret Ambrosi would. Especially if she found him in her little girl's room.

Gingerly she sat on the side of the bed. Now that the stomach issue was over her attention was back on her head, which was pounding. What she needed was another painkiller, because the last one had just been flushed.

Dimly, she registered that despite her express order, Lucas *was* in her room. "I told you not to be here."

He crouched down and eased her slippers off her feet. "Or what? You'll lose that famous temper?"

"That's right." A shiver went through her at the burning heat of his hands on her feet. The chill on her skin made her realize that the next stage of the virus was kicking in. Oh, goody, she thought wearily, Antarctic-cold shivers followed by sweats that rivaled burning desert sands. Exactly how she always wanted to spend a Saturday night.

"I'll take the risk. I survived Thailand, I can survive this."

He pulled her to her feet. Her nose bumped against his shoulder. Automatically, she clutched his lean waist and leaned into his comforting strength. She inhaled, breathing in his scent, and for a crazy moment all she wanted to do was rest there.

A split second later, the sheet peeled back, Lucas eased her into bed and pulled the sheets and coverlet over her.

With a sigh, she allowed her head to sink into the feather pillow. "All I need is another one of the painkillers on the bathroom vanity and some water and I'll be fine." It was surrender, she knew it, but she really did need the pill.

She registered his near silent footfalls as he walked to the bathroom, the hiss of water as he filled the glass, then he was back. His arm came around her shoulders as he propped her up so she could take the pill and drink the water. When she was finished he set the glass down on her bedside table.

She settled back on the pillows. "You know what? You're good at this."

"I had lots of practice in Thailand. Do you need anything else?" His voice was closer now, the timbre low and deliciously gruff.

It was the kind of velvety masculine rumble that, if they had been in bed together, would have invited a snuggling session. Then suddenly she remembered. Lucas was with Lilah now; he no longer wanted her. If he felt anything for her, it had to be pity. A weak, watered-down version of fury roared through her.

She peeled her lids open and peered at Lucas, ready to read him the riot act, then forgot what she was about to say because there was a strange, intent expression on his face. "Nothing. You can leave. Phone's on the coffee table. That was what you came for, wasn't it?"

He was so close she could feel the heat blasting off his body, see his gaze sliding over her features, cataloging her white face and messy hair. For shallow, utterly female reasons she wished that her face was glowing instead of chalky-white and that she had taken the time to brush her hair. Mercifully, the strong painkiller finally kicked in, taking the heat out of the ache in her head and dragging her down into sleep. "I don't want you here."

It was a lie. The virus had made her so weak that she was fast losing the strength to keep up the charade, even to herself.

"I'm staying until I know you'll be all right."

"I would like you to leave. Now." The crisp delivery she intended was spoiled by the fact that the words ran together in a drunken, blurred jumble.

She was certain the soft exhalation she heard had something to do with amusement, which made her even more furious. The mattress shifted as he planted a hand on either side of her head and leaned close. "What are you going to do if I don't? Make me leave?"

For a crazy moment she thought he was actually flirting with her, but that couldn't be. "Don't have to," she mumbled, settling the argument. Her eyelids slid closed. "You've already gone."

Silence settled around her, thick, heavy, as the sedative effect of the pills dragged her down.

"Do you want me back?"

The words jerked her awake, but they had been uttered so quietly she wasn't sure if she had imagined them or if Lucas had actually spoken.

She could see him standing in her bedroom doorway. Maybe she had been dreaming, or worse, hallucinating. "I took codeine, not truth serum."

"It was worth a try."

So he *had* asked the question.

She pushed up on one elbow. The suspicion that he was sneakily trying to interrogate her while she was drowsy from the pills solidified. Although she couldn't fathom why he would be interested in what she really thought and felt now. "I don't know why you're bothering. Thank you for helping me, but please leave now."

He shook his head. "You're...different tonight."

Different? She had been dumped. She had committed the cardinal sin of making love with her ex and could quite possibly be pregnant.

"Not different." Turning over, she punched the pillow and willed herself to go to sleep. "Real."

Six

Ten days later, Carla strolled into the Ambrosi building in Sydney.

When she reached her office, her assistant, Elise, a chirpy blonde with a marketing degree and a formidable memory for names and statistics, was in the process of hanging up the phone. "Lucas wants you in his office. *Now.*"

A jolt of fiery irritation instantly evaporated the peace and calm of four days spent recuperating at her mother's house, the other five in the blissful solitude of the Blue Mountains at a friend's holiday home. "Did he say why?"

Elise looked dreamily reflective. "He's male, hot *and* single. Does it matter?"

Nerves taut, Carla continued on to her desk and deliberately took time out to examine the list of messages and calls Elise had compiled in her absence. Keeping her bag hooked over her shoulder, she checked her calendar and noted she had two meetings scheduled.

When she couldn't stall any longer, she strolled to Sienna's old office, frowning at the changes Atraeus money had already made to her family's faltering business. Worn blue carpet had been replaced with a sleek, dove-gray weave. Fresh paint and strategically placed art now graced walls that had once been decorated solely with monochrome prints of Ambrosi jewelry designs.

Feeling oddly out of place in what, from childhood, had been a cozily familiar setting, she greeted work colleagues.

Directing a brittle smile at Sienna's personal assistant, Nina—Lucas's PA now—she stepped into the elegant corner office.

Lucas, broad shouldered and sleekly powerful in a dark suit with a crisp white shirt and red tie, dominated a room that was still manifestly feminine as he stood at the windows, a phone held to one ear.

His gaze locked with hers, he terminated the call. "Close the door behind you and take a seat."

Suddenly glad she had made an extra effort with her appearance, she closed the door. The sharp little red suit, with its short skirt and fitted V-necked jacket, always made her feel attractive and energized. It probably wasn't the best idea for dealing with Lucas, but she hadn't worn it for him. She had a job interview at five with Alex Panopoulos, and she needed to look confident and professional. His upmarket Pan department stores were branching into jewelry manufacture and he had been chasing her all week to come in for an interview.

She hated the idea of leaving Ambrosi Pearls, but she had to be pragmatic about her position. When Constantine had offered the company back to Sienna on her wedding day they had held a family meeting. In essence, they had agreed to honour their debts, so the transfer of the company to The Atraeus Group had gone through as planned. With Sienna's marriage to Constantine binding both families together, combined with Constantine's assurance that he would keep the company intact, it had seemed the most sensible solution.

As a consequence, Carla now owned a block of voting shares. They would assure her of an income for the rest of her life, but they gave her no effective power. Her current personal contract as Ambrosi Pearls's public relations executive was up for renewal directly after Ambrosi's new product launch in a week's time. She didn't anticipate that Lucas would renew it. Her tenure as "The Face of Ambrosi" was just as shaky, but as she provided that service for free to help the company save money, it was no skin off her nose if Lucas no longer wanted her face on the posters.

Annoyance flickered in Lucas's gaze when she didn't immediately sit. He replaced the phone on its base. "I didn't expect you back in so soon."

She lifted a brow. "I felt okay, so there was no point in staying at home."

"I've been trying to reach you all week. Why didn't you return my calls?"

She shrugged. "I was staying with friends and didn't take my phone." She had left the phone at her apartment on purpose. The last thing she had needed was to have a desperately low moment and make the fatal mistake of trying to call or text Lucas.

There was a small charged silence. "How are you?"

"Fine. A couple of days in bed and the symptoms disappeared." She smiled brightly. "If that's all…"

"Not exactly." His gaze rested on her waist, where the jacket cinched in tight. "Are you pregnant?"

Despite her effort at control, heat flooded her cheeks. "I don't know yet. I have a test kit, but it's early to get an accurate reading."

"When will you know?"

She frowned, feeling distinctly uncomfortable with the subject and the way he was regarding her, as if she was a concubine who had somehow escaped the harem and he had ownership rights. "I should know in another couple of days. But whether I'm pregnant or not, it needn't concern you."

Actually, she could find out right that minute if she wanted. The test kit had said a result could be obtained in as early as seven days. She had studied the instructions then chucked the box in the back of one of her drawers. She still felt too raw and hurt to face using the kit and discovering that not only had she lost Lucas, her life was about to take a huge, unplanned turn. In a few days, when she felt ready, she would do the test.

Anger flickered in his gaze. "You would abort the child?"

"No." She felt shocked that he had even jumped to that conclusion. If there was a child, there was no way she would do anything other than keep the baby and smother it with love for the rest of its life. "What I meant is that *if* there is a child, I've decided that you don't have to worry, because you don't need to be involved, or even acknowledge—"

"Any child of mine would be acknowledged."

The whiplash flatness of his voice, as if she had scraped a raw nerve, was even more shocking. Carla sucked in a breath and forced herself to loosen off the soaring tension. She was clearly missing something here. "This is crazy. I don't know why we're discussing something that might never happen. Is that all you wanted to know?"

"No." He propped himself on the edge of the desk. "Have a seat. There's something else we need to discuss."

There were three comfortable client seats; she chose the one farthest away from Lucas. The second she lowered herself into the chair she regretted the decision. Even though he wasn't standing, Lucas still towered over her. "Let me guess—I'm fired in a week's time? I'm surprised it took you so long to get around to—"

"I'm not firing you."

Carla blinked. Constantine had fired Sienna almost immediately, although his reasons had been understandable. Continuing on as CEO of a company in Sydney while he was based in Medinos had not been viable.

His gaze flicked broodingly over the crisp little suit. "Do you always dress like that for work?"

His sudden change of tack threw her even more off balance. She realized that from his vantage point he could see more than the shadowy hint of cleavage that was normally visible in the vee of the jacket. She squashed the urge to drag the lapels together. "Yes. Is there a problem?"

He crossed his arms over his chest. "Nothing that an extra button or a blouse wouldn't fix."

She shot to her feet. "There is nothing wrong with what I'm wearing. Sienna was perfectly happy with my wardrobe."

He straightened, making her even more aware of his height, the breadth of his shoulders, the incomprehensible anger simmering behind midnight-dark eyes.

"Sienna was female."

"What has that got to do with anything?"

"From where I'm standing, quite a lot.

She didn't know what was bothering him. Maybe a major deal had fallen through, or even better, Lilah had dumped him. Whatever it was she would swear that he was behaving proprietorially, but that couldn't be. He had dumped her without ceremony; he had made it clear he didn't want her. To add insult to injury, the tabloids were having a field day reporting his relationship with Lilah.

His gaze dropped once again to the vee of her jacket. "Who are you meeting today?"

Temper soaring at the lightning perusal, the even more pointed innuendo, she reeled off two names.

"Both male," he said curtly.

"Chandler and Howarth are contemporaries of my father! And I resent the implication that I would resort to using sex to make sales for Ambrosi, but if you prefer I could turn up for work in beige. Or, since this conversation is taking a medieval turn, maybe you'd prefer sackcloth and ashes."

His mouth twitched at the corners and despite her spiraling anger she found herself briefly mesmerized by the sudden jolt of charm. Lucas was handsome when he was cool and ruthless, but when he smiled he was drop-dead gorgeous in a completely masculine way that made her go weak at the knees and melt.

"You don't own anything beige."

"How would you know?" she pointed out, glad to get her teeth into something that could generate some self-righteous anger.

She wasn't vengeful, nor did she have a desire to hurt Lucas. It was simply that she was black-and-white in her thinking. They were either together or they weren't, and she couldn't bear the underlying invitation in his eyes, his voice, to be friends now that he had decreed their relationship was over. "As I recall, you were more interested in taking my clothes off than noticing what I was wearing. You had no more interest in my wardrobe than you had in any other aspect of my life."

His brows jerked together. "That's not true. You were the one who decreed we had to live separate lives."

Her hands curled into fists. "Don't say it didn't suit you."

"It did, at the time."

"Ha!" But the moment of triumph was hollow. She just wished she had realized she wasn't built for such a shallow, restricted relationship.

Pointedly, she checked her wristwatch. "I have a meeting in ten minutes. If there's nothing else, I need to go. With the product launch in two days' time, there's a lot to do."

"That's what I wanted to talk to you about. We've made some changes to the arrangements for the launch party. Nina will be heading up the team running the promotion."

Not fired, Carla thought blankly. Sidelined.

She took a deep breath and let it out slowly, but when she spoke her voice was still unacceptably husky. "Some product launch without the most high-profile component, or have you forgotten that I'm 'The Face of Ambrosi'?"

Broodingly, Lucas surveyed Carla's perfect face, exquisite in every detail from exotic eyes to delicate cheekbones and enticing mouth. Add in the outrageously sexy tousle of dark hair trailing down her back and she was spectacularly irresistible.

Ambrosi had cut costs and cashed in on Carla's appeal, but he found himself grimly annoyed every time he noticed one of the posters. "It's hard to miss when your face is plastered all over the front of the building."

And in every one of the perfumed women's magazines he had been forced to flick through since he'd stepped into Sienna Ambrosi's front office.

Triumph glowed briefly in her gaze. "You can't sideline me. I have to be there." She began ticking off all the reasons he couldn't surgically remove her from the campaign.

His frustration levels increased exponentially with every valid reason, from interviews with women's magazines to a promotional stunt she had organized.

"I have to be there—it's a no-brainer. Besides, the costuming has all been completed to my measurements."

He cut her off in midstream. "No."

Carla's eyes narrowed. "Why not?"

Not a subject he was prepared to go live on, he thought, gaze fixed on the sleek fit of her red suit.

Every time he saw one of the posters, he had to fight the irrational urge to rip it down. The idea that Carla would do a promotional show in the transparent, pearl-encrusted creation he had viewed in front of an audience filled with voyeuristic men was the only no-brainer in the equation.

Over his dead body.

He felt as proprietary as he imagined a father would feel keeping his daughter from hormonal teenage boys. Not that his feelings were remotely fatherly. She could threaten and argue all day; it wasn't going to happen.

"You haven't been well, and you could be pregnant," he said flatly. "I'll do the interviews, and I've arranged for a model to take your place for the promotion. Nina is hosting the promotional show. Elise will take care of the styling."

Styling. He gripped the taut muscles at his nape. A week ago he didn't even know what that meant.

"I'm so well I'm jumping out of my skin. I'm here to work. The launch is *my* project."

"Not anymore."

Silence hung heavy in the air. Somewhere in the office a clock ticked; out on the street someone leaned on a car horn. Carla groped for the fire-engine-red bag that matched her suit.

Lucas's stomach clenched when he saw tears glittering on her lashes. Ah, damn… He resisted the sudden off-the-wall urge to coax her close and offer comfort. He had expected opposition—a fight—but he hadn't been prepared for this level of emotion. Somewhere in the raft of detail involved with taking over Ambrosi and figuring out how to handle Carla, he had forgotten how passionately intense and protective she was about her family and the business. Although how he could forget a detail that had seen *him* sidelined in Carla's life, he didn't know. "Carla—"

"Don't." She turned on her heel.

Jaw clenched against the need to comfort her and soothe away the hurt, he reached the door first. His hand landed on the cream-and–gilt-detailed panel of the door, preventing her from opening it. "Just one more thing. My mother and Zane fly in tomorrow. I've organized a press conference to promote The Atraeus Group's takeover of Ambrosi and the product launch, then a private lunch. As a family member and PR executive your presence is required at both."

She stared blankly ahead. "Will Lilah be there?"

"Yes."

Lucas had to restrain himself from going after Carla as she strode out of his office. His jaw tightened as he noted the outrageously sexy red heels and the enticing sway of her hips as she walked. The fact that he had lost his temper was disturbing, but ten days kicking his heels while she had disappeared off the radar had set him on edge. The second he had seen her in the red suit he had lost it. He had been certain she wasn't wearing anything but a bra under the tight little jacket, and he had been right.

Closing the door, he prowled back to the window and held aside the silky curtains that draped the window, feeling like a voyeur himself as he watched Carla stroll out onto the street and climb into the sports car that was waiting for her.

He had questioned her assistant extensively about her meetings, then, dissatisfied with her answers, had looked both Chandler and Howarth up on the internet.

Elise had been correct in her summation. Both men were old enough to be her father. Unfortunately, that didn't seem to cut any ice with him. They were men, period.

At a point in time when he should have been reinforcing

the end of their relationship by keeping his distance, he had never felt more possessive or jealous.

Instead of moving to Sydney, he should have stepped back and simply kept in touch with Carla. If she was pregnant, whether she told him or not, he would soon have known. Instead he had grabbed at the excuse to be close to her.

The fact that he had lost control to the extent that he had made love to Carla after they had broken up, *without protection,* still had the power to stun him.

Worse, he found the idea that they could have made a baby together unbearably sexy and appealing.

Maybe it was a kickback to his grief and loss over Sophie, but a part of him actually hoped Carla was pregnant.

He dropped the curtain as the taxi merged into traffic. Broodingly, he reflected that when it came to Carla Ambrosi, he found himself thinking in medieval absolutes.

For two years one absolute had dominated: regardless of how risky or illogical the liaison was, he had wanted Carla Ambrosi.

Despite breaking up and replacing her with a new girlfriend—a woman he had not been able to bring himself to either touch or kiss—nothing had changed.

Seven

Carla checked the time on the digital clock in her small sports car. She had ten minutes to reach Alex Panopoulos's office and rush hour was in full swing, the traffic already jammed.

On edge and impatient, Carla used every shortcut she knew, but even so she was running late when she reached the dim underground garage.

Late for an interview that was becoming increasingly important, she grabbed her handbag and portfolio and exited the car.

Her heels tapped on concrete as she strode to the elevator, just as a sleek dark car cruised into a nearby space. The tinted driver's side window was down, giving her a shadowy glimpse of the driver. The car reminded her of the vehicle Lucas's security detail used when he was in town.

Frowning, she stepped into the elevator and keyed in the PIN she had been given. She punched the floor number, then wished she hadn't as the doors slid shut, nixing her view of the driver before he could climb out of the car. Maybe she was paranoid, or simply too focused on Lucas, but for a split second she had entertained the crazy thought that the driver could be Lucas.

She kept an eye on the floor numbers as they lit up. She caught her reflection in the polished steel doors. The scene with Lucas accusing her of dressing to entice replayed in her mind.

Hurt spiraled through her that he clearly had such a bad opinion of her and was so keen to get rid of her that he had replaced her both personally and professionally. She wondered if he intended to escort Lilah to the event, then grimly decided that of course he would.

As a publicity stunt, the move couldn't be faulted. The media would love Lilah fronting for Ambrosi and the further evidence of her close relationship with Lucas. Ambrosi couldn't ask for a better launch gimmick…except maybe an engagement announcement at the launch party.

Her chest squeezed tight on a pang of misery. Suddenly, that didn't seem as ludicrous or far-fetched as it should, given that Lucas and Lilah had only been publicly dating for a couple of weeks. Lucas was legendary for his ruthless efficiency, his unequivocal decisions. If he had decided Lilah was the one, why wait?

The elevator doors opened onto a broad carpeted corridor. Discreetly suited executives, briefcases in hand, obviously leaving for the day, stepped into the elevator as she stepped out.

The receptionist showed her into Alex's office.

Twenty minutes later, the interview over, Carla stepped out of the lift and strode to her car. She had been offered the job of PR executive for Pan Jewelry, but she had turned it down. Five minutes into the interview she had realized that

Alex hadn't wanted her expertise; he had wanted to utilize her connection with the Atraeus family. Apparently, he could double his profit base in two years if they allowed Pan to trade in the luxury Atraeus Resorts.

She had been prepared to withstand his smooth charm, possibly even reject an attempt at seduction. She had done that before, on more than one occasion. Alex had made it clear he was prepared to deal generously with her in terms of position and salary, including a free apartment, if she came to him.

Stomach churning at the sexual strings that were clearly attached to his offer, and because she had missed lunch, Carla tossed her portfolio and purse on the backseat of her car. Flipping the glove box open, she found the box of cookies she kept there for just such an emergency. Part of the reason she had ended up with an ulcer was that she had a high-acid system. She had to be careful of what she ate, and of not eating at all. Stress coupled with an empty stomach was a definite no-no. Popping a chunk of the cookie in her mouth, she drove out of the parking garage.

The car she had thought could possibly belong to Lucas's security guy was no longer in its space, but, as she took the ramp up onto the sunlit street, the distinctive dark sedan nosed in behind her.

Spine tingling with a combination of renewed anger and the flighty, unreasoning panic of knowing someone was following her—no matter how benign the reason—she sped up. The car stayed with her, confirming in her mind that it *was* one of Lucas's men snooping on her.

Still fuming at his high-handed behavior, she pulled into her apartment building. When the sedan slid past the entrance and kept on going, she reversed out and made a bee-line for Lucas's inner-city apartment.

Twenty minutes later, after running the gauntlet of a concierge and one of Lucas's security detail, she pressed the buzzer on Lucas's penthouse door.

It swung open almost immediately. Lucas was still dressed in the dark pants and white shirt he had worn to the office that morning, although minus the tie and with the shirt hanging open to reveal a mouthwatering slice of taut and tanned torso. He leaned one shoulder against the door-jamb, unsubtly blocking her from barging into his apartment.

"Tell me that wasn't you following me."

"It wasn't me following you. It was Tiberio."

"In that case, do you really want to have this discussion in the hallway, where anyone can overhear?"

Cool amusement tugged at his mouth. "I rent the entire floor. The other three apartments are all occupied by my people."

"Let me rephrase that, then. Do you really want to have this discussion where your employees can overhear what I'm about to say?"

His jaw tightened, but he stepped back, leaving her just enough room to march past him. She was in the hallway, strolling across rug-strewn wooden floors into an expansive, airy sitting room before she had time to consider the unsettling fact that Lucas might not be alone. With his shirt hanging open and his sleeves unbuttoned it was highly likely he had company.

Her stomach churned at the thought. She'd had plenty of time on the drive over to consider that Lilah could be here.

She breathed a sigh of relief when she registered that the sitting room, at least, was unoccupied, although that didn't rule out the bedrooms. Until that moment she hadn't known just how much she dreaded seeing Lilah in Lucas's home, occupying the position in his life that until a few days ago she had foolishly assumed was hers.

Fingers tightening on her purse, she surveyed the sitting room with its eclectic mix of artwork and sculpture. Some she knew well; at least two she had never seen. "Nice paintings."

But then that had been one of the things that had attracted her to Lucas. He wasn't stuffy with either his thinking or his enjoyment of art.

As her gaze was drawn from one new painting to the next, absorbing the nuances of line, form and color, her stomach tensed. "A new artist?"

"You know me." His gaze was faintly mocking as he walked through an open-plan dining area to a modern kitchen and opened the fridge. "I'm always on the lookout for new talent."

It occurred to her that the artist could be Lilah, who painted in her spare time, and jealousy gripped her. Before she could stop herself she had stepped closer to the nearest of the new paintings, so she could study the signature. S. H. Crew, not L. Cole.

Her knees felt a little shaky as she moved on to the next painting, also by S. H. Crew. For some odd reason, the thought that Lilah might appeal to Lucas on a creative, spiritual level was suddenly more sharply hurtful than her physical presence would have been.

Lucas loomed over her, the warm scent of his skin, the faint undernote of sandalwood, making her pulse race. "Is it safe to give you this?"

"Not really." Jaw clenching against an instant flashback of the scene on Medinos when she had dashed water over Lucas, and the lovemaking that had followed, she took the glass of ice water. She strolled the length of the sitting room and drifted into a broad hall that served as a gallery. She sipped water and pretended to be interested in the paintings that flowed along a curving cream wall that just happened to lead to the master bedroom. "So why did you have me followed?"

He strolled past her and stood, arms folded over his chest, blocking her view of his bedroom. "I wanted to see what you were up to. Tell me," he said grimly, "what did Panopoulos offer you?"

She blinked at the mention of Panopoulos's name, but it went in one ear and out the other. She was consumed with suspicion because Lucas clearly did not want her to see into his bedroom, and the notion that Lilah was there, maybe even in his bed, was suddenly overwhelming.

Setting the water down on a narrow hall table she marched past him. Lucas's hand curled around her arm as she stepped through the door, swinging her around to face him, but not before she had ascertained that his bedroom was empty. And something else that made her heart slam hard against the wall of her chest.

What he hadn't wanted her to see. A silk robe she had left at his apartment by mistake the last time she had been here almost three months ago, and which was exactly where she had left it, draped over the back of a chair. The aquamarine silk was wildly exotic, sexy and utterly feminine. No woman would have missed its presence or significance and allowed it to remain. The robe was absolute proof that Lilah had never been in Lucas's bedroom.

Her heart beat a queer, rapid tattoo in her chest. "You haven't slept with her yet."

Lucas let her go, his gaze glittering with displeasure. "Maybe I was in the process of getting rid of your things before I invited her over."

Anger flaring, she backed up a half step. The cool solidity of the door frame stopped her dead. "I'm here now, you can hand it to me personally."

"Is that a command, or are you going to ask me nicely?"

Wary of the banked heat in Lucas's gaze, which was clearly at odds with the coolness of his tone, she controlled her temper with difficulty. "I just did ask you nicely."

"I'm willing to bet you were nicer to Alex Panopoulos when you walked into his office in that suit. Did you finally agree to sleep with him?"

"*Sleep* with him?" The words came out as an incredulous yelp. She couldn't help it, she was so utterly distracted by the fact that Lucas thought she could be even remotely interested in Alex Panopoulos, a man she barely tolerated for the sake of business. "Well, I haven't jumped into his bed, yet. Does that make you feel better about me?"

Hot anger simmered through her, doubly compounded by the humiliating fact that Panopoulos *had* wanted to sleep with her.

With a suddenness that shocked her, Lucas leaned forward and kissed her. The sensual shock of the kiss, even though she had half expected it and had goaded him into it, sent a wave of heat through Carla. Until that moment, she hadn't understood how much she had wanted to provoke him, how angry she was at his defection. She was also hurt that he still didn't know who she was after more than two years, and evidently didn't have any interest in knowing, when she was deeply, painfully in love with him.

She blinked, dazed. At some point, she realized, probably that first time they had met, something had happened. After years of dating men and knowing they weren't right, she had taken one look at Lucas and chosen him.

That was why she had broken almost every personal rule she'd had and slept with Lucas in the first place, then continued with the relationship when she knew any association with him would hurt her family. If she had been sensible and controlled she would have stepped back and waited. After all, if a relationship had legs it should stand the test of a little time. But she hadn't been able to wait. She had wanted him, needed him, right then, the same way she needed him now.

Two years. She blinked at the immensity of her self-deception. She had buried the in-love thing behind the pretense that theirs was a modern relationship between two overcommitted people with the added burden of some crazy family pressures. Anything to bury the fact that the sporadic interludes with Lucas in no way satisfied her need to be loved.

Her arms closed convulsively around his neck. She shouldn't be kissing him now, not when she wanted so much more, but in that moment she ceased to care.

"What's wrong?" Lucas pulled back, his gaze suddenly heart-stoppingly soft. "Am I hurting you?"

"No." *Yes.* Her hands tangled in the thick black silk of his hair and dragged his mouth back to hers. "Just kiss me."

Long minutes later they made it to the bed. She dragged his shirt off his shoulders and tossed it aside. Her palms slid across his sleek, heavy shoulders and muscled chest. Giddy pleasure spun through her as he removed her clothing, piece by piece, and she, in turn, removed his.

Time seemed to slow, then stop as she fitted herself against him and clasped his head, pulling his mouth to hers, needing him closer, needing him with her. Late-afternoon sun slanted through the shutters, tiger striping his shoulders as his gaze linked with hers and she suddenly knew why making love with Lucas had always been so special, so important. For those few minutes when they were truly joined it was as if he unlocked a part of himself that normally she could never quite reach, and he was wholly hers. In those few moments she could believe that he did love her.

Cool air swirled around naked skin as he sheathed himself. Relief shivered through her as they flowed together. She was utterly absorbed by the feel of him inside her, his touch and taste, the slow, thorough way he made love to her, as if he knew her intimately, as if they did belong together.

Aside from those few minutes on Medinos it had been long months since they had last made love, and she had missed him, missed this. As crazy as it seemed, despite everything that had gone wrong, everything that was still wrong, this part was right.

His head dipped, she felt the softness of his lips against her neck. Her stomach clenched, the slowly building tension suddenly unbearable as she tightened around him. She felt his raw shudder. In that moment her own climax shimmered through her with an intense pleasure that made tears burn behind her lids, and the room spun away.

Long minutes later the buzzer at the front door jerked her out of the sleepy doze she had fallen into. With smooth, fluid movements, Lucas rolled out of bed, snagged his clothes off the floor and walked through to the adjoining bathroom. Seconds later, he reappeared, fastening dark trousers around narrow hips as he strolled to the door.

Carla didn't wait to see who it was. Snatching up her clothes, including her bra, which had ended up hooked over a bedside lamp, she hurried into the bathroom to freshen up and change. Her clothes were crumpled and her hair was a tumbled mass, but she couldn't worry about that. Her priority was to leave as quickly as possible.

Slipping into her shoes, she searched and found her bag on the floor just outside the bedroom door. She must have dropped it when Lucas had kissed her there. Her cheeks burned with embarrassment as she marched through the sitting room where Lucas was talking in low, rapid Medinian to two of his security personnel.

Lucas said her name. She ignored him and the curious looks of the men, in favor of sliding through the open door and making a dash for the elevator.

Relief eased some of her tension when she saw that the doors were open. Jogging inside, she jabbed the ground floor button as Lucas appeared in the corridor.

"Wait," he said curtly.

The doors closed an instant before he reached the elevator. Heart pounding, Carla examined her reflection in the mirrored rear wall and spent the few seconds repairing her smudged mascara. She winced at her swollen lips and the pink mark on her neck where Lucas's stubble must have grazed her. She looked as if she had just rolled out of bed.

The elevator stopped with a faint jolt. Shoving her mascara back in her bag, Carla strolled quickly through the foyer, ignoring the concierge, who stared at her with a fascinated expression.

She almost stopped dead when she saw Lilah sitting in a chair, flipping through a magazine, obviously waiting. Pretending she hadn't noticed her, Carla quickened her step. Now the two security staff talking with Lucas in hushed, rapid Medinian made sense. Lilah had wanted to go up to Lucas's apartment, but they had known Carla was there.

Mortified, she dimly registered Lilah's white face, the shock in her eyes, as she pushed the foyer doors wide. The sound of traffic hit her like a blow. The sun, now low on the horizon, shone directly in her eyes, dazzling her, a good excuse for the tears stinging her eyes. Her throat tightened as she started down the front steps.

As she stepped onto the sidewalk a hand curved around her arm, stopping her in her tracks.

Her heart did a queer leap in her chest as she spun. "Lucas."

Eight

Carla wrenched free. Lucas was still minus his shirt, his hair sexily tangled. If she looked rumpled, he definitely looked like he had just rolled out of the love nest. "How did you get down so fast?"

"There's a second, private lift."

Her fingers tightened on the strap of her bag. "More to the point, why did you bother?"

His gaze narrowed. "I won't glorify that with an answer. What did you think you were doing running out like that?"

Now that the initial shock of Lucas chasing after her was over, she was desperate to be gone. She needed to be alone so she could stamp out the crazy notion that kept sliding into her mind that there was still a chance for them. She had to get it through her skull that there was no hope. She was the one who got lost in useless emotion, while Lucas remained coolly elusive.

Her gaze flashed. "We were finished, weren't we?" *In*

more ways than one. "Or was there something else you wanted?"

Heat burned along his cheekbones. "You know I never viewed you that way."

"How, then?"

He said something low and taut in Medinian that she was pretty sure was a swear word or phrase of some kind. Not for the first time it occurred to her that for her own peace of mind she really should learn some of that language.

His palm curved around the base of her neck, his fingers tangling in her hair. A split second later his mouth closed over hers.

A series of flashes, the slick, motorized clicking of a high-speed camera jerked them apart. A reporter with an expensive-looking camera had just emerged from a parked car.

A shudder of horror swept Carla. When the press recognized her they would put one and one together and make seven. Before she arrived back at her apartment they would have her entangled in a second-time-around affair with Lucas. By morning they would have her cast off and pregnant or, more probably, since Lucas was involved with Lilah, caught up in some trashy love triangle.

Most of it, unfortunately, was embarrassingly true.

A strangled sound jerked her head around. Bare meters away, directly behind Lucas, Lilah was caught in an awkward freeze-frame.

Carla's stomach lurched as if she'd just stepped into a high-speed elevator on its way down. That was a definite "go" on the love triangle.

Lilah spun on her heel and walked quickly away.

With a final, manic series of clicks the reporter slid back into the car from which he had emerged. With a high-pitched whine reminiscent of a kitchen appliance the tiny hatchback sped away.

Lucas swore softly, this time in English, and released his grip on her nape. His gaze was weary. "Did you know he was out here?"

Her temper soared at what she could only view as an accusation. She gestured at her crumpled clothing and hair, the smeared makeup. "Do I look like I'm ready to be photographed by some sleazy tabloid reporter?"

Lucas's brows jerked together. "You did it once before."

A tide of heat swept her at his reference to her admittedly outrageous behavior in making their first breakup public and the resulting scandal that had followed. "You deserved that for the way you treated me."

"I apologized."

He had apologized. And she had forgiven him, then continued to sleep with him. There was a pattern there, somewhere.

His head jerked around as he spotted Lilah climbing into a small sedan. Slipping a cell phone out of his pants pocket, he punched in a number.

Carla blinked at his sudden change of focus. Feeling oddly deflated and emptied of emotion, she rummaged in her purse to find her car keys. "Before you ask the question, the reporter didn't follow me. Why would he? I'm not your girlfriend."

Lucas frowned and gave up on the call, which clearly wasn't being picked up.

He was no doubt calling Lilah, trying to soothe her hurt and explain away his mistake. Despite the fact that Carla knew she was the one in the wrong for sleeping with Lucas, she found she couldn't bear the thought of Lucas trivializing what they had just shared.

He had the nerve to try the phone number again.

A red mist swam before her eyes. Before she even registered what she was about to do, her hand shot out, closed around the phone and she flung it as hard as she could onto the road. It bounced and flew into several pieces. A split second later a truck ran over the main body of the phone, smashing it flat.

There was a moment of silence.

Lucas's expression was curiously devoid of emotion. "That was an expensive phone."

"So sue me, but I find it insulting and objectionable that the man I've just slept with should phone another woman in my presence. You could have at least waited until I had left."

His gaze narrowed. "My apologies for accusing you of calling the press in. I forgot about Lilah."

"Something you seem to be doing a lot lately. I don't know what you're doing out here with me when you should be concentrating on getting back with her."

A swirling breeze started up, making her feel chilled. She rubbed at the gooseflesh on her arms, suddenly in urgent need of a hot bath and an early night. Technically, she was still recovering from the viral relapse and under doctor's orders to take it easy, not that she would tell Lucas that. She was supposed to take an afternoon nap if she could fit it in. Ha!

She started toward her car. Lucas stepped in front of her, blocking her path.

She stared at his sleek, bare shoulders and muscled chest, the dark line of hair that arrowed down to the waistband of his pants. She was tired, and her body still ached and throbbed in places from what they had done in his penthouse apartment. What they had done was *wrong,* but that didn't stop the automatic hum of desire.

"I have no plans on 'getting back' with Lilah. Do you intend to sleep with Panopoulos?"

She went still inside at the first part of that sentence, although she felt no sense of surprise that Lucas was breaking up with Lilah. If he could gravitate back to her so easily then clearly there wasn't much holding them together. Then a second thunderbolt hit her.

Lucas was jealous.

Make that *very* jealous. She didn't know why she hadn't seen it before, but the knowledge demystified his overbearing reaction to her job interview with Alex Panopoulos. It also cast a new light on the dictatorial way he had decided that she would no longer be "The Face" or act in the promotional play she had planned to stage as part of Ambrosi's product launch. She had thought he was downgrading her both personally and professionally because he didn't want her, but the opposite was true.

A glow of purely feminine pleasure soothed over the hurt he had inflicted by demoting her. The launch was *her* baby. She had meticulously planned every detail, always shooting for perfection, and she needed to be there to make sure everything went smoothly. She still didn't like what he had done, but she understood his reasoning now and, because it involved his emotions for her, she would allow him to get away with being so high-handed.

Her chin came up at the question about Alex Panopoulos, although it no longer had any sting. "You're not my boyfriend," she said flatly. "You have no right to ask that question."

Maybe not. But that situation was about to change.

Lucas's jaw locked as he controlled the surge of cold fury at the thought of Carla and Panopoulos together. When he had asked her before she had said she hadn't slept with him, and he believed her, but he knew Alex Panopoulos. He was wealthy and spoiled and used to having what he wanted. If he wanted Carla, he wouldn't give up.

His hands curled into fists at the almost overwhelming urge to simply pick Carla up and carry her back up to his apartment and his bed. Instead, he forced himself to stillness as Carla climbed behind the wheel of her sports car and shot away from the curb.

He was finished with caveman tactics. Finesse was now required.

He examined his options as he took the stairs into his apartment building and strode through the foyer. They were not black-and-white, exactly, but close.

He stepped into the elevator, which Tiberio was holding for him. It was a fact that ever since he had first seen Carla he hadn't been able to keep his hands off her. His attempt to create distance and sever their relationship had backfired. Instead of killing his desire, distance had only served to increase it to the point that the very thing he had been trying to avoid happened: he lost control.

He could deny the story the tabloids would print and which would no doubt hit the stands by morning, or he could allow the story to stand. If he took the second option, Carla's name would be dragged through the mud. He would not allow that to happen.

Until that afternoon, he had been certain about the one thing he didn't want: a forced marriage to Carla Ambrosi.

But that had been before she had waved Alex Panopoulos in his face.

The elevator door slid open. Jaw tight, Lucas strode to his apartment and waited for Tiberio to swipe the key card.

He walked through to his bedroom, every muscle locking tight as he studied the rumpled bed. He picked up the sexy, exotic silk wrap, his fingers closing on the silk. Her delicate feminine scent still clung to the silk, the same scent that currently permeated the very air of his room and would now be in his bed.

If she had wanted to force his hand, he reflected, she could have done it at the beginning, when the media had published the story about the first night they had spent together. Instead, she had walked away from him. He was the one who'd had to do the running.

He had gotten her back, but only after weeks of effort. His fingers tightened on the silk. It was an uncomfortable fact that he wanted Carla more now than he had in the beginning. With each encounter, instead of weakening, his need had intensified.

Now Panopoulos had entered the picture.

Alex was a clever man who had leveraged a modest fortune into an impressive retail empire. Lucas was aware that he wouldn't miss the opportunity to enhance his bid to place his stores in Atraeus resorts by marrying close to his family.

Lucas reached for his cell phone, and remembered that Carla had destroyed it. He shook his head at the irrational urge to grin. The destruction of personal property, especially his, shouldn't be viewed as sexy.

He found the landline then, irritated because his directory had been on his dead cell and he had to ring his PA on Medinos to find the unlisted number. Frustrating minutes later, he made the call. Panopoulos picked up almost immediately.

Lucas's message was succinct and direct.

If Panopoulos offered Carla any kind of position within his company, or laid so much as a finger on her, he would lose any chance at a business alliance with The Atraeus Group. Lucas would also see to it personally that a lucrative business deal Panopoulos was currently negotiating with a European firm The Atraeus Group had a stake in, deVries, would be withdrawn.

Panopoulos's voice was clipped. "Are you warning me off because Constantine is now married to Carla's sister?"

"No." Lucas made no effort to temper the cold flatness of his reply. "Because Carla Ambrosi is mine."

The instant he said the words satisfaction curled through him. Decision made.

Carla was his. Exclusively his.

He was over making excuses to be with her. He wanted her. And he would do what he had to to make sure that not Panopoulos or any other man went near her again.

Terminating the call, Lucas propped the phone back on its rest.

Panopoulos was smart; he would back off. Now all Lucas had to do was talk to Lilah, then deal with the press and Carla.

Carla wouldn't like his ultimatum, but she would accept it. The damage had been done in the instant the reporter had snapped them on the street.

The following morning, after a mostly sleepless night, Carla dressed for the scheduled press conference and luncheon with care. Bearing in mind the elegance of the restaurant Lucas had booked, she chose a pale blue dress that looked spectacular against her skin and hair. It was also subtly sexy in the way it skimmed her curves and revealed a hint of cleavage. High, strappy blue heels made her legs look great, and a classy little jacket in powder-blue finished off the outfit.

Normally she would dress in a more low-key way for a press conference, but any kind of meeting with Lucas today called for a special effort. The heels were a tad high, but that wasn't a problem; she had learned to balance on four-inch stilettos from an early age. She figured that by now that particular ability was imprinted in her DNA.

She decided to leave her hair loose, but took extra care with her makeup in an effort to hide the faint shadows under her eyes.

Minutes later, after sipping her way through a cup of coffee, she stepped out of her apartment. As she locked the door, she noticed a familiar sleek sedan parked across the entrance to her driveway, blocking her in. Her tiredness evaporated on a surge of displeasure.

As she marched toward the car she could make out the shadowy outline of a man behind darkly tinted windows. It would be one of Lucas's security team, probably the guy who had tailed her to her interview with Alex Panopoulos.

Temper escalating, she bent down and tapped on the passenger-side window. Tinted glass slid down with an expensive hum. Glittering dark eyes locked with hers and a short, sharp jab of adrenaline shot through her. Lucas.

Dressed in a gray suit with a metallic sheen and a black T-shirt, his hair still damp from his shower, Lucas looked broodingly attractive. His hair was rumpled as if he'd run his fingers through it. He looked edgy and irritable, the shadow on his jaw signaling that he hadn't had time to shave.

The irritating awareness that still dogged her despite her repeated efforts to reprogram her mind kicked in, making her belly clench and her jaw set even tighter. "What are you doing here?"

"Keeping the press off." Lucas jerked his head in the direction of a blue hatchback parked on the opposite side of the street.

With an unpleasant start, Carla recognized the reporter who had snapped them outside Lucas's apartment the previous evening. "He wouldn't be here if he wasn't following you."

"He arrived before I did."

Her stomach sank. That meant the press would be going

all out with whatever story they could leverage out of that kiss. "Even more reason for you not to be here."

He leaned over and opened the passenger door. "Get in."

Carla gauged the time it would take to dash to her small garage, open the door and back her convertible out. With the reporter just a few fast steps away it would be no contest.

The flash and whir of the camera sent a second shot of adrenaline zinging through her veins as she slid into the passenger seat and slammed the door. The thunk of the locks engaging coincided with the throaty roar of the engine as the vehicle shot away from the curb. Seconds later, they were on the motorway heading into town and forced to an agonizing crawl by rush-hour traffic.

Carla relaxed her death grip on her purse, strapped on her seat belt and checked the rearview mirror. Anything but acknowledge the fact that she was once more within touching distance of Lucas Atraeus.

And riding in his car.

Although this wasn't his personal car. His taste usually ran to something a little more muscular and a lot faster, like the Maserati, but the intimacy still set her on edge and recalled one too many memories she would rather forget.

The first time they had made love had been in a car.

Two years ago he had given her a lift home from a dinner at a restaurant, a family meet-and-greet following Constantine and Sienna's first engagement.

Accepting a lift with Lucas, when she had expected to be delivered home the same way she had arrived, via hired limousine service, had seemed safe despite his bad-boy reputation with the tabloids. Plus there was the fact that recently he had been photographed on two separate occasions, each time with a different gorgeous girl.

Despite telling herself that he was clearly not on the hunt, when she slid into his car, she had felt a deliciously edgy kind of thrill. Lucas was gorgeous in a dangerous, masculine way, so she was more than a little flattered to be singled out for his attention.

It had taken a good half hour to reach her apartment during which time Lucas had played cruising music and asked her about her family and whether or not she was dating.

When they'd reached her place it was pitch-dark. Instead of parking out on the street, Lucas had driven right up to her garage door and parked beneath the shelter of a large shade tree. An oak overhung the driveway and blocked the neighbor's view on one side. Her security lights had flicked on as Lucas turned off the engine, although they remained encapsulated in darkness since the garage blocked the light from reaching the car.

With the music gone, the silence took on a heavy intensity, and her stomach had tightened on a kick of nerves because she knew in that moment that despite her frantic reasoning to the contrary, he *did* want to kiss her. If Lucas was just dropping her home, he wouldn't have driven right into her driveway, and so far up it that the car was partially concealed.

He had barely touched her all night, although she had been aware that he had been watching her and, admittedly, she had played to her audience.

But all of the time she had flirted and played she had been on edge in a feminine way, her nerves tingling. She was used to being pursued, that went with the fashion industry and the PR job. But Lucas was in a whole different league and she hadn't made up her mind that she wanted him to catch her.

She had turned her head, bracing herself for the jolt of eye contact, and his mouth caught hers, his tongue siding right in. A burning shaft of heat shot straight to her loins and she went limp.

Long seconds later, he had released her mouth. She gulped in air and then his mouth closed on hers again and she was sinking, drowning. Her arms closed convulsively around his neck, her fingers tangling in his hair, which was thick and silky and just long enough to play with. Not a good idea, since playing with Lucas Atraeus was the dating equivalent of stroking a big hunting cat, but the second he had touched her, her normal rules had evaporated.

She'd felt the zipper of her silk sheath being eased down her spine, the hot shock of his fingers against the bare skin of her back.

He'd muttered something in Medinian, too thick and rapid for her to catch, and lifted his head, jaw taut. "Do you want this?"

She realized he was holding on to control by a thread. The realization of his vulnerability was subtly shocking.

From the first her connection with Lucas had been powerful. Cliché or not, she had literally glanced across the restaurant and been instantly riveted.

Head and shoulders above most of the occupants of the room, all three Atraeus brothers had been compelling, but it had been Lucas's faintly battered profile that had drawn her.

She had let out a shuddering breath, abruptly aware of what he was asking. Not just a kiss. Somehow they had already stepped way beyond a kiss.

He'd bent his head as if he couldn't bear not to touch her. His lips feathered her throat, sending hot rills of sensation chasing across her skin, and abruptly something slotted into place in her mind.

She had been twenty-four, and a virgin, not because she had been consciously celibate but for the simple reason that she had never met anyone with whom she wanted to be that intimate. No matter how much she liked a date, if they couldn't knock her sideways emotionally, she refused to allow anything more than a good-night kiss.

Making love with Lucas Atraeus hadn't made sense for

a whole list of logical reasons. She barely knew him, and so there was no way she could be in love, but instead of recoiling, she'd found herself irresistibly compelled to throw away her rule book. On an instinctive level, with every touch, every kiss, Lucas Atraeus felt utterly right. "Yes."

A car horn blasted, shattering the recall, jerking Carla's gaze back to the road.

"What's wrong?"

Lucas's deep, raspy voice sent a nervy shock wave through her. His gaze caught hers, dispatching another electrical jolt. "Nothing."

His phone vibrated. He answered the call, his voice low. A couple of times his gaze intercepted hers and that weird electrical hum of awareness zapped her again, so she switched back to watching the wing mirror. Once she thought she spotted the blue hatchback and she stiffened, but she couldn't be certain.

"He's not behind us. I've been checking."

Which raised a question. "You said he got to my place before you did, so how did you know he was there?"

Constantine inched forward in traffic, braked, then reached behind to the backseat and handed her a newspaper, which had been folded open.

The headline, Lightning Strikes Twice for Atraeus Hatchet Man, sent her into mild shock, although she had been expecting something like it.

They hadn't made the front page, but close. A color photo, which had been taken just as Lucas had kissed her, was slotted directly below the story title.

Her outrage built as she skimmed the piece. According to the reporter, the romantic fires had been reignited during a secret tryst while she'd been on Medinos. An "insider" had supplied the tidbit that the wedding had literally thrown them together and they were now a hot romantic item. Again.

Although the speculation that Lucas would pop the question was strictly lighthearted. According to the "source," if Carla Ambrosi hadn't had what it took to keep Atraeus interested the first time around, the "reheat" would be about as exciting as day-old pasta.

Carla dropped the newspaper as if it had scorched her fingers. The instant she had seen her name coupled with Lucas's she should have known better than to read on.

Two years ago when Lucas had finished with her after that one night, she had been angry enough to go to the press. They'd had a field day with speculation and innuendo. Her skin was a lot thicker now, but the careless digging into her personal life, and the outright lies, still stung.

Reheat.

Her jaw tightened. If she ever found out who the cowardly "insider" was, the next installment of that particular story could be printed in the crime pages.

Folding the newspaper, she tossed it on the backseat. "You should have called me. You didn't have to show up on my doorstep."

Making it look like there really was substance to the story.

"If I'd called, you would have hung up on me."

She couldn't argue with that, because it was absolutely true.

Lucas signaled and made a turn into the underground parking garage beneath the Ambrosi building.

Carla was halfway out of the car, dragging her bag, which had snagged on a tiny lever at the base of the seat, when movement jerked her head up. A man with a camera loomed out of the shadows, walking swiftly toward them. Not the guy in the blue hatchback, someone else. The pale gleam of a van with its garish news logo registered in the background.

Lucas, who had walked around to open her door, said

something curt beneath his breath as she yanked at the strap. The bag came free and she surged upright.

"Smile, Mr. Atraeus, Ms. Ambrosi. Gotcha!"

The camera flashed as she lurched into Lucas.

The touching was minimal—her shoulder bumped his, he reached out to steady her—but the damage was done. In addition to the kiss outside Lucas's apartment the tabloids now had photos of Lucas picking her up from her apartment then delivering her to work.

The day-old pasta had just gotten hotter.

Nine

When Carla stepped out of her office to attend the press conference later on that morning, one of Lucas's bodyguards, Tiberio, was waiting for her in the corridor.

Lucas wasn't in the office. He had left after dropping her off that morning, so there was no one to interpret. After a short, labored struggle with Tiberio's fractured English, Carla finally agreed that, yes, they would both follow Lucas's orders and Tiberio could drive her to the press conference and see her safely inside.

On the way down to the parking garage, she decided that she was secretly glad Lucas had delegated Tiberio to mind her. She had been dreading dealing with the paparazzi when she arrived at the five-star hotel where the press conference was being held.

To her surprise, Tiberio opened the door on a glossy black limousine, not the dark sedan Lucas's security usually drove. When she slid into the leather interior, she was startled to discover that Lucas was already ensconced there, a briefcase open on the floor, a sheaf of papers in his hand.

The door closed, sealing her in. Lucas said something rapid to Tiberio as he slid behind the wheel. There was a discreet thunk, followed by the low hum of the engine.

She depressed the door handle, when it wouldn't budge, her gaze clashed with Lucas's. "You locked it."

His expression was suspiciously bland. "Standard security precaution."

Daylight replaced the gloom of the parking garage as they glided up onto the street. Her uneasiness at finding Lucas in the car coalesced into suspicion; she was beginning to feel manipulated. "Tiberio said you had ordered him to mind me, that he was supposed to drop me at the press conference. He didn't say we would be traveling together."

Lucas, still dressed in the silver-gray suit and black T-shirt he had been wearing that morning, but now freshly shaved, retrieved a cell phone from his briefcase. "Is there a problem with going together?"

She frowned. "After what happened, wouldn't it be the smart thing to arrive separately?"

Lucas's attention was centered on what was, apparently, a swanky new phone. "No."

Her frustration spiked as he punched in a number and lifted the phone to his ear then subsided just as quickly as she listened to his deep voice, the liquid cadences of his rapid Medinian. Reluctantly fascinated, she hung on every word. He could be reciting a grocery list and she could still listen all day.

Minutes later, the limousine pulled into a space outside the hotel entrance. When she saw the media crush, she experienced a rare moment of panic. Publicity was her thing; she had a natural bent for it. But not today. "Isn't there a back entrance we can use?"

Lucas, seemingly unconcerned, snapped his phone closed and slipped it into his pocket.

She flashed him an irritated look. "The last thing we need right now is to be seen arriving together, looking like we *are* a couple."

"Don't worry, the media will be taken care of. It's all arranged."

Something about his manner brought her head up, sharpened all her senses. "What do you mean, 'arranged'? If the media doesn't see me for a few days, the story will die a death."

"No, it won't," Lucas said flatly. "Not this time."

The door to the limousine popped open. Lucas exited first. Reluctantly Carla followed, stepping into the dusty, steamy heat of midtown Sydney.

The media surged forward. To Carla's relief they were instantly held at bay by a wall of burly men in dark suits.

Lucas's hand landed in the small of her back, the heat of his palm burning through her dress, then they were moving. Carla kept her spine stiff, informing Lucas that she wasn't happy with either the situation or his touch, which seemed entirely too intimate.

The glass doors of the hotel threw a reflection back at her. Lucas stood tall and muscled by her side, his gaze with that grim, icy quality that always sent shivers down her spine. With the other men flanking them in a protective curve, she couldn't help thinking they looked like a trailer for a gangster flick.

The doors slid open, and the air-conditioned coolness of the hotel foyer flowed around her as they walked briskly to a bank of elevators. A security guard was holding an empty elevator car. Relief eased some of her tension as they stepped inside.

Before the doors could slide closed a well-dressed female reporter, microphone in hand, cameraman in tow, side-stepped security and grabbed the door, preventing it from closing.

"Mr. Atraeus, Ms. Ambrosi, can you confirm the rumor that Sienna Atraeus is pregnant?"

There was a moment of confusion as security reacted, forcing the woman and her cameraman to step back.

Lucas issued a sharp order. The doors snapped closed and she found herself alone with Lucas as the elevator lurched into motion.

Carla's stomach clenched at the sudden acceleration.

Sienna pregnant.

"Constantine phoned me earlier to let me know that Sienna was pregnant and that it was possible the story had been leaked."

A hurt she had stubbornly avoided dealing with hit her like a kick in the chest.

She didn't begrudge Sienna one moment of her happiness, but it was a fact that she possessed all the things that Carla realized *she* wanted. Not necessarily right now, but sometime in the future, in their natural order, and with Lucas.

But Lucas was showing no real signs of commitment.

Blankly, she watched floor numbers flash by. If she were pregnant she had to assume there would be no marriage, no happy ending, no husband to love and cherish her and the child.

She became aware the elevator had stopped. She sucked in a deep breath, but the oxygen didn't seem to be getting through. Her head felt heavy and pressurized, her knees wobbly. Not illness, just good old-fashioned panic.

Lucas took her arm, holding her steady. The top of her head bumped his chin, the scrape of his stubbled jaw on the sensitive skin of her forehead sending a reflexive shiver through her. She inhaled, gasping air like a swimmer sur-

facing, and his warm male scent, laced with the subtle edge
of cologne, filled her nostrils.

Lucas said something curt in Medinian. "Damn, you *are*
pregnant."

A split second later the elevator doors slid open.

Fingers automatically tightening around the strap of her
handbag, which was in danger of sliding off her shoulder,
she stepped out into a broad, carpeted corridor. Lucas's security, who must have taken another elevator, were waiting.

Lucas's hand closed around her arm. "Slow down. I've
got you."

"That's part of the problem."

"Then deal with it. I'm not going away."

She shot him an icy glare. "I thought leaving was the
whole point?"

He traded a cool glance but didn't reply because they had
reached the designated suite. A murmur rippled through the
room as they were recognized, but this time, courtesy of the
heavy presence of security, there was no undisciplined rush.

Tomas, Constantine's PA, and Lucas's mother, Maria
Therese, were already seated. Carla took a seat next to Lucas.
Seconds later, Zane escorted Lilah into the room.

Her stomach contracted as the questions began. The presence of a mediator limited the topics to the Atraeus takeover
of Ambrosi, Ambrosi's new collection and the re-creation of
the historic Ambrosi pearl facility on the Medinian island
of Ambrus. However, when Lucas rose to his feet, indicating that the press conference was over, a barrage of personal
questions ensued.

Lucas's fingers laced with hers, the contact intimate and
unsettling as he pulled her to her feet. When she discreetly
tried to pull free, wary of creating even more unpleasant
speculation, he sent her a warning glance, his hold firming.

As they stepped off the podium the media, no longer qui-

etly seated, swirled around them. The clear, husky voice of
a well-known television reporter cut through the shouted
questions. A microphone was thrust at Lucas's face.

The reporter flashed him a cool smile. "Can you confirm or deny the reports that you've resumed your affair
with Carla?"

Lucas pulled her in close against his side as they continued to move at a steady pace. His gaze intersected with hers,
filled with cool warning. "No official statement has been
issued yet, however I can confirm that Carla Ambrosi and I
have been secretly engaged for the past two years."

The room erupted. Lucas bit out a grim order. The security team, already working to push the press back, closed in,
forcing a bubble of privacy and shoving Carla up hard against
Lucas. His arm tightened and she found herself lifted off her
feet as he literally propelled her from the room.

Shock and a wave of edgy heat zapped through her as
she clung to his narrow waist and scrambled to keep her
balance. Seconds later they were sealed into the claustro-
phobic confines of what looked like a service elevator, still
surrounded by burly security.

Carla twisted, trying to peel loose from his hold. Lucas
easily resisted the attempt, tightening his arms around her.
In the process she ended up plastered against his chest. The
top button of her dress came unfastened and his hand, which
was spread across her rib cage, shifted up so that his thumb
and index finger sank into the swell of one breast.

As if a switch had been thrown, she was swamped by
memories, some hot and sensuous enough that her breasts
tightened and her belly contracted, some hurtful enough that
her temper roared to life.

Lucas's gaze burned over the lush display of cleavage where the bodice of her dress gaped. "Keep still," he
growled.

But she noticed he didn't move his hand.

She was *not* enjoying it. After the humiliation of the previous evening the last thing she needed was to be clamped against all that hot, hard muscle, making her feel small and wimpy and tragically easy. Unfortunately, her body wasn't in sync with her mind. She couldn't control the heat flushing her skin or the automatic tightening of her nipples, and Lucas knew it.

The doors slid open. Before she could protest, they were moving again, this time through the lower bowels of the hotel. A door off a loading bay was shoved wide and they spilled out onto a walled parking area where several vehicles, including a limousine, were parked.

Her fury increased. Here was the back entrance she had needed an hour ago.

Hot, clammy air flowed around her as she clambered into the limousine, clutching her purse. Lucas slid in beside her, his muscled thigh brushing hers. She flinched as if scalded and scooted over another few inches.

His gaze flashed to hers as they accelerated away from the curb. "All right?"

His calm control pushed her over the edge. She reached for her seat belt and jammed the fastenings together. "Secretly *engaged?*"

A week ago an engagement was what she had longed for, what she would have *loved*. "Correct me if I'm wrong, maybe I blacked out at some stage, but I don't ever remember a proposal of marriage."

She caught Tiberio's surprised glance in the rearview mirror.

Lucas's expression was grim. A faint hum filled the air as a privacy screen slid smoothly into place, locking them into a bubble of silence.

She stared at Lucas, incensed. Thanks to the mad dash

through the hotel, her hair had unwound and was now cascading untidily down her back, and she was perspiring. In contrast, Lucas looked cool and completely in control, his suit *GQ* perfect. "An engagement is the logical solution."

"It's damage control, and it's completely unnecessary." She remembered her gaping bodice and hurriedly refastened the button. "I may not be pregnant."

Her voice sounded husky and tight, even to herself, and she wondered, a little wildly, if he could tell how much she suddenly wanted to be pregnant.

"Whether you're pregnant or not is a consideration, but it isn't an issue, yet."

Something seized in her chest, her heart. For a crazy moment she considered that he was about to admit that he was in love with her, that he didn't care if she was pregnant or not, he couldn't live without her. Then reality dissolved that fantasy. "But what the newspapers are printing is. Do you know how humiliating it is to be offered a forced marriage?"

Irritation tinged with outrage registered in his expression. "No one's *forcing* you to do anything. Marriage as an option can't be such a shock. Not after what happened on Medinos. And last night."

"Well, I guess that puts things in perspective. It's a *practical* option."

Her mood was definitely spiraling down. Practicality spelled death for all romance. Cancel the white wedding with champagne and rose petals. Bring on the registry office and matching gray suits.

"I wouldn't propose marriage if I didn't *want* to marry you."

Her gaze narrowed. "Is that the proposal?"

His expression was back to remote. "It isn't what I had planned, but, yes."

"Uh-huh." She drew a deep breath and counted to ten.

"The biggest mistake I made was in agreeing to sleep with you."

Suddenly he was close, one arm draped behind her, his warm male scent laced with the enticing cologne stopping the breath in her throat. "On which occasion?"

She stared rigidly ahead, trying to ignore the heated gleam in his eyes, the subtle cajoling that shouldn't succeed in getting her on side, but which was slowly undermining her will to resist.

That was the other thing about Lucas, besides the power and influence he wielded in the business world. When he wanted he could be stunningly seducingly attentive. But this time she refused to be swayed by his killer charm. "All of them."

He wound a strand of her hair around one finger and lightly tugged. She felt his breath fanning her nape. "That's a lot of mistakes."

And she had enjoyed every one of them.

She resisted the urge to turn her head, putting her mouth bare inches from his and letting the conversation take them to the destination he was so blatantly angling for—a bone-melting kiss. "I should never have slept with you, period."

He dropped the strand of hair and sat back, slightly, signaling that he had changed tack. "Meaning that if you had played your cards right," he said softly, "you could have had marriage in the beginning?"

Ten

Like quicksilver the irresistible pull of attraction was gone, replaced by wrenching hurt. "Just because I didn't talk about marriage, that didn't mean I thought it would never be on the agenda for us. And what is so wrong with that?"

Silence vibrated through the limousine. She saw Tiberio glance nervously in the rearview mirror. She turned her head to watch city traffic zip by and registered that her stomach felt distinctly hollow.

Glancing at her watch, she noted the time. She'd only had coffee for breakfast and it was after one. She would be eating lunch soon, which would fix the acid in her stomach, but she couldn't wait that long. Fumbling in her purse, she took out the small plastic bag that contained a few antacid tablets and a couple of individually packaged biscuits. After unwrapping a slightly battered biscuit, she took a bite.

"Marriage is on the agenda now," Lucas reminded her. "I need an answer."

She hastily finished the biscuit and stuffed the plastic bag back in her purse.

Lucas watched her movements with an annoyed fascination. "Do you usually eat when marriage is being proposed?"

"I was hungry. I needed to eat."

"I'll have to remember that should I ever have occasion to propose again."

She closed the flap on her purse. Maybe it was childish not to tell him that she had ended up with an ulcer, but it was no big deal and she was still hurt that he hadn't ever bothered to check up on her after he had deposited her on the plane home from Thailand. The memory of his treatment of her, which had been uncharacteristically callous, stiffened her spine. "I don't know why you want marriage now when clearly you broke up with me because you didn't view me as 'wife' material."

His gaze was unwavering, making her feel suddenly uncomfortable about giving him such a hard time.

"As it happens, you've always fulfilled the most important requirement."

She was suddenly, intensely conscious of the warmth of his arm behind her. "Which is?"

Her breath seized in her throat as Lucas cupped her chin with his free hand. She had a split second to either pull back or turn her head so his mouth would miss hers. Instead, hope turned crazy cartwheels in her stomach, and she allowed the kiss.

Long, breathless minutes later he lifted his head. "You wanted to know why marriage is acceptable to me. This is why."

His thumb traced the line of her cheekbone, sending tingling heat shivering across the delicate skin and igniting a familiar, heated tension. His mouth brushed hers again, the kiss lingering. The stirring tension wound tighter. Reflexively, she leaned closer, angling her jaw to deepen the kiss. Her hand slid around to grip his nape and pull him closer still.

When he finally lifted his head, his gaze was bleak. "Two months without you was two months too long. What happened on Medinos and in my apartment is a case in point. I want you back."

Carla released her hold on his nape and drew back. Her mouth, her whole body, was tingling.

It wasn't what she wanted to hear, but the hope fizzing inside refused to die a complete death.

Lucas had tried to end their relationship; it hadn't happened. She hadn't chased him. If he had truly wanted an end, she was in no doubt that he would have icily and clinically cut her out of his life.

He hadn't been able to because he couldn't resist her.

He might label what held them together as sex; she preferred to call it chemistry. There was a reason they were attracted to each other that went way beyond the physical into the area of personality and emotional needs. Despite their difficulties and clashes, at a deep, bedrock level she knew they were perfect for each other.

That they had continued their relationship for two years was further proof that whatever he either claimed or denied, for Lucas she was different in some way. She knew, because she had made it her business to check. Lucas was only ever recorded by the tabloids as having one serious relationship before her, a model called Sophie, and that had been something like five years ago. The fact that he wanted the marriage now, when a pregnancy was by no means certain, underlined just how powerfully he did want her.

It wasn't love, but everything in her shouted that it had to be possible for the potent chemistry that had bound Lucas to her for the past two years to turn to love.

She was clutching at straws. Her heart was pounding and her stomach kept lurching. There was a possibility that Lucas might never truly love her, never fully commit himself to the relationship. There was a chance she was making the biggest mistake of her life.

But, risky or not, if she was honest, her mind had been made up the second she'd heard his announcement to the press.

She loved Lucas.

If there was a chance that he could love her, then she was taking it.

Lucas activated the privacy screen. When it opened, he leaned forward and spoke in rapid Medinian to Tiberio. He caught the skeptical flash of his chief bodyguard's gaze in the rearview mirror as he confirmed that they would be making the scheduled stop at the jewelers.

However, the wry amusement that would normally have kicked up the corners of his mouth in answer to Tiberio's pessimism was absent. When it came to Carla, he was beginning to share Tiberio's doubts. She hadn't said yes, and he was by no means certain that she would.

Carla, who was once again rummaging in her handbag, stiffened as the limousine pulled into the cramped loading bay of a downtown building. "This isn't the restaurant."

Lucas climbed out as Tiberio opened the door then leaned in and took Carla's hand. "We have one stop to make before lunch."

As Carla climbed out he noted the moment she spotted the elegant sign that indicated this was the rear entrance to the premises of Moore's, a famous jeweler. A business that just happened to be owned by The Atraeus Group.

Her expression was accusing. "You had this all planned."

"Last night you knew as well as I that the story would go to press."

Her light blue gaze flashed. Before she could formulate an argument and decide to answer his proposal with a no, Lucas propelled her toward the back entrance.

Frustration welled that he hadn't been able to extract an answer from her *and* that he couldn't gauge her mood, but he kept a firm clamp on his temper. An edgy, hair-trigger temper that, until these past two weeks, he hadn't known existed.

He offered her his arm and forced himself to patience when she didn't immediately take it.

Clear, glacial-blue eyes clashed with his. "What makes you think I'm actually going to go through with this?"

Lucas noted that she stopped short of using the word *charade.* "I apologize for trying to bulldoze you," he said grimly. "I realize I've mishandled the situation."

He had used business tactics to try to maneuver Carla into an engagement. He had assumed that when he proposed marriage she would be, if not ecstatic, then, at least, happy.

Instead, she was decidedly *unhappy,* and now he was being left to sweat.

He acknowledged that he deserved it. If patience was now required to achieve a result, then he would be patient. "The ring is important. I need you to come inside and choose one."

"I suppose we need one because we've been *secretly engaged* for two years, so of course you would have loved me enough to buy a ring."

Ignoring Tiberio's scandalized expression, he unclenched his jaw. *"Esattamente,"* he muttered, momentarily forgetting his English. "If you don't have a ring, questions will be asked."

"So the ring is a prop, a detail that adds credence to the story."

The door popped open. A dapper gray-haired man, elegant in a dark suit and striped tie, appeared along with a security guard. "Mr. Atraeus," he murmured. "Ms. Ambrosi. My name is Carstairs, the store manager. Would you like to come this way?"

Keeping his temper firmly in check, Lucas concentrated on Carla. If she refused the ring, he would arrange for a selection to be sent to his apartment and she could choose one there. What was important was that she accept his proposal, and that hadn't happened yet. "Are you ready?"

Her eyes clashed with his again, but she took his arm.

Jaw clenched, Lucas controlled his emotions with a forcible effort. Fleetingly, he registered Tiberio's relief, an exaggerated expression of his own, as he walked up the steps and allowed Carla to precede him into the building.

She would say yes. She had to.

The turnaround was huge, but now that he had made the decision that he wanted her in his life permanently, he felt oddly settled.

Like it or not he was involved, his feelings raw, possessive. Sexually, he had lost control with Carla from the beginning, something that had never come close to happening with any other woman.

It was also a blunt fact that the thought of Carla with Panopoulos, or any man, was unacceptable. When he had walked into that particular wall, his reaction had cleared his mind. Despite everything that could go wrong with this relationship, Carla was his.

If he had to be patient and wait for her, then he would be patient.

Carla stepped into the room Carstairs indicated, glad for a respite from the odd intensity of Lucas's gaze and her own inner turmoil. For a fractured moment, she had been an inch away from giving up on the need to pressure some kind of admission out of Lucas and blurting out "yes." She would marry him, she would do whatever he wanted, if only he would keep on looking at her that way. But then the emotional shutters she had never been able to fathom had come crashing down and they had ended up stalemated again.

The room was an elegant private sitting room with sleek leather couches offset by an antique sideboard and coffee tables. Classical music played softly. The largest coffee table held a selection of rings nestled in black velvet trays.

Carstairs, who seemed to be staring at her oddly, indicated that she take a seat and view the rings, then asked if she would like coffee or champagne. Refusing either drink with a tight smile, she sat and tried to concentrate on the rings. Lucas, who had also refused a drink, paced the small room like an overlarge caged panther, then came to stand over her, distracting her further.

His breath stirred her hair as he leaned forward for a closer look. Utterly distracted by his closeness, she stared blindly at the rings, dazzled by the glitter but unable to concentrate, which was criminal because she loved pretty jewelry. "I didn't think you were interested in jewelry."

"I'm interested in you," he said flatly. "This one."

He picked out a pale blue pear-shaped stone, which she had noticed but bypassed because it occupied a tray that contained a very small number of exquisite rings, all with astronomical price tags.

He handed it to her then conferred briefly with Carstairs. "It's a blue diamond, from Brazil. Very rare, and the same color as your eyes. Do you like it?"

She studied the soft, mesmerizing glow of the diamond, but was more interested in the fact that he had picked the ring because it matched her eyes. She slipped the ring on her finger. Wouldn't you know, it was a perfect fit and it looked even better on. "I love it."

His gaze caught hers, held it, and for a moment she felt absurdly giddy.

"Then we'll take it." He passed Carstairs his credit card.

Yanking the ring off, she replaced it on its plush velvet tray and pushed to her feet, panic gripping her. "I haven't said yes yet."

Lucas said something in rapid Medinian to Carstairs. With a curt bow, the store manager, who could evidently speak the language, left the room, still with Lucas's card, which meant Lucas was buying the ring, regardless. Simultaneously, an elegant older woman in a simple black dress collected the remaining trays and made a swift exit along with Tiberio, leaving them alone. The blue ring, she noticed, was left on the coffee table.

In the background the classical music ended. Suddenly the silence was thick enough to cut.

Carla shoved to her feet and walked to the large bay window. She stared out into the tiny yard presently dominated by the limousine, and the issue she'd been desperate to ignore, which had hurt more than anything because it had cut into the most tender part of her, surfaced. As hard as she had tried for two years to be everything Lucas could want or need, it hadn't been enough. When the pressure had come on to commit, he hadn't wanted *her*. He had wanted Lilah, who in many ways was her complete opposite: calm, controlled and content to keep a low profile.

In retrospect, maybe she had tried too hard and he hadn't ever really seen her, just the glossy, upbeat side that was always "on." The one time he had truly seen her had been in Thailand. She had been too sick to try to be anything but herself, and he had run a mile. "What about Lilah?"

"I spoke to Lilah last night. Zane is taking care of her."

She met his gaze in the window. "I thought you were in love with her."

He came to stand behind her. "She was my date at the wedding, that was all. And, no, we didn't sleep together. We didn't kiss. I didn't so much as hold her hand."

Relief made Carla's legs feel as limp as noodles. He pulled her back against him in a loose hold, as the palm of one hand slid around to cup her abdomen.

"Marriage wasn't on my agenda, with anyone, but the situation has…changed. Don't forget it's entirely possible you're pregnant."

Lucas's hold tightened, making her intensely aware of his hard, muscled body so close behind her. Their reflection bounced back at her, Lucas large and powerfully male, herself paler and decidedly feminine. "I can't marry solely for a baby that might not exist! There has to be something more. Sienna is married to a man she loves. A man who loved her enough that he kidnapped her—"

"Are you saying you want to be *kidnapped?*"

She stared at the dark, irritable glitter of Lucas's eyes, the tough line of his jaw. Her own jaw set. "All I'm saying is that Constantine loves Sienna. It matters."

There was an arresting look in his eyes. "You love me."

Eleven

Carla inhaled sharply at the certainty in Lucas's voice, feeling absurdly vulnerable that, after two years of careful camouflage, she was so transparent now. She was also hurt by his matter-of-fact tone, as if her emotional attachment was simply a convenience that smoothed his path now. "What did you expect, that I was empty-headed enough that I was just having sex with you?"

"Meaning that was how I was with you?" His grip on her arms gentled. "Calm down. I didn't know until that moment. I'm...pleased."

"Because it makes things easier?"

"We're getting married," he said flatly. "This is not some business deal."

He didn't make the mistake of trying to kiss her. Instead he released her, walked over to the coffee table and picked the ring up.

The diamond shimmered in the light, impossibly beautiful, but it was the determined set to Lucas's jaw, the rock-solid patience in his gaze, that riveted her. "What if I'm not pregnant?"

"We'll deal with that possibility when we get to it."

Her jaw tightened. She didn't want to create difficulties, but neither could she let him put that ring on her finger without saying everything that needed to be said. "I'm not sure I want marriage under these conditions."

"That's your choice," he said flatly, his patience finally slipping. "But don't hold out for Alex Panopoulos to intervene. As of yesterday he has reviewed his options."

The sudden mention of Panopoulos was faintly shocking. "You warned him off."

"That's right." Lucas's voice was even, but his expression spoke volumes, coolly set with a primitive gleam in his eyes that sent a faint quiver zapping down her spine.

Just when she thought Lucas was cold and detached he proved her wrong by turning distinctly male and predatory.

It wasn't much, it wasn't enough, but it told her what she needed to know: Lucas was jealous. Given his cool, measured approach to every other aspect of his life, if he was jealous then he had to feel something powerful, something special, for her.

It was a leap in the dark. Marriage would be an incredible risk, but the past two years had been all about risk and she had already lost her heart. It came down to a simple choice. She could either walk away and hope to fall out of love with Lucas or she could stay and hold out for his love.

Her chin came up. When it came down to it she wasn't a coward. She would rather try and fail than not try at all.

"Okay," she said huskily, and extended her hand so he could slide the ring on her finger.

The fit was perfect. She stared at the fiery blue stone, her chest suddenly tight.

Lucas lifted her fingers to his lips. "It looks good."

The rough note in his voice, the unexpected caress, sent a shimmering wave of emotion through her. "It's beautiful."

He bent his head. Before she could react, he kissed her on the mouth. "I have good taste."

Despite her effort to stay calm and composed and not let Lucas see how much this meant to her, a wave of heat suffused her cheeks. "In rings or wives?"

He grinned quick and hard and dropped another quick kiss on her mouth. "Both."

Lucas shepherded Carla into the backseat of the limousine, satisfaction filling him at the sight of the ring glowing on her finger.

She loved him.

He had suspected it, but he hadn't known for sure until she had said the words. Her emotional involvement was an element he hadn't factored in when he had decided on marriage. He had simply formulated a strategy and kept to it until she had capitulated.

Now that he knew she loved him and had agreed to marry him, there would be no reason to delay moving her in with him. No reason to delay the wedding.

Marriage.

Since Sophie's death, marriage had not been an option, because he had never gotten past the fact that he still felt responsible for the accident.

It had taken a good year for the flashbacks of the accident to fade from his mind, another six months before he could sleep without waking up and reliving that night.

Sometimes, even now, he still woke up at night, reliving their last argument and trying to reinvent the past. He had avoided commitment for the simple reason that he knew his own nature: once he did commit he did so one hundred percent and he was fiercely protective. The night Sophie had died, he had been blindsided by the fact that she had aborted his child. He'd allowed her to throw her tantrum and leave. Maybe he was overcompensating now, but he would never allow himself, or any woman he was with, to be put in that situation again.

Until Carla, he had avoided becoming deeply involved with anyone. The week in Thailand had been a tipping point. Caring for Carla in that intimate situation had pushed him over an invisible boundary he had carefully skirted for five years. He hadn't liked the intense flood of emotion, or the implications for the future. He knew the way he was hard-wired. For as long as he could remember he had been the same: when it came to emotion it was all or nothing.

Now that Carla had agreed to marry him and it was possible that he would be a father, if not in the near future, then sometime over the next few years, he was faced with a double responsibility. He could feel the possessiveness, the desire to cushion and protect already settling in.

With Sophie he hadn't had time to absorb the impact of her pregnancy because it had been over before he had known about it. She hadn't given him a chance. With Carla the situation was entirely different. He knew that she would never abort their child. She would extend the same fiercely protective, single-minded love she gave her family to their baby.

Any child Carla had would be loved and pampered. Unlike Sophie, she would embrace the responsibility, the chills and the spills.

It was an odd moment to realize that one of the reasons he wanted to marry Carla was that he trusted her.

During the drive to the restaurant Lucas had booked, Carla wavered between staring with stunned amazement at the engagement ring and frantically wondering what Lucas's mother was going to think.

Like every other member of the Atraeus family, Maria Therese would know that Carla and Lucas had more than a hint of scandal in their past. Plus, the first and only time they had met, Lucas had been dating Lilah.

Lucas, who had been preoccupied with phone calls for the duration of the short trip to the restaurant, took her arm as she exited the limousine. "Now that we're engaged, there is one rule you will follow—don't talk to the press unless you've cleared it with me."

Carla stiffened. "PR is my job. I think I can handle the press."

Lucas nodded at Tomas, who was evidently waiting for them at the portico of the restaurant. "PR for Ambrosi is one thing. For the Atraeus family the situation is entirely different."

"I think I can be trusted."

His glance was impatient. "I know you can handle publicity. It's the security aspect that worries me. Every member of my family has to take care, and situations with the press provide prime opportunities for security breaches. If you're going to be talking to the press, a security detail needs to be organized. And by the way, I've booked you into the hotel for the launch party. We leave first thing in the morning."

Carla stopped dead in her tracks, a small fuzzy glow of happiness expanding in her chest. Lucas had obviously taken care of that detail before he had asked her to marry him, righting a wrong that had badly needed fixing. She knew she wouldn't be in charge of running the show, but that was a mere detail. She would still be able to make sure everything came off perfectly and that was what mattered. She was finally starting to believe that this marriage could work. "My contract as Ambrosi's public relations executive is up for renewal next week."

"It's as good as signed."

"That was almost too easy."

His arm slid around her waist, pulling her in against his side as they walked into the restaurant. "I was going to renew it anyway. You're damn good at the job, and besides, I want you to be happy."

Her happiness expanded another notch. It wasn't perfection yet—she still had to deal with that emotional distance thing that Lucas constantly pulled—but it was inching closer.

Maria Therese, Zane and Lilah were already seated at the table. Carla's stomach plunged as Lucas's mother gave her a measuring glance. With her smooth, ageless face and impeccable fashion sense, the matriarch of the Atraeus family had a reputation for being calm and composed under pressure. And with her late husband's affairs, there had been constant media pressure. "Does your mother know how long we've been involved?"

"You're an Ambrosi and my future wife. She'll be more than happy to accept you into the family."

Carla's stomach plunged. "Oh, good. She knows."

The resort chosen for the product launch was Balinese in style. Situated in its own private bay with heavy tropical gardens, it was also stunningly beautiful.

The hotel foyer was just as Carla remembered it when she had originally investigated the resort for the launch party. Constructed with all the grandeur of a movie set, it was both exotic and restful with a soaring atrium and tinkling fountains.

When Carla checked in at the front desk, however, she found that the guest room that had originally been booked for her had been canceled and there were no vacancies. Every room had been booked for the launch.

Lucas, casual in light-colored pants and a loose gauzy white shirt that accentuated his olive skin and made his shoulders look even broader, slipped his platinum card across the counter. "You're sharing with me. The suite's in my name."

So nice to be told. Even though she understood that Lucas was behaving this way because he was still unsure of her and he wanted to keep her close, there was no ignoring that it was controlling behavior. Pointedly ignoring the interruption, she addressed the receptionist. "Are you sure there are no rooms left? How about the room that was originally booked for Lilah Cole?"

Lilah had originally been slated to attend the launch. As the head designer she had a right to be there, but she had pulled out at the last minute.

The receptionist dragged her dazzled gaze off Lucas. "I'm sorry, ma'am, there was a waiting list. The room has already been allocated."

Carla waited until they were in the elevator. The feel-good mood of the two-hour drive from Sydney in Lucas's Ferrari was rapidly dissolving. Maybe it was a small point since they were engaged, but she would like to have been asked before Lucas decided she would be sharing his room. Lucas's controlling streak seemed to be growing by leaps and bounds and she was at a loss to understand why. She had agreed to marry him; life should be smoothing out, but it wasn't. Lucas was oddly silent, tense and brooding. Something was wrong and she couldn't figure out what it was.

Lucas leaned against the wall, arms folded over his chest, his gaze wary. "It's just a hotel room. I assumed you would want to share."

"I do."

Lucas frowned. The relaxed cast to his face, courtesy of an admittedly sublime night spent together in his bed, gone. "Then what's wrong? You already know that Lilah and I were not involved."

"It's not Lilah—"

The doors slid open. A young couple with three young children were waiting for the elevator.

Lucas propelled her out into the corridor. "We'll continue this discussion in our room."

Their luggage had already been delivered and was stacked to one side, but Carla barely registered that detail. The large airy room with its dark polished floors, teak furniture and soaring ceilings was filled with lush bouquets of roses in a range of hues from soft pinks to rich reds. Long stemmed and glorious, they overflowed dozens of vases, their scent filling the suite.

Dazed, she walked through to the bedroom, which was also smothered with flowers. An ice bucket of champagne and a basket crammed with fresh fruit and exquisitely presented chocolates resided on a small coffee table positioned between two chairs.

Lucas carried their bags into the bedroom. The second he set them down she flung her arms around him. "I'm sorry. You organized all this—it's beautiful, gorgeous—and all I could do was complain."

His arms closed around her, tucking her in snugly against him. The comfort of his muscled body against hers, the enticement of his clean scent, increased her dizzy pleasure.

The second she had seen what Lucas had done, how focused he was on pleasing her, the notion that there was something wrong had evaporated. Now she felt embarrassed and contrite for giving him such a hard time.

Carla spent a happy hour rearranging the flowers and unpacking. By the time she had finished laying out her dress for the evening function, Lucas had showered, changed into a suit and disappeared, called away to do a series of interviews.

A knock on the door made her frown. When she opened it a young woman in a hotel uniform was standing outside with a hotel porter. After a brief conversation she discovered that Lucas had arranged for the items to be delivered for her perusal. Anything she didn't want would be returned to the stores.

Feeling a bit like Alice falling down the rabbit hole, Carla opened the door wider so the porter could wheel in a clotheshorse that was hung with a number of plastic-shrouded gowns. At the base of the clotheshorse were boxes of shoes from the prominent design stores downstairs. She signed a docket and closed the door behind the hotel employees.

A quick survey of the gowns revealed that while they were all her size and by highly desirable designers, they were definitely not her style. Two had significantly high necklines, one a soft pink, the other an oyster lace. Both were elegant and gorgeously detailed, but neither conformed to her taste. The pink was too ruffled, like a flapper dress from the 1920s, and the oyster lace was stiffly formal and too much like a wedding gown.

The other boxes contained matching shoes and wraps and matching sets of silk underwear. She couldn't help noticing that none of the shoes had heels higher than two inches.

As dazzled as she was by the lavish gifts, nothing about any of them fitted her personality or style. Each item was decidedly conventional and, for want of a better word, boring, like something her mother would have worn.

Her pleasure in unwrapping the beautiful things was dissolving by the second. Aside from the underwear, which was sexy and beautiful, it was clear that Lucas had had one thought in mind when he had had the things sent up: he was trying to tone her down. That brought them back to the original problem. Despite the engagement, Lucas still didn't accept her for who she was. If he couldn't accept her, she didn't see how he could ever love her.

She found her phone and jabbed in the number of Lucas's new phone. He picked up on the second ring, his voice impatient.

She cut him off. "I'm not wearing any of these dresses you've just had sent up."

"Can we discuss this later?" The register of his voice was low, his tone guarded, indicating that he wasn't alone.

Carla was beyond caring. "I'm discussing it now. I resent the implication that I dress immodest—"

"When did I say—"

"I'm female and, newsflash, I have a *figure*. I do not buy clothes to emphasise sex appeal—"

"Wait there. I'm coming up."

A click sounded in her ear. Heart pounding, she snapped her phone closed, slipped it back in her bag and surveyed the expensive pile of items. Hurt squeezed her chest tight.

She had repacked the shoes and started on the underwear when the door opened.

Lucas snapped the door closed behind him and jerked at his tie. "What's the problem?"

Carla glanced away from the heated irritation in his gaze, his ruffled hair as if he'd dragged his fingers through it, and the sexy dishevelment of the loose tie.

She picked up the pink ruffled number. "This, for starters."

He frowned. "What's wrong with it?"

She draped the gown against her body. "Crimes against humanity. The fashion police will have me in cuffs before I get out of the elevator."

He pinched the bridge of his nose as if he was under intense pressure. "Do you realize that on Medinos, as your future husband I have the right to dictate what you wear?"

For a moment she thought he was joking. "That's *medieval—*"

"Maybe I'm a medieval kind of guy."

She blinked. She had been wanting to breach his inner barriers, but now she was no longer sure she was going to like what she'd find. The old Lucas had been a pussycat compared to what she was now uncovering. "I buy clothes because they make me look and feel good, not to showcase my breasts or any other part of my anatomy. If that means I occasionally flash a bit of cleavage, then you, and the rest of Medinos, are just going to have to adjust."

She snatched up the pink silk underwear, which in stark contrast to the dress was so skimpy it wouldn't keep a grasshopper warm. "Are these regulation?"

He hooked the delicate thong over one long brown finger. "Absolutely."

Carla snatched the thong back and tossed the pink underwear back in its box. Retrieving the list of items she had signed for, she did what she had been longing to do—ripped it into shreds and tossed the pieces at Lucas. The issue of clothing, as superficial as it seemed, ignited the deep hurt that Lucas still viewed her as his sexy, private mistress and not his future wife. "You can have your master plan back."

Lucas ignored the fluttering pieces of paper. "What master plan?"

"The one where you turn me into some kind of perfect stuffed mannequin and put me in a room on Medinos with one of those wooden embroidery frames in my hand."

Lucas rubbed the side of his jaw, his gaze back to wary. "Okay, I am now officially lost."

"I resent being treated as if I'm too dumb to know how I

should dress. This is not digging gold out of rocks or sweaty men building a hotel, this is a *fashion* industry event."

His jaw took on an inflexible look she was beginning to recognize. "We're engaged. Damned if I'm going to let other men ogle you."

She threw up her hands. "You're laying down the law, but you don't even know what I plan to wear tonight."

Marching to the bed, she held up a hanger that held a sleek gold sheath with a softly draped boat-shaped neckline. "It's simple, elegant, shows no cleavage—and, more to the point, I like it."

"In that case, I apologize."

Feeling oddly deflated, she replaced the dress on the bed. When she turned, Lucas pulled her into his arms.

Her palms automatically spread on his chest. She could feel the steady pound of his heart beneath the snowy linen of his shirt, the taut, sculpted muscle beneath. Her heart rate, already fast, sped up, but he didn't try to pull her closer or kiss her.

"It wasn't my intention to upset you, but there is one thing about me that you're going to have to understand—I don't share. When it comes down to it, I don't care what you wear. I just don't want other men thinking you're available. And from now on the press will watch you like a hawk."

"I'm not irresponsible, or a tease." She released herself from his hold. The problem was that she had never understood Lucas's mood swings; she didn't understand him. One minute he was with her, the next he was cut off and distant and she needed to know why, because that distance frightened her. Ultimately it meant it was entirely possible that one day he could close himself off completely and leave her.

She began carefully rehanging the dresses, needing something to do. "Why did you never want any kind of long-term relationship with me? You planned to finish with me all along."

He gripped his nape. "We met and went to bed on the same night. At that point marriage was not on my mind."

"And after Thailand it definitely wasn't."

"I compressed my schedule to be with you in Thailand. Taking further time off wasn't possible."

"What if I'd been *really* ill?"

His gaze flashed with impatience. "If you had been ill, you would have contacted me, but you didn't."

"No."

"Are you telling me you *were* ill and didn't contact me?" he asked quietly.

"Even if I was," she said, folding the oyster silk lingerie into the cloud of tissue paper that filled the box, "you didn't want to know because looking after me in Thailand was just a little too much reality for you, wasn't it?"

"Tell me more about how I was thinking," he muttered. "I'm interested to know just how callous you think I am."

Frustration pulling at her, she jammed the lid on the box. Lucas had cleverly turned the tables on her, but she refused to let up. It suddenly occurred to her that Lucas's behavior was reminiscent of her father's. Roberto Ambrosi had hated discussing personal issues. Every time anyone had probed him about anything remotely personal he had turned grouchy and changed the subject. Attack was generally seen as the most effective form of defense.

She realized now that every time she got close to what was bothering Lucas, he reacted like a bear with a sore head. If he was snapping now, she had to be close. "If I wasn't what you wanted before," she said steadily, "how can I be that person now?"

There was a small, vibrating silence. "Because I realized you weren't Sophie."

Carla froze. "Sophie Warrington?"

"That's right. We lived together for almost a year. She died in a car accident."

Carla blinked. She remembered the story. Sophie Warrington had been gorgeous and successful. She had also had a reputation for being incredibly spoiled and high maintenance. She had lost a couple of big contracts with cosmetic companies because she had thrown tantrums. She had also been famous for her affairs.

Suddenly, Carla's lack of control in the relationship made sense. She was dealing with a ghost—a gorgeous, irresponsible ghost who had messed Lucas around to the point that he had trouble trusting any woman.

Let alone one who not only looked like Sophie but who was caught up in the same glitzy world.

Twelve

Half an hour later, after taking her medication with a big glass of water, she nibbled on a small snack then decided to go for a walk along the beach and maybe have a swim before she changed for the evening function. It wouldn't exorcise the ghost of Sophie Warrington or her fear that Lucas might never trust enough to fall in love with her, but at least it would fill in time.

Winding her hair into a loose topknot, she changed into an electric blue bikini and knotted a turquoise sarong just above her breasts. After transferring her wallet to a matching turquoise beach bag, she slipped dark glasses on the bridge of her nose and she was good to go.

Half an hour later, she stopped at a small beach café, ordered a cool drink and glimpsed Tiberio loitering behind some palms. She had since found out that Tiberio wasn't just a bodyguard, he was Lucas's head of security. That being the case, the only logical reason for him to be here was that Lucas had sent him to keep an eye on her.

Annoyed that her few minutes of privacy had been invaded by security that Lucas hadn't had the courtesy to advise her about, she finished the drink and started back to the resort.

The quickest way was along the long, curving ocean beach, which was dotted with groups of bathers lying beneath bright beach umbrellas. As she walked, she stopped, ostensibly to pick up a shell, and glanced behind. Tiberio was a short distance back, making no attempt to conceal himself, a cell phone held to his ear.

No doubt he was talking to Lucas, reporting on her activities. Annoyed, she quickened her pace. She reached the resort gardens in record time but the fast walk in the humidity of late afternoon had made her uncomfortably hot and sticky. She strode past the cool temptation of a large gleaming pool. Making an abrupt turn off the wide path, she strode along a narrow winding bush walk with the intention of losing herself amongst the shady plantings.

Beneath the shadowy overhanging plants, paradoxically it was even hotter. Slowing down, she unwound her sarong and tied it around her waist for coolness and propped her dark glasses on top of her head.

Footsteps sounded behind her, coming fast. Annoyed, she spun, and came face-to-face with Alex Panopoulos.

Dressed in a pristine business suit, complete with briefcase, his smooth features were flushed and shiny with perspiration.

She frowned, perversely wondering what had happened to Tiberio, and suddenly uncomfortably aware of the brevity of her bikini top. "What are you doing here?"

Alex set his briefcase down and jerked at his edgily patterned tie. "I just arrived and was walking to my chalet when I saw you."

She frowned, disconcerted by the intensity of his expression and the fact that he had clearly run after her. "There was no need. I'll see you tonight at the presentation."

"No you won't. My invitation was rescinded."

"Lucas—"

"Yes," he muttered curtly, "which is why I wanted to talk with you privately."

His gaze drifted to her chest, making her fingers itch with the need to yank the sarong back up. "If it's about the job—"

"Not the job." He stepped forward with surprising speed and gripped her bare arms. This close the sharp scent of fresh sweat and cologne hit her full force.

His gaze centered on her mouth. "You must know how I feel about you."

"Uh, not really. Let me go." She tried to pull free. "I'm engaged to Lucas."

"Engagements can be ended."

A creepy sense of alarm feathered her spine. He wasn't letting go. She jerked back more strongly, but his grip tightened, drawing her closer.

The thought that he might try to kiss her made her stomach flip queasily. Alex had frequently made it clear that he was attracted to her, but she had dismissed his come-ons, aware that he also regularly targeted other women, including her sister, Sienna.

Deciding on strong action, she planted her palms on his chest but, before she could shove, Panopoulos flew backward, seemingly of his own accord. A split second later Lucas was towering over her like an avenging angel.

Alex straightened, his hands curling into fists.

Lucas said something low and flat in Medinian.

Alex flinched and staggered back another step, although Lucas hadn't either stepped toward him or touched him.

Flushing a deep red, Panopoulos lunged for his briefcase and stumbled back the way he'd come.

With fingers that shook slightly with reaction, Carla untied the sarong, dragged it back over her breasts and knotted it. "What did you say to him?"

Lucas's gaze glittered over her, coming to rest on the newly tied knot. "Nothing too complicated. He won't be bothering you again."

"Thank you. I was beginning to think he wasn't going to let go." Automatically, she rubbed at the red marks on her arms where Panopoulos had gripped her just a little too hard.

With gentle movements, Lucas pushed her hands aside so he could examine the marks. They probably wouldn't turn into bruises, but that didn't change the cold remoteness of his expression.

"Did he hurt you?"

"No." From the flat look in his dark eyes, the grim set to his jaw, Carla gained the distinct impression that if Panopoulos had stepped any further over the line than he had, Lucas wouldn't have been so lenient. A small tingling shiver rippled the length of her spine as she realized that Lucas was fiercely protective of her.

It was primitive, but she couldn't help the warm glow that formed because the man she had chosen as her mate was prepared to fight for her. In an odd way, Lucas springing to her defense balanced out the hurt of discovering how affected he'd been by Sophie Warrington. To the extent that his issues with her had permeated every aspect of his relationship with Carla.

His hand landed in the small of her back, the touch blatantly dominant and possessive, but she didn't protest. She was too busy wallowing in the happy knowledge that Lucas hadn't left it to Tiberio to save her. Instead, he had interrupted what she knew was a tight schedule of interviews and come after her himself. Despite the unpleasant shock of the encounter, she was suddenly glad that it had happened.

When they reached the room, Lucas kicked the door shut and leaned back against the gleaming mahogany and drew her close.

Carla, still on edge after the encounter, went gladly. Coiling her arms around his neck, she fitted her body against the familiar planes and angles of his, soaking in the calm reassurance of his no-holds-barred protection.

Tangling the fingers of one hand in her hair, Lucas tilted her head back and kissed her until she was breathless.

When he lifted his head, his expression was grim. "If you hadn't tried to get away from Tiberio, Panopoulos wouldn't have had the opportunity to corner you."

She felt her cheeks grow hot. "I needed some time alone."

"From now on, while we're at the hotel you either have security accompany you, or I do, and that's nonnegotiable."

"Yes."

He cupped her face, his expression bemused. "That was too easy. Why aren't you arguing?"

She smiled. "Because I'm happy."

A faint flush rimmed his taut cheekbones and suddenly she felt as giddy as a teenager.

"Damn, I wish I didn't have interviews." His mouth captured hers again.

She rose up into the kiss, angling her jaw to deepen it. This time the sensuality was blast-furnace hot, but she didn't mind. For the first time in over two years Lucas's kiss, his touch, felt absolutely and completely right.

He wanted her, but not just because he desired her. He wanted her because he *cared*.

* * *

Carla showered and dressed for the launch party. Lucas walked into the suite just as she was putting the finishing touches to her makeup.

"You're late." Pleasurable anticipation spiraled through her as he appeared behind her in the mirror, leaned down and kissed the side of her neck.

His gaze connected with hers in the mirror. "I had an urgent business matter to attend to."

And she had thrown his busy schedule off even further because he'd had to interrupt his meetings to rescue her.

The happy glow that had infused her when he'd read Panopoulos the riot act reignited, along with the aching knowledge that she loved him. It was on the tip of her tongue to tell him just how much when he turned and walked into the bathroom. Instead she called out, "I'll see you downstairs."

Minutes later, with Tiberio in conspicuous attendance, she strolled into the ballroom, which was already filled with elegantly gowned and suited clients, the party well under way.

She threaded her way through the crowd, accepting congratulations and fielding curious looks. When she walked backstage to check on the arrangements for the promotional show, Nina's expression was taut.

She threw Carla a harassed look. "A minor glitch. The model we hired is down with a virus, so the agency did the best they could at short notice and sent along a new girl." She jerked her head in the direction of the curtained-off area that was being used as dressing rooms.

Dragging the curtain back far enough so she could walk through, Carla stared in disbelief at the ultrathin model. She was the right height for the dress, but that was all. Obviously groomed for the runway, she was so thin that the gown, which had originally been custom-made for Carla, hung off her shoulders and sagged around her chest and hips.

Carla's assistant, Elise, was working frantically with pins. The only problem was, the dress—an aquamarine creation studded with hundreds of pearls in a swirling pattern that was supposed to represent the sea—could only be taken in at certain points.

To add insult to injury, the model was a redhead and nothing about the promotion was red. Everything was done in Ambrosi's signature aquamarine and pearl hues. The color mix was subtle, clean and classy, reflecting Ambrosi's focus on the luxury market.

"No," Carla said, snapping instantly into work mode, irritated by the imperfections of the model and the utter destruction of the promotion that had taken her long hours of painstaking time to formulate. "Take the pins out of the dress."

She smiled with professional warmth at the model and instructed her to change, informing her that she would be paid for the job and was welcome to stay the weekend at Ambrosi's expense, but that she wouldn't be part of the promotion that evening.

Clearly unhappy, the model shimmied out of the gown on the spot and walked, half-naked and stiff backed, into a changing cubicle. At that point, another curtain was swished wide, revealing the gaggle of young ballet girls, who were also part of the promotion, in various states of undress.

Tiberio made a strangled sound. Clearly unhappy that he had intruded into a woman's domain, he indicated he would wait in the ballroom.

Elise carefully shook out the gown, examined it for signs of damage and began pulling out the pins she'd inserted. "Now what?" She indicated her well-rounded figure. "If you think I'm getting into that dress, forget it."

"Not you. Me."

Nina looked horrified. "I thought the whole point of this was that you weren't to take part."

Carla picked up the elegant mask that went with the outfit and pressed it against her face. The mask left only her mouth and chin visible.

Her stomach tightened at the risk she was taking. "He won't know."

Thirteen

Carla stepped into the gown and eased the zipper up, with difficulty. The dress felt a little smaller and tighter than it had, because it had been taken in to fit the model who was off sick.

She fastened the exquisite trailing pearl choker, which, thankfully, filled most of her décolletage and dangled a single pearl drop in the swell of her cleavage.

Cleavage that seemed much more abundant now that the dress had been tightened.

She surveyed her appearance in the mirror, dismayed and a little embarrassed by the sensual effect of the too-tight dress.

Careful not to breathe too deeply and rip a seam, she fastened the webbed bracelet that matched the choker and put sexy dangling earrings in her lobes. She fitted the pearl-studded mask and surveyed the result in the mirror.

With any luck she would get through this without being

recognized. A few minutes on stage then she would make her exit and quickly change back into her gold dress and circulate.

Elise swished the curtain aside. "It's time to go. You're on."

Lucas checked his watch as he strolled through the ballroom, his gaze moving restlessly from face to face.

Tiberio had informed him that Carla was assisting the girls backstage with the small production they had planned. He had expected no less. When it came to detail, Carla was a stickler, but now he was starting to get worried. She should have been back in the ballroom, with him, by now.

He checked his watch again. At least Panopoulos was out of the picture. He had made certain of that.

Every muscle in his body locked tight as he remembered the frightened look on Carla's face as she'd tried to shove free of him. When he'd seen the marks on Carla's arms, he had regretted not hitting Panopoulos.

Instead, he had satisfied his need to drive home his message by personally delivering the older man to the airport and escorting him onto a privately chartered flight out.

Panopoulos had threatened court action. Lucas had invited him to try.

Frowning, he checked the room again. He thought he had seen Carla circulating when he had first entered the room, but the gold dress and dark hair had belonged to a young French woman. He was beginning to think that something else had gone wrong since the heart-stopping passion of those moments in their room and she had found something else to fret about.

The radiant glow on her face when he'd left her had hit him like a kick in the chest, transfixing him. He could remember her looking that way when they had first met, but gradually, over time, the glow had gone. He decided it was a grim testament to how badly he had mismanaged their relationship that Carla had ceased to be happy. From now on he was determined to do whatever it took to keep that glow in her eyes.

A waiter offered him a flute of champagne. He refused. At that moment there was a stir at one end of the room as Nina, who was the hostess for the evening, came out onto the small stage.

Lucas leaned against the bar and continued to survey the room as music swelled and the promotional show began. The room fell silent as the model, who was far more mouth-wateringly sexy than he remembered, moved with smooth grace across the stage. *Floor show* wasn't the correct terminology for the presentation but he was inescapably driven to relabel the event.

Every man in the room was mesmerized, as the masked model, playing an ancient Medinian high priestess, moved through the simple routine, paying homage to God with the produce of the sea, a basket of Ambrosi pearls. With her long, elegant legs and tempting cleavage, she reminded him more of a Vegas dancer than any depiction of a Medinian priestess he had ever seen.

His loins warmed and his jaw tightened at his uncharacteristic loss of control. He had seen that dress on the model who was supposed to be doing the presentation. At that point the gown, which was largely transparent and designed so that pearl-encrusted waves concealed strategic parts and little else, had looked narrow and ascetically beautiful rather than sexy. He hadn't been even remotely turned-on.

The model turned, her hips swaying with a sudden sinuous familiarity as she walked, surrounded by a gaggle of young ballet dancers, all carrying baskets overflowing with free samples of Ambrosi products to distribute to clients.

Suspicion coalesced into certainty as his gaze dropped to the third finger of her left hand.

He swallowed a mouthful of champagne and calmly set the flute down. The mystery of his future wife's whereabouts had just been solved.

He had thought she was safely attired in the gold gown, minus any cleavage. Instead she had gone against his instructions and was busy putting on an X-rated display for an audience that contained at least seventy men.

Keeping a tight rein on his temper, he strode through the spellbound crowd and up onto the stage. Carla's startled gaze clashed with his. Avoiding a line of flimsy white pillars that were in danger of toppling, he took the basket of pearls she held, handed them to one of the young girls and swung her into his arms.

She clutched at his shoulders. "What do you think you're doing?"

Grimly, Lucas ignored the clapping and cheering as he strode off the stage and cut through the crowd to the nearest exit. "Removing you before you're recognized. Don't worry," he said grimly, "they'll think it's part of the floor show. The Atraeus Group's conquering CEO carrying off the glittering prize of Ambrosi Pearls."

"I can't believe you're romanticizing a business takeover, and it is *not* a floor show!"

He reached the elevator and hit the call button with his elbow, his gaze skimmed the enticing display of cleavage. "What happened to the model I employed?"

"She came down with a virus. The replacement they sent didn't fit the dress. If I hadn't stepped in, the only option would have been to cancel the promotion."

A virus. That word was beginning to haunt him. "And canceling would have been such a bad idea?"

"Our events drive a lot of sales. Besides, I'm wearing a mask. No one knew."

"*I* knew."

She ripped off the mask, her blue gaze shooting fire. "I don't see how."

He took in the sultry display of honey-tanned skin. Cancel the Vegas dancer. She looked like an extremely expensive courtesan, festooned with pearls. *His* courtesan.

It didn't seem to matter what she wore, he reflected. The clothing could look like a sack on any other woman, but on Carla it became enticingly, distractingly sexy. "Next time remember to take off the engagement ring."

The elevator doors opened. Seconds later they had reached their floor. Less than a minute later Lucas kicked the door to their suite closed.

"You realize I need to go back to the party."

He set her down. "Just not in that dress."

"Not a problem, it's not my color." Carla tugged at the snug fit of the dress. Fake pearls pinged on the floor. A seam had given way while Lucas was carrying her, but on the positive side, at least she could breathe now. She eyed Lucas warily. "What do you think you're doing?"

He had draped his suit jacket over the back of a couch, loosened his tie and strolled over to the small business desk in the corner of the sitting room. She watched as he flipped his laptop open. "Checking email."

The abrupt switch from scorching possessiveness to cool neutrality made her go still inside. She had seen him do this often. In the past, usually, just before he would leave her apartment he would begin immersing himself in work—phone calls, emails, reading documents. She guessed that on some level she had recognized the process for what it was; she just hadn't ever bothered to label it. Work was his coping mechanism, an instant emotional off button. She should know. She had used it herself often enough.

She watched as he scrolled through an email, annoyed at the way he had switched from blazing hot to icy cool. Lucas had removed her from the launch party with all the finesse of a caveman dragging his prize back to the fire. He had gotten his way; now he was ignoring her.

The sensible option would be to get out of the goddess outfit, put on another dress and go downstairs and circulate before finding her gold dress and handbag, which she had left backstage. But that was before her good old type A personality decided to make a late comeback.

Ever since she had been five years old on her first day at school and her teacher, Mrs. Hislop, had put daddy's little girl in the back row of the classroom, she had understood one defining fact about herself: she did not like being ignored.

Walking to the kitchenette, she opened cupboards until she found a bowl. She needed to eat. Cereal wasn't her snack of choice this late, but it was here, and the whole point was that she stayed in the suite with Lucas until he realized that she was not prepared to be ignored.

She found a minipacket of cereal, emptied it into the bowl then tossed the packaging into the trash can, which was tucked into a little alcove under the bench.

Lucas sent her a frowning glance, as if she was messing with his concentration. "I thought you were going to change and get back to the party."

She opened the fridge and extracted a carton of milk. "Why?"

"The room is full of press and clients."

She gave him a faintly bewildered look, as if she didn't understand what he was talking about, but inwardly she was taking notes. He clearly thought she was a second Sophie, a party girl who loved to be the center of attention. "Nina and Elise are taking care of business. I don't need to be there."

"It didn't look that way ten minutes ago."

She shrugged. "That was an emergency."

Aware that she now had Lucas's attention, she opened the carton with painstaking precision and poured milk over the cereal. Grabbing a spoon, she strolled out into the lounge, sat on the sofa and turned the TV on. She flicked through the channels till she found a talk show she usually enjoyed.

Lucas took the remote and turned the TV off. "What are you up to?"

Carla munched on a spoonful of cereal and stared at the now blank screen. Before the party she had found reasons to adore Lucas's dictatorial behavior. Now she was back to loathing it, but she refused to allow her annoyance to show. She had wanted Lucas's attention and now she had gotten it. "Considering my future employment. I'm not good with overbearing men."

"You are not going to work for Panopoulos."

She ate another mouthful of cereal. He was jealous; she was getting somewhere. "I guess not, since I have an iron-clad contract I signed only yesterday."

Lucas tossed the remote down on the couch and dispensed with his tie. "Damn. You must be sleeping with the boss."

"Plus, I have shares."

"It's not a pleasing feminine trait to parade your victories." He took the cereal bowl from her and set it down on the coffee table. Threading her fingers with his, he pulled her to her feet.

More pearls pinged off the dress as she straightened. A tiny tearing sound signaled that another seam had given. "You shouldn't take food from a woman who could be pregnant."

His gaze was arrested. "Do you think you are?"

"I don't know yet." She had left the test kit behind. With everything that had happened, taking time out to read the instructions and do the test hadn't been a priority.

"I could get used to the idea." Cupping her face, he dipped his head and touched his mouth to hers.

The soft, seducing intimacy of the kiss made Carla forget the next move in her strategy. Before she could edit her response, her arms coiled around his neck. He made a low sound of satisfaction, then deepened the kiss.

Hands loosely cupping her hips, he walked her backward, kiss by drugging kiss, until they reached the bedroom. She felt a tug as the zipper on the dress peeled down, then a loosening at the bodice. More pearls scattered as he pulled the dress up and over her head and tossed it on the floor.

"The dress is ruined." Not that she really cared. It had only been a prop and it had served its purpose, in more ways than one.

"Good. That means you can't wear it again."

Stepping out of her heels, she climbed into bed and pulled the silk coverlet over her as she watched him undress. With his jet-black hair and broad, tanned shoulders he looked sleek and muscular.

The bed depressed as he came back down beside her. The clean scent of his skin made her stomach clench.

He surveyed the silk coverlet with dissatisfaction. "This needs to go." He dragged it aside as he came down on the bed. One long finger stroked over the pearl choker at her throat down to the single dangling pearl nestled in the shadowy hollow between her breasts. "But you can keep this on."

She had forgotten about the jewelry. Annoyed by the suggestion, which seemed more suited to a mistress than a future wife, she scooted over on the bed, wrapping the coverlet around her as she went. "You just destroyed an expensive gown. If you think I'm going to let you make love to me while I'm wearing an Ambrosi designer orig—"

His arm curled around her waist, easily anchoring her to the bed. "I'll approve the write-off for it."

Despite her reservations, unwilling excitement quivered through her as he loomed over her, but he made no effort to do anything more than keep her loosely caged beneath him.

"Whether we make love or not," he said quietly, "is your decision, but before you storm off, you need to know that I've organized a special license on Medinos. We're going to be married before the week is out."

"You might need my permission for that."

Something flared in his gaze and she realized she had pushed him a little too hard. "Not on Medinos."

"As I recall from Sienna's wedding, I still have to say yes."

Frustration flickered in his gaze and then she finally got him. For two years she had been focused on organizing their time together, taking care of every detail so that everything was as perfect as she could make it, given their imperfect circumstances. Lucas had fallen in with her plans, but she had overlooked a glaring, basic fact. Lucas was male; he needed to be in control. He now wanted her to follow the plan he had formulated, and she was frustrating him.

He cupped her face. "I have the special license. I don't care where we get married, just as long as it happens. Damned if I want Panopoulos, or any man, thinking you're available."

Unwilling delight filtered through the outrage that had driven her ever since she had realized that Lucas had developed a coping mechanism for shutting her out. The incident with Alex seemed a lifetime away, but it had only been hours.

She understood that in Lucas's mind he had rescued her for a second time that day, this time from a room full of men. As domineering and abrasive as his behavior was, in an odd way, it was the assurance she so badly needed that he cared. After watching him detach and walk away from her for more than two years, she wasn't going to freeze him out just when she finally had proof that he was falling for her.

"Yes."

His gaze reflected the same startled bemusement she had glimpsed that afternoon. "That's settled, then."

Warmth flared to life inside her. The happy glow expanded when he touched his lips to hers, the soft kiss soothing away the stress of dealing with Lucas's dictatorial manner. Sliding her fingers into the black silk of his hair, she pulled him back for a second kiss, then a third, breathing in his heat and scent. The kiss deepened, lingered. The silk coverlet slid away and she went into his arms gladly.

Sometime later, she woke when Lucas left the bed and walked to the bathroom, blinking at the golden glow that still flooded the room from the bedside lamp. Chilled without his body heat, she curled on her side and dragged the coverlet up high around her chin.

The bed depressed as Lucas rejoined her. One arm curled around her hips, he pulled her back snug against him. His palm cupped her abdomen, as if he was unconsciously cradling their baby.

Wistfully, her hand slipped over his, her fingers intertwining as she relaxed back into the blissful heat of his body. She took a moment to fantasize about the possibility that right at that very moment there could be an embryo growing inside her, that in a few months they would no longer be a couple, they would be a family. "Do you think we'll make good parents?"

"We've got every chance."

She twisted around in his grip, curious about the bitter note in his voice. "What's wrong?"

He propped himself on one elbow. "I had a girlfriend who was pregnant once. She had an abortion."

"Sophie Warrington?"

"That's right."

"You told me about her. She died in a car accident."

There was silence for a long, drawn-out moment. "Sophie had an abortion the day before she died. When she finally got around to telling me that she'd aborted our child before even telling me she was pregnant, we had a blazing argument. We broke up and she drove away in her sports car. An hour later she was dead."

Carla blinked. She hadn't realized that Lucas had split with Sophie before she had died. She smoothed her palm over his chest. "I'm sorry. You must have loved her."

"It was an addiction more than love."

Something clicked into place in her mind. Lucas had once used that term with regard to her. She hadn't liked it at the time, because it implied an unwilling attraction. "You don't see me as another Sophie?"

His hand trapped hers, holding it pressed against his chest so she could feel the steady thud of his heart. "You are similar in some ways, but maybe that's how the basic chemistry works. Both you and Sophie are my type."

Her stomach plunged a little. There it was again, the unwilling element to the attraction.

She knew he hadn't considered her marriageable in the beginning, because in his mind marriage hadn't fitted with the addictive sexual passion she had inspired in him. Admittedly, she hadn't helped matters. She had been busy trying to de-stress in line with her doctor's orders and keep their relationship casual but organized until the problems between both families had been rectified. In the process she had given him a false impression of her values. He had gotten to know who she really was a little better in the past few days, but that was cold comfort when she needed him to love her.

Fear spiked though her at the niggling thought that, if he

categorized her as being like Sophie, it was entirely possible that he wouldn't fall in love with her, that he would always see her as a fatal attraction and not his ideal marriage partner.

If she carried that thought through to its logical conclusion, it was highly likely that once the desire faded, he would fall for the kind of woman that in his heart he really wanted. "What happens when I get old, or put on weight, or...get sick?"

Physical attraction would fade fast and then where would they be?

She cupped his jaw. "I think I need to know *why* you can't resist me, because if what you feel is only based on physical attraction, it won't last."

He stoked a finger down the delicate line of her throat to her collarbone. "It's chemistry. A mixture of personality and the physical."

She frowned, her dissatisfaction increasing. "If you feel this way about me then how could you have been attracted to Lilah?"

As soon as she said Lilah's name, she wished she hadn't. Despite having Lucas's ring on her finger, she couldn't forget the weeks of stress when Lucas had avoided her then the sudden, hurtful way he had replaced her with Lilah.

"If you're jealous of Lilah, you don't need to be."

"Why?" But the question was suddenly unnecessary, because the final piece of the puzzle had just dropped into place. Lucas hadn't wanted Lilah for the simple reason that he had barely had time to get to know her. She had been part of a coldly logical strategy. An instant girlfriend selected for the purpose of spelling out in no uncertain terms that his relationship with Carla was over.

Fourteen

Carla stiffened. All the comments he'd made about her not needing to worry about Lilah and the quick way he had ended his relationship with her suddenly made perfect sense. "I have no reason to be jealous of Lilah, because you were never attracted to her."

His abrupt stillness and his lack of protest were damning.

"You manufactured a girlfriend." Her throat was tight, her voice husky. "You picked out someone safe to take to the wedding to make it easy to break up with me. You knew that if I thought you had fallen for another woman I would keep my distance and not make a fuss."

He loomed over her, his shoulders blocking out the dim glow from the lamp. "Carla—"

"No." Pushing free of his arms, she stumbled out of bed and struggled into her robe.

She yanked the sash tight as another thought occurred, giving her fresh insight into just how ruthless and serpentine

Lucas had been. "And you didn't pick just anyone to play your girlfriend. You were clever enough to select someone from Ambrosi Pearls, so the relationship covered all bases and would be in my face at work. That made it doubly clear to me that you were off-limits. It also made it look like you wanted her close, that you couldn't bear to have her out of your sight."

The complete opposite of his treatment of her.

Through the course of their relationship she had been separated and isolated from almost every aspect of his personal and business life.

Suddenly the room, with its romantic flowers, her clothes and jewelry draped over furniture and on the floor, emphasized how stupid she had been. Lucas's silence wasn't making her feel any better. "You probably even wanted to push me into leaving Ambrosi, which would get me completely out of your hair."

He shoved off the bed, found his pants and pulled them on. "I had no intention of depriving you of your job."

She stared at him bleakly, uncaring about that minor detail, when his major sin had been his complete and utter disregard for her feelings and her love. "What incentive did you offer Lilah to pose as your girlfriend?"

"I didn't pay Lilah. She knew nothing about this beyond the fact that I asked her to be my date at Constantine's wedding. That was our first, and last, date."

He caught her around the waist and pulled her close. "Do you believe me?"

She blinked. "Do you love me?"

There was the briefest of hesitations. "You know I do."

She searched his expression. It was a definite breakthrough, but it wasn't what she needed, not after the stinging hurt of finding out that he had used Lilah to facilitate getting rid of her.

His gaze seared into hers. "I'm sorry."

He bent and kissed her and the plunging disappointment receded a little. He was sorry and he very definitely wanted her. Maybe he even did love her. It wasn't the fairy tale she had dreamed about, but it was a start.

A few days ago she had been desperate for just this kind of chance with Lucas. Now too she was possibly pregnant. She owed it to herself and to Lucas to give him one more chance.

After an early breakfast, Carla strolled into the conference room Ambrosi had booked for its sales display. Lucas had phone calls to make in their suite, then meetings with buyers. Carla had decided to make herself useful and help Elise put together the jewelry display and set out the sales materials and press kits.

The fact that, if Lilah had been here, setting up the jewelry would have been her job was a reminder she didn't need, but she had to be pragmatic. Lilah was likely to be a part of the landscape for the foreseeable future, and she probably wasn't any happier about the situation than Carla. They would both have to adjust.

Security was already in place and lavish floral displays filled the room with the rich scent of roses. Elise had arranged for Ambrosi's special display cases to be positioned around the room. All that remained was for the jewelry, which was stored in locked cases, to be set out and labeled.

Elise, already looking nervous and ruffled, handed her a clipboard. "Just to make things more complicated, last night Lilah won a prestigious design award in Milan for some Ambrosi pieces. The buzz is *huge*." She snapped a rubber band off a large laminated poster. "Lucas had this expressed from the office late last night." She unrolled the poster, which was a blown-up publicity shot of Lilah, looking ultrasleek and gorgeous in a slim-fitting white suit, Ambrosi pearls at her lobes and her throat. With the pose she had struck and her calm gaze square on to the camera, Carla couldn't help thinking she looked eerily like the Atraeus bride in the portrait both she and Zane had studied at the prewedding dinner.

Elise glanced around the room. "I think I'll put it there, so people will see it as soon as they walk into the room. What do you think?"

Carla stared at the background of the poster. If she wasn't mistaken Lilah's image was superimposed over a scenic shot of Medinos—probably taken from one of the balconies of the *castello*. It was a small point, but it mattered. "Lucas ordered that to be done *late* last night?"

If that was the case, the only window of time he'd had was the few minutes after he had abducted her from the party when he had suddenly lost all interest in her because he had been so absorbed with what he was doing online.

Ordering a poster of the gorgeous, perfect Lilah.

Elise suddenly looked uncertain. "Uh, I think so. That's what he said."

Carla smiled and held out her hand. "Cool. Give the poster to me."

Elise went a little pale, but she handed the poster over.

Carla studied the larger-than-life photo. Her first impulse was to fling it into the ocean so she didn't have to deal with all that perfection. With her luck, the tide would keep tossing the poster back.

"I need scissors."

Elise found a pair and handed them over. Carla spent a happy few minutes systematically reducing the poster to an untidy pile of very small pieces.

Elise's eyes tracked the movement as Carla set the scissors down. She cleared her throat. "Do you want to sort through the jewelry, or would you prefer I did that?"

"I'm here to help. I'll do it."

"Great! I'll do the press kits." She dug in her briefcase. "Here's the plan for the display items. With all of the other publicity about, uh, Lilah, our sales have gone through the roof. We've already received orders from some of the attending clients so some of that jewelry is for clients and not for display. With any luck, they've kept the orders separate."

Carla slowly relaxed, determinedly thinking positive thoughts as she checked off the orders against the packing slip and set those packages to one side. Her mood improved by the second as she began putting the display together, anchoring the gorgeous, intricate pieces securely on black velvet beds then locking the glass cases. Lilah may have designed most of the jewelry, but they were Ambrosi pieces and she was proud of them. She refused to allow any unhappiness she felt about Lilah affect her pride in the family business.

A courier arrived with a package. Elise signed for it, shrugging. "This is weird. All the rest was delivered yesterday."

Carla took the package and frowned. The same courier firm had delivered it, but this one wasn't from the Ambrosi warehouse in Sydney. The package had been sent by another jeweler, the same Atraeus-owned company from which Lucas had purchased her engagement ring. That meant that whatever the package contained it couldn't be either an order for a customer or jewels for the launch.

Anticipation and a glow of happy warmth spread through her as she studied the package. She had her ring, which meant Lucas must have bought her something else, possibly a matching pendant or bracelet.

Her heart beat a little faster. Perhaps even matching wedding rings.

The temptation to open the package was almost overwhelming, but she managed to control herself. Lucas had bought her a gift, his first real gift of love, without pressure or prompting. She wasn't about to spoil his moment when he gave her the special piece he had selected.

She studied the ring on her finger, unable to contain her pleasure. She didn't care about the size of the diamond or the cost. What mattered was that Lucas had chosen it because it matched her eyes. Every time she looked at the ring she remembered that tiny, very personal, very important detail. It was a sign that he was one step closer to truly loving and appreciating her. After what had happened last night, how close they had come to splitting up again, she treasured every little thing that would help keep them together.

Elise finished shoving boxes and Bubble Wrap in the bin liner the hotel had provided. She waggled her brows at the package. "Not part of the display, huh? Looks interesting. Want me to take it to Lucas? I'm supposed to take the Japanese client he's meeting with to the airport in about ten minutes."

"Hands off." Carla's fingers tightened on the package. Despite knowing that Elise was teasing her, she felt ridiculously possessive of whatever Lucas had bought for her.

A split second later, Lucas strolled into the conference room. Immediately behind him, hotel attendants were setting up for morning tea, draping the long tables in white tablecloths and setting out pastries and finger food. Outside, in the lobby, she could hear the growing chatter. Any minute now, buyers and clients would start pouring into the conference room and there would be no privacy. The impulse to thrust the package at Lucas and get him to open it then and there died a death.

Lucas's gaze locked with hers then dropped to the glossy cut-up pieces of poster still strewn across the table. He lifted a brow. "What's that?"

"Your poster of Lilah."

There was a moment of assessing silence.

Lucas was oddly watchful, recognizing and logging the changes in her. As if he was finally getting that she was a whole lot more than the amenable, compartmentalized lover he had spent the past two years holding at a distance.

In that moment Carla knew Lilah had to go completely, no matter how crucial she was to Ambrosi Pearls. If she and Lucas were to have a chance at a successful marriage, they couldn't afford a third person in the equation.

Lucas lifted a brow. "What's in the package?"

"Nothing that won't keep." She pushed the package out of sight in her handbag then briskly swept all the poster fragments into the trash.

Whatever Lucas had bought her, she couldn't enjoy receiving it right at that minute, not with the larger-than-life specter of Lilah still hanging over them.

The weekend finished with a dinner cruise, by the end of which Lucas was fed up with designer anything. Give him steel girders and mining machinery any day. Anything but the shallow, too bright social whirl that was part and parcel of the world of luxury retailing.

He kept his arm around Carla's waist as they stood on the quay, bidding farewell to the final guests.

Carla was exhausted—he could feel it in the way she leaned into him—and her paleness worried him. The last thing she needed was another viral relapse.

He had insisted she fit in a nap after lunch. It had been a struggle to make her let go of the organizational reins, but in the end he had simply picked her up and carried her to their room. He had discovered that there was something about the masculine, take-charge act of picking Carla up that seemed to reach her in a way that words couldn't.

She had been oddly quiet all day, but he had expected that. He had made a mistake with the poster. The second he had walked into the conference room that morning and seen the look on Carla's face he had realized just how badly he had messed up. He had grimly resolved to take more care in future.

Her quietness had carried over into the evening. He had debated having her stay in their suite and rest, but in the end he had allowed her to come on the cruise for one simple reason. If he left her behind, she might not be there when he returned.

Lucas recognized Alan Harrison, a London buyer and the last straggling guest.

He paused to shake Lucas's hand. "Lilah Cole, the name on everyone's lips. You might have trouble holding on to her now, Atraeus. I know Catalano jewelry in Milan is impressed with her work. Wouldn't be surprised if they try and spirit her away from you."

Lucas clenched his jaw as Carla stiffened beside him. "That won't happen for at least two years. Lilah just signed a contract to take on the Medinos retail outlet as well as head up the design team."

"Medinos, huh? Smart move. Pretty girl, and focused. Got her in the nick of time. Another few days and you would have lost her."

Carla waited until Harrison had gone then gently detached herself from his hold. "You didn't tell me you had renewed Lilah's contract."

There was no accusation in her voice, just an empty neutrality, but Lucas had finally learned to read between the lines. When Carla went blank that was when she was feeling the most, and when *he* was being weighed in the balance.

Two years, and he hadn't understood that one crucially important fact. "I offered her the Medinos job a couple of days ago. If I'd realized how much it would hurt you I would have let her go. At the time removing her to Medinos for two years seemed workable, since I'll be running the Sydney office for the foreseeable future and we'll be based here."

"You did that for me." There was a small, vibrating silence and he was finally rewarded with a brilliant smile. "Thank you."

"You're welcome." Grinning, he pulled her into his arms.

Carla slipped out of her heels as she walked into their suite. Her feet were aching but she was so happy she hardly noticed the discomfort.

Lucas had finally crossed the invisible line she had needed him to cross; he had committed himself to her, and the blood was literally fizzing through her veins.

Maybe she should have felt this way when they had gotten engaged, but the reality was that all he'd had to do was say words and buy a ring. As badly as she had wanted to, she hadn't felt secure. Now, for the first time in over two years, she finally did.

The fact that he had arranged for Lilah to work in Medinos because they would be based in Sydney for two years had been the tipping point.

He had made an arrangement to ensure their happiness. He had used the word *they*. It was a little word, but it shouted commitment and togetherness.

Two years in Sydney. Together.

Taking Lucas by the hand, she pulled him into the bedroom, determinedly keeping her gaze away from the bedside bureau where she had concealed the package that had arrived that morning. "Sit down." She patted the bed. "I'll get the champagne."

He shrugged out of his jacket and tossed it over a chair before jerking at his tie. "Maybe you shouldn't drink champagne."

"Sparkling water for me, champagne for you."

"What are we celebrating, exactly?"

"You'll see in a minute."

He paused in the act of unbuttoning his shirt. "You're pregnant."

The hope in Lucas's voice sent a further shiver of excitement through her. Not only did he want her enough that he had bought her a wonderful surprise gift, he really did want their baby. Suddenly, after weeks, years, of uncertainty everything was taking on the happy-ever-after fairy tale sparkle she had always secretly wanted.

Humming to herself, she walked into the kitchen and opened a chilled bottle of vintage French champagne. The label was one of the best. The cost would be astronomical, but this was a special moment. She wanted every detail to be perfect. She put the champagne and two flutes on a tray and added a bottle of sparkling water for herself. On the way to the bedroom, she added a gorgeous pink tea rose from one of the displays.

She set the tray down on the bedside table as Lucas padded barefoot out of the bathroom. In the dim lamp-lit room with his torso bare, his dark dress trousers clinging low on narrow hips, his bronzed, muscular beauty struck her anew and she was suddenly overwhelmed by emotion and a little tearful.

Lucas cupped her shoulders and drew her close. "What's wrong?"

She snuggled against him, burying her face in the deliciously warm, comforting curve of his shoulder. "Nothing, except that I love you."

There was a brief hesitation, then he drew her close. "And I love you."

Carla stiffened at the neutral tone of his voice then made an effort to dismiss the twinge of disappointment that, even now, with this new intimacy between them, Lucas still couldn't relax into loving her.

She pushed away slightly, enough that she could see his face and read his expression, but she was too late to catch whatever truth had been in his eyes when he had said those three little words.

Forcing a bright smile, she released herself from Lucas's light hold, determined to recapture the soft, fuzzy fairy-tale glow. "Time for the champagne."

Lucas took the bottle from her and set it back down on the tray.

He reeled her in close. "I don't need a drink."

His head dipped, his lips brushed hers. She wound her arms around his neck, surrendering to the kiss as he pulled her onto the bed. Long seconds later he propped his head on one elbow and wound a finger in a coiling strand of her hair. "What's wrong? You're like a cat on hot bricks."

Rolling over, Carla opened the bureau drawer and took out the courier package. "This came today."

The heavy plastic rustled as she handed it to Lucas. Instead of the teasing grin she had expected, Lucas's gaze rested on the courier package and he went curiously still.

A sudden suspicion gripped her.

Clambering off the bed she took the package and ripped at the heavy plastic.

"Carla—"

"No. Don't talk." Tension banded her chest as she walked out to the kitchen, found a steak knife in the drawer and slit the plastic open. A heavy, midnight-blue box, tied with a black silk bow, the jeweler's signature packaging, tumbled out of layers of Bubble Wrap onto the kitchen counter.

Not an oblong case that might hold a necklace, or a bracelet. A ring box.

Lucas loomed over her as she tore the bow off. Maybe

it was a set of wedding rings. Lucas wanted an early wedding. It made sense to order the rings from the same place they had bought her engagement ring.

"Carla—"

She already knew. Not wedding rings. She flipped the jewelry case open.

A diamond solitaire glittered with a soft, pure fire against midnight-blue velvet.

Fingers shaking, she slid the ring onto the third finger of her right hand. It was a couple of sizes too small and failed to clear her knuckle. The bright, illusory world she had been living in dissolved.

The ring had never been meant for her. The elegant, classic engagement ring had been selected and sized with someone else in mind.

Lilah.

Fifteen

Carla replaced the ring in its box and met Lucas's somber gaze head-on. "You weren't just dating Lilah to facilitate making a clean break with me, were you? You intended to marry her."

Lucas's expression was calmly, coolly neutral. "I had planned to propose marriage, but that was before—"

"Why would you want to marry Lilah when you still wanted me?" She couldn't say *love,* because she now doubted that love had ever factored in. Lucas had wanted her, period. He had felt desire, passion: lust.

"It was a practical decision."

"Because otherwise you were worried that when Constantine and Sienna tied the knot you might be pressured into marrying me."

Impatience flashed in his gaze. "No one could pressure me into marriage. I wanted you. I would have married you in a New York second."

Realization dawned. "Then lived to regret it."

"I didn't think what we had would last."

"So you tied yourself into an arrangement with Lilah so you couldn't be tempted into making a bad decision."

His brows jerked together. "There was no 'arrangement.' All Lilah knew was that I wanted to date her."

"With a view to marriage."

"Yes."

Because she wouldn't have gone out with him otherwise. Certainly not halfway across the world to a very public family wedding.

Hurt spiraled through her that Lucas hadn't bothered to refute her statement that marrying her would have been a bad decision. And that he had so quickly offered Lilah what she had longed for and needed from him.

Throat tight, eyes stinging, Carla snapped the ring box closed and jammed it back into the courier bag. She suddenly remembered the odd behavior of the manager of Moore's. It hadn't been because their engagement was so sudden, or because of the scandal in the morning paper. The odd atmosphere had been because Lucas had bought *two* engagement rings in the same week for two separate women.

Blindly, she shoved the courier bag at Lucas. "You were going to propose to her *here,* at this product launch." Why else would he have requested the ring be couriered to the hotel?

Carla remembered the flashes of sympathy in Lilah's gaze on Medinos, her bone-white face outside of Lucas's apartment when the reporter had snapped Carla and Lucas kissing. Lilah had expected more than just a series of dates. She wouldn't have been with Lucas otherwise.

"You were never even remotely in love with Lilah."

"No."

Her head jerked up. "Then, why consider marriage?"

His expression was taut. "The absence of emotion worked for me. I wasn't after the highs and lows. I wanted the opposite."

"Because of Sophie Warrington."

"That's right," he said flatly. "Sophie liked bright lights, publicity. She loved notoriety. We clashed constantly. The night of the crash we argued and she stormed out. That was the last time I saw her alive. I shouldn't have let her go, should have stopped her—"

"If she wasn't your kind of girl, why were you with her?"

"Good question," he said grimly. "Because I was stupid enough to fall for her. We were a mismatch. We should never have been together in the first place."

Carla's jaw tightened. "You do still think I'm like her," she said quietly. "Another Sophie."

His expression was closed. "I…did."

The hesitation was the final nail in the proverbial coffin. Her stomach plummeted. "You still do."

"I've made mistakes, but I know what I want," Lucas said roughly.

"Me, or the baby I might possibly be having?" Because if Lucas still didn't know who she was as a person, the baby seemed the strongest reason for marriage. And she couldn't marry someone who saw his attraction to her as a weakness, a character flaw. She stared blankly around the flower-festooned room. "If you don't mind, I'd like to get some sleep."

Stepping past Lucas, she walked into the bedroom and grabbed a spare pillow and blanket from the closet.

"Where are you going?"

"To sleep on the couch."

"That's not necessary. I'll take the couch."

She flinched at the sheer masculine beauty of his broad shoulders and muscled chest. She had fallen in love with a mirage, she thought bleakly, a beautiful man who was prepared to care for her but who, ultimately, had never truly wanted to be in love with her. "No. Right now I really would prefer the couch."

His fingers curled around her upper arms. "We can work this through. I can explain—"

She went rigid in his grip. The pillow and blanket formed a buffer between them that right now she desperately needed because, despite everything, she was still vulnerable. "Let me go," she said quietly. "It's late. We both need sleep."

His dark gaze bored into hers, level and calm. "Come back to bed. We can talk this through."

She fought the familiar magnetic pull, the desire to drop the pillow and blanket and step back into his arms. "No. We can talk in the morning."

A familiar cramping pain low in her stomach pulled Carla out of sleep. A quick trip to the bathroom verified that she had her period and that she was absolutely, positively not pregnant.

Numbly, she walked back to the couch but didn't bother trying to sleep. Until that moment she hadn't realized how much she had desperately needed to be pregnant. If there was a child then there had been the possibility that she could have stayed with Lucas. Now there wasn't one and she had to face reality.

Lucas had broken up with Sophie when she had aborted his child. He had also proposed marriage when he had thought she could be pregnant. For a man who had gone to considerable lengths to cut her out of his life, that was a huge turnaround. She could try fooling herself that it was because he loved her, even if he didn't quite know it, but she couldn't allow herself to think that way. She deserved better.

Now she knew for sure she wasn't pregnant. There were no more excuses.

Her decision made, she opted not to shower, because that would wake Lucas. Instead, she found her gym bag, which was sitting by the kitchen counter and which contained fresh underwear, sweatpants, a tank and a light cotton hoodie. She quickly dressed and laced on sneakers. Her handbag with all her medications was in the bedroom. She couldn't risk getting that, but she had a cash card and some cash tucked in her gym bag. That would give her enough money and the ID she needed to book a flight back to Sydney. She had plenty of medication at home, so leaving the MediPACKs in her purse wasn't a problem. She would collect her handbag along with the rest of her luggage from Lucas when he got back to Sydney.

Working quickly, she jammed toiletries into the sports bag. She paused to listen, but there was no sound or movement from the bedroom. She wrote a brief note on hotel paper, explaining that she was not pregnant and was therefore ending their engagement. She anchored the note to the kitchen counter with the engagement ring.

Picking up the sports bag and hooking her handbag over her shoulder, she quietly let herself out of the room.

Within a disorientingly short period of time the elevator shot her down to the lobby. The speed with which she had walked away from what had been the most important adult relationship of her life made her stomach lurch sickly, but she couldn't go back.

She couldn't afford to commit one more minute to a man who had put more creative effort into cutting her out of his life than he ever had to including her.

A small sound pulled Lucas out of a fitful sleep.

Kicking free of the tangled sheet, he pushed to his feet and pulled on the pair of pants he'd left tossed over the arm of a chair.

Moonlight slanted through shuttered windows as he walked swiftly through the suite. His suspicion that the sound that had woken him had been the closing of the front door turned to certainty when he found a note and Carla's engagement ring on the kitchen counter.

The note was brief. Carla wasn't pregnant. Rather than both of them being pushed into a marriage that clearly had no chance of working, she had decided to give him his out.

She had left him.

Lucas's hand closed on the note, crumpling it. His heart was pounding as if he'd run a race and his chest felt tight. Taking a deep breath, he controlled the burst of raw panic.

He would get her back. He had to.

She loved him, of that fact he was certain. All it would take was the right approach.

He had messed up one too many times. With the double emotional hit of discovering that he had intended to propose to Lilah then the shock of discovering that she wasn't pregnant, he guessed he shouldn't be surprised that she had reacted by running.

Like Sophie.

His stomach clenched at the thought that Carla could have an accident. Then logic reasserted itself. That wouldn't happen. Carla was so *not* like Sophie he didn't know how he could have imagined she was in the first place.

But this time he would not compound his mistake by failing to act. He would make sure that Carla was safe. He would not fail her again.

He loved her.

His stomach clenched as he examined that reality. He couldn't change the past; all he could do was try to change the future.

Sliding the note into his pocket along with the ring, he strode back to his room to finish dressing. He pulled on shoes and found his wallet and watch. The possibility that he could lose Carla struck him anew and for a split second he was almost paralyzed with fear. Until that moment he hadn't understood how necessary Carla was to him.

For more than two years she had occupied his thoughts and haunted his nights. He had thought the affair would run its course; instead his desire had strengthened. In order to control what he had deemed an obsession, he had minimized contact and compartmentalized the affair.

The strategy hadn't worked. The more restrictive he had become in spending time with Carla, the more uncontrollable his desire had become.

She wasn't pregnant.

Until that moment he hadn't known how much he had wanted Carla to be pregnant. Since the out-of-control lovemaking on Medinos, the possibility of a pregnancy had initiated a number of responses from him. The most powerful had been the cast-iron excuse it had provided him to bring her back into his life. But as the days had passed, the thought of Carla losing her taut hourglass shape and growing soft and round with his child had become increasingly appealing. Along with the need to keep Carla tied close, he had wanted to be a father.

Pocketing his keys, he strode out of the suite. Frustration gripped him when he jabbed the elevator call button then had to wait. His gaze locked on the glowing arrow above the doors, and he scraped at his jaw, which harbored a five-o'clock shadow.

Dragging rough fingers through his rumpled hair, he began to pace.

He couldn't lose her.

Whatever it took, he would do it. He would get her back.

He recalled the expression on Carla's face when she had found the engagement ring he had ordered for Lilah, her stricken comment that Constantine had wanted Sienna enough that he had kidnapped her.

Raw emotion gripped him.

Almost the exact opposite of his behaviour.

Carla walked quickly through the lobby, which was empty except for a handful of guests checking out. She had wasted frantic minutes checking the backstage area. It had been empty of possessions, which meant either Elise or Nina had her things.

Too fragile to bear the stirring of interest she would cause by waiting inside, she avoided the concierge desk and made a beeline for the taxi stand.

Not having her medication wasn't ideal. She hadn't taken any last night, and now she would go most of the day without them. Antacids would have to do. She could wait out the short flight to Sydney and the taxi ride home, where there was a supply of pills in her bathroom cupboard.

A pale-faced group of guests, obviously catching an early flight out, were climbing into the only taxi waiting near the hotel entrance. Settling her gym bag down on the dusty pavement, she settled herself to wait for the next taxi to turn into the hotel pickup area.

Long seconds ticked by. She glanced in at the empty reception area, her tension growing, not because she was desperate to escape, she finally admitted to herself, but because a weak part of her still wanted Lucas to stride out and stop her from going.

Not that Lucas was likely to chase her.

Shivering in the faint chill of the air, she stared at the bleak morning sky now graying in the east as a cab finally braked to a halt beside her.

She slipped into the rear seat with her bag, requested the cab driver take her to the airport and gave the hotel entrance one last look before she stared resolutely at the road unfolding ahead.

Why would Lucas come after her, when she was giving him the thing he had always valued most in their relationship, his freedom?

Lucas caught the flash of the taxi's taillights as it turned out of the resort driveway and the panic that had gripped him while he'd endured the slow elevator ride turned to cold fear.

Sliding his phone out of his pocket, he made a series of calls then strode back into the hotel and took the elevator to the rooftop.

Seconds later, Tiberio phoned back. He had obtained Carla's destination from the taxi company. She was headed for Brisbane Airport. He had checked with the flight desk and she had already booked her flight out to Sydney.

The quiet, efficient way Carla had left him hit Lucas forcibly. No threats or manipulation, no smashed crockery or showy exit in a sports car, just a calm, orderly exit with her flight already arranged.

He felt like kicking himself that it had taken him this long to truly see who she was, and to understand why she was so irresistible to him. He hadn't fallen into lust with a second Sophie. He had fallen in love for the first time—with a woman who was smart and fascinating and perfect for him.

Then he had spent the past two years trying to crush what he felt for her.

Issuing a further set of instructions, Lucas settled down to wait.

Carla frowned as the taxi took the wrong exit and turned into a sleepy residential street opposite a sports field. "This isn't the way to the airport."

The driver gave her an odd look in the rearview mirror

and hooked his radio, which he'd been muttering into for the past few minutes, back on its rest. "I have to wait for someone."

Carla started to argue, then the rhythmic chop of rotor blades slicing the air caught her attention. A sleek black helicopter set down on the sports field. A tall, dark-haired man climbed out, ducking his head as he walked beneath the rotor blades.

Her heart slammed in her chest. She had wanted Lucas to come after her. Contrarily, now that he was here, all she wanted to do was run.

Depressing the door handle, she pushed the door wide and groped for the cash in the side pocket of her gym bag. She shoved some money at the driver, more than enough to cover his meter, and dragged the sports bag off the backseat. A split second later the world flipped sideways and she found herself cradled in Lucas's arms.

Her heart pounded a crazy tattoo. The strap of the sports bag slipped from her fingers as she grabbed at his shoulders. "What do you think you're doing?"

His gaze, masked by dark glasses, seared over her face. "Kidnapping you. That's the benchmark, isn't it?"

Her mouth went dry at his reference to the conversation they'd had when she had listed the things Constantine had done that proved his love for Sienna. Her pulse rate ratcheted up another notch.

She stared into the remote blankness of the dark glasses, suddenly terribly afraid to read too much into his words. "If you're afraid I'm going to do something silly or have an accident, I'm not. I'm just giving you the out you want."

"I know. I read the note." He placed her in the seat directly behind the pilot. "And by the way, here it is."

He took out a piece of the hotel notepaper, tore it into

pieces and tossed it into the downdraft of the blades. The scraps of paper whirled away.

"What are you doing now?" she asked as he started to walk away from the chopper.

The noise muffled his reply. "Getting your shoes and makeup and whatever else it is that makes you happy."

Seconds later, he tossed her sports bag on the floor at her feet and belted himself in beside her.

"Where are we going?" She had to yell now above the noise from the chopper.

Lucas fitted a set of earphones over her head then donned a set himself. "A cabin. In the mountains."

A short flight later the helicopter landed in a clearing. Within minutes the pilot had lifted off, leaving them with a box stamped with the resort's logo on the side. Lucas picked it up. She guessed it was food.

Carla stared at the rugged surrounding range of the Lamingtons, the towering gum trees and silvery gleam of a creek threading through the valley below. "I can't believe you kidnapped me."

"It worked for Constantine."

Her heart pounded at his answer. It wasn't quite a declaration of love, but it was close.

She followed Lucas into the cabin, which was huge. With its architectural angles, sterile planes of glass and comfortable leather couches it was more like an upscale executive palace than her idea of a rustic holiday cottage.

He placed the box on a kitchen counter then began unloading what looked like a picnic lunch. A kidnapping, Atraeus-style, with all the luxury trappings.

Frustrated by his odd mood and the dark glasses, she walked outside, grabbed her sports bag and brought it into the house. She could feel herself floundering, unable to ask the questions that mattered in case the hope that had flared to life when he had bodily picked her up and deposited her in the helicopter was extinguished. "It's not as if this is a real kidnapping."

He stopped, his face curiously still. "How 'real' did you want it to be?"

Sixteen

"We're alone. We're together." Lucas reached for calm when all he really wanted was to pull her close and kiss her.

But that approach hadn't worked so far. Carla had actually tried to run from him, which had altered his game plan somewhat. Plan B was open-ended, meaning he no longer knew what he was doing except that he wasn't going to blow this now by resorting to sex. "We can do what we should have done last night and talk this out. Have you eaten?"

"No." She stared absently at the rich, spicy foods and freshly squeezed juice he had set out then began rummaging through her gym bag just in case there was a stray pack of antacids in one of the pockets.

Lucas, intensely aware of every nuance of expression on Carla's face, tensed when she picked up the phone on the counter. "What's wrong? Who are you calling?"

She frowned when the call wasn't picked up. "Elise. She can get me some medication I need."

"What medication?" But suddenly he knew. The small bag of snacks she carried, her preoccupation with what she was eating and the weight loss. "You're either diabetic or you've got an ulcer."

"The second one."

He could feel his temper soaring. "Why didn't you tell me?"

"You weren't exactly over the moon when I got ill in Thailand."

"You had a virus in Thailand."

"And the viral bacteria just happened to attack an area of my stomach that was still healing from an ulcer I had two years ago. Although I didn't find that out until the ulcer perforated and I got to hospital."

He felt himself go ice-cold inside. "You had a perforated ulcer?" For a split second he thought he must have misheard. "You could have died. Why didn't you tell me?"

Her gaze was cool. "After what happened in Thailand I didn't want you to know I was sick again." She shrugged. "Mom and Sienna didn't know about you, so it was hardly likely they would call you. Why would they? You had no visible role in my life."

That was all going to change, he thought grimly. From now on he was going to be distinctly, in-your-face visible.

He felt like kicking himself. In Thailand he had distanced himself from Carla when she was sick because the enforced intimacy of looking after her had made him want a lot more than the clandestine meetings they'd had through the year. Pale and ill, sweating and shivering, Carla hadn't been either glamorous or sexually desirable. She had simply been *his*.

He had wanted to continue caring for her, wanted to keep her close. But the long hours he had spent sitting beside her bed, waiting for her fever to break, had catapulted him back to his time with Sophie.

He had not wanted her to be that important to him. He hadn't wanted to make himself vulnerable to the kind of guilt and betrayal his relationship with Sophie had resulted in. He could admit that now.

"When was the last time you had your medication?"

She punched in another number. "Lunch, yesterday. That's why I'm calling the resort. Either Nina or Elise can go to the suite and find my handbag, which is where I keep my Medi-PACKs. I'm hoping Tiberio or one of your other bodyguards could drive up with it."

"If you think I'm taking two hours to get you the medication you need, think again." Lucas's cell was already in his hand. He speed dialed and bit out commands in rapid Medinian, hung up and slipped the phone back in his pocket. "Our ride will be here in fifteen minutes."

She slipped her phone back in her handbag. "I could have waited. It's not that bad. I just have to manage my stomach for a few weeks."

"You might be able to wait, but *I* can't. What do you think it did to me to hear that you almost died in hospital?"

"I didn't *almost* die." She grimaced. "Although it wasn't pleasant, that's for sure. It wasn't as if I wasn't used to dealing with the ulcer. It just got out of hand."

He went still inside. "How long did you say you had the ulcer?"

"Two years or so."

Around the time they had met. His jaw tightened at this further evidence of how blind he had been with Carla. He knew ulcers could be caused by a number of factors, but number one was stress. In retrospect, the first time they had made love and he had found out she was a virgin he should have taken a mental step back and reappraised. He hadn't done it. He hadn't wanted to know what might hurt or upset

Carla, or literally eat away at her, because he had been so busy protecting himself.

"News flash," she said with an attempted grin. "I'm a worrier. Can't seem to ditch the habit."

He reached her in two steps and hauled her close. "The woman I love collapses because she has a perforated ulcer," he muttered, "and all you can say is that it *wasn't pleasant?*"

Carla froze in Lucas's arms and, like a switch flicking, she swung from depression and despair to deliriously happy. She stared, riveted by his fierce gaze, and decided she didn't need to pinch herself. "You really do love me?" He had said the words last night but they had felt neutral, empty.

"I love you. Why do you think I couldn't resist you?"

"But it did take you two years to figure that out."

"Don't remind me. Tell me how you ended up with the ulcer."

"Okay, here it goes, but now you might fall out of love with me. I'm a psycho-control-freak-perfectionist. I worked myself into the ground trying to lift Ambrosi's profile and micromanage all of our advertising layouts and pamphlets. When I started color coordinating the computer mouses and mouse pads, Sienna sent me to the family doctor. Jennifer gave me Losec and told me to stop taking everything so seriously, to lighten up and change my life. A week later, I met you."

"And turned my life upside down."

"I wish, but it didn't seem that way." She snuggled in close, unable to stop grinning, loving the way he was staring at her so fiercely. "All I knew was that I was running the relationship in the exact opposite way I wanted, supposedly to avoid stress. If you'd arrived in my life a couple of weeks early, you would have met a different woman."

"I fell in love with you. Instantly."

She closed her eyes and basked for just a few seconds. "Tell me again."

"I love you," he said calmly and, finally, he kissed her.

During the short helicopter ride, Lucas insisted on being given a crash course on her condition. When they reached the doctor's office, which was in a nearby town, Carla took Losec and an antibiotic under the eagle eye of both the doctor and Lucas.

At Lucas's insistence, the doctor also gave her a thorough checkup. Twenty minutes later she was given a clean bill of health.

They exited the office and strolled around to the parking lot to wait for the rental vehicle that Tiberio, apparently, had arranged to have delivered.

Lucas had kept his arm around her waist, keeping her close. "How are you feeling?"

"Fine." She leaned on him slightly. Not that she needed the support, but she loved the way he was treating her, as if she was a piece of precious, delicate porcelain. She could get used to it.

Lucas cupped her face, his fingers tangling in her hair. "I need to explain. To apologize."

Carla listened while Lucas explained about how her illness in Thailand had forced him to confront the guilt and betrayal of the past and had pushed him into a decision to break off with her.

His expression was remote. "But as you know, I couldn't break it off completely. When Constantine told me he was marrying Sienna, I knew I had to act once and for all."

"So you asked Lilah to accompany you to the wedding."

"She was surprised. Before that we had only ever spoken on a business level."

"But she guessed what was going on the night before the wedding."

"Only because she saw us together." He pulled her close, burying his face in her hair. "I'm not proud of what I did but I was desperate. I didn't realize I was in love with you until I read the note you left in the hotel room and discovered that you had left me. It was almost too late."

He hugged her close for long minutes, as if he truly did not want to let her go. "I've wasted a lot of time. Two years."

"There were good reasons we couldn't be together in the beginning. Some of those reasons were mine."

He frowned. "Reasons that suited me."

Gripping her hands gently in his, he went down on one knee. "Carla Ambrosi, will you marry me and be the love of my life for the rest of my life?"

He reached into his pocket and produced the sky-blue diamond ring, which he must have been carrying with him all along, and gently slipped it on the third finger of her left hand.

Tears blurred Carla's eyes at the soft gleam in Lucas's gaze, the intensity of purpose that informed her that if she said no he would keep on asking until she was his.

Emotion shimmered through her, settled in her heart, because she *had* been his all along.

"Yes," she said, the answer as simple as the kiss that followed, the long minutes spent holding each other and the promise of a lifetime together.

* * * * *

CAUGHT
IN THE
SPOTLIGHT

BY
JULES BENNETT

Published in Great Britain 2012
by Mills & Boon, an imprint of Harlequin (UK) Limited,
Eton House, 18-24 Paradise Road, Richmond, Surrey TW9 1SR

© Jules Bennett 2012

ISBN: 978 0 263 89204 8
ebook ISBN: 978 1 408 97197 0

51-0812

Harlequin (UK) policy is to use papers that are natural, renewable and recyclable products and made from wood grown in sustainable forests. The logging and manufacturing processes conform to the legal environmental regulations of the country of origin.

Printed and bound in Spain
by Blackprint CPI, Barcelona

Jules Bennett's love of storytelling started when she would get in trouble as a child and would tell her parents her imaginary friend Mimi did it. Since then, her vivid imagination has taken her down a path she'd only dreamed of.

When Jules isn't spending time with her wonderful supportive husband and two daughters, you will find her reading her favorite authors. Though she calls that time "research." She loves to hear from readers! Contact her at authorjules@gmail.com, visit her website at www. julesbennett.com or send her a letter at PO Box 396, Minford, OH 45653, USA. You can also visit her fan page on Facebook or follow her on Twitter (@Jules-Bennett).

One

When a dripping-wet female yelled his name, Bronson Dane didn't even try to stop his eyes from roaming over all of her.

With only a short white towel covering her glistening dark, Italian skin, his mother's personal assistant of only six months certainly knew how to catch a man's attention.

"Mr. Dane," she repeated, clutching the towel to her chest with both hands. She'd stopped short as she'd stepped from the bath when she saw him standing at the desk in his mother's adjoining office.

"Formalities are unnecessary when you're only wearing water droplets and a towel. Call me Bronson." He shoved his hands in his pants pockets, thankful he'd shed his jacket because, damn, the temperature just rose at least ten degrees. "Where is my mother and why are you showering in her private bath?"

Wide eyes, nearly as dark as her ebony hair, blinked in

rapid succession. "Olivia is gone for the day. I often use the gym, and since I'm working this afternoon, she told me just to freshen up here instead of running back to my guest cottage."

Bronson muttered a curse at his naive mother. It was bad enough Mia Spinelli lived on the Dane estate, but now she was given free rein of the house? Hadn't his mother learned her lesson from the last "loyal" assistant? When would the woman realize she couldn't trust everyone who looked innocent?

This was Hollywood, for pity's sake. Lies and manipulation were as common as breast implants and collagen injections.

"I'm sorry, Mr. Dane. I had no idea anyone would be coming by," Mia continued, squaring her shoulders as if having a conversation wearing only a scrap of terry cloth was normal. "Weren't you supposed to be shooting in Australia until next week?"

"Call me Bronson," he reminded her, gritting his teeth at the floral aroma wafting from the bathroom. "The movie wrapped a week early. I stopped by to talk to my mother about the film festival next week. Did she say when she'd be back?"

"She'll be back later in the afternoon. She's having lunch with her attorney to go over the final contract for her next book." The knuckles on the hand fisting her towel between her breasts turned white as she crossed the room. "If you'll excuse me, I dropped my toiletry bag on the desk chair when I came in because the phone was ringing."

Before she could pass by him, he blocked her and reached for the simple black bag from the leather desk chair. She grabbed for it, but he held the small bag out to the side, away from her grasp.

He didn't trust her, especially since she'd just come off

the heels of working for the one man he despised in the industry, Anthony Price. He loathed the man with every fiber of his being. But he certainly didn't want to think about all those reasons now.

His mother had assured him that Mia was "a doll" and completely trustworthy and dependable. His sister, Victoria, had jumped on the Mia bandwagon as well, stating that Mia was such a joy and pleasure to be around. When they'd chatted on the phone last, Victoria had gone so far as to say that she'd instantly clicked with their mother's new assistant.

Granted, Mia had been around for six months, but was that enough time for his mother and sister to be such die-hard Mia Spinelli fans?

Bronson wasn't blind, though. Anthony sending his assistant here to snoop was really sinking to a low he never expected.

The rumors of Mia and Anthony's relationship were anything but businesslike. And that irked him even more. The fact his mother had hired Mia while he'd been on location in Australia still grated on him. True, his mother could have any assistant she chose, but why bring in one fresh from his nemesis?

The Hollywood rumor mill had pegged the mesmerizing Mia as the main problem in Anthony's rocky marriage. Whom Mia slept with was none of his concern, but it *was* his business if she was taking Dane family secrets back to her lover.

Bronson and his mother were secretly working on a huge film that he knew the media would die to get their hands on. He and his mother had worked for years honing this project, and he had no doubt Anthony Price, Hollywood's top director, wanted to know just what the big secret was.

Just because his mother wasn't suspicious didn't mean he'd be letting his guard down any time soon.

Bronson intended to find out just what this conveniently placed assistant's intentions were before she uncovered the script and slid back in between Anthony's sheets with it in hand. The thought of this sexy siren in bed with the devil made his stomach knot up.

He thrust the bag her way because he needed her to get dressed. Whether he trusted her or not had no bearing on matters; she was fresh from the shower smelling of something sexy and floral—her own because that certainly wasn't his mother's scent—and he was having a hard time focusing on the task at hand.

Not to mention that he was not one bit happy with the immediate physical attraction he felt to his enemy's lover.

"Get dressed. We'll talk."

With a slight nod, she turned, crossed the room and entered the still-steamy bath, shutting the door at her back. He had no room on his plate for lustful feelings, and he was a damn fool for even letting them creep into his thoughts. His main concern right now was to keep his mother and his fashion designer sister out of any more scandal.

His mother's last assistant had stolen nearly half a million dollars from Olivia's personal account over the span of several months. The media loved feeding off the Dane name right now, which is why they needed to be a bit more cautious about whom they let into their lives—especially if he had any hopes of keeping this script under wraps.

Was it any wonder his blood pressure had soared since he stepped into his mother's office? Olivia Dane was an icon, and the media would love to get some dirt on her—though he doubted there was any. They had a way of twisting even the innocent to make them look sordid.

Olivia Dane had been Hollywood's sweetheart, had

starred in more films than any other female in the industry and had been dubbed the "Grand Dane" years ago. The
media loved her. Which is precisely why he needed to keep
a close watch on her new assistant.

The bathroom door opened once again and Mia emerged
wearing crisp white capris and a black, sleeveless button-
down shirt. She had twisted her long dark hair into some
sort of knot at the nape of her neck. Her feet were still bare,
except for the subtle pink polish on her toes. A simple gold
locket lay in the open V of her shirt.

Everything about this woman screamed innocence and
simplicity, so how the hell did she end up working for the
most glamorous woman in Hollywood?

Olivia had told him how impeccable Mia's credentials
were and Mia's reasons for leaving her job with Anthony.
Supposedly she didn't want to be the cause of any more
rumors and aid in destroying Anthony's marriage.

His mother had said she admired a woman who put
others' needs ahead of her own. She assured him the background check also confirmed her initial thoughts—Mia
was flawless and perfect for the job.

A background check could easily make a person look
good on paper, and Mia had certainly appeared to be innocent as an angel, but Bronson wanted to get to know
more about the quiet, subtle Miss Spinelli. The one who,
no matter what line she fed his mother, still may be sleeping with—and possibly spying for—his enemy.

And fate had just handed him the perfect opportunity.
What better way to get to know someone than a little one-
on-one time? With the exotic, sexy ambiance of the Cannes
Film Festival next week, how could she resist succumb-
ing to his charms as his escort? He hadn't been dubbed
People's Sexiest Man Alive for nothing.

"I have a proposition for you," he told her. "You're traveling to Cannes with my mother. Correct?"

Mia nodded.

"There are ceremonies every evening with parties afterward. I want you to escort me to those events."

"Escort you?" she asked, eyes wide. "But I'm only going to work with Olivia, and I hadn't planned on attending any of the evenings' festivities."

He hadn't planned on asking her to be his escort, but he also hadn't planned on his first impression of her covered in iridescent droplets and wearing nothing but a piece of terry cloth. God knows he could invite any woman he knew, but he really didn't want to have to entertain and make sure some diva was properly pampered. This woman, this virtual stranger, would be the ideal companion. He'd been on location nearly the entire time she'd been employed by his mother. He couldn't think of a better venue to get to know Mia than to have her as his "date" for five nights in a row.

"I don't think this is a good idea," Mia said, taking a seat behind his mother's desk and booting up the computer. "I'm pretty busy with Olivia, and I know we'll be working just as hard in Cannes because she's trying to finish this book by midsummer."

Bronson stood on the other side of the desk, watching Mia's delicate, ringless fingers fly over the keyboard. "I assure you, my mother will have no problem with your being my escort. You just worry about getting to the plane on time and packing light. I'll have Victoria ship all the dresses you'll need. She's a whiz in a pinch."

She looked up from the screen, licking her naked lips. "But why me?"

"Why not you?" he countered, liking this idea more and more.

"I'm just an assistant."

Bronson shrugged. "All the more reason. Unless you don't want to be seen with me because of your recent scandal with your previous employer." He leaned in close and whispered, "Or you have a jealous lover."

Mia's eyes widened. "I can't believe that out of all the women you know, you'd want to take me."

Her swift dodge of his question wasn't very subtle, but he'd let it pass. For now.

"I won't lie." Leaning on his palms on the edge of the mahogany desk, Bronson offered a crooked grin and eased back just a bit so he didn't seem too overbearing. "I'm protective of my mother. I'm using this as a prime opportunity to get to know you better."

A sinful, beautiful smile spread across her face. "I understand being protective about family. In that case, I'd love to attend with you, as long as Olivia doesn't mind."

Bronson stood straight up and returned her smile. "She won't. Trust me."

Trust me.

It had been four days since Bronson had flashed his sexy smile and charmed her into turning her working trip into something more social.

And she should've flat-out told him no. He wouldn't have asked her to attend parties and ceremonies with him, and he sure as hell wouldn't have asked her to trust him, if he knew the secret she held. A secret that would ruin his family's tight bond.

Mia shook the guilt off and concentrated on her immediate mission: she was in Cannes and she was going to be waltzing into glamorous events on the arm of Hollywood's sexiest bachelor. She had to look better than her best.

Which shouldn't be a problem. Looking back at her

were five—yes, five—glamorous Victoria Dane original designs. Mia took a step back in her luxurious suite, unable to catch her breath. Olivia had told her that Victoria always kept multiple designs on hand for any star who needed a dress last minute.

Cinderella and her fairy godmother had nothing on Mia and this amazing array of glitzy dresses.

She had to keep reminding herself that she was just an assistant, but Mia certainly felt like a star as she spun in a little-girl-like circle, giddiness overwhelming her.

Was this really happening? Was she really in Cannes working for Olivia Dane by day, dressing up in a Victoria Dane gown at night and mingling with celebrities on the arm of hotshot producer Bronson Dane? Did she hit the job jackpot or what?

She and Olivia had worked a couple hours on the long flight over and Olivia had given Mia the rest of the day off. Of course, Mia figured Olivia was shopping at all the specialty shops.

Mia smiled as she recalled how surprised, yet excited Olivia was when she'd learned Mia was escorting Bronson to the parties and awards ceremonies. The Grand Dane had smiled, clasped her jeweled fingers together and said, "Wonderful."

Everything about working for the Grand Dane was incredible. Mia had been scared to leave Anthony at first, but now she knew this was the best decision for everyone. She'd come to love him like family—though not in the way the family-wrecking tabloids had portrayed their relationship. She hoped he could put his marriage back together.

Mia's heart ached for Anthony. Never once had their relationship turned intimate, but the tabloids assumed and printed the worst, in turn hurting his wife. Yes, they'd spent a lot of time together, but they were always working.

Mia knew Olivia believed her, but what about Bronson? Did he also assume the worst about her? More than likely. There was no love lost between the two Hollywood big shots, which meant he probably believed the rumors. He'd already implied as much.

Hopefully, her actions would win his trust in time. He'd had his fair share of scandal in the media. Surely he didn't believe everything he heard or read. Hollywood certainly wasn't known for honesty.

And she'd never expected anything like this when she'd come to work for Olivia. When she'd been employed by Anthony, she'd traveled with him to film sites, but never, ever to a glamorous film festival. And here she was in Cannes. Just the trip itself was thrilling, but adding all the extras on top of that was fabulous.

First, she'd expected a simple room, not a suite, and she never, in her wildest dreams, thought she'd be treated like a princess when she was just…an assistant. But she'd take this once-in-a-lifetime opportunity and not question the whys.

With a delicate touch, because God knew she'd never be able to cover the expense of just one of these dresses, even though her pay was very generous, she looked over the gowns as she envisioned dancing the night away in each one.

Spending money on clothes was not a priority in Mia's life, unlike many women who lived in Hollywood. But she certainly wouldn't turn down the opportunity to wear these classy, elegant designs.

Would she be dancing with Bronson all night? Would her body press against his as they swayed? She'd be lying to herself if she pretended she hadn't thought of being close to him, feeling his arms around her.

More than likely he had a whole slew of women who

danced with him at such events, but he'd chosen her to escort him. What did that mean? And he'd gone to the trouble of getting his sister involved. Did he just want to get to know her better, as he'd said? She could understand that, but somewhere deep inside she thought he must find her attractive or he wouldn't have asked her to accompany him every single night.

The memory of his eyes taking in her bare skin when he'd caught her coming out of the shower had her body humming. She wasn't vain, but she also wasn't stupid. Bronson hadn't been immune to the fact she'd been pretty much naked.

Reality check.

To think that Bronson Dane found her attractive sounded absurd, even in her own head. He worked with movie starlets, dated models and had literally seen women who exemplified perfection in the flesh. He'd even been engaged to a stunning makeup artist. But still, his eyes had widened on seeing her, and the muscle had ticked in his jaw. Her body heated again when she recalled how close they'd been as he'd held her bag away from her. He'd smelled so...masculine, powerful. Sexy.

Mia pulled the short, black, chiffon dress from the closet and held it in front of her as she turned to the full-length mirror. This would be for the first party. All the dresses were gorgeous, but this one—this would make the biggest impact. She wanted Bronson's first impression of her in Cannes to be memorable.

The simplicity of the black gown and her black hair would complement each other and hopefully help her blend in with the rich and famous. She certainly didn't want to be an embarrassment on Bronson's arm. She may have immature thoughts, but she wanted him to notice her as more than his mother's assistant.

Nerves danced around in her belly. How could she even compare to the arm candy Bronson normally had draped over him?

A laugh escaped her as she hung the dress back up. Had she just compared herself to arm candy? She wasn't here to try to win Bronson over as her boyfriend or even her lover...but that didn't stop her from wishing to be noticed by Hollywood's sexiest bachelor. What woman wouldn't want to be desired by such a strong, powerful man who ranked his loving family at the top of his priority list? There wasn't a woman alive who wouldn't want to be part of his inner circle.

But amid the excitement and arousal, guilt gnawed away at Mia as she pulled another dress from the closet. How could she take so much from this family when she knew a secret that could very well destroy their perfect happiness?

Unfortunately, the secret wasn't hers to reveal. And since she had come to care about all the key players, she felt torn between her loyalty to her former employer and her loyalty to her current employer.

Right now all she could do was keep her own counsel and enjoy herself in one of the most exotic, memorable places on earth. Borrowing trouble that was utterly out of her hands wouldn't help ease the guilt or make the nearly forty-year-old secret disappear.

Mia's cell rang, breaking into her thoughts. She pulled her phone from her pocket and hit the Talk button.

"Hello?"

"I trust you found the dresses to your satisfaction."

Mia's gaze traveled back to the open closet. "Yes, Bronson, they're gorgeous. I could never thank you or Victoria enough."

"And the jewelry is all to your liking?" he asked. "If not, I can call the jeweler and have some pieces traded out."

Mia's eyes went to the dresser where velvet boxes were stacked. She hadn't even opened them, but she knew the contents were surely more glamorous than anything she'd ever seen.

She fingered the simple locket around her neck. "Everything is more than I'd hoped for. Thank you."

"Tonight's viewing begins at seven-thirty," he went on. "We have to be on the red carpet by quarter to seven, so I'll meet you down in the lobby by the elevator at six-thirty."

Without another word, he hung up. Mia didn't quite know what to make of his abruptness. On the jet en route to Cannes he'd made idle chitchat—nothing personal. At times she'd feel someone staring at her and turn to see those crystal-blue eyes on her as if he were just as intrigued with her as she was with him—at least, she liked to think that was the reason. And when she caught him, he didn't even pretend that he hadn't been studying her. But why would a strong, powerful playboy be shy or coy? He could have any woman he wanted, and that woman would gladly follow those endless baby blues anywhere. She was no exception.

She was finding, in the few encounters she'd had with Bronson, that he was a hard man to get to know, especially when he delivered a twenty-second phone call that was straight and to the point and hung up before she could even ask a question.

Mia sighed as she padded to the bath. A nice, long bubble bath would do her nerves some good. With Olivia out shopping with some friends for the day, Mia could just relax.

Or as much as she could relax with a damning secret preying on her mind. She'd had nothing but high hopes when she'd accepted this job as assistant to the Grand Dane of Hollywood. But then she'd accepted the position nearly a week before learning Olivia's best-kept secret. If only she'd left Anthony sooner and not worked during her two weeks' notice, she wouldn't have this guilt weighing on her.

So many times over the last six months she wished she didn't know the secret. Then maybe her job wouldn't be so difficult. But she did know. And eventually the truth would come out and damage Hollywood's most beloved family. The Danes.

All this secrecy bubbling inside her forced her mind back to another time, another secret that had hurt those she loved.

Her mother had once asked her to keep a secret, but at the tender age of five, Mia didn't think that meant to keep it from her father. Ultimately, the truth tore her family apart, taking the lives of her parents and sending Mia into a long line of foster homes. And even after twenty-five years, the guilt and heartache that followed her, haunted her, was just as strong and powerful as ever.

She knew she needed to keep this secret. No way would she cause another disaster. And this explosion she could see coming. She would keep this secret out of loyalty to a friend and respect to the key players.

After pouring an enormous amount of jasmine-scented bubblebath into the running water, Mia stepped into the round, sunken tub with a one-way window overlooking a lavish garden. She settled down into the skin-tingling hot water and sighed as she looked out the glass.

What would Bronson think once he saw her tonight? Would he be disappointed? Would he be attracted? Anthony had reminded her about Bronson's playboy style. He'd warned her not to get involved or, worse, attached to a man who was known for the revolving door in his bedroom.

Even though she'd worked for Anthony for three years,

she'd never once seen Anthony and Bronson in the same room. She'd certainly seen the tabloids showcasing the bitterness between the two Hollywood powerhouses, but anytime she questioned Anthony about it, he'd laugh it off. He was always joking, always carefree. The very opposite of Bronson.

But the tabloids' speculation about their alleged affair was no laughing matter. Neither she nor Anthony found the assumptions amusing. She'd seen firsthand the destruction a photo and boldface caption could cause.

She was eternally grateful that Olivia had given her a chance, and believed in her ability to do her job, and not focused on what the rumor mill portrayed her as—a liar.

And now she was in Cannes getting ready for one of the largest film festivals in the world.

With excitement and curiosity spiraling through her, Mia slid a handful of hot bubbles up over her shoulders. She only hoped the two men didn't get into another verbal altercation. The press was always so greedy when it came to pictures of the two most powerful men in movies having a public disagreement.

There had to be a way to bridge the hatred between Bronson and Anthony, and with her current position she could be that link. Because once Bronson learned that Anthony was the child Olivia had given up for adoption nearly forty years ago, he'd have even more hatred for the man than he did now.

She hadn't been able to save her own family, but maybe, just maybe, she could bring this family together.

Two

Bronson's breath caught. He knew his mouth had dropped open, but nothing could pull his gaze from the sight coming toward him.

He hadn't thought it possible, but as Mia walked toward him in a Victoria Dane original, she looked even sexier than she had in just a towel.

Mia wore his sister's design as if she'd been made to model the one-of-a-kind dress on a runway in Milan or Paris. Or as if she'd been made to torture unsuspecting men like him.

He'd been feeling guilty about not picking her up at her suite, and now he knew that was a wise decision because there were very few steps from the door to the bed.

"I have to say, it's not often I'm speechless." Bronson lifted Mia's slender hand to his lips. "I'm glad you're going in on my arm."

Mia offered a sexy, confident smile. "Well, that makes two of us."

If this were any woman other than his mother's assistant, an assistant he still had serious doubts about, Bronson could've talked her out of that thin, flowy dress in a matter of seconds. And, who knows, he still could get her out of that dress. They were here for nearly a week, and this was only the first night. After all, he did need to spend some one-on-one time with her, didn't he?

Damn if she wouldn't be turning some heads tonight. Jealousy stabbed him in the chest. What did he care that men looked? So long as they didn't touch. For now, she was his. Anthony's loss made this seduction all the more enjoyable.

"Shall we?" he asked, slipping her arm through his.

She fit against him as they walked through the open lobby toward the glow of the sunset streaming in the etched-glass doors. Her heels clicked against the marble floor, the jasmine scent he'd associated with her wafting around him. Everything about her mocked him. He wanted her, but he didn't trust her. His emotions were all jumbled because of this intriguing woman, and he didn't like this lack of control. That in itself should make him dislike her, but she oozed sex appeal and confidence, and Bronson knew he would have her before the week's end.

When they reached the door, he placed a hand on the small of her back to escort her out...and encountered bare skin. If he thought she was sexy from the front with that low cowl-neck design that enhanced her perfect breasts, she was sinful from the back with the chiffon draping as low as legally possible without being indecent.

A sexy back got him every time. Of course, he was beginning to think every physical attribute of this Italian beauty got to him. Great. Just what he needed, an out-of-control libido to hinder his judgment about this woman…as if he weren't having enough issues with that. The fact she may have slept with his enemy should have been enough to turn him off. But damn if he wasn't stubborn and all the more defiant when he saw something, or someone, he wanted.

He had to hand it to his sister. When she'd picked the dress, she'd nailed the style that accentuated Mia's height, curves and sensual features. That's why Victoria was so sought after by every star in America—and why men were sent reeling by the women who wore the designs.

"Victoria sure knows how to make a woman feel pretty," Mia told him, seeming to read his mind as they walked beneath a canopy of lush palms and thick foliage beside the water's edge that led toward the red carpet. "I have to admit, I tried on every single one of those dresses. They're all my favorite."

Bronson hadn't removed his hand from her back and he didn't intend to. She was too soft, too feminine, too…everything.

The perfect spy for Anthony.

"Victoria knows how to make beautiful women look even more breathtaking."

Mia's gaze shot to his. "Thank you."

He stepped in front of her just before they reached the area with the camera flashes of the paparazzi and the red carpet. "I should be thanking you," he told her, then bent to whisper in her ear, "Because of you, I'll be the envy of every man here tonight."

A soft, visible shudder produced a shaky smile. "I doubt that, but thank you again."

She was serious. Most women in Hollywood loved showing off their bodies…God knows they'd paid enough for their enhancements. But as he studied Mia's dark, sultry eyes, he realized she was the minority. She may have trembled at his words, but she didn't believe him.

That was just fine, since he was still leery of her, as well. But he would uncover the true Mia soon enough. And if uncovering her from that wispy black dress was involved, well, that wouldn't be a hardship.

Anything to stick close to the alluring Mia Spinelli.

Flashes of lights, clicks of cameras and shouts of Bronson's name from every direction followed them as they made their way up the red carpet toward the steps leading into the Marché du Film Theater.

Mia couldn't believe this. Simply couldn't believe she was in Cannes, wearing a Victoria Dane design on the red carpet with Bronson's strong hand on her bare back. She took mental images of every moment because she knew, once she got back to the real world of "assisting," this would all be a wonderful, distant memory.

Though, she had a feeling the tingling from Bronson's touch would linger long after tonight. And that was just fine with her. Mercy, the man was potent.

She allowed him to lead her from camera to camera, giving a subtle nudge to her back when he wanted to move on to the next one. Did celebrities ever tire of this attention? Did they enjoy being photographed at every twist and turn? Probably not, but this was all so new to her, she was loving every minute.

But she'd worked in the industry, albeit in the background, long enough to know the camera caught everything. Would viewers see the Cinderella-like euphoria she drifted in? Would it capture the smile on her face that said she was having the time of her life, even though she hadn't been to a viewing, ceremony or post-party yet? She certainly hoped the sometimes unforgiving lens didn't zero in on her nerves and shaky hands.

"They're wondering why you're here on my arm," Bronson whispered in her ear as they turned to another camera. "Relax."

"Easy for you to say," she whispered.

His thumb stroked her back. "I've seen you wearing a scrap of terry cloth and water droplets, surely you can relax for a few cameras."

Did he have to keep bringing up that mortifying experience? Or perhaps he brought it up because he wasn't totally unaffected by her....

"You aren't the one who's been accused of having an affair with your boss." A horrifying experience.

He laughed, flashing his signature charming smile, no doubt giving the greedy paparazzi the snapshot they'd been after. "That's what makes you even more intriguing. They don't know what to expect."

They moved down the red carpet as more celebrities arrived, pleasing the rest of the media that awaited. Mia couldn't believe all the stars standing so close to her looking glamorous and flawless. Everyone smiled, waving to various cameras and gave brief interviews to the press.

True, she didn't like the limelight, but the recent rumors had given her no choice. The media ate up any type of scandal. And while Mia wasn't thrilled with having her life in the news, she would sacrifice her privacy if it meant taking the heat off Anthony long enough for him to rebuild his marriage. The media would no doubt speculate about her being a bed hopper, but she knew the truth.

"Let them speculate," she murmured. "I have nothing to be ashamed of."

"Let's head on inside," he told her and waved as a camera flashed in their faces. "I'm sure my mother is already wondering why we're not in our seats. She's always an hour early for these things so she can mingle."

Mia held on to Bronson's arm as she started up the red-carpeted steps. "And you don't like to mingle?"

He shrugged. "I mingle plenty at the after parties."

Mia laughed. "You're a man of few words. Aren't you?"

"When it's time to talk, I talk. Time to work, I work." He looked down at her, steely blue eyes darting to her lips. "Time to play, I definitely play."

A shiver rippled up her spine, stemming straight from that powerful stare. Fantastic. Just one heavy-lidded bedroom gaze and she had zings shooting through her body into every nook and cranny, making her even more attracted to the playboy on her arm.

"Any more questions?" he whispered in her ear, so close his warm breath tickled her cheek.

He may be quiet, but perhaps that's why he had a reputation as the master seducer. The subtle brush of his fingertips across her bare back, the whispers and those ocean-blue eyes—the man was charming seduction in stealth mode.

She turned, their mouths nearly touching. "I'll take a rain check."

Bronson leaned back just a hair and laughed. "And I'm sure you'll redeem it soon."

She smiled as they entered the grand foyer. "Count on it."

"Vous êtes trop genre."

Bronson jerked his head around at the flawless French that came from Mia's glossy lips as she spoke to a popular French producer. She laughed, patted the elderly man's beefy arm and turned back to Bronson.

"Sorry about that," Mia told him, beautiful smile still in

place. "On my way back from the chocolate fountain Mr. du Muir stopped me and we started chatting."

Chatting? In French? First she shows up in the lobby looking like sin in stilettos, teasing him with upswept hair and a bare back that just begged his hands to explore more, and then she conducts a conversation in French that sounded as if she'd been living in France her whole life.

"I forgot you were fluent in French," he told her, taking a champagne flute as a waiter walked by. He handed her the glass and an embossed napkin. "Mother told me you have an ear for languages." Not to mention he'd seen it on her background reports.

"I speak French, Spanish and Italian." She took a sip of champagne, leaving her plump pink lips moist, inviting.

"You even had the sexy accent down. You sure you're not an actress?" He only half joked.

Not once at the Marché du Film opening night film earlier or since they'd entered the Icon Picture party had she acted shy or uncomfortable. She'd lit up the red carpet with her smile and sultry gaze into the cameras, and Bronson knew without a doubt that when he saw their pictures in a tabloid, his eyes would be glued to this Italian beauty. There wasn't a man drawing breath who would blame him for being infatuated with her.

How many times over the past few years had she escorted Anthony Price to events? He'd never seen her, but then he hadn't been looking and didn't care who Anthony entertained. At least not at that point.

"Not an actress," she assured him with a smile. "I just find speaking another language romantic and mysterious."

"Romantic and mysterious?" Bronson leaned in so only she could hear. "The perfect description of my date tonight, wouldn't you say? Makes me want to uncover more of you."

Bronson leaned back, eager to see her eyes, even more

eager to hear her response. But Mia's dark gaze darted over his shoulder. Bronson turned to see what she was looking at, and the moment was gone.

"Oh, there's your mother." Mia waved, standing on her tiptoes.

"Darling!" Olivia closed the gap and kissed Mia's cheek. "So sorry I've been scarce since the showing. I've been catching up with old friends. There's quite a buzz about the beauty on my son's arm. There's not a man who can keep his eyes off you, my dear."

Mia laughed. "Oh, please. Every woman here is stunning."

Not like you. God, the words nearly came out of his mouth. But it was true. There wasn't a woman in Cannes right this minute who compared to Mia.

Focus. He wasn't here to get played by this woman—he was here to see what the hell she truly wanted from his family. There wasn't a doubt in his mind that Anthony had some kind of agenda behind Mia's career move. But he didn't have to worry about his mother saying anything to her personal assistant about the script they'd been working on. It was just as important to her that nothing be revealed until they were both ready.

And, if Mia turned out to be as clean and innocent as her background check indicated, then he would let her be. But if he found out she was indeed working for Anthony, they both would rue the day they decided to cross the Danes.

Bronson kissed his mother's cheek. "It's a shame Victoria couldn't join us this year."

Olivia smiled. "Working hard on a big celebrity wedding trumps us, darling. That girl does work herself to death."

Bronson laughed. "Says the pot about the kettle."

Olivia wrapped an arm around Bronson's waist in a half hug. "I'm proud of all my children for their hard work."

Bronson was about to say something else, but his thought was lost as he looked to Mia. A flash of pain darted through her eyes.

"You're all very lucky to have each other." Mia took a sip of champagne. "Does Victoria usually attend, as well?"

"Almost always," Olivia said. "She designed many of the dresses you see here tonight, and she loves nothing more than to admire her work up close."

Bronson didn't know about the other clients, but he was sure as hell happy with the dress she'd chosen for Mia. And he couldn't help but wonder what other taunting designs would adorn Mia during their trip. What dress he would ultimately unwrap her from.

God help him. This was only night one.

"It's getting late." Olivia lifted her face, placing a kiss on Bronson's cheek. "See you tomorrow. Mia, I'll see you first thing in the morning."

Mia smiled and nodded. "I'll be at your suite by eight."

As his mother disappeared beneath sparkling chandeliers into the sea of glitz, glamour and overflowing champagne fountains, Bronson turned back to Mia, who was placing her empty flute on the tray of a passing waiter.

Mia smothered a yawn. "I'm still a bit jet-lagged."

He hated that the evening was drawing to a close, but it was late and he had an early meeting. "Then I'll escort you to your room."

With a warm smile that threatened to lure him in, Mia placed a slender hand on his arm. "No need to leave because I am, Bronson. I'm sure you have many more associates who'd love to chat with you."

He shrugged. "It's well after midnight as it is. You're not the only one who needs to be well rested."

Taking her soft hand, he laced her arm through his and escorted her through the party. He didn't miss the fact that men seemed to keep their gaze on Mia a little longer than necessary…he knew the feeling of wanting to capture a mental picture of this beauty.

Mia, on the other hand, seemed oblivious to the attention.

"And here I thought all you Hollywood hotshots never slept," she went on, smiling up at him.

Those dark-as-night eyes could make a man forget any scruples he had. The sweet floral scent radiating off all that bare skin made his mouth water. If the woman was this potent after one evening, how would he survive the rest of the trip?

Dammit. He hated being vulnerable, and Mia was working her way fast and hard under his skin.

"I won't lie," he told her. "We do burn the midnight oil quite often. Which is why we need to sleep when we can."

As they stepped out into the warm night air, Bronson tasted the saltiness of the sea on his lips. He couldn't help but wonder if Mia would taste the same.

Yachts lined the docks and bobbed gently with the subtle ripples of the Mediterranean. Thousands of twinkling lights glistened off the black water, setting a romantic ambiance seen in movies.

Obviously, a realistic effect.

"This place is amazing." Mia snuggled closer to him as she looked out over the water. "I could live here and just stare at that gentle rolling tide all day."

"We have coastline at home, as well."

She looked back at him and tilted her head. "True, but there's something romantic and glamorous about Cannes. I love Hollywood, but it's all so…fake."

Bronson laughed. "Fake? You've never faked anything?"

"No," she said without hesitation. "What you see is what you get."

His eyes roamed over her, then landed back on her flawless face. "The exterior is perfect without faking anything. But what about on the inside? You've never lied? That's faking the truth. No?"

Mia looked back to the sea. "We all lie about something at some point, Bronson. It's human nature not to reveal the truth when a lie can benefit us."

Bronson stepped in front of her, keeping his hand on her arm. When she turned her gaze to face him, moonlight sparked off those deep, chocolate eyes. If he weren't careful, he'd fall into them and lose the battle he was fighting with himself.

"What are you faking now, Mia?" he whispered.

A soft breeze from the water lifted a tendril of her hair and sent it dancing. He tucked the strand behind her ear, stroking a finger down the side of her face, down her neck until her breath caught.

"I told you." She licked her lips, mocking Bronson because he wanted to be the one to lick that salty sea air off her parted mouth. "What you see is what you get."

"What I get, huh?" he asked with a slight grin.

Bronson slid his hand up her bare arm, cupped the back of her neck and captured her lips beneath his.

Perfect. Absolutely…perfect.

God, he'd been so right in believing her lips would taste amazing. Soft, giving. Mia may be holding a secret, but if it had anything to do with her sexuality, he'd just uncovered it. There was a passion brewing beneath this confident, yet private woman.

She wrapped her fingers around his biceps, whether to push him away or hold on as he continued assaulting her mouth he didn't know. But he wasn't going to stop unless she made him because one taste, just one, had him pulling her against him. His hands roamed up that bare back that had mocked him all evening. Damn this dress. He wanted it off her. Now.

With their bodies only separated by his tux shirt and thin layers of chiffon over her breasts, Bronson could feel the effect he had on her.

A snap and flash had him pulling back just in time to see a paparazzo running in the other direction.

Damn.

"Oh, God, did he…"

"Yeah." Bronson gritted his teeth, taking a step back to put some space between them. "He snapped our picture and now he's probably running back to whatever rag he works for."

Mia held a hand over her mouth, eyes wide as she stared back at him. "Oh, Bronson, I'm so sorry."

"Sorry because we kissed or sorry because we got caught?"

She smoothed that dangling strand of hair back. "Is that your way of finding out my feelings about what just happened? I'm not sorry we kissed. Surprised, but not sorry. I am sorry if what just happened ends up in the newspaper and causes more grief for your family in the press, especially with my recent scandal."

Her concern seemed genuine—but so had her French accent.

Bronson shrugged. "My body blocked your face, so as far as the media's concerned, you're a nameless woman."

But now that he'd had a sample, Bronson wanted the rest of what she had to offer.

Three

Nameless woman.

Mia wished those words from two nights ago still didn't cut right into her heart, but they did. Is that how Bronson saw her? Was he just kissing her as a prelude to a passing fling? How many women walked away from this Hollywood playboy on weak knees, nursing a broken heart?

God knew hers were still shaking from that toe-curling kiss. But would she just be a statistic when this week was all over? How flattering.

Mia touched up her lip gloss over lips that ached for more of Bronson's touch and examined herself in the ballroom's bathroom mirror. The short, deep plum dress with one shoulder bare and the other with a long, flowing sleeve made her feel just as sexy and feminine as the previous dresses.

Night three of the festival was no different than the others...except that she was aching even more for Bronson, and she knew she was every kind of a fool for feeling this way.

She was realistic, though. He may want her physically, but that's where their relationship ended. That didn't stop her from daydreaming, and their smoldering kiss certainly hadn't done a thing to diminish her attraction. Bronson Dane was every woman's walking fantasy, and her hormones were no different than those of any other female who'd had the fortunate opportunity to be close to the Hollywood powerhouse.

Mia smoothed a hand over her belly, trying to calm her jumbled nerves. Only a few more days and they would be back in Hollywood, and Bronson would be off to meetings about his next movie prospect.

She'd watched him charm actresses and build up actors' egos, though Mia knew it was just for leverage if he wanted them in a film one day. Hollywood was all about getting everything you wanted, no matter who you had to play to get it. And Bronson played the game like a pro.

But she doubted he needed to do all the charming. Bronson Dane was a force to be reckoned with in the industry. Turning down a chance to work with him would be an idiotic career move for anyone.

Mia smiled at an elderly woman and exited the bathroom. Just as she turned at the end of the hallway, she ran into Anthony Price.

"Mia." He pulled her into his strong arms for a friendly hug. "I thought I saw you the other night, but discounted the idea. I didn't know you'd be here."

She jerked back. "You can't do that. What if someone had taken a picture?" What if Bronson had seen them?

Anthony glanced around. "Paparazzi aren't allowed in here, but I do apologize. I was just shocked and happy to see you. Are you here with Olivia?"

Mia smiled at her previous employer. "And Bronson."

Anthony's smile dimmed. "Really. Do they—"

"I haven't said a word, Anthony." She knew he was nervous about opening a nearly forty-year-old secret and potentially ruining lives—she didn't blame him. "I told you I wouldn't reveal the secret and I keep my word."

"I know you do." He sighed. "I just haven't figured out how to handle this. I mean, after all these years, lives will be changed forever. Not only that, but with my situation at home…"

Glancing behind her, Mia offered a smile. "I know. I'm here for you any time you need me. Don't think because I'm not working for you that I'm not available to talk."

"I appreciate that, Mia." Anthony smiled. "I'm still trying to figure out why I let you go."

"Because your marriage is more important than your assistant," she reminded him. "You'll be just fine, Anthony. You both need some time. But I should get back to the party before Bronson starts looking for me or someone sees us. It certainly won't help your case."

"You're right. I can't afford to lose Charlotte. But it was so good to see you again."

"Perfect timing."

Mia jerked around at Bronson's deep voice. "Bronson."

"Don't let me interrupt," he told her, his gaze on Anthony. "I was wondering if you were okay, but now I see you are."

Why did she feel like she'd been caught doing something she shouldn't have? Damn. Could she not talk to a close friend without someone assuming something more sinister was going on?

Mia was smack dab in the middle of two of the most powerful men she knew. The air around them crackled with tension. Now that she could see them both up close, she studied their faces.

Yes, the resemblance was there. Subtle, but it was there.

Ironic that biological half brothers, raised in two separate families, could both grow up to be Hollywood moguls and totally despise each other.

"I didn't realize Mia was your date," Anthony told Bronson. "You're a lucky man."

Bronson's gaze narrowed. "Yes."

Mia couldn't handle the awkward silence. God, if she was this uncomfortable, she couldn't imagine how Anthony felt, having known the truth for the past six months.

When Anthony chose to reveal the secret to Olivia, he'd told Mia he would not cause a big scene and make more scandal than necessary. Even though he and Bronson despised each other, Anthony had always expressed his respect and admiration for the Grand Dane and wouldn't do anything to purposely hurt her. Though he would confront her, eventually. He had a lot of questions for her.

Well, Mia knew one thing. She didn't want these two together any longer. All they needed to do was have an argument about anything at all and news of it would be sent to every media outlet within moments—complete with pictures that would fuel the press even more.

She moved over to Bronson, placing a hand on his arm. "You ready? I could use some champagne."

The muscle in Bronson's jaw ticked. Mia gave a subtle tug on his arm.

"It was great to see you, Anthony," she said.

"You look beautiful, as always, Mia." Anthony leaned over and kissed Mia on the cheek. "I'm sure I'll see you again before the festival is over."

Mia smiled and, thank God, Bronson led her toward the

champagne fountains. Celebrities mingled, sipping drinks, laughing, and all Mia could think of was how hard her heart was pounding over being in the middle of Bronson and Anthony. Mercy, they were something remarkable to look at, but she certainly wouldn't want to be on the receiving end of either of their angry stares.

As long as she just focused on her job and let Anthony handle everything, she had nothing to worry about. Yes, she wanted to help blend these two broken siblings, but that was not her place. Because she knew—God did she know—how much damage could be done by letting a life-altering secret slip.

Mia stopped at the champagne fountain and turned to Bronson. "Relax."

His piercing blue gaze landed on her. "I'm relaxed."

"You were until you saw Anthony. Now you're shooting daggers."

"It's no secret that we don't get along," Bronson told her. He took a delicate flute and filled it with champagne. "Besides, I thought you two were finished. Or don't you care who sees you?"

"I worked for him. We're friends. That's the extent of our relationship." Mia took the drink he offered.

"You two looked cozy when I found you." Bronson lifted a brow, tilting his head. "And the media says otherwise."

Mia didn't even pretend not to know what he was talking about. Her eyes narrowed. "You should know you can't believe everything the Hollywood tabloids print. Why do you care anyway?"

Bronson shrugged, eyes roaming over the crowd. "None of my concern what you did with your ex-employer as long as it doesn't trickle over into my family."

His close-to-the-truth words nearly had her choking on

her champagne. Mia quickly composed herself as his eyes came back to settle on her.

"Nothing gets in the way of my job," she assured him. "I'm thrilled to be working for your mother."

His silence combined with his intense stare left her unsettled.

"There's something more, isn't there?" she asked. There had to be. Anger radiated off Bronson. "You look ready to—"

"Leave it alone, Mia."

His firm tone left no doubt he wasn't happy with her observation. There was something deeper than just not getting along on set, but Bronson was private and there's no way he would tell Mia...nor was it any of her business. Yet she couldn't help her curiosity.

"Why did my talking to Anthony get you so riled up?"

"No concern of yours." Bronson closed his eyes briefly, then opened them and settled them on her. "Just had a flashback of another time. Another place."

Another woman. The words hung in the air, just the same as if he'd said them. Jealousy from Bronson Dane was certainly not something she expected, but she had a strong feeling past and present were getting jumbled together.

"It's getting late," he told her. "I'll walk you to your room."

Mia handed her glass off to a passing waiter. "Of course."

Something had transpired between those two men, and more than likely no one knew about it but them. She certainly hadn't heard anything while working with Anthony...at least nothing out of the ordinary.

If Bronson was this angry now, she could only imagine how furious he would be once he found out Anthony was his older brother.

* * *

Bronson didn't know what he wanted more—to know what secret Mia and Anthony had been discussing or whether or not they'd been involved.

No. That was wrong. What he wanted most right now was Mia. Naked. Whatever had happened between her and Anthony in the past was irrelevant to what he wanted now. He refused to relive any part of the last relationship he'd had with a woman he'd trusted. Trusted her so much he'd been ready to spend his life with her and their child.

Their child. That turned out to be another lie.

Bronson rid his mind of that painful time and concentrated on something he understood. Lust. Good old-fashioned lust. He wanted the sexy, sultry Italian woman who'd taunted him with her radiant beauty, her teasing jasmine scent and the power she held over him.

Ushering Mia off the elevator, Bronson snaked his arm around her waist, guiding her toward her suite at the end of the wide hall.

Silence had accompanied them from the party, though the sexual tension had been apparent between them on the ride up. Now there was just one thing on his mind.

Mia pulled her key card from her small silver clutch and opened the door.

"Do you want to come in?"

And that was all the invitation he needed.

"Yes," he said before he palmed her face and pulled her hard against him.

This was what he'd fantasized about since seeing her wearing droplets. Desired since she'd come to Cannes and strolled into the lobby wearing that draped-back dress. But this dress, this one-shouldered number, would be so easy to peel off her. And he would be shedding her dress in a matter of seconds.

Right now, though, he concentrated on her mouth. Her perfect lips that gave all he took. The lips he'd ached for since he'd tasted them two long nights ago.

He backed her into the suite, her clutch falling from her grasp just as the door slammed behind them. Her hands clenched around his biceps and squeezed just as she let out a soft moan.

Bronson lifted his mouth just a fraction. "I've wanted you for days. Tell me you're not still with Anthony."

"I never have been," she assured him before she captured his mouth again.

Mia was just as hot and passionate as he'd anticipated, and even more so than the other night. Perhaps because they were behind a closed door now. And Bronson had every intention of taking advantage of this privacy. No paparazzi, no media. Pure, utter privacy.

He couldn't take in enough of her at once. He wanted her. Naked. Now.

He continued moving her into the room until the backs of her legs bumped into the decorative table in the living area. All power was lost, all control vanished. His mouth traveled down her jawline to her neck, from her bare shoulder and on to the top of the clingy dress.

Mia placed her hands behind her on the table and arched into him, offering herself up as if she'd been needing, craving this moment as much as he had.

He lifted his head and slid the thin material down her arm until she freed herself of the unwanted sleeve. An ache he didn't remember having in a long, long time encompassed every part of him. Taking the hem of her dress, he eased it up as Mia shifted from side to side to assist.

"I don't have protection with me," he told her, cursing himself for being ill-prepared.

"I have some in the cosmetic bag on the table behind you."

God bless a prepared woman. He shuffled through the bag in a hurry, found the foil wrapper and smacked it on the table next to Mia's hip.

She'd moved the dress farther up to her waist, giving him more than a glimpse of what she wore beneath.

"Beautiful," he whispered as his eyes landed on the small scrap of lace in the same shade of purple as her dress. He slid the garment down her toned legs and over the stilettos. The fantasy shoes had to stay.

"You don't know how much you've driven me crazy." Bronson made quick work of his pants while Mia nipped along his jawline.

"Then kiss me because I'm going just as crazy waiting."

She scooted to the edge of the table as he donned protection. Her long legs wrapped around his waist and he lost no time in taking her.

Yes...yes. Her body moved perfectly against his, and Bronson had to work to keep from being too rough, too fast. He wanted this feeling of euphoria to last. The anticipation building up to this paled in comparison to having Mia draped all around him.

He realized then that the past two days had all been foreplay leading up to this moment. And each one of those stepping-stones, from the subtle touches to the harmless flirting, was mild when he had Mia right where he wanted her.

With her body wrapped around his, Bronson set the rhythm, pleased when an audible sigh escaped her full, moist lips.

It was those lips that had driven him crazy. Hell, the entire package made him feel like a horny teenager, but those lips mocked him when they smiled, when they talked. When they moaned.

Bronson kept the pace fast because nothing, absolutely nothing could slow him down now. He feasted on Mia's mouth. She grabbed hold of his shoulders, gripping the tux shirt he still wore because being inside her had taken precedence over being fully undressed.

Sweat drenched the skin beneath his shirt, and a fine sheen covered Mia's shoulders as he moved his lips down to one freed breast.

He didn't care that this was his mother's assistant, didn't care if she'd had or hadn't had a relationship with Anthony. All Bronson knew was that he wanted this woman, and what he wanted, he took. And Mia, the intriguing, dark-eyed beauty, had been onboard from the first kiss.

When her body shivered, shook, Bronson stopped holding back and let go. As they crested together, he knew this was not a one-time thing.

When their trembling ceased, Mia opened her eyes and smiled. "I have to say, I like how you walk me to my room."

Bronson nipped at her swollen, moist lips. "I should warn you: I intend to do this again as soon as I recover."

Trembling fingers toyed with the buttons on his shirt. "Maybe we could be skin to skin this time."

Anticipation rippled through him. "Absolutely."

No, Bronson didn't care that Mia was his mother's assistant, didn't care that he didn't trust her. And he sure as hell didn't care if she was now or ever had been involved with Anthony Price.

Because he wasn't getting his heart involved with anyone ever again. Not after his last relationship. His ex-fiancée had walked away after miscarrying a child he'd thought was his.

His ex-fiancée had met Anthony on a movie set, where she'd been the makeup artist, ironically the same way Bronson had met her. When Bronson and she began arguing after the death of the baby, and their relationship became strained, she'd thrown the supposed affair in his face once she'd walked out on him.

So, no, there was no love lost between Anthony and him. And any potential for future relationships was completely destroyed after that whole fiasco.

Lust and sex. That's all Bronson had room for in his life, and the very naked woman in his arms would fill that void nicely.

Four

Six weeks later...

What had she eaten?

Mia groaned. Closing her eyes, she let her head fall back against the plush sofa cushions. In the seven months she'd worked for Olivia, never once had she asked for a day, or even an hour, off. But today there was absolutely no way she could've made it through the afternoon without falling over or running to the bathroom and hugging the commode—not qualities a personal assistant to the Grand Dane should possess.

Olivia had taken pity on her and sent her home, with the promise Mia would call if she felt worse or needed anything at all. Mia would've promised anything to anyone if it meant she could crawl back onto her comfy sofa and lie perfectly still. Why did the house keep shifting?

Yeah, there was no way at all she could've kept up with the fast-paced, never-tiring Olivia Dane. Not today.

With the majority of her work on her laptop, she was just fine right here in her own living room. Well, she would be fine if the room would stop tilting and her stomach would stop rolling. Seriously, all she'd had for dinner the previous night was a piece of baked fish and some steamed veggies. Nothing at all to prove fatal, yet death was surely knocking at her door because concentrating on these fan emails was taking the last bit of energy she had.

Mia lifted her head and clicked on another email with a sigh. The message, like hundreds of others, wanted to know when Bronson would produce a film with his mother playing the lead role. The public loved this close-knit Hollywood family, and the fact that the Grand Dane and the best producer in the business hadn't worked together yet kept people interested.

Why did everything circle back to Bronson? In the six weeks since he'd left Cannes to go on a business trip for his next film, she hadn't heard a word from him. She'd been in the room once when he'd called to chat with his mother, but that was as close as she came to the man who'd given her the most spine-tingling night of her life.

Obviously, he'd been able to move on, so why was she still hanging on to the memories of his touch, his kiss? His taste. She lived in Hollywood. Sexual partners came and went. Unfortunately, sex had always meant more to Mia that just a casual coupling.

But, she reminded herself, he'd stressed that he didn't want anything personal, and she completely understood. For one night of passion with Hollywood's hottest bachelor, she'd put her moral compass aside and taken one for the team.

Though deep down, there was that little girl inside her

who wished for the old Hollywood fairy tale, the handsome man to sweep her off her feet, the mansion where they'd live happily ever after. Of course she'd keep all her wishes and dreams to herself, but she couldn't help the fantasies that flitted through her mind.

Unfortunately this was Hollywood. Unfulfilled fantasies were everywhere. But she didn't care if wanting her dreams to become reality made her naive. She'd continue to be a hopeless romantic.

She clasped the locket around her neck, the image of her parents' picture inside flooding her mind. They'd chased their dreams when they'd come to America from Italy. So what if she was a dreamer? That only made her work harder for what she wanted. And a part of her did want Bronson. Granted, she didn't know him that well, but she'd like to get to know him better. He'd been so attentive, so giving with his affection, not to mention he'd been a true gentleman the entire week they'd spent together.

But had she seriously thought Bronson would sleep with her, find himself falling madly in love and they'd ride off into the sunset in a town that was full of lies and deceit? Even couples who'd been married for a number of years seemed to fall into the bottomless pit of divorce.

And why was she wasting a workday fantasizing about weddings, divorces and Bronson's thrilling touch?

Mia's hands flew across the keyboard as she replied to the interested fan. There was nothing in the works for Olivia and Bronson, but that didn't mean it wasn't a possibility. And Mia knew the two would love to work on a film together, they just hadn't found the right one—or so she'd been told.

This was the part of her job she dearly loved—hearing from all the people around the world who reminisced about old Grand Dane movies and still enjoyed seeing her on the big screen with the hottest up-and-coming young stars. No doubt about it—when Olivia Dane made an entrance on to the screen, the audience loved her. No one could ever overshadow her beauty, class or intelligence. She reigned supreme even over today's hottest stars.

As she read more fan mail exuding love for this successful, bonded family, guilt washed over her.

When would Anthony tell Olivia he knew the truth? On one hand, Mia wanted it to be out in the open so she didn't have to hoard all this guilt. But, on the other hand, once the truth was out, how many lives would be ruined? Would the Danes be able to move on? They were such a tight-knit family and had lived through minor scandals, but something of this magnitude could cause tremendous upheaval. Anthony and Bronson already loathed each other. Informing Bronson they were brothers would surely prove to only drive that hatred to a deeper level.

And ruining Olivia's flawless image wouldn't solve anything.

Mia's stomach churned again. Between the constant fear of how these two families would cope with a forty-year-old secret and whatever stomach bug she'd picked up, Mia was ready to crawl back into bed and call it a day. Unfortunately, it was only ten in the morning and she still had about fifty more emails to get to and some phone calls to return for Olivia's TV talk show appearances to promote the new movie she had a cameo in. No rest for the dying.

Just as she opened another email, the doorbell sounded throughout the cottage. *Cottage* was a silly word for the five-thousand-square-foot guesthouse, complete with its own swimming pool, hot tub and movie room with a floor-to-ceiling movie screen. However, compared to the main house, at twenty-two-thousand square feet, this was definitely a cottage.

Mia came to her feet, thankful the room had stopped tilting for the time being, glanced down to her less-than-professional attire and shrugged. She'd changed into something more comfortable when Olivia had sent her home and hadn't expected to see anyone else today.

Oh, well. More than likely if it wasn't Olivia herself, then she'd sent one of the staff to check on her. Mia loved that Olivia cared for her in that motherly way...a way her own mother never had the chance to. She only prayed the cook hadn't brought food, as Olivia had suggested. The thought sent her stomach revolting—again.

The cool tile beneath her feet as she crossed the foyer felt refreshing, considering she was getting a bit light-headed again. Maybe she needed to crank up the AC or get a cool cloth for her head.

Mia twisted the lock and opened her door to see Bronson in all his gorgeous glory bathed in the sunlight falling over his shoulder. With his California tan, styled "messy" hair, green polo and dark designer jeans, he looked every bit of perfect. So opposite her. Oh, wait, she had the messy hair, just not in the stylish way he sported it. No, hers was more of the get-out-of-my-face-because-I'm-going-to-be-sick mess in a topknot with stray pieces hanging down.

"I called up to the house. Mom told me you were sick," Bronson said, leaning against her doorjamb. "Is there anything you need?"

Really? He'd rushed here after not a word in weeks? A phone call would've proved just fine and then she wouldn't have to worry about how deathly she looked while he, as usual, looked drop-dead sexy. If he hadn't put their sexual encounter out of his mind already, one look at her would surely have him running for the next starlet.

"Mia. Do you need anything?" he asked again.

Yeah, for him to leave and only return when her makeup

was on, her hair was done and her breath couldn't be used as a weapon.

"I'm good." She smiled. "Did you come over just to see how I was?"

Bronson shrugged. "I just got back into town a couple days ago and I was going to stop by to see you anyway."

"Really?" Considering the six-week gap since they last saw each other, she was a little skeptical. "Why?"

"Honestly?"

Mia grabbed the edge of the door for some stability and lifted a brow. Yeah, she wouldn't mind a little honesty from the man she'd slept with and couldn't get out of her mind.

Bronson threw her that billion-dollar, white-tooth smile. "I wanted to see you again. I was hoping for dinner at my place, but if you're sick, we can postpone."

If she'd had the energy to jump up and down, she probably would have. Even the giddy girl inside her was wiped out this morning.

"I haven't even agreed to see you again and you're already making plans to postpone?" she asked. "My, my. Awfully full of yourself."

Reaching into his back pocket, he whipped out a well-worn, folded-up tabloid.

Mia took it, unfolded it and saw the cover. A cover with the two of them in a heated embrace, kissing. Their first kiss that some paparazzo schmuck had captured and exploited. Not only was that picture blown up as the main feature, but there were also smaller pictures surrounding the perimeter. Snapshots from the red carpet, one picture of the two of them when they'd been waiting to meet with his mother for lunch—but, of course, Olivia wasn't in the photo.

The headline read, "DANE'S NEW LEADING LADY?" She'd seen these images and more intrusive headlines on the internet, but they'd only popped up for a few days. More Hollywood drama had unfolded since then, and their little week in Cannes had been pushed aside.

Mia's eyes darted to Bronson. "Why would this make you so confident I'd want to see you again? Aren't you the one who wanted to keep things to that one night?"

Bronson's bright baby blues roamed over her, heating her and making her feel just a wee bit better. "I do prefer simple, but after I saw these pictures, I knew I needed to see you again. The way you're looking at me, the way we look kissing—it's hard to deny that there's some real chemistry between us, Mia. And the camera picks up everything."

Shivers rippled one after another through her body as she slapped the the tabloid down onto the small table by the door. "In most of these we're looking at each other. I'd say the chemistry isn't completely one-sided."

"As I said, the camera picks up everything." One corner of his kissable mouth tilted. "Which is why I'd like to see you again."

And today she was not feeling, or looking, her best. Was this fate's way of telling her to take the night she had and move on without getting too involved with this man? She did know a secret that would crumble the solid foundation his world was built upon. On the other hand, she wanted to see this charming, sexy man again, away from the romantic, alluring ambiance of Cannes. She wanted to see if this chemistry was real.

"I'll call later to check on you," he told her. "If you're feeling up to it, I've got a great dinner planned."

Mia's eyes widened. "You're going to cook?"

"I've been banned from my own kitchen because I'm so terrible at cooking. But I assure you my chef will prepare a feast you'll never forget." His eyes grew dark, and a smile curved at his lips. "But my staff will have the night off when you're there. I promise you my undivided attention. If you're not feeling well, we can reschedule. Tomorrow?"

"No, I'll be fine. I'm sure I just need to rest."

Bronson stepped over the threshold, forcing her to take a step back. His finger trailed down her cheek, as if she needed a reminder of how spine-tingling his touches were. Those touches had driven her mad in Cannes, and she couldn't wait for an encore. Please, God, let her feel better after a nap and some Pepto.

"You look a bit pale." His brows drew together. "We'll do it tomorrow."

Great, here she'd been thinking of the last time he'd touched her with those talented hands and he was commenting on how deathly she looked. Didn't she just reek sex appeal?

His hand came back to her forehead and she swatted him away, but not before his palm rested over her head and cheek.

"Really, Bronson, I'm not in the mood to play doctor-patient. Tomorrow I'll feel better and we can have that dinner at your place. Maybe I'll bring my stethoscope."

A grin tugged at the corner of his mouth. "I'd like nothing more than to see your bedside manner again, but let's get you feeling better. Okay?"

"Fine," she agreed. "Tomorrow. I'll be there."

"I'll pick you up," he told her. "Five o'clock."

He turned and strolled back to his sleek, black sports car, leaving her standing in her doorway. That man had whipped back into her life as fast as he'd left and here she was panting after him just like the last time.

Oh, well. She didn't care what she looked like, she only cared about being with Bronson again because that man held more arousing power in his lips and fingertips than most men held in their entire bodies.

She was not going to let Anthony's secret or this stupid virus keep her from seeing him tomorrow. Because there was no way she would miss a repeat of the Cannes event. If Bronson had thought of her since then—and he obviously had or he wouldn't be carrying around that tabloid—then he wanted her just as much as she wanted him.

Dinner invite to his place? That just screamed for her to wear her best lingerie.

Bronson dove headfirst into his Olympic-size pool. Getting his laps in not only kept him in great shape, but allowed him to unwind after a long day. One of his favorite places in this Beverly Hills home was the pool. And each time he came home from business, he spent his evenings here. Even when the sun set and the stars came out twinkling, he found the water refreshing and could reflect on the happenings in his life.

And right now Mia Spinelli was happening in a big way.

Never before had a woman distracted him from his work. But in the weeks since the one they'd shared in Cannes, she'd done just that.

The first tabloid he'd seen nearly had him cringing, but that was just a knee-jerk reaction to the ever-looming media. Once he looked more closely at the picture, or *pictures,* rather, he'd seen something he couldn't deny. He wasn't lying when he'd told her the camera picks up everything.

Bronson pushed off the concrete wall and began the backstroke. The paparazzo had captured that first kiss at just the right moment and just the right angle to keep Mia's face a mystery. More pictures had shown her with her back to the camera, and that's when he'd noticed just how he'd been looking at her.

With lust. Pure and simple. He couldn't deny the attraction, and since he'd had her that's all he'd been able to think of. Luckily, his business trip hadn't taken as long as he'd thought and now he could concentrate on luring the seductive Mia into his bed once more.

Beyond that, he needed to keep an eye on her because he still wasn't convinced that she wasn't hiding something or out to benefit from working with his rival and now his mother.

As he came to rest with his arms on the side of the pool, Bronson vowed if Mia was hiding something, or working some angle, he'd uncover it…and, along the way, uncover her.

The next morning came with a vengeance as Mia threw back her covers and raced to the bathroom.

Just in time.

Good grief. She'd been fine yesterday afternoon and evening. Why was she feeling this way for the second morning in a row?

Mia's hands froze as she reached to flush the commode. Oh, no. No. This timing had to be coincidental. Fate wouldn't be this cruel to her…would it?

Easing back on her heels, her mind raced, calculating the date.

Oh, God.

Her period had always been on an odd cycle, but she'd never gone this long without one. Her eyes immediately went to her stomach. Surely there wasn't a baby growing inside her. She refused to believe it. Unfortunately, the facts were piling up fast, leaving her heart beating heavy against her chest, giving her a whole new reason to be nauseous.

Damn, she didn't have one of those at-home pregnancy tests on hand. She never thought she'd need one. But even if she ran out and bought one, were they 100 percent accurate? She had no clue what to do here. She'd never found herself in this predicament.

She needed to get to the doctor. Now. She needed to know the truth.

On shaky legs and with her thoughts moving through her mind faster than she could process them, Mia washed her face, brushed her teeth and threw on a strapless yellow sundress and flip-flops.

Grabbing her keys and handbag, she raced to the attached garage, pulling her cell out of her purse. By the time she got in her car, the receptionist told her they could do a walk-in test, no appointment needed. Thank God. She only hoped her sickness eased off long enough for her to find out the results.

Wait, shouldn't she be hoping for a negative test? An upset stomach was the least of her worries right now.

Mia raced down palm-lined streets, never more afraid or eager to go to the doctor. Once this scare was behind her, she could focus on her dinner with Bronson tonight and everything that went along with it.

But this night could have a totally different outcome if the pregnancy test came back positive.

Another scandal with her name all over it was the last thing she wanted. She was still trying to recover from the media painting her as the "other woman" in Anthony's marriage. Damn the paparazzi for adding to the already growing personal issues for Anthony and his wife. Not to mention the lies they made up about her all for the sake of a story.

Mia pulled into a parking spot on the street and tried not to run to the door, but a brisk walk was absolutely necessary. After entering the cool, air-conditioned building, Mia took the elevator to the third floor where her doctor's office was located, and thankfully had weekend hours.

She entered the carpeted waiting room and signed in on the walk-in tablet. In no time a nurse called her name and Mia started feeling queasy all over again. She could do this. She had to know.

Thirty minutes later when Mia stumbled out of the office, she rested against the wall in the empty hallway, trying to fathom what her life would be like now.

Because in thirty-four weeks, she and Bronson were going to have a baby.

Scandal with a Hollywood Hotshot: Take Two.

Five

Mia wanted nothing more than to forget the date with Bronson and hide in her house for the duration of her pregnancy.

Her pregnancy. She never thought those words would come to her mind when she wasn't in love, wasn't married and wasn't planning for a baby. But there was nothing she could do now except move forward and be upfront and honest with Bronson. And she would have to tell him… sooner rather than later.

But no matter how Bronson reacted, she wouldn't think of this baby as a mistake or a burden. The baby didn't ask to be conceived by two people who couldn't control their emotions.

Talk about a mood spoiler. Mia didn't put on her ugliest, lounge-around-the-house bra and panties, but her plans for her best lingerie were swiftly abandoned. After she dropped this bombshell tonight, she seriously doubted

Bronson would want to see how she filled out her newest Victoria's Secret purchase. And why was she even having those thoughts? That's the same path of destruction that had gotten her in this situation.

Dammit, they'd used a condom.

If she thought she'd been nervous before she found out the results, that anxiety was nothing compared to the thought of telling Bronson that he was going to be a father. She recalled that he'd been engaged before and they'd been expecting a baby, but his ex-fiancée had miscarried. What would he feel now? How would he react to another baby?

She'd rehearsed in her head over and over just the right way to say it, but was there really a right way to upend someone's life? She certainly wasn't his fiancée, was barely his lover. So how were they going to handle this arrangement?

Not only that, this scandal would send the media into another feeding frenzy. First she's accused of sleeping with Anthony and breaking up his marriage, and now she's carrying Bronson's child.

Just wait until the media circus discovered the two men were brothers. Wouldn't that just burn up the phone lines from reporter to reporter? She didn't want to even think about the headlines surrounding her when that time came.

Mia nearly laughed at the irony. Now she knew two secrets that would surely have Bronson reevaluating life and the hand it dealt him.

When her doorbell rang, she jumped. With a calming breath and a quick prayer, Mia left the comfort of her bedroom, smoothed a hand down her blue halter dress and went to answer the door.

She greeted Bronson with a smile, but just seeing him caused an ache she hadn't expected. She truly cared what he would do and say, but she was especially interested to see how he would handle this news emotionally, because soon another bomb would drop in his life that was just as big as him being a father.

His eyes raked over her. "You have no idea how glad I am we aren't going out. You look amazing."

Mia swallowed the lump of guilt and tamped down the arousal from his words. "Thank you."

She closed the door behind her and accepted his hand as he led her to his black luxury SUV. Just as she grabbed for the handle, he reached around her and opened the door. But before she could climb in, he took her shoulders and turned her back against the side of the car.

"I can't wait any longer for a sample."

Bronson's lips came down on hers and Mia had no choice but to melt into him. His hands settled on her waist as he pulled her lower body against his. With a grip on his muscular biceps, Mia returned the kiss with all the passion she had because—baby or no baby—she still craved this man like no other.

Obviously, their time apart hadn't banished her from his mind. In a sense she was thrilled that the ever-present attraction wasn't one-sided, but his feelings were likely going to change when he learned about the baby.

Bronson stepped back. "We may have to have the main course first."

Mia didn't even have to ask—she knew the main course was *not* something his chef had whipped up in the kitchen.

She climbed up into the SUV, sighing when he closed her door. She could do this. Millions of women broke the news of pregnancy all the time. Once the secret was out in the open, they'd be able to move on and deal with the consequences of their night together.

Bronson climbed in and brought the engine to life. When they were on the freeway headed to his Beverly Hills mansion, he took hold of her hand. "Everything okay? You seem awfully quiet."

"Everything's fine," she told him, nerves growing stronger with each passing second. "Just ready to relax."

Yeah, as if that were possible.

"You're not still feeling sick are you? Did that pass?"

Mia suppressed the groan. "It passed." *But it'll be back in the morning.*

"Great, because my cook made the most amazing Alfredo lasagna with a freshly tossed salad and vinaigrette dressing. I also have Italian bread and tiramisu for dessert."

Impressed, Mia smiled. "Wow. You know I'm Italian, right? I'm a harsh critic."

He gave her hand a gentle squeeze and laughed. "I always aim to please, Mia, and I know you'll enjoy everything I have in store for this evening."

The Mia who'd initially agreed to come have dinner with him would no doubt enjoy everything he had to offer. The pregnant, shocked, petrified Mia…not as eager. She had a feeling a lot of harsh words might be spoken and feelings would be hurt before the end of the night.

But when did she announce the news? Before dinner when they'd barely had a chance to talk? Or after when he'd no doubt put those seductive moves on her?

Definitely between the dinner and before the moves, because Mia knew once he started roaming those talented hands over her body, she'd be done. And it would be very, very wrong to take advantage of the situation when she had information that would almost certainly change the mood.

But would he be excited about the baby, about another Dane entering the dynasty? Mia hadn't paid that much attention to the press when he'd been engaged and lost a baby before, since she'd worked for Anthony at that time. But she knew a little bit about Bronson. He was a family man, and that loss of a child had to have nearly destroyed him. How would he accept another baby? And Mia couldn't help but selfishly wonder where she factored into this equation.

As they pulled into his gated drive, Bronson punched in a code and the lacey gates, complete with wrought-iron initials, parted and slid to either side of the drive.

She didn't know what to expect of Bronson's house, maybe a version of his mother's in that sleek white, Mediterranean style. But Bronson's three-story home exuded masculinity with the dark brick and large windows on each floor. Tall palms surrounded the curved home with a circle drive. No frilly flowers for him. Everything was green, lush and thriving.

"Your home is beautiful, Bronson."

He pulled into the attached four-car garage, closing the door behind them, sending them into darkness. "I'm not here often enough to enjoy it, but I do love it."

Would she be too forward if she asked about someday filling a home this large with a wife and children? Probably not the way to approach the topic of her pregnancy. God, she just had to say it. Once the words were out, they could deal with it, but her courage had failed to accompany her tonight.

She toyed with the locket around her neck, as if to draw strength from the two loving people pictured inside.

They exited the car and Bronson led her into the house through the kitchen any chef would die to just spend one day in—four built-in stoves, a brick pizza oven, three sinks mounted beneath gray concrete countertops. Dark mahogany cabinets made the large space look and feel masculine.

"Do you know what I'd do to have a kitchen like this?" she asked, running her fingertips along the grooved edges of the counter. "I love to cook in my spare time. I think I subscribe to every cooking magazine there is. With all this counter space, the stoves... My mind is working overtime."

Bronson tossed his keys onto the counter. "Feel free to come over anytime and let that imagination run wild. I'm a disaster in the kitchen."

She doubted that invite would last once she told him about the baby. Amazing how quick she'd gotten used to saying the words in her head without feeling the need to scream or cry. But they were going to have a baby, so why worry about something she couldn't change?

"Everything smells delicious," she told him. "Is it going to taste just as good?"

Bronson extended his hand toward the open eating area at the end of the kitchen. "Let's go find out."

She smiled at the round black table with high-back chairs, a simple white orchid in a slender glass vase and bright white plates waiting for the meal.

"Table for two?" she asked, throwing a smile over her shoulder. "You did go all out, didn't you? Or should I say your chef did."

Bronson pulled a chair out for her, brushed her hair from her shoulder and placed a gentle, tingling kiss right below her ear. "I may not have made the meal, but the rest is all me. I never need help impressing a woman."

Excitement mixed with guilt curled low in her belly. "Is that what you're trying to do? Impress me?"

"How am I doing?"

Exceptional. Wonderful. Perfect.

And why couldn't this night end the way she wanted, ached for it to? Why couldn't she have discovered the pregnancy tomorrow? Just one more night with him would've fulfilled her fantasies for years to come. Because she knew, once she dropped this bombshell, that would kill anything that had sparked weeks ago.

"Doing well so far," she told him, easing down into the chair.

Bronson brought over two full bowls of salad with dressing and fresh bread. Mia couldn't taste much, not for the secret on the tip of her tongue. She was a fraud, a liar. The kind of woman she despised.

Finally, she dropped her freshly buttered bread back onto the plate. "I can't do this."

With his fork halfway to his mouth, Bronson froze, eyes coming up to meet hers. "I'm sorry?"

Unable to stay seated any longer, Mia came to her feet and stood behind her chair, gripping the back. "I can't sit here and pretend this is going to go somewhere when I know it can't."

Bronson's fork clattered to his salad bowl. "What are you talking about, Mia? Are you having second thoughts about spending the evening with me?"

"Not at all, but you may have second thoughts about me when I tell you that…"

God, it was so much harder to say the words out loud, instead of just in her head. She'd never spoken them before and now that she was ready…well, she wasn't ready.

Bronson came to his feet, too, crossed to her and took her hands. "Come into the living room. You look like you're ready to pass out."

Funny, that's exactly how she felt and it had nothing to do with the morning sickness she'd been having.

Bronson led her to one of the two oversized leather sofas. She eased down, praying to find the right words, praying he wouldn't treat her differently. Praying he'd accept this baby.

And in all honesty, that's what everything boiled down to. With her background of foster homes and an unstable lifestyle, she just wanted this baby to be accepted and loved by Bronson. If he didn't love her, that was fine, but this baby didn't deserve to be shunned or kept from knowing his family.

He took a seat next to her, grabbing hold of one of her hands and bringing it to his lips. "Did something happen? Yesterday you seemed fine when we discussed our dinner date."

"That's because yesterday I was fine." Other than morning sickness. "And I'm fine today." Other than the morning sickness. "It's just my life has changed drastically since you saw me last."

His eyes roamed over her body and back up to her face. "You look the same. What is it?"

"I'm pregnant."

There, the words were out in the open and the world hadn't stopped spinning. Well, hers hadn't. She couldn't say the same for Bronson, who had just gone a shade paler.

"Pregnant?" he repeated.

Mia nodded slowly, afraid of what he'd say or do next.

"Now I understand why you're hesitant to be here with me." He came to his feet, as if he were afraid to sit next to her, touch her hand as he was. "Have you told the father? I mean, you two obviously aren't still involved or you wouldn't have agreed to come here, right?"

Mia placed an arm around her abdomen, trying to keep the hurt from seeping in even more. He didn't understand what she was saying. She'd never thought of that scenario when she'd rehearsed all of this in her head.

"Actually, we are still somewhat involved," she told him, looking up because she had to say this to his face and be brave. "You're the father, Bronson."

Six

Bronson heard the words, but he couldn't believe life could be this cruel. Another woman, another baby flashed through his mind and along with that came the hurt and betrayal he'd worked so hard to bury.

"I'm not the father, Mia."

Mia jerked, eyes wide. "Excuse me?"

Bronson shoved his hands in his pockets. "I believe you're pregnant, but I'm not the father. We used protection." And then he remembered and that pit in his stomach deepened. "*Your* condoms."

In an instant, she was on her feet, standing mere inches from him. "Are you implying I did this on purpose? Do you remember that night? Do you remember how I said good night and it was you who kissed me? You who backed me into the room and hiked up my dress?"

Bronson remembered…all too well, in fact. He remembered the rush to get her dress off, the rush as he fumbled with the condom and the pleasure he'd experienced like no other.

All the accusations surrounding her and Anthony flashed through his mind. How she'd supposedly broken up his marriage, how their affair had lasted several years.

"I know how it went down, Mia." Nausea threatened to overtake him, but he couldn't back down. "We used your condoms and now you're pregnant. Pretty coincidental, don't you think?"

In a flash, her palm connected with his cheek. The sting didn't even compare to the spearing pain running through him. He couldn't handle another baby that wasn't his. He could not, would not go down this path again. Nor would he be trapped, if somehow he really was the father, into a relationship or blackmailed for money.

"You expect me to take your word about something this serious?" he asked, rubbing his jaw.

Was that her angle? Was she trying to get money so she didn't have to work or so she could get into some headlines?

God, either scenario was a mess and fodder for all the gossip rags. He didn't know her angle, didn't care. His attorney would eat her alive and hopefully they would keep this insane accusation out of the media's hands.

How the hell had he let his guard down so fast, so easily with this woman? He'd wanted to stay close because he didn't trust her. Damn. How had his plan so completely backfired? Now he certainly didn't trust her.

"What is your angle, Mia?" Bronson crossed his arms over his chest, narrowing his eyes at her. He may as well be direct. "Was this your plan all along? To trap me? Does Anthony know you're pregnant, supposedly with my child?"

Mia stepped back. "Anthony? Why would I tell him? You're the first person I've told."

He had a hard time believing that. "You two looked pretty cozy when I found you together in Cannes. How do I know the baby isn't his?"

"How dare you? I am not a liar and I am not out to trap you into anything. I'm laying all the facts out there so we can deal with this baby who didn't ask to be brought into this world and I will not..."

Her words ended on a very persuasive hiccup as tears filled her eyes. She spun around, dropping her head to her chest.

Wow. Maybe he should cast her in his next film. She was damn convincing, but he wasn't falling for any of her theatrics.

"I want a DNA test as soon as possible," he told her. "I've been down this road before, Mia, and it didn't end well for me. Though I'm sure you already knew about the baby I lost."

Mia turned back to him, wiping her damp cheeks. "I do remember hearing about your ex-fiancée who lost the baby. I'm so sorry about that, but I assure you I love this baby already and will do everything to keep it safe."

Her soft tone made him want to believe she was truly sorry, but still, he didn't want to revisit the past with his ex-fiancée and the baby that ended up not being his, and he sure as hell didn't want to be living this nightmare again.

"I won't go through this again, Mia. I won't start a family with a woman I can't trust."

Mia's face paled at his words. "I'm just as shocked and scared as you. I never intended to get pregnant. If you don't want to be part of this child's life, that's your loss. But I will love this child and I will provide for it with or without your help. I've been alone my entire life. I'm used to it."

A sliver of Bronson wanted to believe this baby was his. Though he wasn't in love with Mia, he'd always wanted children to carry on the Dane dynasty, a wife to love. He wanted what his parents had had before his father's death.

But he had to be realistic. Mia probably saw this as her way to extort money from him, even if she claimed to not want part of his fortune.

"I won't pay you anything until I know for sure who this baby belongs to," he told her, not caring one bit that she looked like she was on the verge of tears again.

"I would never ask for anything from you," she said through gritted teeth. "I thought you should know, but if this is the attitude you're going to take, I don't even want you in my baby's life. We deserve better."

A psychological ploy used many times by thousands of women to trap the man into giving in. He wasn't falling for it. Now more than ever he needed to stay close to figure out exactly what her angle was.

"I assure you, Mia, if this baby's mine, I will be part of his life." He stepped closer to the woman who drove him insane on so many levels. "And if this baby's mine, whether I like it or not, I will be part of your life. Count on it."

Mia's lips thinned. "I don't want you in my life. Not after the accusations you've just hurled at me. I would never lie about something as serious as a baby. And I assure you, I haven't been with another man in over a year and, no, it was not Anthony. He was my employer and friend, that's all."

Yet again, she sounded and looked so convincing. And there was that part of him that wanted to believe her. He didn't even want to think of Anthony Price's hands on her willowy, soft body. Didn't want to think of another man's baby growing inside her. Not that he wanted a baby with her, either. Other than the sexual, physical attraction, what did they have in common?

Sure, before this bombshell, he'd considered seeing where that attraction could lead. But now…

Dammit. Why? Just…why?

Mia moved past him, charging back to the kitchen.

"Where are you going?" he asked, following her.

"To call a cab." She pulled her cell from the purse she'd left on the center island. "I think it's best if we both cool down and think rationally before talking about this again."

"I'll drive you home." He took the cell from her hand and hit the End button. "There's no need to call a cab. The paparazzi would get wind of your leaving here in tears and who knows what story they'd make up."

Mia stared at him, her face red from crying, her makeup smeared in one corner of her eye. And she was still beautiful. Alluring and simple all in one. But the most important question was, Was she a first-class liar who'd set out to trap him?

Only time would tell.

The pain sliced through her. Agony, frustration, despair. Even a week after dropping the news on Bronson, she still had that sickening pit in her stomach.

Mia curled up on her four-poster bed, refusing to cry. Expecting a child should be a joyous time in every woman's life, but this moment was anything but joyous.

Toying with the bronze beading on her comforter, Mia thought about the life growing inside her. Most women ran to their mothers for advice, or a sister or best friend. Who did she have? Seriously? She'd purposely engrossed herself in work so she could forget that she'd never had anyone in her life who cared…other than her parents, who'd died when she'd been only five years old. Her few friends had busy lives of their own. Too busy to call and share the news or borrow a shoulder to cry on.

Never before had being alone bothered her; she actually enjoyed being independent. But now, when her life was taking a dramatically sharp turn, she truly wished she had someone.

She hadn't expected Bronson to take the news well, but to accuse her of sabotaging the condom to trap him? That was beyond absurd. Once Bronson calmed down and could think rationally, would he believe her? Would Olivia and Victoria be happy or just as skeptical?

Oh, God. Would Olivia still let her remain in such a personal, intimate position? She needed this job, especially now with a baby coming—no way would she take any money from Bronson. That certainly wasn't the reason she'd told him.

No, she'd told him out of consideration and, dammit, because it was the right thing to do. So why was she allowing all this guilt to consume her?

Her blood pressure soared once again at the thought of his believing the worst. But stepping back and looking at it from his point of view, she could somewhat understand how he'd distrust her. They had used a condom—her condom—and he really didn't know her.

But the accusations he threw at her still cut deep. She prided herself on honesty and built her life on always telling the truth. Of course, that was before she saw the damning, life-altering file on Anthony's desk mere days before she started working for Olivia.

On a groan, Mia rolled onto her back and stared up at the ceiling. Her locket slid around her neck and tickled her ear.

Why did her life have to end up so complicated? Why couldn't she be like millions of other women who felt the joy and elation of having a baby? She'd always fantasized about telling the man of her dreams he would be a daddy. Now all her fantasies were shot.

But what did she expect, going to bed with a man she barely knew? Karma surely wasn't this cruel. She hadn't wanted any personal involvement with Bronson, especially until the secret of his illegitimate brother came out, and now she'd thrown herself smack dab in the center of his life—whether he wanted to admit it or not.

Mia glanced over at her clock and knew she couldn't avoid the inevitable. Monday morning came too fast, and now she had to get ready to head to the main house, spend the entire day with Olivia and pretend she wasn't hiding two major secrets from this woman.

As she made her way to her adjoining bath, Mia figured she deserved the good pity party she'd thrown for herself all weekend, but now it was time to take charge and stand strong. This was her life, she was bringing a baby into it and she needed to have a firm, solid foundation for them both to stand on.

Once Mia was ready, both with her appearance and mind-set, she headed to the main house where she would work just as she did any other day.

Should she mention the pregnancy?

From a boss/employee standpoint, absolutely. But this was Bronson's mother, which forced the situation into personal territory. She honestly didn't know how to handle this delicate matter.

She and Bronson needed to have an adult conversation that didn't involve accusations and other harmful words in order to head in the right direction for this baby.

A wave of giddiness overwhelmed her as she followed the wide, palm-lined sidewalk to the patio doors of Olivia's office. For once in her life, Mia had someone to focus on other than herself. The thought both thrilled and terrified her. She didn't have the best examples of parenting growing up and she'd never been around babies, but she knew, without a doubt, that this baby would never, ever wonder if it was loved.

Love. Isn't that all anybody ever wanted? To be loved, unconditionally, just for who they are and not for their accomplishments or what they could give in return.

One day, Mia vowed, she would find that love.

"Ah, there's my beautiful assistant." Olivia poured herself a small glass of juice from the tray the cook provided every morning with fresh juices and fruit. "Care for something?"

Mia shook her head. Thanks to the crackers by her bed, she'd been able to make it here. No way was she going to jinx her good luck with anything else.

"I'm fine right now. Thanks."

Mia started to leave the office and head to her own when Olivia stopped her. "Is something wrong, dear?"

Cringing at the guilt that consumed her, Mia smiled. "Didn't sleep well last night. I'll perk up in a bit."

With a smile on her nearly wrinkle-free face, Olivia nodded. "As long as you're feeling better. Did you just have a twenty-four-hour bug?"

More like the nine-month kind.

Mia shrugged, unable to think of a way not to lie, but not to reveal the truth, either. "I'm just glad I'm able to come in today. Working from home isn't the same. I feel more productive in my office here. I did manage to complete your itinerary for the next two months and we can go over it just as soon as I get my computer booted up and check for an email confirmation for one more interview."

Fleeing before she had to stay in the same room with the woman who was her baby's grandmother, Mia went straight to her spacious office overlooking the Olympic-size pool.

The more time she could spend in here, alone, the better. Once she and Bronson had a plan, then she wouldn't feel so jittery around Olivia.

Mia sat down and turned on her computer. On a sigh she glanced at the gold-framed photograph hanging above the chaise at the other end of her office. The timeless portrait had been made into posters and paintings for decades. A young, smiling Olivia with her glossy, dark, upswept hair and body-hugging gold dress as she posed with her first Oscar...which, according to the time line Mia now knew about, was almost two years after giving up Anthony in a secret, well-paid adoption.

Mia looked at this picture in a whole new light now. A hand slid around to her flat abdomen as she thought of the fear and worry Olivia must've experienced. Mia couldn't even imagine giving up a child, but she knew Olivia must've had her reasons. What had changed in Olivia's life from that adoption to four years later when she'd given birth to Bronson?

All Mia knew was Bronson and Victoria's father had been Olivia's one and only husband. Perhaps her career and relationship status combined, forced her into giving up Anthony.

Mia couldn't help but wonder how Olivia had felt the second time she gave birth to a son. Having Bronson probably brought bittersweet memories.

Mia's thoughts always drifted back to Bronson and that night in Cannes when he'd entered her suite. She should've told him no, considering what she knew regarding Anthony, but how could she when his mouth had taken over and his hands had started their journey up her dress?

Sometimes she thought of that night and it moved through her mind in a haze of slow motion, almost as if it was a dream. Making love all night. The soft, heated whispers in the dark. The kisses. Ah, the kisses had rendered her speechless. The man had captivated her.

They had an amazing night of sex with no promises and in the final days of the festival, they'd appeared together for the cameras. Simple, no complications.

And now she was pregnant. So much for keeping it simple.

She wished more than anything that she could keep her personal feelings out of this, but she couldn't. Even though Bronson had said some hurtful things to her, she was still every bit as attracted to him as she'd been in Cannes. Perhaps if she could get that night out of her head, she'd be better off.

Except that's all that consumed her thoughts. Her days, her nights. Bronson Dane and his smooth touches, his Prince Charming–like qualities.

"Mia, darling."

Olivia's buttery-smooth voice drifting from across the grand mahogany desk pulled her from the memories of Cannes back to the fact that her lover's mother stood across from her.

"You've been staring at the screen for two minutes, and I said your name twice." Olivia smiled, crossed her arms over her ivory pants suit and tilted her head. "Would you like to talk about whatever it is that has your mind elsewhere?"

Mia closed her eyes, wishing Bronson would stay out of her head so she could work. "I'm sorry, Olivia."

The Grand Dane slid off her diamond-studded reading glasses and smiled. "My dear, you have nothing to be sorry about. Now, let's talk. What's bothering you, darling?"

Mia sighed, acknowledging that this woman was relentless in getting what she wanted. She'd given birth to three very successful children, raised two and didn't get to the top of her game by not reading other people.

Mia could talk about some things, but not the main thing.

How did she start?

"You think I don't recognize the signs?"

Mia froze. "Olivia—"

The starlet smiled. "I know when a woman is infatuated with a man. Especially when that man is my son."

Mia breathed a sigh of relief and came to her feet. "I'm not infatuated with Bronson. I'm just…" Having his baby.

"Mia, honey, I know you don't have people in your life. I know you grew up under extreme circumstances, which makes me all the more proud of how you've excelled." Olivia rested her hands, palms down, on the glossy desktop. "I was young once and I know all about matters of the heart. So, believe me when I say I've been where you are."

If only she knew how true that statement was.

Olivia had been where Mia was now. Pregnant, unwed, in a very promising career. God, how Mia wished this weren't Bronson's mother. She'd love nothing more than to confide in Olivia, to seek advice from someone who'd been in her shoes.

Mia went to the floor-to-ceiling windows and blew out a breath as she looked down to the lavish gardens and pool below. "And where am I?"

The question had been turning over and over in her mind since her world came to a crashing halt Saturday morning in her doctor's office.

"Only you can answer that," Olivia said, coming to stand beside her. "And if you can't, perhaps you should be talking to Bronson so you can get your mind back on work."

Okay, hard to take advice from a woman who didn't know all the facts. But she was right. Mia did need to talk to Bronson again. Why hadn't he called? Was he still convinced this baby wasn't his? Wouldn't he feel like an ass when he discovered she'd been telling the truth?

A gentle arm wrapped around Mia's shoulders, reminding her of how much she missed having her own mother in her life. "My darling, I can tell when another woman is at war within herself. I just want you to find some peace. And feel free to talk to me, not as your employer, not as Bronson's mother, but as a friend."

Mia looked back at their reflection in the window as tears pricked her eyes. Stupid hormones. As if the thought of having a loving family of her own weren't always on her mind, now she was coming to love the Danes a little too much. They were all seeping into her heart and she feared—no, she knew—she would end up hurt.

"I do think of you as a friend, Olivia." Mia turned, smiling at her baby's grandmother. "I have so few and I appreciate your taking time to give me advice."

"Anytime, my love." Olivia's smile was replaced by a scowl. "Now, have you told Bronson how you feel? Men can be so dense at times."

How she felt? Oh, no, this was not a conversation she was going to have. Honestly, Mia wasn't entirely sure. She certainly had some kind of feelings for Bronson, but beyond that, she couldn't say. Right now, whatever feelings she may or may not have weren't the issue. This baby had to be first and foremost on her mind.

Before she could answer, a wave of nausea overwhelmed her. Mia swayed, holding a hand up to the glass to steady herself, but Olivia took hold of her hands.

"Mia?"

"I'm okay," she assured Olivia. "I just got dizzy or something."

She closed her eyes, willing the moment to pass. Deep breath in. Deep breath out.

"Why don't you sit down." Olivia guided her to the leather desk chair. "You got awfully pale all of a sudden."

Mia took a seat, thankful the room had stopped spinning. "Really, Olivia, I'm fine."

Fine. Well, as fine as she could be, considering that the father of her baby had accused her of being a liar and having an affair with his illegitimate brother.

"Doing better now that you're sitting down?"

As if getting off her feet would make her condition better.

"Yes," Mia offered with a smile. "I'm sure I just need some juice or something. Why don't we go back to your office and I'll see what the cook put on the tray?"

"Perfect." Olivia stepped back, allowing Mia to get to her feet. "You snack and get your strength back up so we can chat about why you're hiding a pregnancy from me."

Mia's eyes darted to Olivia's steely blue ones. "Olivia, I…" She wanted to lie, she really did, but she couldn't. "I'm not hiding it. Honestly, I just found out myself."

Olivia reached out and squeezed her hands. "I'm not going to pry, because I know this is a scary time, but please know that you can come to me and discuss anything. I want to be here for you."

Mia couldn't help the tears that sprang up like a leaky faucet. "Oh, Olivia, you don't know how much I need someone to talk to."

Olivia opened her arms and Mia sank into the woman's embrace. How many times had she needed this—the love of an understanding woman? Just one hug shot straight to Mia's heart.

"I assume the baby belongs to my son." Olivia pulled back, meeting her eyes. "I saw how the two of you looked at each other in Cannes. The sparks practically singed everyone around you. Does he know?"

Mia nodded. "He does. We haven't really had a chance to talk rationally. We're both letting this sink in. And considering those rumors about me and Anthony, I'm not sure where I stand with Bronson."

"Come to my office." Olivia wrapped an arm around her shoulder and led her toward the hall. "You have a lot you need to get off your chest."

Oh, she had no idea. But at least the pregnancy was out in the open. Too bad the forty-year-old baby secret was still locked up tight. Mia had a bad feeling that Olivia would push for something between her and Bronson. But Mia refused to be in a relationship out of obligation or pity. And no way would she be with Bronson just because he or anyone else said so.

Call her naive, but she was waiting for love. She would find love, and that man would accept Mia and her baby.

Seven

When Bronson had returned from his lunch meeting with his attorney—just to discuss his options if he was indeed the father of the baby—his assistant had informed him he had a call from Mia Spinelli, stating that he had to be at her place by six o'clock. No exceptions.

Another urgent message, this time from his mother, said she needed to see him tonight, as well. Again, no exceptions. Since when did he allow his life to be controlled by demanding women?

Obviously, the baby secret was no longer a secret. He was not ready to discuss this with his mother, not until he knew all the facts and where he stood.

Bronson had barely dropped his hand after knocking when the door to the cottage swung open. There stood Mia wearing another one of those simple little strapless cotton dresses. No matter that she looked amazing, he was certainly not in the mood. And considering the current circumstances, he'd better learn to control his hormones around this woman because he would not be forced deeper into her devious plan.

"Telling my mother about the baby is your new tactic?" he asked, barging past her into the house.

Mia spun around to face him, sending the door slamming behind her. "Did she tell you that?"

So, she really had told his mother. He was just guessing by the urgency of the phone calls. Dammit, he wasn't ready for anyone to know, especially considering the last baby debacle.

"Actually, I haven't talked to her. She called my office and demanded I come to the house tonight. I'm assuming that means she knows, and I sure as hell didn't tell her."

Bronson kept his hands on his hips, ready for another fight. This was his life, his reputation. There was no backing down, no letting Mia have the upper hand. And now more than ever he needed to keep his sights on her. No way would he allow her to destroy his family…or whatever the hell else her intentions were.

"Look, I didn't call you here to argue." Mia moved past him and led him through the thick white columns separating the foyer from the living area. "We need to sit down and discuss, like adults, what we're going to do and what part you want to take in the life of our baby."

Bronson remained standing when Mia took a seat in the wing-back chair. "Let me set a few things straight, Mia. My mother's last assistant extorted nearly a million dollars from her before she was caught and imprisoned. And two years ago my ex-fiancée betrayed my trust. So you're sorely mistaken if you think, even for a second, that I'm just going to believe you when you say the baby is mine. Scandal is nothing new in Hollywood, so don't think you're

going to get away with the most popular form of entrap-
ment known."

Mia crossed those long, tanned legs. "If you're finished,
I'd like to say something, too."

Bronson shoved his hands in his pockets and nodded,
testing his willpower by keeping his eyes off those legs.
"Fine."

"My parents were killed when I was five. After several
foster homes, I realized that the only way I would ever have
a family was to grow up and have one of my own."

Mia turned her head, but not before he saw the moisture
gather in her eyes. He waited for her to turn back, fully engaged in a crying session in an attempt to gain his sympathy. But when she looked back up, the tears were still there,
only unshed and Mia tilted her chin just a bit as if defying
them. Damn, he didn't want to respect her strength.

"Family means everything, Bronson," she went on, her
voice thick with emotion. "I've always dreamed of finding
the perfect man for me. We'd settle down in a nice house,
we'd create babies out of love and grow old together. I
assure you, this scenario was not my dream. You can believe me, or you can choose to believe that I'm just as con-
niving as other women you've grouped me with. That's up
to you. I want this baby to know its father, and I'd hate for
you to miss out on the life of your child simply because
you're afraid and this deceitful town has made you cynical."

Bronson turned toward the wall of windows and wished
like hell she was telling the truth—and that she hadn't
pegged him so easily. She wasn't the only one who'd had
the idea of a family. He'd come from a loving home, one
of the few the industry hadn't tainted. He'd love to someday fill his spacious home with a woman he loved and their
babies. So, yeah, Mia wasn't the only one with dreams.

But his work had always come first, something his ex-fiancée had thrown in his face. And since then, he *had* turned cynical—disturbing how Mia homed in on that aspect.

"I totally understand your reasons for not believing me," she went on as he continued to stare out the window. "I can only hope my actions back up the truth. I won't ask for a dime from you, Bronson, or your family. I will continue to work for your mother and support the baby. This baby's needs have to come before your feelings."

She was right. Whether the baby was his or not, the baby didn't ask to be born, and Mia's baby had to have top priority.

So, for now, until he had medical proof, he'd assume what she said was the truth and keep a close watch on her. Because if this baby was his, there was no way in hell Mia was going to raise this child on her own.

"How are you feeling?" he asked, surprised that he really cared when, for all he knew, she was a first-rate scam artist.

A soft smile spread across her lips. "Better once lunch passes. I've been reading online, and mine is a typical pregnancy. This is all so new to me because I've never been around babies. I just can't devour enough information."

Bronson swallowed the lump of emotion. Hearing her excitement made him feel like a jerk, but he had to be cautious. His heart couldn't take another beating…or another baby ripped from his life.

"The baby is only the size of a pea right now," she added, her hand moving to her flat stomach. "Strange how something so tiny can throw off my whole system."

"I found a doctor I'd like you to start seeing. She's the best, and she will keep things quiet if this baby turns out to be mine. I don't want the press hounding you."

Mia's hand froze on her stomach, and her eyes turned to slits. "I don't want your doctor, Bronson. I have a doctor I'm quite pleased with and, I assure you, the office won't reveal who the baby's father is because I haven't said a word. Besides, it's not as if the office will ever know it's you anyway."

Bronson closed the space between them and took a seat next to her on the sofa. "I'm going to your doctor's appointments, Mia. While I'm not totally convinced this baby is mine, on the chance that it is, I want to be around for every appointment and the birth."

For a minute, Mia simply stared. Her natural beauty left him breathless—so flawless, so timeless. The camera would love her. The camera *had* loved her. He had tabloids with snapshots from Cannes to prove it.

"I will not have you believe the worst of me and expect me to let you control and watch over my pregnancy," she told him through gritted teeth. "You can either act like a father or stay away. You can't have it both ways, Bronson."

Oh, he could and he would. But she'd learn that in time. No need to argue right now.

"Fine," he agreed. "You stick with your doctor, but I'm coming to all the visits and I will ask questions if I see fit. I will also have my assistant call to make sure your appointments are kept quiet and we get right in. We shouldn't be seen in the waiting area."

Mia rolled her eyes. "They have private waiting areas, Bronson. No need to get all guard dog on me. Besides, you need to talk to your mother and sister. We can't prolong the inevitable. The media is going to find out soon anyway when I start showing."

Bronson could just imagine Mia with a rounded stomach, carrying a baby—possibly his baby. She'd be just as stunning, just as breathtaking.

Dammit, he hated being torn like this. How could he want something he'd never even had? Granted, he'd more than gotten used to the idea of being a father when his ex-fiancée was pregnant. But when she'd lost the baby, and the truth had come out that it hadn't even been his, Bronson had buried those crushed emotions and vowed never to be caught up in something that wasn't his again.

And here he was insisting he attend all of Mia's appointments for a baby that could very well be Anthony's—the very man his ex threw in his face as a potential candidate for being the father.

All the more reason to loathe the man and be suspicious of his ex-assistant.

"I'm going to the main house as soon as I leave here," he told her. "I left a message for Victoria to come over, so I'm hoping she'll be there, as well. Do you want to join me?"

Mia's eyes widened as she let out a soft gasp. "I'm not…I…Bronson, I'm not sure I'd be very good at this family meeting."

He hadn't really intended it as a question. "You'll come with me because if this baby is mine, you have bonded yourself to the Danes for the rest of your life." God help him being tied to this seductive woman forever.

"I'm so sick of your trying to control me," Mia told him, coming to her feet. "And quit acting like you're not sure you're the father. You know you are. Deep down, Bronson, you know. And it hurts me that you would deny this baby even for a second." She turned, heading toward the foyer. "Let's get this family meeting over with."

With a smile on his face, Bronson watched Mia storm out of her cottage. If his life weren't in such chaos at the moment, he'd admire her take-charge attitude and independent stance. But since his family was on the line, he needed to focus.

No way was he letting this temptress under his skin again. From now on he'd be on guard and ready for whatever she threw his way.

Dread, excitement, fear and anxiety all rolled into one big ball of nerves and settled deep into Mia's stomach as she and Bronson entered the main house.

Olivia stood in the formal living room next to the wall of shelves that housed many pictures from her early days in movies as well as several professional pictures of Victoria and Bronson as children. Most of the photos were personal, showcasing the movie family in real life. Swimming in the pool as children, Victoria as a teen ballerina, a young Bronson on the shoulders of his father.

Mia pulled herself out of the Dane family snapshots and into reality. One day maybe her child would be in a frame in this very room. Mia hoped so. That was one of the things she'd missed as an adult. There were very few pictures of her as a child, though she still had the two photos of her and her parents when they'd first come to America. Those captured moments were something she treasured every day.

She slid a hand over her locket, reminding herself that she was never alone in life's endeavors, even if she felt that way at times.

Soft laughter pulled Mia from her thoughts. Victoria sat in the white club chair on her cell phone speaking French and laughing at someone named Jacques. But once Mia and Bronson fully entered the room, Olivia's face softened with a genuine smile and Victoria ended her call.

"I'm assuming Mother told you the news about the baby." Bronson eyed Victoria who simply nodded. "I just want to get this all out so there's no confusion as to where I stand and what's going on."

Mia wanted to throw up. Undoubtedly Bronson would

start the same song and dance she'd heard the past two days about "if" the baby was his. No matter how harsh those words sounded and how she hated him for saying them, she knew he was just as scared as she was.

"I will assume this baby is mine for now," he went on. "But we will get a DNA test to determine the father."

"I never agreed to that," she piped in. "You assumed I would, but since I don't want your money, it's a moot point."

Bronson turned on her. "You will have a DNA test done on the child, Mia. Forget yourself for a minute, will you? If this child is a Dane, he has a sizable fortune he's set to inherit."

"Are you kidding me?"

Mia glanced around to Victoria who was now on her feet, hands on her hips. "You're acting like this is a business arrangement. You're talking about a child for crying out loud, Bron. *Your* child. You may have been caught off guard the last time, but I believe Mia. She wouldn't lie about the paternity."

A bit of elation spread through Mia at Victoria's confidence that she wasn't trying to swindle anything from this family, especially since they'd only known her about seven months. But what did she mean about "last time"?

"You just want the baby to be mine," Bronson said. "Don't start sewing designer Onesies."

"You want the baby, too." Olivia moved toward them. "There's no need to deny it, Bronson. I know you're scared to death to admit this is your child for fear of losing another baby. But I agree with Victoria. Mia isn't lying. I've gotten to know her very well, and this is an honest, loyal woman."

She wasn't feeling so loyal at the moment, considering the secret she held. Oh, she was being honest about *this* baby, but not so much about the baby Olivia gave up nearly forty years ago.

Talk about intense. This was why Mia didn't want to do family meetings. First of all, she wasn't in the family and, second of all, old wounds always reopened and Mia certainly didn't want to add that dash of salt into Bronson's.

But what was all this talk of the baby he lost? They made it sound as if that baby wasn't his. But surely if his ex-fiancée was pregnant, the baby had been his. Hadn't it? Good Lord, was there another buried Dane scandal? What kind of mess had she stepped into?

"I'm not here to discuss my past," Bronson declared, eyeing his mother and sister. "I'm here to let you all know that this baby is between me and Mia for the time being. I don't want you two fawning all over her and getting attached to someone who may not even belong in this family."

"Excuse me," Mia chimed in. "This baby is as much a Dane as it is a Spinelli. If your mother and sister want to get *attached,* let them. Just because you are choosing to keep your distance doesn't mean they have to. My whole life I wanted to be part of a family." Mia clutched her locket and choked back tears. "My whole *life.* Do you know what that's like?"

Mia stared at Bronson, not caring a bit that Olivia and Victoria were listening, not caring that her voice was cracking. She was standing up for her child, as no one had done for her after her parents' death, and she was starting now. This child would know love and security from day one.

"I never really felt a sense of belonging. Once my parents were killed…" She hesitated, praying the tears stinging her eyes wouldn't spill over. "I will not have our child wondering where he or she belongs. I want nothing but love for this child. You can keep every last dollar. Just don't deny the fact this child does belong here just as much as you do. Don't deny our baby the bond only a loving family can provide."

Mia caught sight of Olivia and Victoria, and both women had glistening tears and soft smiles. Bronson, on the other hand, still wore the signature scowl he'd had in place since he'd learned the truth. What would it take to get him to look on the bright side? Try to make this a positive time?

"I'm sure you all need to talk, so I'll let you have your privacy."

Mia turned on her heel and left the room. She didn't slow down until she was far enough away from the house that no one would see her break into tears.

She'd never been much of a crier. Life had toughened her up at a young age, but lately she couldn't stop the tears. Whether it was the uncontrollable hormones or the fact that she just didn't want her baby to feel neglected and abandoned, she didn't know. What she did know is that it was quite obvious the Dane women were perfectly comfortable with the idea that this baby belonged in the family. Too bad Bronson believed the worst.

And that's what hurt the most. Had he always believed the worst in her? When he'd slept with her, had he just been passing time?

Mia hated the thought that she'd slept with Bronson out of pure lust. She'd never slept with a man only because she found him attractive. But it wasn't just that Bronson was curl-your-toes sexy. He had been so smooth, so seductive, and with the ambiance of Cannes and all the romance surrounding them, she'd been caught up in a whirlwind. But she'd be damned if she let her lack of good judgment affect her child's life or what Bronson thought of her.

This baby would have everything she never did: stability, unconditional love and family. Mia would settle for nothing less.

Eight

The next month flew by without any major drama—baby or otherwise. Anthony still hadn't confronted Olivia, and Bronson was still as personable as a bedsheet when he'd call twice daily to ask how she was feeling.

But today was the day of her first prenatal visit, and Bronson would be picking her up any minute.

This should be a fun ride.

As if the strained phone conversations weren't enough, now she had to sit in close proximity to the man she found both insufferable and devastatingly attractive at the same time. She couldn't blame any of this on her hormones. Bronson was still just as sexy, and every time she looked at him she couldn't help but remember their night together.

She so wished she could forget how amazing his hands felt as they'd glided over her body. The way he held her, giving so much of himself. Mia had never before experienced anything like it, and she had a feeling she never would again. Yes, the sex had been hurried, frantic, but Bronson had been so in tune with her body, so perfect for her.

When Mia's doorbell rang, she grabbed her purse and keys and opened the door to a still-sexy Bronson. She reset the alarm and closed the door behind her. Without a word, Bronson led her to his two-door sports car. At least he had the decency to open the passenger door for her.

"This'll be a blast," she muttered to the empty car as he walked around the hood.

As soon as he got in and brought the engine to life, Mia twisted in her seat. "You don't have to go. No one will think anything if you just stay away. I've already given you the out you obviously want. I expect nothing from you."

Bronson's grip tightened on the wheel, the muscle ticking in his jaw. "I said I'd be there for every appointment in case the baby is mine. I meant it. My assistant has already called to ensure we will be taken back immediately."

Mia wasn't going to argue. In truth, she wanted to share this glorious time with someone, she just wished that someone shared her excitement.

And she was excited—more and more every day. The baby was coming whether she'd planned for it or not. True, the fear still overwhelmed her at times, but in all honesty, she was happy about this little person growing inside her. She'd even had a burst of giddiness this morning when her skirt had been snug.

"You're happy?"

Mia glanced back over to Bronson. "Excuse me?"

He threw her a glance. "You were smiling. You're happy about this."

"The baby, yes. The situation, not really." She smoothed her short cotton skirt over her knees. "I won't lie. The more I think about this baby, the more excited I get. But I do wish I was at a different place in my life. I've always en-visioned myself married before having kids."

He said nothing, and Mia wasn't sure she even wanted to know what he thought. Other than her giving him direc-tions to the doctor's office, nothing else was discussed. Ob-viously, he didn't want things to get too personal, and that was fine with her. If he was going to be a jerk about this, she didn't want to open up her feelings to him. He didn't deserve to be privy to her thoughts.

Once they were in the office, Bronson's tension meter skyrocketed as his shoulders stiffened and his gaze moved around the room. They were immediately shown to a pri-vate waiting area, complete with a closed door. Considering Hollywood's lame attempt to keep things hush-hush, Mia assumed every doctor's office had private waiting areas like this one.

"You okay?" she whispered as she filled out all the doc-uments about her medical history.

"Fine."

Mia let it go and proceeded with the questions. She knew her information, but when it came to the father, she was a bit uncomfortable asking.

"Could you um…" She nudged the clipboard and paper onto his lap and handed him the pen. "I need you to fill this section out."

His eyes darted down, then back up to her. "Can't you leave it blank?"

"If I didn't know who the father was I would. But since you're here, fill it out and pretend this isn't torturous."

She'd seriously had it with his take on the pregnancy. He didn't want to acknowledge the baby was his because he was scared of losing another one. But the least he could do was be supportive of her. Not financially, but some con-versation or even a smile now and then would help.

Lord have mercy, would he ever believe that she wasn't out to sabotage his family? She could only hope time and her actions would prove her innocence.

He grabbed the pen, began reading then checking the appropriate boxes next to family history of illnesses and diseases. Mia stared at the paper, jealous that he actually had a family history that he knew about, had heard stories about. That is what she wanted for her child. That sense of family, a unit.

Mia had only been able to answer the questions strictly on what she had been told about her birth parents. Beyond them, she knew nothing about her family back in Italy. Her mother had been a diabetic, but other than that, she didn't know about any major health issues.

Tracing a finger over the scar on her hand, Mia silently vowed to her unborn baby that there would always be stability, always a place to call home.

"Here." Bronson handed the clipboard back to her. "I'm done."

She took the forms out to the receptionist and within minutes they were called back to the exam room. When the nurse told Mia to change into the gown, her eyes darted to Bronson. He merely lifted a brow as the nurse left the room.

"I'll just change in here." She motioned to the bathroom.

As Mia put on the paper-thin gown, she nearly laughed at how modesty now overtook her. The man had touched, tasted and savored every inch of her body. And he would probably be in the delivery room.

Yeah, modesty definitely had no place here. Her needs were no longer a priority. Her baby trumped everything and everyone.

Mia put on the hospital footies and padded back out to the exam table, holding her gown together with a fisted hand. Bronson's presence filled the room as he sat in the corner in a plastic chair.

"What will they do today?" he asked.

Mia's heart softened a little. She knew he was nervous. He'd lost a baby once before. He may have his doubts about whether or not he was the father, but she could tell he was getting more used to the idea.

"I think they listen for a heartbeat and maybe do an ultrasound to see exactly how far along I am."

"I came to a couple appointments the first time…" He trailed off, looking her in the eye. "Never mind. Let's just focus on now."

Mia wanted to say something, to not let this intimate moment pass her by. For a split second he'd thought of opening up to her, and she realized she wanted that more than she'd thought. She did want a connection to Bronson, other than a physical one, if for no other reason than for the sake of the baby. Could they work backward and attempt at least a friendship? Would he ever feel comfortable enough to not close up when personal issues arose?

The door swung open and Mia smiled at her doctor.

"Good afternoon, Mia," Dr. Bender said. "How are you feeling today?"

Mia nodded. "I'm adjusting to the morning sickness and I know to keep food by my bed and eat before I even think about standing up."

The doctor washed and dried her hands at the sink in the corner. "You should be nearing the end of the queasiness. Not many women have morning sickness through their entire pregnancy."

The entire pregnancy? Mia couldn't even fathom that. She prayed she had the typical first trimester kind and the sickness would end soon.

Dr. Bender moved around the exam table. "Just lie back

here and let's listen for the heartbeat." She eased Mia down and glanced over to Bronson. "You're the father?"

Mia didn't look at him, didn't want to see his denial, but she was even more crushed when he spoke.

"How soon can a DNA test be done?" he asked.

The doctor placed a sheet over Mia's legs, then folded the gown up to expose her belly and squirted some cool gel onto her stomach. She began to move the Doppler around, spreading the sticky gel, obviously not fazed by Bronson's question.

Mia, on the other hand, wanted to cry. How dare he humiliate her like this? Even worse, how could he deny this baby in public? Besides making it sound as if she slept around, he was disrespecting their child.

"That depends," Dr. Bender said. "There is one test called chorionic villus sampling, which can be done between ten and fourteen weeks. The other is called an amniocentesis, which is done between fourteen and twenty weeks. I can go over the procedures and the risks involved if you'd like before you make a decision."

Amid all the static of the Doppler machine and the doctor telling Bronson about the testing, Mia heard it. The rapid thump, thump, thump of her baby's heartbeat.

Her baby. Her eyes darted to Bronson. Their baby.

"Baby's heart rate is right at the norm for eleven weeks." The doctor wiped off the gel from Mia's stomach. "Sounds like you've got a healthy one. Are you experiencing any other symptoms, other than morning sickness?"

"Just some slight cramping," Mia told her. "I get dizzy sometimes."

"You never told me that," Bronson piped up, suddenly more concerned.

Eyes wide, Mia threw him a look. Now was certainly not the time to discuss why she hadn't told him—because he'd barely given her two minutes when he'd called on the phone. Besides, if he'd acted halfway as if he genuinely cared, she would have made the time to open up to him.

"That's fairly normal," the doctor told her, taking a seat on her black stool. "Your uterus is stretching, so that will cause some cramping. Try to rest as much as possible. If a miscarriage happens, it's more than likely going to happen within the first twelve weeks from conception. I don't say that to scare you. I just want you to listen to your body and take good care of yourself."

"I'll see that she does."

Mia fisted her hands at her side. Now he chose to step up? Now he wanted to offer to help? And what did he mean by *he'd see that she takes care of herself?* Did he plan on spending more time with her?

When the rest of the exam was done and she got herself dressed, Mia scheduled an ultrasound for next month and didn't wait for Bronson before she made quick steps back to his car.

She wasn't sure what she was most angry at. His abrupt questioning about the DNA, that he acted like he cared once she'd mentioned her symptoms or that he had the doctor laughing at his witty charm by the end of the appointment.

Damn that man. She just wanted to throttle him for making her so aware that her feelings weren't slacking at all…if anything they were growing stronger.

The man oozed sex appeal, he charmed everyone he came in contact with and he'd starred in nearly all her dreams since they'd left Cannes. One would think, in light of the situation, she'd learned her lesson not to fall for the charm, but unfortunately her mind and her heart were not receiving the same memo.

So now she wasn't only angry with him for his accusations and attitude toward her, she was furious with herself for getting all tied up in knots over a man she'd let work his way into her life. Permanently.

By the time Bronson pulled in front of Mia's cottage, he knew he was not going to get an invite inside. He also knew that wouldn't stop him.

He opened her car door, took her hand to help her out and kept holding it, even when she tugged. He wasn't letting her off the hook that easily.

She'd driven him crazy from the second she'd stepped out of her house. Immediately he'd noticed the change in her body from her fuller breasts to her thicker waist. She'd looked completely simple in layered colorful tanks that hugged her slightly rounded belly and a plain cotton skirt, showcasing those killer legs. Her ensemble was utterly sexy.

Added to that, her protectiveness of the baby, her adamant stance that she wanted a stable life for her child— maybe his child—was just another aspect that made her even more attractive.

Everything about her was sexy, and Bronson wished like hell he could get those thoughts out of his mind.

But how could he when she was very likely carrying his child? How could he deny that he still wanted this woman, whether she was lying or not? And how the hell had he let his emotions slip from his grasp? He seriously had no control as far as Mia was concerned, and that could prove to be catastrophic.

Every time he thought of the baby, he thought back to Cannes, when he'd wanted her and nothing else mattered. He always got what he wanted; there were never consequences. Until now.

Mia unlocked her door and reached in to type in her security code. "Thank you for taking me," she told him, obviously trying to block him from coming in. "I have a lot of work to catch up on after taking a few hours off."

Bronson knew his mother cared more about this baby, which could be a Dane heir, than whatever work she'd put on Mia's schedule.

"I'm coming in."

She eyed him and he waited for the argument. Surprised when she moved from the door, Bronson followed her in.

"In case you missed my not-so-subtle silent treatment, I'm not in the best of moods right now," she told him, heading to the kitchen. "I cannot believe you asked the doctor about a DNA test. I just can't…"

Because she really didn't want him to uncover the truth or had that question really upset her?

Mia had made this kitchen her own with an array of cooking magazines spread open on the counter next to the stove. A very impressive spice rack sat next to an even more impressive knife set.

"You know it has to be done, Mia." He watched as she reached for a handful of M&M's from a glass candy dish on the center island. "The sooner we know, the sooner plans can be made."

She laid out an assortment of colors, moving the green ones to the side. "I do know, Bronson. I know you're the father. I don't care about having a test after the baby is born, if it will ease your mind, but I will not put this baby in jeopardy right now just to satisfy you. The doctor went over the risks. I'm not willing to chance a miscarriage or harm this baby in any way."

"Then we'll have the test as soon as the baby's born," he told her, watching her pick through her candy like a child. "No excuses then."

Intrigued, he watched as she ate all the other colors, but saved the green ones for last. "You don't like green?"

She eyed the candy, then looked up to him. "They're my favorite. I always save the best for last."

He watched her dainty, pink-polished fingertips pick up one green piece at a time and pop it into her mouth. Why did he have this urge to feed them to her? She could very well be playing him. But damn if he wasn't starting to have doubts about that. Emotionally, he couldn't afford to go down this path again.

He tried not to think of her phoning Anthony to discuss how quickly and easily she'd gotten so personal with Bronson's family. But he couldn't dismiss the reality that she could be doing just that. So many emotions—both for and against Mia—and he didn't know where to place them all. Unfortunately, they'd conglomerated into one large ball of anger and frustration. What he needed to do was stay focused on work…the one aspect of his life he had control over lately.

He'd met with his mother this week, and they'd finalized the movie script and budget. Now he had to put the wheels in motion to produce it, and then they could make the grand announcement. The media had their ideas about the secret project he was working on, considering he'd been so private about it, but they hadn't guessed yet.

And he intended for no one to find out until he and his mother were ready. That included the stunning woman standing across from him, possibly carrying his child. His mother had really done some work to keep this project a secret from Mia.

"You're awfully quiet for someone who came in uninvited." She spoke without looking up as she pulled out another handful of candy and proceeded to separate them. "Something on your mind?"

The fact that he still wanted her just as badly as he had in Cannes. Liar or not, this woman turned him on by simply standing there. Hadn't he learned his lesson after the last deceitful beauty?

Bronson knew he needed to keep a closer eye on Mia. If she were out to destroy him, he'd break her. And if not, well, they could at least have some fun along the way.

But that seed of doubt had been planted in his mind once he saw how genuine she was regarding this child. Was she telling the truth? Had this pregnancy been unplanned and was he indeed the father?

Common sense told him no, but his heart was starting to get involved as far as this child was concerned, and he wanted so much to believe her.

Taking a seat at the wrought-iron barstool, he reached for one of her precious green M&M's. "I actually thought we should spend some time together. You are so adamant this baby's mine, so I'd like to know what you expect from me. You've stressed it's not money. What is it?"

Mia's hand froze as she reached for another green piece. "I don't want anything from you, Bronson. Not for me anyway. I want this baby to have a loving father. That's all."

She met his eyes on those final words, and the sincerity he saw nearly put a choke hold on him. Either he was becoming a pushover or she was telling the truth. Time would tell.

"I promise, if this baby is indeed mine, he will know no stronger or deeper love."

That was something Bronson didn't have to think about. This baby would be a Dane and have everything at his disposal. He'd never lack for stability or love.

"What about for yourself, Mia?" Bronson stood, came

around the bar and leaned against the counter right next to her. "What do you want?"

Her hand trembled as she placed the glass lid back on the candy dish. "Nothing. I already told you."

She was crumbling. Now he just had to push a little harder. If she were lying, he'd discover it, and God help her if he didn't like what he found.

With his index finger, he grazed her cheek, her chin, until she turned to look at him. "If this baby's mine, there can't be any lies between us. Starting now. What do you want, Mia?"

"Nothing." Her eyes betrayed her as they darted down to his mouth and back up. "There's nothing I...need."

That statement alone just proved she was a liar. And he didn't know if he was pushing her to torment her or himself, but he had a feeling they were both equally uncomfortable right now.

Which was all the more reason for him to take charge.

Bronson couldn't stop his lips from claiming hers any more than he could stop the arousal that punched him whenever he so much as thought of her.

He hadn't gotten to where he was in life by riding on the coattails of his name. Nor had he gotten there by being weak.

But Mia was working her way into his life, causing a weakness he couldn't afford.

Literally.

Nine

Mia had wanted to feel those lips on hers again but never thought she would. So she'd lied when she said she didn't want anything. She couldn't very well tell Bronson she wanted him again, could she? He was so skeptical of her, and if she wanted that family she'd dreamed of, she'd have to take it slow and make him see she was the real deal.

As Bronson's hands slid up to cup the sides of her face, Mia realized that's exactly what she wanted. She wanted to see where this attraction would lead. He couldn't very well deny that he was physically attracted to her…she could feel the evidence.

Mia wrapped her arms around his neck and gave in to the kiss as Bronson changed the angle. She arched her back, pressing her sensitive breasts against his solid chest.

What had happened to make him turn from being so irritated at her to devouring her in her kitchen?

Mia eased back. "What was that for?"

Dark eyes filled with desire stared back at her. "You may not need anything, Mia, but I do. I've tried to keep my hands off you. I've tried to keep my distance because I didn't want to complicate anything with this pregnancy, but I can't."

Really? Was this a game or was he sincere?

"But you don't believe me."

Bronson rested his forehead against hers and sighed. "I want to, God do I want to. I want this baby to be a Dane."

Mia's heart clenched at the battle he waged within himself. And he'd admitted his fears aloud—that shocked her. His frustrated tone and moment of vulnerability revealed more about his state of mind than he'd probably intended.

She reached up, grasping his biceps. "Then let yourself believe and I swear to you, you won't get hurt."

At least not about this. About Anthony being his biological brother...that wasn't her secret to tell, and she could only pray her loyalty and vow of silence didn't blow up in her face.

Bronson stepped back, shoving his hands in his pockets. The muscle ticked in his jaw as he glanced out the French doors to the hot-tub area. "All I can offer is a physical relationship, Mia. I have nothing else to give a woman at this stage in my life. I promise if this child's mine, I'll love it beyond measure. But if you're under the impression that you and I can forge a relationship—much less a marriage—we can't."

She hadn't been under that impression. Of course, that didn't stop her from hoping and dreaming for a family of her own. But she wouldn't push—that's not how she wanted to obtain her family. She would hold out for love.

So while spending more time with Bronson might exact a toll on her emotionally, she was willing to take the chance because she believed there was so much more than physicality to explore between them.

"I just want us to get along for the sake of the baby," she told him. "If anything happens between us, physical or otherwise, we'll deal with that when the time comes. For right now, this baby is my main concern. Not your needs and not mine."

Bronson's eyes came back to her. "You're going to be a great mother."

Mia's throat tightened, and her belly fluttered. She was going to be a mother. What she wouldn't give to be able to go to her own for advice right now.

She could get through this on her own. She had no choice. Although she had a feeling that getting her heart involved with Bronson was going to lead to a bigger heartache than she could ever imagine.

After three weeks of life getting back to normal, Mia thanked God every day that her morning sickness didn't rear its ugly head. Nausea occasionally followed her around like an unwanted friend, but other than that, she felt fine. Bronson had called and stopped by, but nothing intimate had even come close to transpiring again, and her hormones were screaming for one more touch.

Just as Mia was turning off her computer for the day, Olivia stepped into her office. "Do you have a minute or do you need to go?" she asked.

"I'm in no hurry. I'm just going home to try a new recipe I saw in a magazine." Mia sat back down in her chair. "Something wrong?"

"Not at all. I want to commend you for how well you're handling this pregnancy, considering my son's doubts."

Mia really didn't want to get into what she and Bronson discussed. Working with the grandmother of her child while wanting Bronson more in her life could get a bit awkward.

"I'm not trying to pry," Olivia said, as if reading her thoughts. "But I do want to offer some money to help with the baby's furniture, clothes, whatever you want to buy."

Mia came to her feet. "Oh, no. I'm not taking any money, Olivia. What you pay me is more than enough, and I've been setting some aside in my savings for anything this baby may need."

"I didn't think you'd take it, but I had to offer."

"No, you didn't. I will be just fine and so will the baby, no matter what Bronson decides."

Olivia crossed her arms over her bright orange silk tunic. "Well, I don't care what my son or you say, I will be spoiling my grandchild, so you tell me when you decide on furniture or a nursery theme. I have a wonderful designer, if you're interested."

Mia laughed. "I hadn't even thought that far ahead yet."

"Oh, yes, you have."

"Okay, maybe I have," Mia conceded. "But not much. I want to find out the sex of the baby before I decide on the colors. And I'd really like to do everything myself."

Olivia shook her head. "Stubborn and independent. My son has his work cut out for him. At least say you'll hire someone to paint. You don't need to be smelling those fumes."

How could anyone not love this woman? She was so caring, so take-charge, so motherly.

"I promise."

Olivia moved around the side of the desk and came within a foot of Mia. "I have to tell you this because I'm a mother and because I love my son and have come to care about you like family. Don't let Bronson's attitude deter you if you want him in your life."

"Pardon?" Olivia wasn't really going to attempt her hand at cupid's bow, was she?

Olivia laid a gold-ringed hand on Mia's arm. "This baby has scared him more than he'll ever admit. The last time... it didn't end well. There are things you don't know, and it's his place to tell you if he chooses. I just don't want you to think everything is as it seems with him."

"I won't pry into his past, Olivia." Mia smiled, touched that this Hollywood icon valued her family more than any-thing else. "Right now we are getting along for the sake of the baby. What I want, what he wants, doesn't matter."

Olivia cupped Mia's cheek. "Oh, my darling, you're so wrong. You're a unit whether you like it or not. Everyone's happiness counts. Don't shove your own desires aside, es-pecially now when you need people in your life."

Mia knew she needed people. She'd never wanted to need anyone, but she had to think realistically and see that she was out of her league here. She would need help and guidance with this child.

"I'll let you know about that painter," Mia said, hugging Olivia.

Mia left her office and walked out through Olivia's as she always did. The summer evening breeze wasn't quite so stifling tonight, and Mia lifted her face to the sky, feel-ing confident she was heading in the right direction with her life.

For now there was no turmoil, or not as much as there had been, and that suited Mia just fine. She hated drama—ironic since she loved working in Hollywood.

As she walked along the wide concrete path back to her house, she resisted the urge to call Anthony. She wanted to share her good news with him because they were friends, but she didn't want to add any more issues to his home life.

She also wished she could talk to him about broaching

the delicate subject with Olivia. The guilt she carried was pointless since she couldn't say anything. How she wished she could go back to that day in Anthony's office and *not* open that file he'd had on his desk. Why did she have to uncover a secret that had been buried for decades?

"Good evening."

Mia squealed, jumping back with a hand to her heart. "Bronson! You scared me to death."

If she hadn't been so lost in thought, she would've noticed him sitting on her porch looking sexy as ever. Of course, he'd show up out of the blue. That's what he did. Oh, he called every morning, but with his crazy work schedule, which changed from day to day, she never knew when he'd make a surprise visit.

"I didn't mean to scare you." He came to his feet and took her hand as she ascended the steps. "Were you lost in thought?"

Yeah, thinking about your brother.

"Something like that," she told him as she fished out her key from her bag. "How long have you been waiting?"

"Just a few minutes."

She led him inside, turned off the alarm and set her purse and keys on the foyer table. "I was just going to fix dinner. You hungry?"

A slow, cautious, sexy smile spread across his face. "Starving. I'd help, but the cook always kicked me out when I was a kid. So maybe I'll just observe."

Mia laughed as she toed off her heels and headed toward the kitchen. "I can turn on the TV if you'd like to watch something."

She moved toward the flat screen on the wall between the breakfast nook and the kitchen.

"No, I'd rather have conversation or silence. My brain is on overload right now."

Mia didn't question what was wrong. He didn't want to do personal and she could live with that...for now. But he was here, wanted to stay for dinner. Something drew him to her and she wasn't going to question it.

She pulled one of her cooking magazines from her stack beside the fridge and turned to the earmarked page. As she bustled around the kitchen pulling out ingredients and double-checking the list, she was hyperaware of his presence. He didn't say a word, but the shuffling of his rolling up the sleeves of his white dress shirt and the smell of his masculine aroma filled her kitchen.

"Feeling okay today?" he asked as she preheated the oven.

"I'm fine. I can't wait until the ultrasound." Mia pulled out a mixing bowl and stared across the island at Bronson. "I just want to see her."

"Her?" he asked, raising a brow.

Mia laughed. "I go back and forth using her or him. I don't care what we have."

Bronson's shoulders tensed.

"Sorry." Mia cringed as she turned to get a pan. "I didn't mean to make you uncomfortable."

Silence settled in once again as she mixed and poured everything into the baking stone. Once she had the dish in the oven, she wiped her hands on a towel and turned to Bronson.

"That has to bake for about an hour. Do you want some wine or a drink?"

"No, I'm good."

Mia couldn't take it another minute. She just had to uncover the truth Olivia spoke of.

"I know it's not my place to pry, but I need to know about your ex-fiancée and the baby."

Bronson's eyes turned dark as he jerked his gaze to hers. "No, you don't. There's nothing that concerns you."

Mia wet a rag and wiped off the counter. She needed a prop for her nervous hands. "Actually, it does involve me, considering you're hesitant about everything because of your past. Your ex-fiancée is always in the room with us, whether you realize it or not."

"Leave it alone, Mia."

For once she was not going to back down. "You know all about my life. You know why this baby means so much to me. I want to know why this baby scares you to the point that you can't even discuss it without tensing up."

Bronson came to his feet, running a hand through his stylishly messy hair. "I don't know why you think now is the time to rehash all this."

"I've been wondering for a while, Bronson, and today your mother—"

He jerked around. "My mother? You've got to be kidding. Did she tell you I loved that child, that his name was chosen and that I could hardly work for all the anticipation surrounding my upcoming marriage and baby?"

Mia tossed the rag into the sink. "She just said that—"

"What?" He threw his arms out to the side. "She said what? That my ex-fiancée was sleeping around behind my back and the baby wasn't mine? Oh, and did she tell you how I believed the baby belonged to Anthony?"

Breath caught in Mia's throat. Anthony the father? That couldn't be. He loved his wife more than anything and was fighting to save his marriage.

She placed her palms on the island and stared into his tormented eyes. "Oh, God, Bronson. I had no idea."

"No, but you had to push and push until I gave in. Well, congratulations. Now you know my secret." He muttered a curse. "I don't know how that wasn't leaked to the media.

They all assumed we split over her losing the baby, that the stress was too much."

Mia remembered reading that, hearing those rumors. Now she understood why this DNA test was so important... especially considering the rumors about *her* and Anthony and after he'd seen them talking in Cannes.

"That's why you don't believe me," she whispered. "All of that in your past, added to my history with Anthony, has stacked the deck against me and instantly put you on guard. In Cannes, even, you probably thought I was working for the enemy. You slept with me with all these hateful thoughts in your head. I swear, Bronson, I never even entertained thoughts of sleeping with Anthony."

Mia turned, holding a hand over her slightly rounded stomach. She didn't want any of this ugliness to touch her baby.

"Maybe dinner was a bad idea." She kept her gaze down, her body facing away from him. She couldn't look him in the eye right now. Not when she knew so much hurt was swimming in hers. "I honestly didn't meant to hurt you, to make you relive that nightmare. But I can't be around someone who believes everything I say is a lie."

Bronson's hands came up to her shoulders. "Dinner isn't a bad idea at all. I want to spend time with you, Mia. I didn't mean to yell at you. I just wanted you to see where I'm coming from."

Mia allowed those strong hands to turn her around, and she studied those eyes that showed so much emotion. It was probably a good thing he was on the other side of the camera. No way could he ever hide his true thoughts.

"I see a lot of pain," she told him, smoothing the line between his brows. "I see a man who wants to hope and is afraid to. If you'll look back at me, really look, you'll see we aren't so different."

And then she did something she'd been dying to do—
even with the accusations, the lies, the uncertainty.

Taking control of the situation, she rose on her bare toes
and kissed him.

Ten

He was toast.

Bronson knew when he'd been waiting on her porch that if she so much as hinted that she wanted physical contact, he'd be all over her. He'd been wanting her for weeks. Not just a kiss, either.

And her pressing her lips, her body, against his was much more than a hint—it couldn't get more obvious than that.

Bronson wrapped his arms around her waist and picked her up, holding her body against his. She'd read into his feelings, his emotions too well, and that scared the hell out of him. He didn't want to be under her scope—he didn't want pity.

He wanted to know if she was trying to trap and destroy him.

But most of all he wanted to know what she wore beneath her simple black skirt and sleeveless pink top.

Mia framed his face with her palms and moaned as his mouth traveled from her lips down her neck. She arched into him, sending all kinds of jolts throughout his body.

"Bronson, we—"

"Need fewer clothes."

He hated the loss of control he had as far as she was concerned. Hated that she had the power to ruin him.

But right now, Mia's breathy sighs and pants in his ear clearly overrode common sense.

"Dinner…"

He nipped at her lips. "Still has a while and I need you now."

Mia's eyes widened, then softened as a smile spread across her face. "I didn't think you liked me."

Bronson palmed her breasts through her silk top. "I like you, Mia. I still can't trust that you're telling me the whole truth, but right now, I don't give a damn."

She started to protest when his mouth settled over hers. He didn't want to hear excuses or reasons they should not be together. He knew them already and chose to ignore them.

He slid his hands around to the waist of her skirt and moved the zipper down. She wiggled those mesmerizing hips until the unwanted garment fell to the floor with a whoosh. She pulled the silk top over her head and tossed it toward the breakfast area, leaving her in a sexy, pink, lacey bra-and-panty set. Her rounded belly wasn't the only sign of pregnancy. Her breasts nearly spilled over the top of the lace.

"You destroy me," he muttered before pulling her body back against his. "Utterly destroy me."

He devoured her mouth as her hands made quick work of his belt and pants. He kicked off his shoes and stepped out of his pants, then lifted her onto the kitchen island and stepped between her legs.

"Just to be clear, I'm going to have you again tonight on a bed."

Mia smiled, tracing his lips with her fingertip. "Count on it."

He pulled her bra cups aside and slid his hands over her bare breasts, pleased when she moaned and arched into his touch. Wrapping one arm around her waist, he pulled her against the edge of the counter.

"Do we need a…" She trailed off, her eyes questioning.

"It's a little late for that," he told her. "Besides, I've always used one and I just had a routine physical. I'm clean."

"Me, too. I had complete bloodwork for my prenatal appointment."

He smiled, easing into her. "That settles it then."

Mia's arms came around his neck as her hips tilted against his. This woman was becoming a drug in his system that he couldn't get enough of. Those little moans, the sighs and the way she fit against him only proved to him how much she wanted this. She wasn't immune to their sexual chemistry.

He slid into her slowly, wanting this to last, knowing it wouldn't. He'd desired her, ached for her since Cannes. Wondered if he'd imagined how good they were together.

He hadn't. No, those dreams he'd had every night since were spot-on.

Bronson shoved aside all thoughts, focusing on the woman writhing in his arms, whispering his name. In no time she shuddered against him, sending him into his own tailspin. He held on to her until they both stopped shaking and silently vowed to make this better later in that promised bed.

As he eased back, he couldn't help but wonder how this would affect their...what? Relationship? They didn't really have a relationship. They'd supposedly made a child, but what should he call what they had?

Regardless of what this arrangement was called, he knew he wanted Mia again and he had no intention of leaving her house tonight. And the deeper he became involved with her, the more he wanted to trust every word that came out of her mouth.

Mia poured an after-dinner drink for Bronson and moved into the living room where he'd settled and was flipping through to find a movie, his gloriously tanned broad shoulders and bare chest on display for her to appreciate.

"Really?" she asked, setting his drink on the glass side table. "A movie?"

He eyed her. "We can start one, but if you try seducing me, I reserve the right to turn it off."

Was he actually going to stay? Did he want to play house? Mia was so confused by his actions because they contradicted his words. She didn't want to play games, didn't want to wait around until he decided where they stood. She just didn't have the emotional stamina for it.

"We need to talk," she told him, sitting down beside him. "I'm all for what happened before dinner, but I have to be honest—I'm not looking for a fling, Bronson. I think there could be something between us if we could just be honest with each other and not keep this so shallow."

His hand froze on the remote before he laid it down on the table. "I've told you I can't offer more to a woman, Mia. I just can't. You know why."

"I know what happened in your past," she retorted. "Let

go of it and move on. Let those wounds stay covered and stop reopening them."

He turned his head and sighed. "Mia, I'm not looking for happily-ever-after. I used to, but that's gone. Now I'm focused on work, and I have more than one project going. What I have to offer is minimal."

Meaning sex. Mia placed a hand on his arm. She knew he was softening—she'd seen it in the doctor's office when he'd heard their baby's heartbeat. She also knew their chemistry was amazing. So many elements to make for a wonderful family if he would just open his eyes to the possibility.

Patience. She had to learn patience if she wanted to forge a family with Bronson. And if the compatibility wasn't there, then she'd let it go. But she had to try. Her heart had already gotten entangled with him.

Mia started unbuttoning Bronson's dress shirt, which she'd thrown on before dinner. One by one his eyes traveled the path of her fingers.

"Then I'll take what you have to offer," she told him, shrugging out of the oversized shirt. "But I won't stop trying to make you happy and to show you how good we could be together."

She came to her feet, allowing the garment to slide down her arms and puddle on the floor. With a quirk of her brow, she walked from the room, knowing he'd follow.

She wanted him in her bed. She wanted to pull him just a bit deeper into her personal space. Little by little, she wanted him to realize that she meant business. Seduction came in all forms and Mia planned on using them all to get her man.

The couch rustled and she didn't have to turn to know he was only steps behind. She padded down the hall into her master bedroom. The evening sun glistened in her high windows, casting a pale glow onto her bed.

By the time she'd removed her mound of silk throw pillows and turned, Bronson stood in the doorway, gloriously naked. Mia extended her hand, inviting him to join her.

He closed the space between them, taking her hand in his. And as they came together, Mia knew in her heart this is where she was meant to be, where they were meant to be.

Bronson kissed her with so much passion, so much hunger, Mia nearly wept with anticipation. There was no way this man could be so giving and caring and only have physical feelings for her. She refused to believe it.

Grasping his broad shoulders, Mia eased down onto the bed, pulling him with her. She sank into the duvet, reveling in the delight of his weight on top of her.

He pulled up as if to move. "The baby?"

"Is fine," she assured him. "You're not hurting either one of us. I like you here."

Gently, he eased back down, trailing kisses over her face, her neck, her collarbone. Mia slid her hands up and down his muscular back as she lifted her knees.

In one smooth, toe-curling move they were one. Mia held tight to this man she was coming to care about more and more. She knew it wasn't a stretch to say she was falling in love with him.

Perhaps that was just the baby situation talking, but she didn't think so. He was caring, though cautious. He was loyal to everyone in his life and expected the same in return.

She'd tried to steel herself from falling for Bronson. Good Lord, considering his past, she didn't blame him for having trust issues. But that vulnerability beneath his alpha exterior had her melting, and she could see, could feel, that he was coming around. If he truly didn't believe her, he wouldn't be with her so much. And if she didn't think he had feelings for her—beyond sexual feelings—she wouldn't let him sleep with her.

Mia would prove, beyond a shadow of a doubt, that she wasn't lying about her feelings for him or about the baby.

But as pleasure consumed her, a niggling thought invaded her mind. She was lying, and that lie did involve Anthony.

Bronson took Mia's hand as he led her into the doctor's office for the ultrasound. The test was delayed for a week because the ultrasound tech had been ill, which irked Bronson, but here they were and Mia was fifteen weeks pregnant. He'd seen the little stars on her calendar hanging by the fridge. Every Thursday had a star with a number. He knew Mia was excited about the baby. And he hated to be pessimistic, but he had to rein in his own excitement until he knew for sure where he stood.

A part of him screamed that she was not lying, would never lie to him. But another part kept butting in and reminding him of the last woman who claimed to be carrying his child. Why couldn't he separate the two in his mind?

They took a seat in the private waiting room until it was their turn, which wasn't very long. As they went into the ultrasound room, Bronson helped Mia step up onto the table.

"Good afternoon," the tech said, coming in right behind them. "Feeling okay, Mia?"

Mia nodded. "Morning sickness has been gone for about a month, and I've never felt better."

The tech smiled as she laid Mia back and pulled her shirt up to her bra. "You're into your second trimester. Most women have a huge burst of energy during this time. No cramping or anything?"

"Not anymore."

Bronson stood beside the table, and when the tech put the scope on Mia's stomach and pointed to the screen, his heart literally constricted. He grabbed Mia's hand as he looked at the small, beating heart.

"I'll take some measurements to be sure of the due date, but it looks like your baby has a nice, strong heartbeat."

Bronson looked down to Mia, who was staring at the screen with watery eyes. "That's so amazing," she whispered.

The tech tapped a few buttons, moved the scope and tapped some more. "You're exactly fifteen weeks and one day. Looks like your due date is Valentine's Day."

Good Lord, that seemed so far away. This was just the start of September.

"A Valentine's baby?" Mia asked. "How appropriate, since I love her so much already."

The tech laughed. "We can schedule your next appointment for one month out and at that time we'll see if we can determine the sex of the baby. Assuming you want to know."

Mia looked to Bronson. "I'd like to. Would you?"

The sex? That would make this child all the more real to him, but as he glanced up at that little beating heart, he knew he was already sucked in. This baby was real and, he hoped, his.

"I'd like that," he said.

Mia's smile spread across her face. Between seeing this child and spending so much time with Mia lately, he was starting to fall into a role he wasn't sure he was ready for. And he was beginning to see Mia as the honest woman his mother had always claimed she was.

The tech wiped off the gel she'd put on Mia's slightly

rounded belly. "The receptionist will make that appointment on your way out."

Once they made the appointment and left, Bronson settled Mia in the car.

"Would you like to go out for a late lunch?" he asked.

"I'd love to, but I've got so much I need to do. Can you just drop me off at the main house?" she asked.

Disappointment speared through him, not something he expected. "Sure."

Mia stared down at the glossy black-and-white pictures the tech had given them. "I don't know that I'll get much done today. I may just have to look at our baby."

Our baby. He was getting used to those words.

"If you show those to my mother, I guarantee nobody will be working."

"I wasn't sure you'd want me to show them."

Bronson spared her a glance, hating how he always saw uncertainty in her eyes. "She knows we went."

He didn't want to admit that his mother had no doubts about this child's paternity. How could the woman be so sure? Granted Mia never gave him reason to doubt her. But in his mind the black mark against her was her relationship—whatever it may be—with Anthony Price.

"It's okay, Bronson. I don't mind keeping these to myself. I understand that you don't want her to get attached yet."

Mia's words sent an ache through him. He knew she wanted to share her excitement. After all, she really had no one else in her life.

And that right there was all the more reason for her to try to trap him into a family.

Dammit, he wished he weren't so cynical, but he had to be careful. He hated the thought of more scandal coming to his family.

Eleven

Déjà vu?

Bronson slammed the paper down onto the dark wood tabletop. He'd come to Saturday brunch at his mother's and had been greeted with today's "news"—a picture of him and Mia coming out the back door of the doctor's office. As if the image of Mia, a hand protectively on her belly, with him at her side weren't telling enough, the damning article went on to talk about "Dane's second chance at a family" and Mia "bed hopping from one Hollywood hot-shot to another."

This was the only drawback to his career. He couldn't even have a private life. Of course, after Mia's rumored affair with Anthony, she was great fodder for the media, as well.

"I'm sorry, Bronson."

Bronson turned from his cushioned chair to see Victoria standing next to him. As always, she appeared the picture of chic with her wraparound, sleeveless navy dress, gold jewelry and perfectly coiffed blond hair held back by her sunglasses.

Her eyes darted back down to the paper. "I just saw that earlier and tried to reach you, but my call went to your voice mail."

"Don't be sorry, Tori." Bronson came to his feet, placing a peck on his sister's cheek. "It's not your fault the media sniffed out this story. It was bound to happen. I just hope they leave Mia alone."

Victoria took a seat next to him and smiled. "I knew you cared for her."

"Yes," he said cautiously, because Victoria always had love on the brain. "I care. We're not planning a wedding or even playing house together. But I do care."

A little more than he was comfortable with.

Victoria waved a hand in the air. "I know you like to keep your feelings to yourself, so I won't say I told you so when you propose."

"Propose?"

Bronson groaned as he turned to see his mother only a few feet away. "No. There's no engagement. Tori's just fantasizing. Again."

Olivia kissed both her children on the cheek before taking a seat at the patio table under the bright California sun, shielded by a vibrant orange umbrella.

"Well, I for one would be all for bringing Mia into the family," Olivia declared. "She's a wonderful woman."

This was not what he was in the mood for today. He'd already lost sleep the past several nights over conflicting feelings for Mia. He needed to work this out on his own without his mother or sister influencing him. For pity's sake, he was a grown man who produced multimillion-dollar blockbusters. Surely he could decide how to handle a petite, Italian beauty who had his stomach in knots.

"I've drawn up a budget for the film," he told his mother, stopping midthought when the waitstaff approached because only three people knew about this project and they were all sitting at this table.

"Not a subtle change of subject, but a necessary topic." Olivia smiled up at the waitstaff as the two ladies brought out carts complete with soufflés, fresh fruit, breads and juice. Once they were out of earshot, she spoke again. "Have you chosen a director?"

"I've got two in mind." He took his napkin and placed it in his lap. "I'd like to discuss that with you."

"Allow me to throw my choice in." Olivia leveled her gaze at Bronson. "Anthony Price."

Victoria's audible intake of breath could barely be heard over the ringing in his ears. He set his cup of juice on the table, wishing for something a little stronger in his glass if this was the way his day was going to go. First the newspaper and now this preposterous request from his mother? She couldn't be serious.

"Hear me out," Olivia said, sitting straight up in her seat. "I have something important to tell you both, something that no one knows, and I'd prefer it stay that way."

Every nerve ending in his body prickled as he glanced at Victoria, who seemed to be just as nervous about this impending declaration as he was.

"I've had some tests that have come back unsatisfactory, according to my doctor." She looked from Victoria to Bronson. "I don't expect this to be anything more than a nuisance, but I am having further testing to rule everything out."

"What tests? What symptoms are you having?" Victoria asked.

"You've gotten a second opinion, right?" Bronson asked at the same time.

That genuine smile that had won her Oscars and worked its way into the hearts of millions spread across her face. But Bronson didn't care about the audiences who'd come to love her. This was his mother, and if her health was in jeopardy, he wanted her healed. Now.

"This is why I didn't want you two to know," she told them. "I don't want you to worry, and I don't want you to look at me the way you are now. I assure you, I feel fine, and I'm convinced this next round of tests will prove the others wrong.

"I've been having some slight chest pain, and I just attribute it to stress. My stress test came back a bit off, and the doctor wants to go in a take a look."

"When?" he asked.

"Monday."

Bronson tried to grasp that his mother wasn't invincible, as he'd thought. He'd been so self-absorbed lately, he'd ignored his mother and sister, trying to get his own life under control. Fear squeezed his chest as he stared at the woman who'd been his rock and source of strength for so long.

Which is why he had a hard time trying to comprehend what this had to do with Anthony Price.

"I'll clear my schedule," Victoria told her. "But what does Anthony have to do with any of this?"

Something flickered in Olivia's eyes, something he couldn't identify, which both worried and irritated him. She was hiding something.

"This medical nuisance has had me thinking." She looked Bronson dead in the eye. "You're the best producer in the business. No question. You cannot deny that Anthony is the best director. I want the best for the film we've written loosely based on my life, and I want you and Anthony to bury this animosity long enough to make this the best film ever."

Fury burned through him. "Why are you so insistent? There's more to this than your medical scare."

Olivia reached for the butter and began to layer a very minimal amount onto her freshly baked banana bread. "This will be my last film, Bronson, and this is what I want."

"Mother," Victoria piped in. "You're not retiring. Don't even suggest this is the last film you'll do."

"Darling, as much as I love to be in front of the camera, it's time for me to call it quits. I want to go out on top, and what better way than with my own story?"

Bronson stared down at the newspaper with the headline that continued to mock him.

He'd certainly had better days.

"You know why I hate Anthony. Asking him to work on this film is unacceptable." Bronson came to his feet. "We'll discuss directors after your appointment Monday, once we see what the doctors say. Until then, this topic is closed." He turned to Victoria. "See you later, Tori."

Walking away, Bronson didn't know where to go from here. He needed to calm down from his mother's request, he needed to grasp that his mother may have a heart problem and there wasn't a damn thing he could do about it.

But first things first. He needed to go see Mia and talk to her about that damning picture on the front page of the newspaper.

Mia couldn't believe the headline. She hadn't heard from Bronson, but she knew he'd be up having brunch with his mother and sister. She'd so hoped this pregnancy wouldn't get out until they were ready. The last thing she wanted was to cause more heartache for Bronson or to have the progress she'd made in getting him to open up encounter a setback.

She had a feeling he'd be dropping by after his brunch with his family. What she didn't have a clue about was the mood he'd be in when he arrived.

Rubbing the swell of her baby bump, Mia tried to relax by the pool. She'd donned her black string bikini, not caring that her waistline was expanding more quickly than she'd expected. Her cell sent out a shrill ring, jarring her from her thoughts. Why hadn't she left that thing inside?

Her fingers felt along the chaise until she found the phone tucked by her thigh. "Hello?"

"Tell me this isn't true."

Mia sat up, sliding her sunglasses onto the top of her head as Anthony's low voice interrupted her thoughts. "You saw the paper."

"You're not carrying Bronson's baby, Mia. Tell me you're not."

"I can't do that."

"You two have gotten close," Anthony said. "Obviously closer than I thought you would. You didn't…"

Mia came to her feet. "I didn't tell him, Anthony. I told you I wouldn't."

His frustrated sigh resounded through the phone. "How did you get entangled with him at all? I warned you, Mia. You knew what a ladies' man he was."

She tried to block that from her mind, especially since she was falling in love with that "ladies' man."

"I can't stop my feelings, Anthony. You of all people know that."

He let out a bitter laugh. "I'm not talking about my rocky marriage. I'm worried that you're getting in over your head here."

Touched, Mia turned toward the beckoning, clear water

of her pool. "I assure you, I've got everything under control."

"So when are you due?"

"Valentine's Day."

"Really? That seems so far away."

Mia glanced at her belly. "I have a feeling it'll be here before we know it."

"You sound happy."

She couldn't help the smile as she clutched her cell. "I really am. I'm not sure where we're going, but I'm happy and for now that's enough."

"Just don't sell yourself short."

Mia pulled her sunglasses back down to block the bright rays. "When will you talk to Olivia?"

The pause of silence didn't surprise her. She knew this was more than likely all he thought about. Well, that and how to keep his marriage intact.

"Anthony?" she urged. "You have to talk to her. I know this is your place to tell her, but I've gotten in deeper with this family. It's way beyond employer/employee, and it's putting a strain on me that I can't afford."

"I'd already decided to call her. Charlotte will be gone next week with some friends at our Tahoe home, so I'm going to call Olivia and set up a time to chat."

"You tell me when and I'll make sure her schedule is clear that day," Mia assured him. "I know it will be hard, but I really think it's for the best."

"I know it is. I just don't know what to say."

Mia sighed, not envying his position—or Olivia's, for that matter. "I'm sure once you tell her you know, she'll do all the talking."

Anthony talked for another few minutes while Mia listened. She knew he had no one else to talk to about this because he hadn't even told his wife. He'd claimed he didn't want to add any more of a strain on Charlotte and their marriage. She was already so sick of all the Hollywood hype. How would she react when he told her he was the biological son of Hollywood's Grand Dane?

Once she hung up with Anthony, she felt a bit more confident now that he'd assured her he was going to confront Olivia. She prayed the outcome wouldn't cause an explosion. She prayed even harder that Bronson would try to see a new side to Anthony and not hate her for keeping the secret.

Mia set her sunglasses and cell on the chaise and dove into the refreshing water. She loved relaxing by the pool and didn't feel the least bit guilty for spending her day doing absolutely nothing. A girl deserved a little "me time" every now and then. And with all she had on her plate right now, she most certainly deserved it.

The cool water calmed her as she swam a few laps. The doctor had told her she should continue any forms of exercise she normally did and not worry about too many activities.

"Too bad I don't have my trunks."

Mia jerked to a stop in the pool, sending the water rippling around her. "Bronson. I thought you were at brunch."

The tension practically radiated off his stiff shoulders, the muscle ticking in his jaw and the clenched fists in the pockets of his designer jeans.

"I was," he told her. "But this looks like much more fun."

Okay, so he didn't want to discuss what was wrong. She could take the hint, but that didn't mean she'd let it go for good or that his lack of openness didn't hurt her feelings. She longed for the day when he could talk to her without feeling as if she was going to double-cross him.

"You don't need a suit to get into my pool," she told him,

reaching behind her neck to undo the strings. "I'm game if you are, Mr. Dane."

A wicked smile spread across his lips. "I never was one to give in to peer pressure."

She flung her top, hitting him square in the chest with a sloppy, wet smack. "But you will now."

"I always said I'm willing to try anything."

And within seconds he joined her in the pool wearing only a tan and a smile.

Bronson drove home, top down on his sporty Mercedes, and reflected on the bits and pieces he'd overheard of Mia's conversation with Anthony. Obviously, this was Anthony's first inkling about the pregnancy.

A sharp pain had stuck in his chest when he'd come upon Mia's patio and overheard her telling Anthony something about keeping her word and clearing a schedule—Bronson assumed that meant his mother's schedule.

Did this have something to do with the film he and his mother were working on? Surely Mia and Anthony didn't know about that.

So what else would Mia need to clear Olivia's schedule for? And what the hell did Anthony have to discuss with his mother? Had she already told him about the film?

Something was going on, and Bronson had a sickening feeling that whatever it was, he wasn't going to like it.

Now more than ever, he intended to keep Mia close. Every part of him wanted to believe her. In fact, he had started to, but how could he be so certain after overhearing that conversation?

He had to get her away from here. They needed some one-on-one time where he could tap into those honest feelings of hers and see just where they stood on the loyalty platform. He wanted to build from there, but he could go no further until he knew why she was having private conversations with his enemy.

But first he'd have to lay himself on the line and hope he didn't get burned again.

Twelve

Monday morning Mia knew something was up. Olivia, Bronson and Victoria all said they'd be unreachable for the next few hours. Well, Bronson told Mia she could call in an emergency, but other than that, the three were out of commission for the day.

What was going on? Had Anthony decided to talk to Olivia early and now they were all in a family meeting?

Mia didn't know, and honestly, she didn't want to know. She just wanted to do her work and try to remain stress-free so she could have the healthiest, happiest baby ever.

And just like every other time she thought of the baby, she began to daydream. As always she chose the best features of Bronson and her. Not just physical, but character traits, too.

She hoped the baby had her Italian skin tone and dark hair with Bronson's blue eyes. She hoped their child had strength and determination from both of them. The classy, regal style of Olivia and the romantic and creative side of Victoria.

Mia's desk phone rang, and she pulled herself from the fantasy and remembered she was at work. Alone, but still at work.

"Hello."

"How fast can you pack?"

Mia smiled at Bronson's low, sexy tone. "Pack for what?"

"A trip. Five days and the destination is a secret. I have clothes at your service. All you need is essentials."

Was he for real? Who did this ever happen to?

"Well, I'm working today and for the next several days. And I thought you were not available to take calls right now."

Bronson laughed. "Our plans finished sooner and better than we'd hoped. I'll fill you in on the plane. I've already gotten you a hall pass from your demanding employer, so when can you leave?"

If he was that anxious to get her somewhere, hopefully alone, then she could be ready five minutes ago.

"I'll be ready in thirty minutes," she told him.

"I'll send my driver and meet you at the airport."

And with that he hung up.

Mia stared at the handset for a second before she burst out laughing. Sometimes that man just amazed her. A surprise trip complete with wardrobe? Did he even know what size her swelling body wore?

If her waistline continued to grow the way it was, she'd be going to Omar the tent maker to get her fall and winter wardrobe.

Mia saved the spreadsheet she was working on and shut off her computer. She couldn't get to her cottage fast enough to pack.

By the time she'd pulled her suitcase out and thrown in necessities—and sexy lingerie was the first necessity—she still had ten minutes to spare. She double-checked everything, including her passport, just in case, as the driver pulled up and took her bags.

Giddiness swept through her on the ride to the airport. Were they going on a cruise? Maybe a trip to Aruba? Oh, she hated waiting. Did the man not know how rude dangling the proverbial carrot was? Patience had never been her strong suit.

Okay, so that was a trait she didn't want to pass down to the baby.

At nearly five months along, Mia couldn't wait for the next few weeks to fly by so she could find out the sex of the baby. Back to that waiting game again.

The driver pulled into the private section of the airport and there was Bronson standing next to his jet, talking with a man she assumed was the pilot. A thrill of anticipation shot through her. Spending time alone with Bronson anywhere on earth would be fine with her, but the thought that he'd gone to the trouble to keep a surprise really threw her for a loop. Did she dare hope he was falling for her and not just feeling obligated to spend time with her for the baby's sake?

Bronson opened her door as the driver got her bags and passed them on to the pilot.

"Glad you're quick," he told her, kissing her cheek. "You ready?"

She smiled. "For you to tell me where we're going, yes."

"Oh, you'll find out soon enough. I just hope you're as excited as I think you'll be."

"I'm getting five days off to spend with you and not work? I'm already excited."

Bronson led her up the stairs of the private jet, and she settled into her plush leather seat. "How long is the flight?"

"Long enough for us to eat, sleep and have a stop to refuel before we arrive to our destination. I already called your doctor to clear your travels." He smiled as he looked down at her. "I thought this would be a good time for us to discuss baby names."

Mia froze, fastening her seat belt. "Baby names?"

"Yeah." He took the seat across from her and leaned forward, taking her hands in his. "The baby has to have a name. And I have to admit this is something I've been thinking about a lot lately."

Was he serious? Was he really ready to have their first parentlike discussion? Could he actually want this family to work?

Great, now she was going to tear up all because he was whisking her away and wanted to talk baby names.

"I didn't think you'd want to be that involved until you knew…"

"My involvement is inevitable." He kissed her hand. "And I want to do this. This baby will be an important part of the Dane legacy."

Did that mean he believed her now? Did she dare hope he'd quit lumping her together with his ex-fiancée, who'd betrayed him? Could they be more?

"Mr. Dane. We are ready for takeoff," the pilot said over the loudspeaker. "If you both would take your seats and buckle up, we'll be in the air in minutes. Beautiful, clear day. Should have a smooth flight."

Bronson fastened his seat belt and sat back. "So what do you think of the name Herbert?"

Mia's gaze darted to his, only to find him laughing. A humorous side? Who knew? This was going to be an interesting flight.

* * *

Bronson watched Mia's eyes light up at his joke. He only hoped he hadn't offended her and she didn't have some long-lost friend with that name.

"I know you've thought of names," he told her as the plane began to taxi down the runway. "I'll bet you've even scribbled some down to see what they look like."

"Maybe just a few." Mia laughed. "This is a big deal. We'll live with this name for the rest of our lives—and so will the baby. I want something classy and timeless, but not far out there."

Every day that passed, he was coming to think of this baby as his own. He couldn't pinpoint when he'd let the unknown override his feelings for this baby. Somehow Mia had not only pulled him into her web, but into this innocent baby's, as well.

And his mother and Victoria always questioned him about the child—that didn't help. Those two were so willing to look past everything and believe the best of Mia.

Couldn't they see how this would crush them if Mia was lying? Oh, he'd love to believe Mia, love to know he had a second chance at being a father. Love to know that this woman he was coming to care more and more about was not deceitful.

Truth was, he was ready to jump from the pessimistic ship he'd been sailing and get onboard with his family. But he also had to remain realistic to keep his heart from taking another beating.

"I have this feeling the baby is a girl," she went on. "So I've been thinking more girl names."

Bronson smiled. He could easily see Mia holding an infant in her likeness with dark hair, flawless Italian skin and those midnight eyes that looked straight through to your heart. His own heart constricted at the thought.

"Such as?" he asked as the plane lurched into the air.

She crossed her legs, smoothing her skirt down over her thighs. "Well, what do you think of Katharine or Audrey?"

"Classic movie stars, loved by millions."

Mia's silky laugh floated through the plane. "Get your mind off films for a minute. We're talking baby names. I want a name that will carry her from childhood to adulthood. Something strong, yet feminine."

"You're that sure it's a girl?"

She bit at her bottom lip, the lip he was dying to kiss. "I'm not sure, but maybe I'm just hoping."

Honestly, he didn't care, so long as the baby was his. Damn, he was going to be heartbroken if...

"Hey, you didn't tell me what was going on with your mom and sister this morning." Mia's brows drew together in worry as she leaned forward in her seat. "Everything okay?"

Bronson sighed, not wanting to think about the fact that after she came out of her same-day surgery with glowing reviews from the doctors, his mother had again asked him to consider Anthony as the director.

"My mother had a heart cath this morning."

Mia jerked up in her seat. "Oh, Bronson. I had no idea. She's never said a word to me that she was having cardiac issues. Is she okay?"

Bronson knew Mia's love for his mother was genuine and that only added to his confidence that she was trustworthy. And he was starting to care more for her than he ever intended.

"Her stress test showed something was off, so this was just a precaution. I assure you, she's fine and the doctor said she looks perfect."

Mia's visible sag of relief warmed him all over. She loved his family without question. But how would his heart take it if she was lying? He was getting in deeper every day and couldn't emotionally afford to lose her.

No, no. He didn't want love or any such emotion to be involved. No way was he ready for anything like that.

"Tell me where we're going," she begged. "Just a hint."

He'd gotten her this far, might as well give in. He'd always been a sucker for a woman begging.

"Tuscany."

Mia's eyes widened a split second before they misted. "Where my…"

He leaned across, taking her hands in his. "I know that's where your family was from. I thought you might want to see your birthplace before you begin your own journey as a parent."

"Bronson," Mia whispered as one lone tear trickled down her cheek. "I've never felt so appreciative or grateful. I don't know what to say."

Moved by her honest emotion, he unbuckled his seat belt, shifting to sit next to her and buckling in there. "You don't have to say anything. I've wanted to do this for you, but when Mom dropped this bombshell of her procedure the other day, I had to wait to see if we could still go. I wasn't sure what was going to happen with her."

Mia's delicate hand cupped his cheek. "You're the kindest man I've ever known. Our baby is going to have the best father."

Bronson swallowed the lump in his throat, grabbed Mia's hand and kissed it. "I have other surprises while we're there, but I refuse to tell you. Those you will have to wait for."

Mia sniffed, laid her cheek against their joined hands and smiled. "You've given me more than I'd ever hoped for."

He knew she wasn't just talking about the trip, but the

baby. A baby he could hardly deny any longer was his. He'd been sliding down a slippery rope since he found out Mia was expecting and he was hanging on by a strand.

He needed to know more about her on a personal level. Needed to try to develop the trust he so desperately wanted to have.

Mia's first impression of Tuscany was everything she'd dreamed. Rolling green hills, beautiful villas on hillsides and a sense of calm and serenity. Sunshine kissing the tops of trees, roads wet after a brief shower. And the beauty made that nineteen-hour plane ride worth every minute.

"How far is our villa?" she asked once they were settled into the car Bronson had rented.

"No villa."

"Are we camping in a tent?" She laughed.

Bronson smiled as he wound through the narrow streets. "I've rented a castle."

"A *castle?*" Mia tried to grasp the implications of that. "You're kidding."

"Not at all."

Mia watched the old city fly by. "But this was such short notice. How did you manage a room in a castle?"

He threw her a look as if to say, "Look who you're dealing with."

"We didn't get a room," he told her, turning back to the road. "The entire castle is ours until Friday."

Mia eased deeper into her seat. This man was nothing short of amazing. He'd gone through some trouble to whisk her away to the town in which her parents had met, fallen in love and started their young family. He'd rented an entire castle all to be alone with her. She didn't believe he went through all this just to sleep with her again.

He cared for her—that much was obvious. But did he

love her? Mia didn't know and had a feeling he was unsure himself. She had to be patient and let him figure out on his own where he wanted this to go.

When he pulled into the drive that wound up the hill, Mia gasped. "This is beautiful, Bronson."

"We used some of the grounds in a film I produced about five years ago. I've always wanted to stay here but never found a reason to."

Until now.

The words hung in the air just as if they'd left his lips. A wave of giddiness swept through her. Yes, he was falling in love with her. The emotions may be slow in coming, but they had started taking root in his heart. Of that she was sure.

"Every castle has a name," he informed her as he parked the car. "Welcome to Castello Leopoldo."

Mia didn't wait for him to come around and open her door, she hopped out and took in the Old World beauty. Light brick and stone with vines wound up and over the entryway. She could almost sense the magic from this place and couldn't wait to see what awaited them inside.

Bronson came up beside her. "There are eleven baths and ten bedrooms."

Mia glanced at him. "Are all those rooms on the agenda?"

With a quick kiss on her lips, Bronson murmured, "Count on it."

Thirteen

Mia stretched, smiling at the memory of how Bronson had already started making good on that multiroom promise.

Silk sheets swished softly as she shifted her bare legs. Bright rays slashed through the opening in the drapes and slanted sunlight across the bed.

Mia rolled on her side, tucking her arm beneath her head as she stared at a peaceful, sleeping Bronson. Dark lashes feathered his skin, a wisp of black hair fell over his forehead and those talented—mercy, were they talented—lips parted ever so slightly.

Swallowing a lump of fear, reality set in. She knew Anthony would be talking to Olivia this week. By the time she and Bronson returned from their romantic getaway, decades worth of secrets would be exposed and one by one the details would trickle out, giving the media the story of the century.

And leaving Bronson…what? Brokenhearted? Bitter? Destroyed?

As she studied his face, his bare shoulders and chiseled chest, she knew without a doubt she'd fallen in love with him and would do anything in her power to make sure he knew she was here for him.

But would he see her as a liar? Would he feel betrayed that she'd known the secret and hadn't told him?

How had she come to be wedged so tightly in the middle of this mess?

A flutter in her stomach made her gasp. Her hand flew over her abdomen as the light movement tickled her from the inside.

She jerked up in bed, laughing as she experienced her baby's first movement.

"What? What's wrong?"

Mia turned to Bronson, who'd sat up beside her. "Nothing. Everything is perfect. I just felt the baby move."

His eyes widened and darted to her stomach. "Are you serious?"

Mia nodded. "I'd read where the first signs of life are just a little flutter, and I felt it twice since I woke up. This is so amazing. I've never experienced anything like it."

Bronson's gaze came back up to hers. "Thank you."

Everything in her stilled. "For what?"

"For being you," he told her, moving in to wrap an arm around her and guide her back down. "For loving this baby so much the light shines in your eyes. For being genuine and honest."

Closing her eyes at the irony of his words, Mia forced herself to keep quiet about the secret. It wasn't her place to tell. Anthony and Olivia needed to work it out first.

"I do love this baby," she told him, looking back up into his blue eyes. "And I love you."

Bronson didn't stiffen as she thought he would at her declaration. Instead a flash of pain shot through his eyes a second before he closed them, as if to keep the hurt away.

Mia cupped his cheek, softly kissing his lips. "I don't say that to cause you more confusion or pain. I say it because I want to be open about my feelings for you. I don't expect you to say anything. My love is a gift, free for you to take."

He reached up, holding on to her hand. "I care about you and this baby—more than I wanted to. But that's all I can give, Mia. All I have in me."

The war he waged within himself spoke volumes about his love for her. If he didn't love her, he wouldn't be so torn and apologetic, so caring and nurturing.

He gently kissed her lips, then eased back. "I have some very nice surprises for you today."

"I hope one involves clothes, since you told me not to pack any."

Desire filled those eyes as his gaze darted down to her bare chest. "Pity, but yes, clothes are involved."

Mia smacked his arm. "Tell me, you know I hate waiting."

"There's a suitcase for you in the first bedroom we were in last night. You'll find Victoria Dane original maternity clothes."

"What?" Mia nearly jumped out of bed, dragging the sheet with her. "Your sister made me maternity clothes? But she only does evening gowns and wedding gowns."

Bronson, in all his fabulous naked glory, stretched out on the bed with a smile. "I happen to know the designer personally, and she did it as a favor. There are only a few pieces because she didn't have time for much and because she will make more as the pregnancy goes along."

Mia laughed. "That was a very nice way around telling

me I'm going to be a whale, but I'm so overwhelmed with gratitude and surprise, I don't care."

"Do you want to go get the clothes or do you want to hear what else I have in store?"

Decisions, decisions. "I'm greedy. Tell me what else."

He rolled to his side, propping his head up on his hand. "I've arranged cooking lessons from Italy's top chef, Chef Ambrogio Ricci. He'll be here around noon."

His words sank in and Mia raced back to the bed, hopping up on her knees. "You're kidding! Oh, my God, Bronson. This is amazing. I can't believe you did all this for me."

One tanned finger trailed down her bare arm. "It's only nine. I think we have plenty of time for you to show your thanks before our guest arrives."

Mia moved the silky sheet aside. "I don't know," she said, shoving him down to straddle him. "I'm pretty thankful."

A wicked smile donned his face as she set out to show just how grateful she was.

All doubts about his love were cast aside. He may not be able to say the words, but his actions were telling.

And speaking of action…

Bronson put the finishing touches on one of the bedrooms they hadn't made use of…yet. He'd greeted Chef Ricci and introduced him to Mia, then he'd given the two of them some privacy in the gourmet kitchen.

While they'd been preparing something that had sent a tantalizing aroma through much of the first floor of the castle, Bronson set up an intimate table on the balcony of one of the bedrooms on the top floor.

The elation in Mia's eyes when he'd told her about the

cooking lessons had taken his breath away, much like the moment when she'd felt the baby move. Their baby.

Bronson laid an exotic purple lily he was lucky enough to find in one of the lush gardens across Mia's plate and swallowed the lump in his throat. He could do this. He wanted to do this. He wanted to be the father of her baby, he wanted to get to that place in his life where he was comfortable enough with her to express his feelings.

Of course, for that to happen, he had to address those feelings within himself. Love was too strong for him to admit right now, but he'd never felt this way about another woman. Never truly cared and put her needs first. But over the past twenty-four hours, he'd really come to see Mia for the honest, loyal woman he'd hoped she was.

Once Bronson set out one last surprise on the table, he went to see how the lessons were going.

He'd made several phone calls and actually got a little work done while Mia was learning how to make authentic red sauce, homemade noodles and tiramisu from the top chef.

The lesson should be drawing to a close, and Bronson was more than eager to have Mia all to himself again. He was ready to tell her that he believed her about the baby.

Bronson may not trust Anthony, but he did trust Mia, and he knew in his heart that Mia wouldn't have slept with a married man. Even though she still kept in contact with Anthony, Bronson's gut told him the two were merely friends. She truly was one of the most honest people he knew. Why hadn't he seen how genuine she was before? She wore that loving heart of hers on her sleeve.

He only hoped he didn't break it. His track record with love wasn't all that great. In fact, it sucked. And right now, this journey he and Mia were on scared him to death, but he'd never backed away from a challenge, or fear. Or love.

And if he was scared, he could only imagine how Mia felt. She literally had no one else. He had a family who loved him, and he knew he could turn to them at any time—something he'd always taken for granted until he saw a glimpse into Mia's life.

Just as Bronson reached the first floor, he saw Mia closing the front door, a huge smile spread across her beautiful face.

"I take it from your smile and the aroma that your lessons went well."

Mia turned to him, still beaming. "Oh, Bronson, that was one of the best experiences of my life." She closed the space between them and wrapped her arms around his neck. "I'll remember this forever. Thank you."

Bronson's cheek rested against her silky hair, and he couldn't help but smile, too. "You are more than welcome, but I did this for selfish reasons."

Pulling back, Mia quirked a brow. "Oh, really?"

"I wanted authentic Italian food and I didn't want to have to leave the castle to get it."

Mia playfully slapped at his chest and turned back toward the kitchen. And, as always, Bronson followed those swaying hips.

"Grab a plate and see if my lessons paid off," she told him, removing the lid from the pot of sauce.

"I have a better plan."

Bronson pulled out some bowls and poured sauce into one and the pasta into another. He grabbed the bread and laid everything on a serving tray. "Get your dessert and follow me."

"Where are we going?" she asked.

"Trust me."

Two words that had really come to mean so much in their relationship.

Relationship? He guessed that's exactly what they had, and he was becoming more and more comfortable with that notion. Actually, the idea had him smiling even more as he led the way to the third-floor bedroom where he'd set up the romantic table on the balcony.

"Bronson," Mia gasped as she stepped through the doorway. "This is beautiful."

He set the tray down on the dresser just inside the bedroom. "I thought you might like the view from up here. Besides, we haven't used this room, yet."

Mia set her tiramisu on the dinner table and moved into him. "I don't know what I did to deserve all this. Words cannot express just how thankful I am."

She slid an arm around his waist, leaned her head on his shoulder and looked out over the view of the rolling green hills and the breathtaking countryside.

"I'm all for your showing me your thanks if words aren't enough."

He slid his arms around her waist, encountering that slight belly bump he just couldn't quite get used to. Each time he saw it, touched it, a lump rose in his throat. He was falling in love with this child, with this woman. But what if something happened to one of them? He couldn't afford to go through that nightmare again.

"I have to tell you something," he whispered into her hair. "I know this baby is mine. I know it because I've come to know you. You're genuine, honest. I also believe that you and Anthony are friends—probably better friends than I'd like, but that's your business."

Mia looked up at him, her eyes swimming with unshed tears. "Bronson, you can't know what that means to me. I want us to have trust. I want to be able to give this baby stability."

"We will," he assured her.

He couldn't wait to show her the final surprise he had in store. More than once he'd almost let it slip, but he wanted to see the expression on her face when he revealed the gift he'd been working on.

Mia didn't want this moment to end. Wrapped in Bronson's arms, looking on to the Tuscan countryside, feeling the soft flutter of their baby in her belly, nothing else in life mattered right now. There were no problems, no secrets. Nothing to keep her from happiness.

But as he pulled away to assist her with her chair, reality set in. There *was* a problem and there *was* a secret. She wanted to tell Bronson, wanted to tell him while they were in this magical place where the outside world couldn't touch them. But she was bound by loyalty to another man to keep his secret, and no matter how deep the love she had developed for Bronson, she would never go back on her word.

Bronson moved the flower to the side of her plate before dishing out hefty helpings of pasta.

"You okay?" he asked.

She forced a smile. They were in this magical castle, and she refused to think about what would be waiting for them upon their return home.

"I'm fine," she assured him. "Just nervous about your trying my first authentic Italian meal."

As he came back with bread, Mia poured a glass of water from the pitcher he'd had on the table. "What's this?" She tapped on the stainless-steel bowl with lid.

"Open it," he told her, taking a seat across from her.

Mia lifted the lid, stared at the contents and laughed. "All green M&M's?"

He shrugged. "Just in case your homemade dessert didn't turn out, I knew you liked those."

Mia's heart swelled even more. There was no question

Bronson loved her. How many ways had he shown her? Did she need him to say the words? They would be nice to hear, but she knew he wasn't ready to say them, and his actions had seriously spoken louder than three simple words could.

But what she prayed for more than anything was that he trusted her. And that he would still trust her when he discovered the truth about Anthony. That he would come to her, let her comfort him and explain why she hadn't been able to tell him what she knew.

Because if she lost Bronson from her life, she truly doubted that she would ever find love like this again.

Fourteen

"Another surprise, Bronson?" Mia asked as she climbed into the sporty silver rental car.

After a night of passionate lovemaking and testing her scrumptious dessert in bed, Bronson woke her with orders to get dressed and be ready in an hour.

"Trust me," he told her as he started the engine. "You may love this surprise most."

"More than a castle getaway, the cooking lessons, my own bowl of green M&M's?"

He smiled, steering them down the narrow street. "More."

Now that had her even more intrigued. "Can you tell me what it is?"

Reaching over, he grabbed her hand and laughed. "You have really got to learn some patience, Mia."

"I will. Tomorrow. Now tell me where you're taking me."

The infuriating man merely laughed as he drove. They

traveled for nearly an hour before coming to a beautiful little town with bistros and specialty shops.

"What are we doing here?" she asked once he'd parked.

"Shopping."

Mia jerked around. "You like to shop?"

"Not really, but I love seeing you happy. We're looking for baby furniture."

Mia squealed. "Baby furniture?" She glanced out the window at the small, locally owned shops. "Do they have a furniture store here?"

"Even better. They have a store where you can custom-order your furniture and it's all made and shipped to you."

Was this a dream? And she'd thought in Cannes she'd outdone Cinderella. This was much, much bigger than anything she could've ever imagined.

"The owner has made some pieces for my mother and Victoria," Bronson told her as he unbuckled his seat belt. "I've never been to his store, but I've spoken with him on the phone a few times with this day in mind."

Unable to contain the excitement bubbling within her, Mia shoved open the car door. "Let's go."

Bronson came around, took her hand and led her to the store down the block. "I called Fabrizio yesterday and informed him we'd be in. He's fluent in English and is known worldwide for his baby furniture collection."

Anticipation spread through her as Mia entered the quaint store, a small bell chiming overhead. Sample pieces of intricate headboards made of solid oak sat along the wall. Tables of all shapes, sizes and various stains were all around them. Classy chairs and sofas upholstered in an array of fabrics anchored the room, drawing her eye to the middle-aged man coming toward them.

"Mr. Dane, welcome." The man closed the gap, shaking Bronson's hand. "And you're the lovely Mia. I'm so thrilled you chose to come here. It doesn't seem like that long ago I was building a crib for your parents."

Mia's breath caught as she risked a glance to Bronson, who merely smiled and nodded. He'd planned this. Love flooded her as she looked back to Fabrizio.

She slipped into Italian so easily. *"Avete conosciuto I miei genitori?"* You knew my parents?

The elderly man smiled. *"Ero un amico d'infanzia con il tuo padre."* I was childhood friends with your father.

Mia couldn't stop the tears from collecting. "I'm honored to meet you," she told him, switching back to English. "I'm even more honored you're going to make my baby's furniture."

"Oh, my pleasure. My Viviana and I had eight children of our own. There's nothing as special as welcoming a child into this world."

He motioned for them to follow as he made his way toward the back of the store. "Come into my office. I've pulled some books for you to look at. Some old designs, some new."

Mia followed the Italian man with a heavy accent and graying temples. Of course with eight kids, it was a wonder the man wasn't bald.

Mia rubbed the side of her belly as a little flutter tickled her. She couldn't wait to see her baby, to savor the treasure of motherhood and communicate with her child face-to-face.

They went into a small office where many binders and loose pictures were displayed across the desk. Mia took a seat in a cozy, curved, velvety chair and picked up one of the pictures.

"These are amazing," she murmured, truly taken aback by the beauty. "I've never seen anything like them."

"After Mr. Dane called me, I wanted to give you a variety." He leaned a hip on the edge of his desk. "If there's something you like in more than one picture, we can try to combine styles or colors. Whatever you like, I'll try to make it happen."

After several minutes of looking in silence, Mia choked up as she studied the perfectly round crib with a little pink canopy over the top. Easily she could see her baby snuggled in a deep slumber beneath the silky canopy.

As she looked through more pictures, Bronson remained standing, not saying a word. Did he want to distance himself from this? Was he just letting her choose because he still had doubts about whether this baby was his?

No. If he didn't believe he was the father, he wouldn't have done this for her and their baby. She had no doubt he was still frightened that something would happen to the child, but still, she wished he'd say something. Take some part in this decision.

Mia went back to the first picture that had captured her attention. The soft colors and delicate woodwork were appropriate for either gender.

"I want this one."

Fabrizio nodded with a smile. "Any changes you'd like made?" he asked.

"None. But I don't know if I'm having a boy or girl, so I'm unsure of the bedding."

"You can call me and let me know, or we can choose a unisex color for the bedding. There are so many nice materials for a universal crib."

Mia's mind worked overtime, thinking of the layout of her cottage, the way the windows let the morning sun in and how that would affect the color scheme.

"Could I see the materials and pick one for a boy and one for a girl and let you know?"

The man smiled. "Of course. It will take a few weeks for me to complete this design. But I'll try to have it ready in two weeks because you are a special client."

"We have an appointment in two weeks to learn the sex of the baby," Bronson told the man. "I'll give you a call."

"Fine." Fabrizio motioned for them to follow him out of the office and onto the showroom floor. "Now let's look at fabrics."

After choosing all the necessary materials and designs for either sex of the baby, Mia couldn't help but impose on Fabrizio another few moments to question him about her parents. This was the closest connection she'd had to them, other than the locket around her neck, and she wanted to hold tight to that thread of similarity.

Bronson stepped outside the office, giving them privacy, and Mia delighted in hearing childhood stories about her father, then about how he and her mother were so excited to be having a baby.

Mia choked up a few times, but Fabrizio was a gentleman and offered her a tissue as he continued reminiscing.

Before long, an hour had passed. Mia apologized and promised to keep in touch and send baby pictures once her little one was born.

Now more than ever Mia knew Bronson loved her. He'd purposely found this man who knew her father. He'd set up this meeting, this day, all so she could have that glimpse into her past as it collided with her future.

So many emotions whirled around inside her, and she just didn't know how to react. One thing was certain, though, she needed Bronson to still feel he could trust her once they returned home and he discovered the truth she'd been hiding from him. She hadn't come this far to lose him now.

* * *

After lunch at a small bistro and some more shopping in the cute little specialty stores, Mia was thankful to be back at the castle and put her feet up.

"I had no idea a baby could zap so much energy from your body," she said, sinking into the leather sofa in the main living room. "This is all starting to seem so real. The baby, I mean."

Bronson laughed, settling in beside her. "You mean the morning sickness wasn't a sign of it being real?"

She shuddered at the thought. "Oh, yeah. That was real enough, but this trip, being here with you, feeling the baby move, picking out furniture. Everything just seems so... right."

As Bronson wrapped an arm around her, Mia settled in closer to his side. They only had one more day here, and Mia had so much she wanted to tell him. So much she needed him to see about her life so he would understand her actions when he discovered the truth.

She rubbed the scar on her hand, as if to draw courage from the fateful night that had changed her life, molding her into the person she was today.

"You know I'm not lying about this baby." Silence answered her, sending a stabbing pain through her chest. "I need to know you believe me, Bron."

"I do." His voice, thick with emotion, enveloped her. "I've been afraid to admit it for fear of losing another baby I loved, but I know."

Months' worth of worry, of fear, evaporated at his heart-felt declaration. He loved this child.

"I know this is probably hard for you, but I promise nothing is going to happen to this baby." Mia rested her hand on Bronson's denim-clad thigh. "I don't know how to thank you for all you've done for me. Introducing me to Fabrizio... I'll never be able to thank you enough."

"You don't have to thank me." He toyed with the ends of her hair. "I care about you and this baby. I wanted you to get a glimpse of your past. I have my family, and I'm glad I got to show you a side of yours."

Mia glanced up at him. "You'll be a wonderful father. You have such a loving family, and you're all so close. This baby won't want for anything."

"My father passed away when I was ten," he told her. "The media actually handled it better than my mother thought they would by letting us have our privacy. I always wanted to be like him. He was the man of the house, and it didn't bother him at all that my mother was a Hollywood icon. Some husbands would've been jealous, but he was so proud of her."

Mia watched a play of emotions cross Bronson's face. "I knew my career in the film industry would come before anything, but once I had my footing, I wanted a wife, a mother for my children, and I wanted to be my dad. Devoted, loyal, loving."

Why couldn't he see he was all those things and more?

"I met Jennifer on a movie set and thought I'd found the one," he went on, staring into the fireplace as if watching the movie unfold before him. "Then she lost the baby. We argued about everything. Looking back I know we weren't compatible, but lust screws up the senses. She knew about my feelings toward Anthony—hell, everyone in the industry knows we don't get along on set. She'd worked on a film with him in the past and told me he was the father of the child."

Mia's heart ached for him and for Anthony. This entire fiasco between these two was, she feared, going to get a whole lot worse before it got better.

"You know she was lying, right?" Mia asked. "I mean about Anthony. I can't say if she had an affair or not with someone else, but I know Anthony and I know how much he loves his wife. I've seen firsthand how hard he fights for their marriage."

Bronson snapped his gaze down to hers. "I never thought of her lying about the father, but when she threw that in my face—true or not—it shattered what little relationship we had left."

"I'm not her, Bronson." Mia lifted her hand, cupped his cheek and eased her body around just a bit more to face him. "I'm not lying to you. I assure you, Anthony and I are, and always have been, just friends. That's why I stopped working for him—because I saw the struggle he was going through with Charlotte, and I knew he loved her or he would've just walked away at the first sign of scandal."

Bronson's blue eyes, which never failed to impress her, studied her face. "I know you're not her. You're a fighter and stand up for what you believe. You're loyal and honest."

Tell him, the voice in her head practically screamed, but Mia couldn't do it. She couldn't betray the trust of a friend. She just had to believe that Bronson would understand her reasoning once the truth came out.

"I'm not sure what kind of mother I'll make," she told him, easing back down against his side. "I mean, I haven't had an example, and I've never really been around babies. One of my foster homes had a toddler, but I wasn't there long enough to get attached."

"You were bounced around a lot?"

Mia nodded. "Yeah. After my parents died, I was placed into four foster homes by the time I was ten. When I turned ten, I was placed in a home with other kids waiting to be adopted. I was there until I turned eighteen, and then I decided it was time to take control of my life and do something that pleased me. I had no one else to please or answer to."

"I'm amazed at the woman you've become, Mia, considering you were so young when your parents were killed."

Mia nodded, rubbing her scar. "Yeah. I was five."

He slid a finger alongside hers. "And that's where this came from?"

"I only had minor injuries, but my parents were killed. Sometimes life isn't fair," she murmured. "I may not be the best mother, but I will love this baby with every fiber of my being and always put her needs before my own."

Bronson moved in front of her, taking her hand in his. "I have no doubt you'll be a fantastic mother, Mia. I'm not worried about that one bit. You go into everything in life with excitement at full throttle and give 110 percent.

"That's one of the reasons I brought you on a getaway." He leaned forward, placing a soft kiss on her lips. "I want you to know that I believe you, that I trust you and that I want to see where this thing between us will lead. That's all I can offer, but I hope you'll be patient with me."

Love speared through her, nearly bursting to get out. She'd never, ever felt like this—so alive, so happy. She wrapped her arms around Bronson, choking back tears.

"Love is patient," she whispered in his ear. "I'm not going anywhere."

She eased back, noting the desire in his eyes, knowing hers matched his. Sealing the new milestone in their journey was logical, and Mia hoped every time they made love he could see, feel, just how much she did love him.

Bronson's strong hands slid up the skirt of the tunic-style dress Victoria had made for her. Warmth spread through her as he leaned in to capture her lips again, massaging her thighs.

Mia broke the kiss, coming to her feet. Gripping the

hem of the garment, she pulled it over her head and tossed it aside. Desire shot straight through her as Bronson's gaze slid up her body, pausing at her matching yellow bra-and-panty set.

"You always have the most amazing things on under your clothes," he told her, coming to his feet.

Mia slid his polo shirt off as he worked his jeans down and kicked them aside. He palmed her shoulders and tugged her toward him until she fell against his hard, solid chest. Mia looked up just as his lips came crashing down on to hers.

The swell of her belly brushed against him as their bodies molded together. Mia poured her emotions, her desires, her love into the kiss.

Bronson eased back, bent down and picked her up to carry her. "Where to?"

"Bronson, I'm getting too heavy for you to carry," she scolded. "Put me down."

"You've barely gained anything, and if I want to carry my family, I will."

Mia's eyes stung as she stared back at him. "Your family? In that case, take me anywhere you want."

Hope sprang to life within her. He thought of them as a family. Did he intend to make them a family in the legal way?

Oh, God. Her dreams of a family, a real unit, could come true and with a man she was totally in love with. She realized she'd never want a family with anyone but Bronson.

He carried her down the narrow, stone hallway out one of the back doors. "I want to make love to you outside, in the open, under the stars."

Mia knew there was no one around to see since the castle sat on a huge lot and they were the only residents.

He set her on her feet, wrapping his arms around her. "Look at me, Mia."

She lifted her face, knowing her love shone in her eyes.

"Know that I care for you, know that what is between us is real to me and that I'm giving all I can emotionally."

Mia smiled, holding his face between her hands. "I know, Bronson. I know more about you than you know about yourself. Make love to me."

With soft, tender touches, he kissed her as he rid her of her bra and panties. Once she stood wearing only a kiss of the moonlight, Bronson placed his hands on her belly. He leaned down, kissed her stomach and murmured, "I love you" to the baby.

Mia choked back tears, knowing he was taking a giant leap outside his comfort zone by declaring his feelings aloud. His vulnerability was now out in the open for her to see. Which told her right there that he trusted her—and possibly loved her, too.

Bronson came up to his full height, framed her face with his hands and kissed her, backing her up until her legs hit the outdoor sofa. He spun them around and took a seat, urging her down to straddle him.

Mia hovered with her face above his, looking into his eyes, needing him to know that her love was genuine. "I love you."

As they became one, Bronson's eyes closed. Mia leaned down to kiss him as he stroked his hands up and down her bare back. The crisp night air pricked her skin, sending even more sensations surging through her.

She tilted her hips, arching her back as she lifted her face to the night sky. Bronson's talented hands found her breasts and sent Mia over the edge. She cried out and let the climax spread through her.

In no time Bronson's body stiffened as he grabbed her

shoulders and pulled her back against him, capturing her mouth.

Mia held on to his shoulders as their tremors merged into one and knew that this was the man she was meant to spend her life with. There would be heartache, she had no doubt about that, but she intended to fight for him, for their family.

He loved her. Now she just had to pray that love was strong enough to get them through the next few days.

Fifteen

Once Bronson's jet landed back in L.A., Bronson dropped Mia off at her cottage because his mother had called his cell and told him to come to the house before going anywhere else. She assured him her health was fine, but they urgently needed to talk in private.

He hadn't told Mia about the message because he didn't want to alarm her. What else could be wrong? If her health was fine, what else could she have to discuss that was so important?

Even though his mother was a Hollywood icon, she'd never been one for personal drama. Twice in one week she'd needed to see him in private—that made him a bit nervous.

Bronson entered the main house, smiling at one of the staff as they passed each other on the wide, curved stairs. As he entered the grand study where his mother spent nearly all her time, he noticed two things right off the bat:

one, his mother had been crying and two, Anthony Price stood right next to her.

"What the hell is going on?" he demanded.

Olivia gestured toward the sofa where his sister sat. "Please, Bronson, sit with your sister. There's something you both need to know"

Remaining on his feet, Bronson eyed Anthony. "What's he doing in your house? Did you go around me and hire him for the project? We were supposed to discuss this when I returned."

Olivia's eyes, now misting back up, turned to Anthony. "No, this has nothing to do with the film."

A sickening pit bottomed out in his stomach. Nothing, absolutely nothing good was going to come from the next few minutes. Of that he was certain.

"Why are you upset?" he asked, fear of the unknown gripping at his chest.

"These are tears of joy," his mother assured him. "And a little of fear, I must say."

"Come sit, Bronson." Victoria shifted on the sofa and smiled. "I'm sure whatever Mom has to say is very important."

"If it's that important, maybe just family should be here."

Why was Anthony looking so…comfortable? What the hell did the man have to do with anything that his mother could have to say?

"Actually, that's precisely what I need to talk to you both about," Olivia said. "Family. Bronson, I want you to promise not to speak until I'm done talking."

He never, ever liked the sound of that, especially coming from his own mother. Who wanted to give up the right to interrupt when the conversation wasn't going in a satisfactory direction?

"Bronson?" she asked.

"Fine."

Olivia came to her feet, crossed the room to stand in front of the French doors that opened on to the patio. Silence settled into the room and Bronson knew his mother was having a hard time voicing her thoughts. Whatever she wanted to say obviously upset her.

And there was no script to follow in real life.

Olivia smiled. "I never thought this day would come. I dreamed of how I'd handle it, but I never thought it would be a reality."

Victoria reached over and grabbed Bronson's hand, and honestly he wanted that connection. Who knew what was going to come next from his mother's lips.

"I was at a pivotal point in my career nearly forty years ago," she went on. "I had one of the biggest roles of my life handed to me without an audition. The industry adored me. I had never been so alive, so happy. I was only twenty years old, and I was pregnant by a man I didn't love enough to marry."

Bronson drew his brows together, biting his tongue because that wasn't right. His mother was twenty-five when he was born, and he knew she'd loved his father.

"I panicked because I was not ready to be a mother. I was still working on my career and knew that if I had a baby, I wouldn't put his needs before mine. I admit I was selfish, but I also admit that an abortion was out of the question. I wanted this baby to have a good life, and I was wealthy enough that I could buy a private adoption and pay any lawyer and judge to keep this from leaking to the press.

"And I did."

Victoria squeezed Bronson's hand. Whether she was

scared or because she wanted him to keep his promise of silence, he didn't know.

"Anthony is the son I gave up for adoption."

"This is preposterous." Bronson came to his feet. "Price, what have you told my mother? Did you dig up this dirt on her about an adoptive child and now you're blackmailing her?"

Anthony shook his head. "What would I blackmail her for, Bronson? I have everything I want and I could buy anything else."

"Then what the hell *do* you want?"

Olivia stepped forward. "Bronson, calm down. I've known Anthony was my son from the moment I gave birth to him. I gave him up for adoption and kept track of him all this time. He's not lying, and quite honestly, I'm shocked he found out and came to me. I paid a lot of money to keep this hidden."

Anthony sighed. "It wasn't easy. I've had my attorneys and a detective looking for my birth parents for well over a year. I didn't think they'd uncover anything, but about nine months ago they did."

Nine months?

"You've known for all this time?" Bronson clenched his fists at his side. "Why wait this long to come forward?"

Bronson stared at the man he'd loathed for so many years. Now that he knew the truth, he noticed they had exactly the same eyes and facial structure...just like their mother.

Anthony ran a hand through his hair. "Honestly, my home life hasn't been the best, as I'm sure you've heard. I'm trying to work on my marriage, and I'm fumbling through assistants since mine came to work for Olivia."

Mia. Another time line perked Bronson up even more.

"Does Mia know about this?"

Anthony stared without saying a word, and dammit, Bronson knew.

How the hell could she keep something like this from him? Maybe this really was some scheme devised by Anthony and Mia.

The mother of his child.

One crisis at a time.

"So now what?" Bronson asked, turning to his mother. "I hope you don't expect me to accept him as my brother. I never liked him before, and I sure as hell don't like him now."

"Bronson," Victoria's soft, smooth voice cut through his anger. "Nobody is asking you to do anything. The truth is out there, now we just have to deal with it."

"The truth?" He laughed. "If Mother had been so worried about the truth, she would've told us years ago."

"And disrupt the only life Anthony had ever known?" Olivia interjected. "I made my choice to give him a better life, and I wasn't going to push my way back in. I couldn't afford to tell anyone."

"All these years Bronson and I feuded were hell on you, I'm sure," Anthony said to Olivia.

Olivia's eyes filled, and one tear slid down her aged cheek. "It was torture to see my children always at odds."

"This isn't happening," Bronson muttered to himself. "This cannot be happening."

"I assure you," Anthony said. "I'm no more thrilled that we're related than you are."

Bronson walked to his mother, angry at her for keeping something so…life-altering from him all these years, but at the same time heartbroken because he couldn't imagine giving up a child.

"Mom." He wrapped his arms around her. "I honestly don't know what to say here. I want to be angry with you, but I can see you're at war with yourself. I can't welcome him into the family. I just can't."

Olivia sniffed against his polo and nodded. "I know, son. My only wish is that you two will cease this feud and at least try to get along."

Bronson doubted that would happen, but he'd appease his mother. "I'll do my best."

He eyed Anthony over his mother's shoulder. The illegitimate brother stared back, a knowing look passing between them. Anthony wasn't any more eager to have Bronson for a brother, and that was perfectly fine.

Because this whole brother thing was a non-issue as far as he was concerned. What *was* a concern was Mia. The woman he'd made a baby with, trusted and started falling in love with.

She'd betrayed him even more than his mother—though he hated to call what his mother had done betrayal. She'd given up the child nearly forty years ago and had reasons for keeping it a secret.

Mia, though, had known from the second she'd stepped out wearing only a towel that he was Anthony's brother. And she'd never said a word. Never even hinted at the fact.

Bronson eased back, keeping an arm around his mother's shoulders. "What did you promise Mia for keeping silent about this?" he asked Anthony.

"Nothing. I asked her to keep this to herself until I had a chance to talk to Olivia."

Bronson laughed. "And she just agreed to it?"

The muscle in Anthony's jaw ticked, his dark eyes narrowed. "And here I thought you knew her. You know nothing about Mia if you have to ask that."

That's exactly what Bronson was beginning to see. Just how well *did* he know Mia?

He knew her body better than she did. He knew she lit

up like a child at green M&M's. Her culinary skills were amazing, and she kept the locket with a picture of her parents around her neck at all times so she could always have them with her.

That much he knew.

What he didn't know was how deep her love for Anthony ran—platonic or not. He didn't know if she truly had an agenda as far as he and his family were concerned and the pregnancy threw a wrench in her plans.

At this point he knew nothing except his life had just done a one-eighty and now his worst enemy was his brother and a woman he thought he knew was carrying his child.

"Leave Mia out of this," Olivia said. "If she knew, then I'm even more impressed with her for keeping this to herself."

"Impressed?" Bronson wasn't impressed at all right now. He was angry, hurt, betrayed. "After all she and I have been through, she should've told me."

"Loyalty is something Mia prides herself on," Anthony said. "And even though right at this moment you're angry with her, she'd be just as loyal to you if you asked her to keep something to herself."

Bronson turned toward Anthony. He was the dead last person Bronson wanted to have a conversation with regarding Mia.

"This changes nothing." Bronson narrowed his eyes. "You want to spend time with my mother and try to form some sort of bond, that's up to her. I'm not feeling very brotherly."

"Bronson." Victoria came to stand beside him, placing a delicate hand on his arm. "Don't say things right now that you don't mean. We've all sustained a shock. Let's just think this through, let it all settle and then we'll decide how to proceed."

He glanced down at his sister who had a loving heart for everyone. "Tori, my feelings won't change for him just because we share a mother. I've never trusted him, and I'm not going to be buddies with him. You and Mom are free to do what you want with this newfound relationship, but I want no part of it."

Unable to stay in the same room with the tension, the lies and the hurt, Bronson turned to leave.

"No," Anthony said. "I'll go."

Bronson looked over his shoulder. "What?"

His illegitimate brother crossed the room. "I'll go. You three have a lot to discuss and you don't need me here. I realize I'm not part of this family, and it's certainly not my intention to break anything up. I know this will take a lot of time to deal with."

Bronson was shocked at Anthony's gracious action, volunteering to leave. He wouldn't have thought the man would step aside at a time like this. Bronson was grateful... though he wouldn't admit it.

He nodded to Anthony, who then turned to Olivia. "I hope I can call or stop by again soon."

Olivia's face lit up as a smile spread across her face. "Anytime, my darling."

"Goodbye, Anthony," Victoria said with a tender smile.

Anthony spared Bronson one last look before leaving.

Bronson turned back to his mother. "You've always known?"

Olivia lifted her chin. "Yes, and I'm not ashamed of my actions because I'd do the same thing again to give my child the best start at life."

Anger, confusion and hurt spread through Bronson. He wished he had somewhere to place the blame, but he didn't want to castigate his mother. In his heart, he knew his mother had made the hardest decision of her life, and making her pay for it nearly forty years later wouldn't fix anything.

"Oh, Mother, I wish you'd said something." Victoria wrapped an arm around their mother's shoulders. "The pain you must've felt all these years with all the turmoil between Bron and Anthony. Why didn't you at least tell us? We never would've told a soul."

"Because if Anthony never came to me, I would've died with this secret." Olivia smiled at Victoria. "I do have him in my will, and I even had letters to each of you that you were supposed to receive if something happened to me. I gave specific instructions for you to read the letters well before the reading of my will so you wouldn't be as stunned."

"Letters, Mother?" Bronson asked, resting his hands on his hips. "I never took you to be afraid of anything, yet you couldn't tell us this?"

Those sparkling blue eyes that had dazzled the camera for decades turned to him. "To be honest, I didn't want either of you to be disappointed in me. I was human. I met a man I thought I loved, got pregnant and knew I was in no position to raise or care for a child properly. It wasn't until a couple years later I met your father, and I told him everything before we married. He tried to get me to reclaim Anthony then, but I couldn't do that. I'd given him up to a loving family, and I refused to tear them apart."

Bronson swallowed, unable to even fathom giving up a child. He'd lost one and thankfully had the chance to be a father again. But to willingly give the baby up so he could have a better life?

He wrapped his arms around two of the most important women in his life. "You're the bravest woman I know," he whispered to his mother. "I'm glad you don't have to carry this secret anymore. Just please don't expect me to change overnight."

Olivia clutched his shirt at his back and hugged him to her side. "I won't, son. But promise you'll try to make amends with Anthony. For me."

For his mother he'd try anything. But first he had another woman in his life to deal with.

Sixteen

Mia opened her door to a very tense, angry Bronson. The muscle ticking in his jaw, the thin lips and narrowed eyes were all directed at her.

Her heart stopped and she knew the secret was out. Now was possibly her one and only chance to salvage their relationship and prove that her love for him was never in question.

"You saw your mother?"

"Would you ever have told me, Mia?"

Mia's gaze darted down to her bare feet, then back up. "No."

"My mother said the same thing," he whispered. "Betrayal from all sides. This secret just gets better and better."

A flash of pain tore through Bronson's eyes before he pushed past her and entered her house. With a heavy heart and a sickening pit in her stomach, Mia shut the door and followed him.

"Your mother knew?" Mia asked, shocked.

He spared her a glance as he moved into her living area. "She's known the whole time."

Bronson stood looking out on to her patio, his back to her. "You want to tell me again that there was never anything between you and Anthony? Why your loyalty is stronger for your previous employer than the father of your baby?"

She would not fight. There was no reason to start arguing, Mia told herself. He was hurting and looking for a place to lay blame, and she was in the path of his destruction. She had to be strong to keep this relationship afloat on these rocky waters.

"I've never lied to you about my involvement with Anthony," she told him in a soft voice. "I love Anthony like a brother, and I saw him struggle with this secret. I happened to stumble across the information just about a week before I was set to leave and come work for your mother. I assure you, more than once I wished I'd never known the truth."

"But you did." He turned, hands on his hips. "You knew the truth that would change my life. You slept with me, made a child with me and professed your love for me all the while knowing this."

How could she deny anything?

"Yes."

He threw his arms in the air, his voice boomed through her house. "How can I trust what you say, Mia? How can I ever trust you to be open and honest with me? You of all people know how important family is."

Okay, that was low, but she refused to let him pull her into a fight, refused to throw away this family she'd already come to love.

"Bronson, family means everything to me, too." A soft

flutter slid through her stomach as her baby moved. "But this was not my secret to tell, and if Anthony had decided to never open up, then my spilling the secret would've ruined everything."

"Did you know he was going to talk to my mother?"

"Yes. He told me last week he'd be talking to her in the next few days."

Bronson's lids fluttered down, and a curse slipped through his lips. "So the whole time we were gone you knew what was happening back here?" he asked, directing those blue eyes at her.

Mia nodded. "I was so worried what we'd come home to, but I wanted that time with you, Bronson. I wanted that time with just us because I have fallen in love with you. Not because of the baby, but because of us."

Bronson laughed. "There is no us, Mia. *Us* implies a unit, and I'm not going to be part of a team where I can't trust my partner."

The burn in Mia's throat quickly spread to her eyes, but she wasn't giving up. She'd known going in this would be hard, but she had never been a quitter.

"If you look back, you'll see I did nothing to make you not trust me, Bronson. If you think that you can't see where this relationship would go, then fine. Walk out that door and don't look back. Don't give me a second thought. But I know you can't do that."

"Not when you're carrying my baby," he threw back.

Anger fueled Mia. "The baby may have brought us together, but this baby is not the reason I want to be with you or the reason I love you. And you cannot tell me you aren't in love with me, Bronson."

"I'm not."

"Now who's lying?" she whispered through tears. "You make love to me like I'm the most important thing in your life. You whisk me away to a castle for a week when I know you never take that much time off work. You surprise me with all of my favorite things and you take me shopping for custom-made, Italian furniture. Don't even deny those are signs of love."

That gaze bore into her, but Mia held her ground. Her future, their baby's future, was at stake.

"Leave if you want," she told him, praying he'd come to his senses. "But know that no one will ever love you as much as I do. No one will ever be as faithful and loyal to you as I will. And know that you are throwing away a family that would've made you a lifetime of memories."

The muscle in Bronson's jaw ticked as he stared her in the eyes. Tension-filled silence enveloped Mia, but she hadn't come so far in her own life by backing down from getting what she wanted.

"'Throwing away' implies I had something to begin with." Bronson stepped away from the windows and crossed the wood floor to stand before her. "Yes, we have a baby, but that's all. As far as I'm concerned, there's nothing else between us. There never was, and there never will be."

He brushed past her, careful to turn his shoulder so he didn't even come in contact with her. Mia stood stone-still as his shoes clicked on the tile in the foyer. She didn't even move when he opened the door and closed it.

It wasn't until the roar of his engine died that she sank back onto the couch. Tears slid down her cheeks, one chasing after the other. But Mia didn't feel defeated. She hadn't lost this fight yet, and she certainly didn't intend to.

Bronson just needed time to think. He needed time to adjust to all that had been thrown at him in one day. Mia couldn't expect him to deal with her when she had no doubt the relationship with his mother was probably now strained.

Mia's heart ached for Olivia. Protectively, she slid a hand around her baby. Mia couldn't fathom giving this baby away, even if it meant a better life for the child. Olivia's courage forty years ago astounded Mia, and she only hoped Bronson saw how his mother had always put her children's welfare first.

Because if Bronson didn't make peace with his mother and Anthony, there was no hope for her and the baby.

For the last hour Bronson had stared at his computer screen. Actually, at the title page of the script he and his mother had worked on, to be exact.

Everything had changed since they began working on writing their own film over a year ago. The script had been very loosely based on his mother's life in the movie industry. She'd been adamant about keeping her personal life from the script. At first he'd assumed it was simply because she wanted to keep their personal family life to herself.

Now he knew she didn't want to get into the fact that she'd given up her first child for adoption.

Bronson closed the script and came to his feet. His life had changed dramatically in the last three weeks, and he still hadn't figured out what steps to take next. Who the hell did he trust? Victoria had certainly taken the news better than he had, but Victoria had always had a heart of gold and gave everyone a chance. One of these days she was going to get her heart broken.

There was nowhere for him to direct his anger. The emotion seemed to shoot out in so many different directions. He wanted to hate his mother for keeping something like this from him, but at the same time he knew she lived her own hell by not being with a child she'd given birth to and then by seeing her two sons turn into rivals in the public eye.

As for his feelings for Anthony, Bronson honestly didn't know what to feel. Anger crept up from any emotion he battled with lately, but it wasn't Anthony's fault. He'd been given up for adoption and just recently discovered his mother was Hollywood's most beloved star. As much as Bronson hated to admit it, Anthony was a victim of fate, too.

But Mia, the woman who carried his child and claimed to love him, had known for months. In all that time, she'd worked her way into his life with that innocent smile and loving nature. She'd simply glowed whenever talking about the baby.

Bronson ran a hand through his hair, turning to look out the wide window behind his desk. And now he was back to doubting the baby's paternity. How could he trust her with anything? Did loyalty mean nothing to people anymore? How could he be so naive as to fall for another woman's lies?

Dammit. How many times had he lectured himself not to get too attached to another child? He'd known going in that Mia's past working relationship with Anthony made her questionable.

But he'd gone and fallen in love with the child anyway, and he knew, looking back, there was no way around it. The first time he'd seen the baby on the screen, the little heartbeat thump that resounded through the tiny exam room, there was no way anyone could avoid falling in love with that moment, that baby.

Bronson hated this helpless feeling that had plagued him since he'd come back from Italy and discovered the truth. Hated that control had been taken from his life and he'd had no way to stop it.

But he intended to get his life back in order, and the only

way he knew to start was to confront each of the key players: his mother, Anthony and Mia.

The war raged within him, but he knew the person he needed to start with was the one who'd had the shock of his life, too.

Bronson didn't call, didn't want to think about his plan. He ran down to the kitchen, grabbed the keys to his two-door sports car and headed toward Anthony's house before he could talk himself out of confronting him.

If Anthony wasn't home, then Bronson would go to his mother. But right now he was too angry, and he didn't want to talk to his mother when there was a good chance he'd say something he regretted. As far as offending Anthony, Bronson didn't care. There was no love lost there to begin with.

In less than twenty minutes Bronson arrived in front of Anthony's gated home. He pulled next to the guard's post and rolled down his window.

"Is Mr. Price in?"

The guard's eyes widened in recognition and he nodded. "Is Mr. Price expecting you, Mr. Dane?"

Bronson shook his head. "No, but if you tell him I'm here, I'm sure he'll see me."

The guard disappeared into the small post and within seconds the long, black wrought-iron gate slid open, allowing him access.

Bronson hadn't even come up with a course of action, but he had a feeling once he was in the same room with Anthony their conversation would take on a life of its own.

The palm-lined drive led Bronson to the light brick, three-story home—a place where Bronson had never envisioned himself.

Anthony stood in the doorway and something clenched in Bronson's gut as he stepped from his car. This man was his brother. There was no escaping the truth, no matter how much he wanted to. So now he had to deal with this information as best he could and not make this any more uncomfortable for his mother.

Besides, this would eventually leak to the press, and he wanted them all to appear as a united front. No need to make things more difficult on everyone.

"I wondered if you'd be by," Anthony said as Bronson approached. "Come on in."

Anthony led him into a formal sitting room just off the open foyer. Two large leather sofas faced each other for an intimate conversation setting, but Bronson hoped he wouldn't be here long enough to get that cozy. This was already way beyond his comfort zone, but he had to step outside the box if he wanted to get his life back on stable ground.

Anthony motioned to the wet bar in the corner. "Need a drink?"

"No, thanks."

Bronson took a seat on one of the sofas and leaned forward on his knees. "How did you find out?"

Taking a seat opposite him, Anthony sighed. "I've always known I was adopted. My parents were upfront about that from as far back as I can remember. But it wasn't until about a year and a half ago, when my own parents passed away, that I just wanted to know where I came from. Now that my adoptive parents are gone, it's just me and my sister. I didn't want to disrupt a family, but I wanted to know."

Bronson listened as Anthony poured out his past, his heart. A little bit of that hatred that had built up for years started to ebb. He'd come here ready for war, but seeing Anthony, listening to how much he wanted to find out where he came from, Bronson couldn't get angry. This was just a man looking for some answers, and the answers happened to weave around Bronson's life.

"When my investigators came up with Olivia's name, I made them check again," Anthony went on. "I mean, I just didn't believe it. She'd done a very thorough job of keeping things under wraps."

Bronson's heart clenched. His mother had secretly watched over her son, and she'd shared that grief, that love, with no one but Bronson's father. When he died, she'd had no confidant at all.

"So why didn't you confront her months ago when you discovered the truth?"

Anthony's gaze faltered before coming back up to meet Bronson's. "It's no secret that my personal life is falling apart. My marriage is a disaster, and I was trying to get my feet under me before I approached Olivia. Unfortunately, that's not happening any time soon. I had to take back control in some part of my life. I wanted one-on-one time with her so we could decide where to go."

Damn. He hated the burst of jealousy that speared through him. Because of all the people on this earth, his sworn rival turned out to be the brother he never knew he had. And if Bronson were in Anthony's shoes, he'd be doing the exact same thing. Trying to regain control and determined to find some answers.

"And what did you two decide?"

Anthony shrugged. "Right now we're taking it one day at a time. Mostly phone calls, though, because we don't want the press to question why we're talking. Nobody needs that right now, with my marriage on the rocks, you and Mia expecting a baby."

Bronson sat straight up. "I wondered how long it would take you to weave Mia into the mix."

"There's no weaving her," Anthony said, eyes narrowing. "She's in it thanks to you."

"Me? I'm not the one who sent her to work for my biological mother all the while knowing about this secret."

Anthony shook his head. "No, you're the one who got her pregnant and probably broke her heart. Have you already confronted her about the fact that she knew?"

Bronson gritted his teeth. "What Mia and I discuss is none of your concern."

"She's too good for you," Anthony threw back. "I told her that when she told me who she was going to work for. I told her you'd try to sink your playboy claws into her, and I tried to warn her."

"And what were you warning her for? Because you wanted her for yourself? Because your wife wasn't enough—you had to get Mia, too?"

Anthony came to his feet. "I've never, *ever* cheated on my wife, and I'm damn sick of being accused of it. I love Mia like a sister, and I know these rumors are killing her, especially now that she's pregnant."

Bronson didn't know what to believe. A few weeks ago he did, but now…did the truth matter anymore? Another supposed "truth" would just come along later and void the previous one.

So what the hell was he supposed to do?

"I know your mind is turning a hundred miles an hour," Anthony went on. "And I know we've never gotten along, but I assure you I never, ever laid a hand on Mia in a personal, intimate way. She was like my assistant, best friend and sister all rolled into one and I hated to see her go. She chose to leave because of the strain the rumors were putting on my marriage. In my opinion, that's a hell of a woman to put others' needs first."

Bronson came to his feet and paced around the room. "It was Mia's idea to come work for my mother—not yours?"

"Mine?" Anthony laughed. "I begged her to stay. I never wanted to lose her."

Balls of tension built in Bronson's neck. He twisted it to the right, to the left, trying to relieve the pressure. God help him, he was starting to believe Anthony. Either he was a fool or he'd finally opened his eyes.

Bronson turned to face Anthony. "You've never cheated on your wife?"

"Never. Not with Mia, not with anyone."

"Not with Jennifer?"

Anthony jerked his head back. "Heavens, no. Why would you ask that?"

He was telling the truth. The stunned reaction, the shock in his tone told Bronson all he needed to know. Jennifer had played him.

"No reason."

No way did Anthony need to know what Bronson's ex-fiancée had accused him of. Which meant either she'd slept with someone else...or that baby had been his.

Dammit, why did his life keep circling back to lies and confusion, hurt and betrayal?

"I know there's no love lost between us," Anthony said, resting a hip on the edge of the sofa. "But whatever happens with Mia, be careful with her. She tries to be tough, but she's not. She has a tender heart and she truly has no one she can rely on."

Bronson ran a hand through his hair. "I won't talk about Mia's heart with you, Anthony."

"Fine, but know that she means a lot to me."

Bronson swallowed and nodded. She meant a lot to him,

too. Damn if he wasn't in the same scandalous situation he'd been in two years ago.

Except this time, his feelings for the woman were completely different.

Seventeen

Mia settled onto the exam table, more than ready to find out the sex of her baby. She'd hoped this would be a happy day, one with Bronson at her side, holding her hand while beaming at the screen. But that was not to be. She hadn't talked to him in the three weeks since he'd stormed out of her house, and she was not going to go to him. Once he had time to think, to process all this information, he could come to her. If he still wanted her.

Just as the ultrasound tech walked into the room, Bronson fell into step behind her and entered.

Relief surged through her. God, how she'd wanted him here, wanted him so bad she wondered if she didn't just wish him to appear.

"Am I late?" he asked, coming to stand beside the table.

The tech smiled. "Not at all. I'm just getting started."

Mia glanced up to Bronson. "I didn't think you'd come."

"I told you I'd be part of this baby's life."

She'd hoped Bronson was here out of his concern and love, not obligation. Had he changed his mind? Did he question her again about who the father was?

He didn't reach for her hand, didn't even look at her again as the tech moved the probe over her belly.

"There's the heart." The tech pointed on the screen. "All the arteries and vessels look good. Let's take some measurements so we can determine the approximate weight."

Mia watched, waiting with anticipation to make sure everything on her baby was healthy and normal. Nothing else mattered but the welfare of her child. Not Bronson's anger, not the secret she'd kept. Nothing.

"Your baby weighs about nine ounces and has a very healthy heart and organs." She adjusted the probe. "Now let's see if we can determine the sex."

Mia glanced back to Bronson, who kept his eyes on the screen. She might as well be here alone. He showed no sign of affection toward her, no brush of his hand against hers, no eye contact. The words he'd spoken were cold.

"Looks like we have a girl."

Mia's gaze jerked back to the screen. "A girl? Are you sure?"

The tech pointed to the screen. "Positive. The new imaging machines make this so easy to determine. See?"

Mia saw indeed. "Is she putting her toes in her mouth?"

The tech laughed. "She is. Most babies develop personalities in utero. Your little one is playful."

Just then the baby turned, exchanging toes for a thumb. Mia's eyes misted as she watched her baby's activity. A new life she and Bronson had created. How could he not want to reach out and touch her hand? Had he already distanced himself that much? Was he completely through with her?

"I've printed some pictures for you to take with you," the

tech said. "I'd like to do another ultrasound closer to thirty-two weeks if you want to go ahead and get that scheduled. Do either of you have any questions?"

Mia shook her head.

"No," Bronson answered, taking the photographs the tech held out to him. "Thank you."

"I'll just step out and let you dress," she told Mia.

Mia climbed down from the table and started toward the small bathroom off the exam room.

"Mia."

She turned, looking into the eyes of the man she feared she'd always love, but could never have. "Yes?"

"I meant what I said. I'll be here for the baby."

"Just the baby, Bronson?" Mia clutched the paper-thin gown to her chest, trying to keep the hurt from entering her heart. "You may not want to admit it because you feel I betrayed you, but you know I did nothing wrong. I understand you want to place blame somewhere, but don't use me and this baby as your targets."

"How am I supposed to feel, Mia?" He stepped closer, the muscle ticking in his jaw. "I've been lied to and manipulated in a situation just like this before."

Pulling all her courage to the surface, Mia swallowed any fear and knew she needed to explain where she was coming from. "I've already told you I was in the car when my parents were killed. I overheard my mother on the phone telling someone she was expecting a baby. I was so excited, and I asked her about it. She said not to tell anyone, but I didn't think she meant I couldn't tell my dad. I mentioned it in the car because I couldn't hold it in any longer. They immediately started arguing. At the time I didn't know what they were so upset about, but I remember my father saying something about the baby not being his because he'd had surgery."

Mia leaned against the doorway to the bathroom, pray-ing Bronson understood her actions, hoping he'd realize just how much she did love him.

"I replayed that conversation over and over in my head for years," she went on. "I still do. If I'd kept my mouth shut, kept my mother's secret, they'd still be alive. I vowed that day that I would never tell another secret. And I haven't. I love you, Bronson, but if you can't understand and forgive me for not sharing Anthony's secret with you, then I don't know if there can be a future for us."

Before he could say anything, Mia turned to the bath-room and shut the door. With shaky hands she dropped the gown into the laundry bin and redressed. She wanted to be with Bronson more than anything, but this battle he waged with himself could not be part of their relationship…if they had one left to salvage.

In her heart, Mia believed all was not lost and Bronson still cared. Somewhere beneath his rage and torment, he cared, more than likely even loved her. She had to believe, to hold on to that love because it was the single weapon she had to use to keep this family alive.

She smoothed her Victoria Dane custom-designed sun-dress over her rounded belly and opened the door. Bron-son was nowhere to be found, and the pictures of the baby were lying on the counter near her purse.

Mia slid a finger over the picture of the baby's face and vowed to do everything in her power to keep this baby in a stable, loving home, no matter what the future held for her and Bronson.

She only hoped her plan to push him away long enough to think and allow him to sort out his feelings about his upturned life would pay off. For both her and their baby.

Bronson made a late-night trip to his mother's house. After seeing the baby on the ultrasound earlier in the day, he'd done nothing but think about his mother and the decision she'd made decades ago.

That's not true. He'd also thought of the hurt he'd seen in Mia's eyes. Bronson knew there was nothing more she wanted than her own family, but he wasn't here to be part of a fairy tale. This wasn't a script, this was his life, and he honestly had no clue what the ending would be.

He found his mother sitting in the formal living room, reading. The timeless Hollywood icon sat with her legs folded beneath her on a white chaise. An oil painting of a young Olivia holding her first Oscar hung on the wall opposite the doorway. His eyes traveled from the portrait to the woman, a smile spread across his face. Not much had changed. His mother had truly grown more graceful with the years.

"Mom."

Startled, Olivia jerked her head toward the door. "My heavens, you scared me." She set her book, open side down, over her leg. "I've been waiting for you to come back once you had time to think."

Bronson moved into the room, too restless to sit, too exhausted to pace. There was no happy place for him lately—except when he'd seen the baby on the screen.

"We're having a girl," he blurted out.

Olivia clasped her hands together. "Oh, how wonderful, Bronson. I'm so glad you and Mia patched things up. Is she excited?"

Bronson walked to the wet bar, tempted to get a drink, but knowing no alcohol could change his fate. He leaned an elbow against the dark wood bar.

"We haven't patched things up," he informed her. "I went to the appointment and left after I found out the sex and that the baby was healthy. I promised Mia I would be there for the baby."

Olivia moved her book to the coffee table and swung her legs down. "Just the baby? Mia doesn't warrant the same devotion?"

Bronson shrugged. "I'm not quite ready to take Mia at face value, considering the circumstances."

"Oh, son. You know in your heart she was in a rough position. Why torture yourself and Mia? She's just as torn up about this as you are. I guarantee she battled with herself over whether to tell you because I can assure you, that woman loves you with every ounce of her being."

Bronson raked a hand through his hair. He didn't want to hear about Mia's loyalty or love for him when she also had loyalties to Anthony. Besides, love was based on trust. Plain and simple. And he'd finally begun to trust her before this latest life-altering blow.

"I'm here to talk about you," he told her. "Mia can take care of herself."

Olivia's eyes closed. "If you truly think that, then you don't know the girl at all."

He couldn't get into this. He was still trying to come to grips with everything and sort through his feelings. Couldn't people understand that he couldn't take another betrayal?

"When I saw the baby on the screen today, I thought of you." Bronson pushed off the bar and moved across the wide room to sit in a wing-back chair across from his mother. "How you must've felt to give up a child, how selfless the act was."

"The act was utterly selfish, Bronson. I gave Anthony up because I was starting a promising career and was rising fast in the movie industry. I knew I wanted a career first and a family later, and I wasn't even in love. I had a fling—plain and simple. I was a selfish woman."

"That's not selfish, Mom, that's love."

Olivia batted a hand in the air. "Maybe so, but I knew giving him to a family who wanted a child would be best. Soon after, Anthony's parents discovered they were going to have a baby of their own. Giving him up was the hardest decision of my life, and I questioned myself every day, but I know, looking back, I did what was right."

Bronson leaned forward on his knees. "Tell me the truth. Did you not tell me and Victoria because you thought we'd be disappointed or because Anthony and I are rivals and you were afraid of the outcome?"

With misty eyes, Olivia smiled. "Both. I was afraid if you found out Anthony was your half brother, you'd hate him more. But mostly I feared you and your sister would look at me with disappointment in your eyes. I worried what you'd think of me."

Bronson's heart melted. "I think you're human. Do I like that you kept this from us? No. Do I like that Anthony is a blood relation? Hell, no. But I love you, Mom. Unconditionally and forever."

A cry escaped Olivia as she closed her eyes against the tears. "You don't know how much I wanted you to feel that way, to understand my actions and not hate me."

Bronson moved to sit next to his mother. Wrapping an arm around her, he pulled her to his side. "When I saw that baby today I realized that I would do anything to ensure a good, stable life for her. That's when I realized you had to have battled this guilt for years. All you wanted was to give Anthony a good life with a loving family."

Except for when his father died of a sudden heart attack, Bronson had never seen his mother this vulnerable, this emotional.

"Please, Bronson," his mother sniffed. "Please don't throw away what you have with Mia. Try to make this work. She loves you and she loves this baby."

"How can I be sure she won't deceive me?"

Olivia sat up, looked him in the eye. "If she were out to deceive you or she had something going on with Anthony, don't you think she would've gone to the tabloids the second she uncovered the truth?"

Bronson swallowed. "I suppose. I just can't live with another broken heart."

"Who says you have to?" Olivia patted her damp cheeks. "I can almost guarantee that if you go to Mia, she'll not only welcome you with open arms, she'll forgive you for doubting her. That's how true love works. It's forgiving. You've forgiven me, haven't you?"

Bronson smiled. "There's nothing to forgive."

"And that's how Mia will feel. Don't shut her out when you need each other most. Believe me—love only comes once. Don't waste time arguing over my past sins."

Pulling his mother into another hug, Bronson kissed her cheek. "Quit blaming yourself for this. All your children turned out fine. We all love you and we're going to be okay. Somehow, this will all work out."

"What do we tell the media?" Olivia asked, fear lacing her voice.

"Nothing." He pulled back. "We wait until we are comfortable talking about this, until we all can stand before a camera as a united front."

Her eyes bore into his. "Can you do that? Can you bury your hatred for Anthony?"

Bronson swallowed. "I'm beginning to realize he's not the man I thought he was. True, we clash on film sets, but as for the private life he's led, it's not nearly as wild and deceitful as I'd thought."

"So you'll make this work?"

The hope in Olivia's eyes, in her voice had Bronson nodding. "But first I have to get my own life straightened out."

He kissed his mother one last time on the cheek. He might have a great deal of groveling in his immediate future, but the end result with Mia and his baby in his life was all that mattered at this point.

Eighteen

Nearly six months along in the pregnancy and Mia had never felt better. Other than her disappearing waist, she had no complaints. But every time she felt a kick or a swift movement from her baby girl, the waistline was all but forgotten and joy filled her.

The baby name book wasn't giving her any suggestions she thought she—or the baby—could live with for the rest of her life. She'd been through the thing at least five times and nothing resonated with her.

Of course, her heart hadn't really been in the search because this was not something she wanted to decide on her own. She wanted Bronson at her side, giving suggestions, laughing when she chose silly name combinations.

But since she'd seen him in the doctor's office yesterday, he'd only called to double-check on her next exam appointment. Other than that, he'd said nothing on a more personal level.

And there was only so long she would wait before she marched to his mansion and made him see what he was throwing away because of pride and fear. She'd tossed down the proverbial gauntlet, so why hadn't he picked it up?

Why did men let such negative emotions rule their love lives? And speaking of negative emotions, Mia was still reeling from Anthony's phone call earlier when he'd told her that he and Charlotte had separated. But she couldn't dwell on that now.

Mia glanced at the boxes sitting in the room she'd had painted a very pale pink. The furniture had arrived yesterday, and she'd instructed the deliveryman to put everything in here. The bedding would arrive shortly if Bronson called Fabrizio to tell him the baby's gender.

When she and Bronson had ordered the crib and bedding, she certainly hadn't expected to be the only one putting it all together. She'd envisioned them working as a team, taking an occasional break to feel the baby moving within her belly, sharing a smile of recognition that they were going to be parents in just a few short months.

Mia moved into the room. There was no way she could move anything by herself. Maybe some of Olivia's staff would come help.

Mia tore into the boxes and smiled. The circular crib was going to look perfect tucked into the corner between the windows. Trailing a finger along the edge, Mia couldn't wait to see her baby all snuggled up, safe in her bed with the chandelier-type mobile hanging overhead.

She moved to the smaller boxes and opened them, curious to know what else there might be. The second her eyes landed on the pale-pink-and-ivory bumper cover, Mia's breath caught. The soft swirl pattern was so much more delicate and precious than she'd hoped.

As her finger slid over the ruffled edge, tears clogged her throat. This was supposed to be a joyous time, a moment every woman would remember.

She looked deeper into the box to find her boy bedding. A note attached to the bumper read, "Send back what you don't need…or keep for the next *bambino*. Love, F."

For a second, Mia closed her eyes, giving in to the tears. She was so happy for this baby to come into her life and didn't regret a moment of being with Bronson. She just wished she hadn't allowed herself to open her heart so freely when she knew she was going to get hurt. She'd known from the start that she carried a secret that would change his life. How could she blame him for being so angry and not believing anything she said now?

On a sigh, Mia wiped her damp cheeks. "I can do this on my own. I'm stronger than I think."

"Yes, you are."

Mia spun around to see Bronson standing in the doorway of the nursery. "What are you doing here?"

Casual as you please, he lifted a shoulder, but kept those mesmerizing eyes focused directly on her. "I wasn't sure if I'd be welcome, so I let myself in since I knew your code."

With slow, easy steps, he crossed the room to stand directly in front of her. Mia tipped her head back to look up into those eyes she'd so easily fallen in love with.

Bronson slid a thumb over her cheek, wiping away one lone tear. "Are those tears over me, sweet Mia?"

The words may have sounded cocky if he hadn't delivered them with such agony in his own tone, such torment in his eyes.

Mia blinked and cleared her throat. "My tears are over a lot lately."

His eyes roamed over her face and she just knew she looked like a mess. At this point, though, what did it matter? She was turning into a whale. But, God, she'd waited for him to come to her. Waited and prayed.

"You're not sleeping well," he told her, running a fingertip below her eyes. "I'm sorry."

Mia jerked away, shocked those two words came from his mouth. "What are you sorry for?"

She turned back to the boxes, unable to be so close to him.

"Everything," he whispered in her ear as his hands came to cup her shoulders, pulling her back against his chest. "I'm sorry for everything. For denying this child is mine, for not being the man you needed me to be, but most of all for not returning the precious gift you so freely offered me."

Mia's head dropped to her chest. So much for holding those tears back. "And what gift was that?"

Bronson turned her around, lifting her chin with his fingertip. "Love. Your unconditional gift of love was so rare to me. I didn't believe it, didn't believe in you or us."

Hope speared through her, but fear accompanied it. Could she allow herself to let her guard down again? Bronson wouldn't be here if he didn't believe her and, dare she hope, love her.

"I know what I did may not have been the right decision, but Bronson, it wasn't my place to say."

"I realize that now." He kissed the top of her head. "If I'd been in your shoes, I can't say what I would've done, but I know that what you did was right. There aren't many people who make the right decision when they're under pressure. I was so angry I wasn't sure if I could forgive you."

Bronson stared back at her, then reached to pull her into his strong, warm embrace. Mia fell against his chest and sighed.

"And now?" she dared to ask, tipping her head back to look into his eyes.

"Now I've fallen in love with a woman who only eats green M&M's, who has persevered through life no matter what the odds and who I want to spend the rest of my life with so she can try amazing new recipes in my gourmet kitchen. I want to spend the rest of my life showing you how much you mean to me, how much your loyalty and integrity have made me a better person." He swiped a lone tear that trickled down her cheek. "I want to wake up every morning and see you next to me. I want to make more children with you so we have a house full of love that can come only from the bond we have. But most of all, I want you to know that I was a fool for ever doubting you. Let me spend the next fifty years showing you how much I love you."

Mia's breath caught. "Is that a proposal?"

Bronson stepped back, reached into his pocket and held out a locket. "It's not to replace the one you have, but I thought you might want a picture of your new family to keep with you."

"Oh, God."

Bronson smiled. "How am I doing in making up for being a jerk? Because I'll grovel more, Mia. I'll do anything to make you see just how serious I am about loving you and committing myself to our family."

"Our family," she repeated.

His image blurred as her eyes collected with more tears than she could hold. They fell down her cheek, one after another, as a laugh escaped her. "You're amazing. The locket is… God, Bronson, I don't know what to say."

Bronson slid the chain around her neck and fastened it, then pulled a small box from his pocket.

"Just how much do you have in those pockets for me?" she joked through tears.

"Not nearly enough to make up for my actions," he told her, opening the velvet box. "This is the ring my father gave my mother."

"What? Bronson, I can't take her ring."

"When I told her my plans, she insisted. This isn't her original engagement ring—that one she'll never part with. He gave her this on the night I was born for this purpose right here. To pass down to the woman I will marry." He took her hand, sliding the ring on. "Perfect fit."

Mia eyed the ring on her finger. The glistening diamonds stole her breath, but had someone else worn this before?

"No," he said, as if reading her thoughts. "I didn't give this to my ex-fiancée. She wanted a new ring, and when she asked to go ring shopping, I didn't even mention that I had this. I should've known then she wasn't the one."

Unable to contain her excitement one more second, Mia threw her arms around Bronson's neck, but their baby stopped her from getting too close.

"Oh, sorry." She laughed. "Bella is growing pretty fast these days."

Bronson raised a brow. "Bella?"

"Um, I call her that. It means—"

"Beautiful," he whispered before capturing her lips for a brief kiss. "Just like her mother."

His kiss never failed to send a jolt of love and hope through her.

"Let's start our life together," he murmured against her lips.

Epilogue

"Are you ever going to put her down?"

With a radiant smile on her face, Bronson's wife of two months rocked their sleeping daughter. A sight he never tired of seeing.

"She's just so sweet," Mia whispered. "I could look at her all day."

Bronson knew exactly how she felt. He eased off the door frame and crept into the room, loving the look of his family—Bella, with her mother's dark wispy hair and almond-shaped chocolate eyes, and Mia with her glow that never ceased to clutch his heart.

He knelt down beside the plush rocker they'd ordered on their trip to Italy. "You're going to have to let her sleep on her own, you know."

Mia's lips brushed the top of Bella's head. "I know. I just want her to know how much she's loved."

"I'm sure she knows." Bronson wrapped an arm around

Mia, leaned his head against hers and watched his child sleep, nestled against Mia's chest. "I love you, Mia. Love you more every day."

"I love you, too."

"I just hung up with Anthony."

"Bella's a heavy sleeper. Tell me." Mia's rocking slowed. "Did you ask him to work with you on your mother's film?"

"We've talked about it. We're taking this one day at a time. We know how important this is to Mom, and we can't let our past differences affect the movie. We both want this to be the best film either of us have ever produced and directed."

Mia adjusted the white blanket over Bella's tiny hands. "I think that says a lot about where the two of you are now in your journey."

"Yeah, it does." Bronson cleared his throat. "I want him to help me produce it, not just direct."

Mia's misty gaze came up to meet his. "Oh, Bronson. That's wonderful."

Bronson's heart clenched at the sight of his wife, his daughter and this talk of producing a movie with his half brother. "I haven't asked him, but I plan on it."

"I'm so happy for the two of you."

Bronson kissed the tip of her nose. "I'm happy for me, too. I never imagined I could have everything I ever wanted, but I do."

Mia's smile lit her up from within. "Trust me, I know all about dreams coming true."

* * * * *

A sneaky peek at next month...

Desire™

PASSIONATE AND DRAMATIC LOVE STORIES

2 stories in each book - only £5.49!

My wish list for next month's titles...

In stores from 17th August 2012:

☐ The Temporary Mrs King — Maureen Child

& The Paternity Proposition — Merline Lovelace

☐ A Perfect Husband — Fiona Brand

& A Scandal So Sweet — Ann Major

☐ Relentless Pursuit — Sara Orwig

& Ready for Her Close-up — Katherine Garbera

☐ Unfinished Business — Cat Schield

& The Ties that Bind — Emilie Rose

Available at WHSmith, Tesco, Asda, Eason, Amazon and Apple

Just can't wait?

0812/51